RISING PHOENIX

KYLE MILLS

HarperCollins*Publishers*

RISING PHOENIX. Copyright © 1997 by Kyle Mills. All rights reserved. Printed in the United States of America. No part of this book may be used or reproduced in any manner whatsoever without written permission except in the case of brief quotations embodied in critical articles and reviews. For information address HarperCollins Publishers, Inc., 10 East 53rd Street, New York, NY 10022.

HarperCollins books may be purchased for educational, business, or sales promotional use. For information please write: Special Markets Department, HarperCollins Publishers, Inc., 10 East 53rd Street, New York, NY 10022.

Designed by Ruth Lee

Library of Congress Cataloging-in-Publication Data

Mills, Kyle, 1966–
    Rising Phoenix / Kyle Mills.
       p.   cm.
    ISBN 0-06-101248-3
    I. Title.
PS3563.I42322R57   1997
813' .54—dc21   97-20633

97 98 99 00 01 ❖/HC 10 9 8 7 6 5 4 3 2 1

To my dad
The get-things-done guy

ACKNOWLEDGMENTS

I have been told, on a number of occasions, that the care and feeding of a first-time novelist is no small task. I would like to thank the following people for all their help and/or tolerance:

Darrell Mills for unwittingly immersing me in the FBI culture for most of my life—see, I do pay attention. Also, for putting his inexplicable marketing genius to work for me. I never doubted for a second.

Elaine Mills for her unwavering confidence that I could translate my grade school short story career into an adult novel, as well as for her occasionally scathing editorial comments.

My "test market" critics: Steven Summers, Chris Bruno, and Lori Adams.

Kelly Meier, my Baltimore connection, and Deb Michael for a brief lesson on the criminal justice system at the Wharf Rat.

Robin Montgomery at the FBI's Critical Incident Response Group for his help with the FBI's SWAT capabilities.

Tim Sandlin for spending God knows how many hours combing though my manuscript and scrawling comments. I promise not to stick you with the next one.

Allen Thomas for his many inspired title ideas.

Tom Clancy, for helping to put me in touch with the right people and for all his support.

John Silbersack and Caitlin Blasdell at HarperCollins for their insightful editorial comments and for teaching me a little about the business.

Robert Gottlieb and Matt Bialer, my miracle worker agents at William Morris, for taking a chance on a first time novelist and borderline climbing bum from Wyoming. And, of course, Maya Perez for always being there to answer a dumb question.

And finally, my wife, Kim, for reading the manuscript more times than I had a right to ask and for always prefacing criticism with, "It's really good, but . . ." For doing my chores while I hammered away at my keyboard, and, of course, for everything else.

There is nothing more difficult to take in hand, more perilous to conduct, or more uncertain in its success, than to take the lead in the introduction of a new order of things.

—Niccolò Machiavelli
The Prince

PROLOGUE

Baltimore, Maryland,
August 23, 1985

Mark Beamon jabbed at the air-conditioning button one last time as he eased the car to a stop next to a faded yellow curb. It was pointless, he knew—the mechanic who cared for the FBI's pool cars hated him. One little practical joke and he was condemned for the rest of his time in Baltimore to driving these subtly sabotaged vehicles. In the summer it was always the air-conditioner. In the winter, of course, it was the heater. Spring and fall usually found the windshield wipers disconnected.

Some people just had no goddam sense of humor.

He stepped from the car and stood motionless on the sidewalk for a moment, enjoying the gentle, salt-scented breeze coming off the water. He wasn't familiar with the neighborhood, but it didn't really look any different from most others in this part of town. The endless brick row homes that set Baltimore apart from other major U.S. cities also contributed to a mind-numbing architectural monotony.

Beamon jogged quickly across the street, his sweat-soaked shirt slapping audibly against his skin. He slowed to a walk when he reached the sidewalk, already slightly out of breath. The house he was looking for was halfway up the block.

He rapped hard on the door. No answer. He tried the knob and, finding it open, entered. It took a moment for his eyes to adjust to the gloom inside the narrow living room.

John Hobart, the DEA agent he had been temporarily partnered with, was sitting on the sofa at the far right. A younger, painfully thin man was lying on the dirty carpet at Hobart's feet. Beamon assumed the man on the floor was the informant that Hobart had suggested he meet.

"Nice of you to show up, Mark."

Beamon pushed at the door behind him. It was warped with age, and took nearly his full weight before it clicked shut. "Yeah, yeah. Too goddam hot to rush." He nodded toward the figure on the floor. "Is this Peter Manion?"

"That's Peter."

Beamon walked over to the young man and peered down at him. "What's wrong? Didn't get his fix today?"

Hobart remained silent as Beamon crouched down to get a better look at Manion's face. He pulled on the young man's arm, trying to roll him over, but let go when Manion cried out.

"Jesus, John, what happened?" Beamon asked, poking at Manion's arm again and getting a similar response.

"Peter here was bullshitting me." Hobart leaned forward on the couch. "Weren't you, Petey?"

Manion whimpered a noncommittal response as Beamon examined his arm. A delicate-looking bone was protruding from the top of his wrist. The blood drying onto Manion's hand had a distinct waffle pattern.

"What the fuck's going on here, John?" Beamon said, tying his handkerchief around Manion's wrist.

Hobart's face remained serene. He didn't reply.

Beamon stood and looked down at his partner. At first glance, he didn't look like he was capable of this kind of violence. He stood less than five foot eight in stockinged feet and couldn't have weighed more than one hundred and forty pounds. His size, combined with his sharp features and fine skin, made him look almost feminine. This impression was quickly dispelled, though, by his seething intensity. The little quirks that combined to form a person's humanity seemed to be lacking in him.

The vague misgivings that Beamon had had about his new partner's soul, though, had been lost in his admiration for Hobart's uncanny eye for detail and unwavering dedication to his work.

Until now.

"Take it easy, Mark," Hobart said finally. "The arm was an accident. He fell into the edge of the table."

"Then why are your fucking shoe prints all over his hand?"

Hobart shrugged. "His wrist was already broken, Mark. Might as well take advantage of it."

Beamon opened his mouth to say something but Hobart cut him off. "Come on, Mark. I was there when you slapped Terazzi around, remember? Don't even think of lecturing me about this."

"Bullshit! There's a difference between slapping a mob enforcer a couple of times and this." He pointed to Manion. "Terazzi was intimidation. This is torture."

Hobart crossed his legs and stretched his arms across the back of the sofa. "You say tomato . . ."

Beamon stared at his partner, slack-jawed. He'd seen it before, but usually in cops who had been on the beat for twenty years. Hobart had completely distanced himself from Manion and others like him. He no longer saw them as human, only as problems to be solved.

Beamon stooped down and grabbed Manion by the back of his shirt. The young man cried out in pain as Beamon dragged him to his feet, but managed to stand with minimal support. Beamon wrapped an arm around Manion's torso and began hobbling for the door.

"Where the hell do you think you're going, Mark?"

Beamon turned to face his partner. "To the hospital."

Hobart shook his head slowly. "Manion's the key to this investigation. You know that. I'm not going to let you blow this bust just because you have a weak stomach."

Beamon's eyes narrowed. "Blow this bust? I'm gonna blow your entire career, you sadistic son of a bitch."

Beamon began to turn back toward the door but stopped when Hobart reached for the gun resting on the coffee table in front of him.

"What are you gonna do? Shoot me?" Beamon had to struggle to keep the nervousness out of his voice.

Hobart put his feet up on the coffee table and rested his gun hand on his knee. The barrel, and Hobart's eyes, were pointing directly at Beamon's chest.

Beamon turned and began moving slowly for the door, pulling Manion's near deadweight along with him. He held his breath as he reached for the knob.

1

*Washington, D.C.,
October 15, Present Day*

Things were looking good for Wile E. Coyote. His rocket-propelled roller skates gushed fire as he streaked across the dramatic desert landscape. It didn't matter, though. In the end he'd lose, left in the dust by that smart-ass Road Runner.

Leroy Marcus understood the coyote. He understood wanting and not having. And, though he had only just turned fifteen, he understood disappointment.

He punched the volume button on the remote, effectively drowning out the loud coughing coming from his mother. It looked like the coyote was about to take another spectacular fall to the earth, and he loved the low whistle that always seemed to accompany The Plunge.

"Leroy, get your mama some sugar."

He ignored her and stabbed at the volume button a couple more times.

"Leroy. Did you hear me? I need me some sugar!" The quiet desperation in her voice cut through the screech of ACME rocket skates.

He thought back to the days when his mother used to come home from work and ask for sugar. He and his older brother would run to her and bury their faces in her skirt and she would laugh and pat their heads affectionately.

But his brother had been dead for almost a year, and his mother no longer rushed out the door every morning, fussing that she was late. Now when she asked for some sugar she wanted more than a kiss. She wanted her fix.

"Leroy!"

He turned his head slowly and peered around the overstuffed chair that engulfed him. His mother sat in the kitchen, legs splayed out unnaturally under the table. She stared back at him with watery eyes.

The volume of the television increased again, this time on its own. The cartoons were over, replaced by a small leprechaun extolling the virtues of Lucky Charms. He turned away from his mother and pulled his knees to his chest.

"What you waitin' on, boy?"

Reluctantly he lowered his feet to the floor and maneuvered through the worn and broken toys that his five-year-old sister had scattered across the room. He paused for a moment to look down at his mother. She turned away and reached for a pack of cigarettes.

His sister appeared in the doorway of their mother's bedroom and ran to him. He knelt down and ran a hand through her hair.

"What you been up to, Diedre? Your braid's already falling out. Took me a half an hour this morning to make you all pretty."

She giggled and chewed on her knuckle.

"I gotta go out for a little while, okay? You gonna be good for Mama?"

She nodded. Her smile had a way of making him forget who he was. He took care of her—and that made him as important as any rich white man. Maybe even more important.

"Okay. I'll be back in an hour. If you're good, I fix that braid. If not, you have to walk around all lopsided for the rest of the day."

She turned and ran back to their mother's bedroom. He watched her until she disappeared, and then he punched the redial button on his cellular phone.

The wind that had been flowing through the streets like a river for the past two days had finally blown itself out, leaving

Washington blanketed in a cold mist. Leroy surveyed the dark sky from the doorway of the housing project that had been his home since he was born. His 'hood was particularly depressing in the rain. It was true that the sun accentuated peeling paint and cracked sidewalks, but it also spurred activity. Children ran across asphalt-covered playgrounds. Teenagers smoked and drank on street corners. Even the foul smell that the sun wrung from the neighborhood was something. Rain made it all look like a faded black-and-white photograph.

He shoved his hands into baggy jeans and began splashing slowly down the stairs. At the bottom he turned right and started up the street, covering his head with the hood of his sweatshirt. Through the mist, he could just make out another lone figure framed by a severely leaning doorway. As he approached, the figure came to life and started toward him. "Tek! Whassup?"

Leroy had earned the moniker a little over a year ago from his prolific, though less than skillful, use of a Tec-9 machine pistol. It was his weapon of choice, and an item that he was never without.

"Ain't nothin' goin', 'Twan. You ready?" The wet air seemed to suck up sound.

"Shit, yeah. Nothin' much doin' on a day like this."

They continued up the street, not talking. It took less than ten minutes to arrive at the small white house that was their destination. They paused on the sidewalk, scanning for danger signals.

The house's roof looked ready to cave in. The thick boards covering the windows seemed to be the only structurally sound materials that had been used on it. There was no yard to speak of, just wet garbage clinging to overgrown weeds. To the uninitiated, the house would have appeared abandoned. They knew better.

'Twan held back by the street as Tek walked casually to the front door, resisting the urge to look around him. He rapped three times with his knuckles, paused, then hit the door twice with the soft flesh on the side of his fist.

"Yeah, who is it," came a muffled voice on the other side of the door.

"Yo, man, it's Tek. Open up, it's fucking pouring out here!"

The door opened about two inches, stopped, then opened the rest of the way.

"Who's that?"

Tek examined the man pointing at his friend on the sidewalk. He looked like a mountain.

"He's with me," Tek explained simply, trying unsuccessfully to step around the man and out of the rain.

"You come in. He stays out."

Tek gave his friend a quick wave. 'Twan remained motionless, staring at him through the dark wraparound sunglasses that seemed to have become part of his face over the years.

The light in the room was dim, supplied by a single shadeless lamp in the corner and what little daylight could filter in through the boarded-up windows. The interior of the house was divided in two by a single wall, making it impossible for Tek to see into the back room from his position by the door. There was no furniture, though he imagined that behind the wall was a table full of the stuff he was there for.

A tall man with mottled skin appeared from the back. Tek had met him twice before and knew him only by his street name—DC.

"Tek, my man! How you doin?" His warm smile made Tek vaguely uneasy.

DC turned away for a moment and spoke to the large man who had positioned himself in the far corner of the room. "Hey, Split— this is my man Tek. He's the exclusive supplier to the Waring apartments." Split nodded in Tek's direction. If he was impressed that someone Tek's age could control such a prestigious territory, he didn't show it.

"What can we do for you?" DC asked. His tone was light.

"I could use some rock, man. Havin' problems with my supplier and I thought we could do business."

"Love to, man, love to. What you need?"

"Got a thousand, man. What'll that get me?"

"A thousand! Shit, maybe I can get you our preferred-customer volume discount. Allow me to confer with my associates." He disappeared into the back again, and Tek was left under Split's watchful eye.

A few minutes passed before DC poked his head back around the wall. Tek was feeling more and more exposed standing in the empty room.

"You lookin' to buy right now?"

Tek nodded impatiently. Why else would he be here?

DC walked back into the room with an exaggerated look of disappointment on his face. "We don't have that much stuff ready, man, but it's no problem. Tell you what—why don't you just leave the money here, and I'll have Split come by in a couple of hours and bring you what you need."

Tek's heart began to pound forcefully in his chest, though his face remained expressionless. DC knew damn well that he wasn't going to leave a thousand dollars in cash with a man he had never done business with.

Out of the corner of his eye Tek saw Split's arms drop to his sides. He quickly sized up the situation, once again becoming aware of the comforting weight of the machine pistol tucked under his rain-soaked sweatshirt.

There was no way he was getting out without shooting his way out. 'Twan could be trusted to back him up, but the door had been locked behind him when he'd entered. The trick was going to be surviving the twenty seconds it would take for his friend to run to the house and take out the lock.

"Thanks anyway, man," he heard himself mumble. "I'll just come back later and pick it up myself." He looked directly at DC when he spoke, but his mind was focused on his peripheral vision and Split.

"Shit, man, it's no problem. Split would be happy to do it. Wouldn't you, Split?"

The mountain nodded but didn't look enthusiastic.

DC's words confirmed Tek's first impression. Talking was a waste of time. Better to go for his gun first and get the edge.

Tek stepped slowly out from in front of the door that he hoped 'Twan would be shooting at in a few seconds. With one quick motion, he reached under his sweatshirt and leveled the machine pistol at Split's chest. He'd gotten more of a drop on them than he'd expected. Taking full advantage of his good fortune, he pushed the gun out in front of him and squeezed the trigger.

Through the flash of the muzzle, Tek watched his target clawing for the gun stuffed in his pants. He ignored DC, who was diving for the back room, reaching under his jacket as his body twisted through the air.

Split's gun had cleared his pants and was nearly level with Tek's chest when it was torn from his hand. A second bullet impacted his chest, spinning him around to the right. He hit the wall face first and was suspended there for a moment, framed by fresh bullet holes.

Tek turned his attention to more pressing matters as Split's lifeless body slid slowly down the wall, ending up crumpled in the corner. DC hadn't reappeared and Tek stood motionless for a few seconds, ears ringing in the sudden silence. He thought for a moment that he'd lucked out, that DC had taken off through the back door and was at that moment sprinting through the wet streets.

The moment didn't last. As he turned to make a grab for the front door, someone started shooting at random through the wall that separated them. The rate of fire suggested some kind of fully automatic machine gun. Tek dove onto the floor and shot back through the wall. Behind him, pieces of the front door began tumbling through the air as 'Twan fired relentlessly at the lock.

In front of him, the wall was becoming so riddled with bullet holes that he was beginning to be able to make out movement on the other side. The realization that he wasn't going to survive another fifteen seconds struck him without warning. The feeling of immortality that seemed to go hand in hand with youth drained from him. For the first time, he could picture his own death.

It was getting hard to breathe and progressively harder to see. The lamp that had stood in the corner hadn't survived DC's first volley. Gun smoke and particles of shattered drywall floated lazily in the air, choking him and burning his eyes. Tek dropped the empty pistol and rolled onto his stomach. The smell of mold in the carpet mingled with the overpowering smell of gunpowder.

It was time to get out. The boarded-up window in front of him emanated a few small beams of natural light that were quickly swallowed up by the thick air. Holding his breath, he jumped to his feet and ran crouching though bullets and flying debris, throwing himself headfirst at the window. He fully expected either to be shot in midair or to hit the boards covering the window and bounce back into the gauntlet. To his surprise, the combination of dry rot and gunfire had weakened the boards to the point that they offered no more resistance than glass.

He landed hard in the garbage-strewn side yard of the house, but managed to struggle to his feet and begin limping around to the front. As he came around the corner he saw 'Twan standing in the now open doorway, holding his Uzi sideways in front of him, spraying bullets wildly into the room and shouting obscene insults at no one in particular.

"Let's get out of here!" Tek shouted over the crackling gunfire.

Miraculously, his friend heard him, and they began running, side by side, back the way they'd come. Tek grabbed his friend's gun and began firing blindly behind them as they ran, hoping to discourage pursuit.

In a house two doors down from the one the two young men were fleeing, Katerina Joy Washington was sleeping on a couch in her cluttered living room. Gunfire was no more unusual to her than the sound of laughter or car engines, and she barely stirred. Yesterday had been her third birthday, and she was still clutching the doll her mother had given her. It hadn't been out of her hands all day.

If someone had been standing next to the sofa, looking into her serene face, they probably wouldn't have noticed anything unusual. Her head jerked slightly as though she had sneezed. Or maybe it was a bad dream. Then she lay perfectly still, a crimson stain spreading out behind her head like a halo.

2

Greenbelt, Maryland,
October 15

The Reverend Simon Blake felt the sweat trickling down his back as he paced back and forth under the glaring stage lights. He stopped short, wiping his brow with an exaggerated flick of his hand.

"I have something important I want to talk to you about. It's something that threatens our families, our country—threatens Christ himself," he confided to the five thousand eager faces looking up at him. Continuing his pacing, he pulled the microphone close to his mouth.

"It's Satan's greatest weapon. His greatest curse—drugs."

Blake was near the end of his weekly service. In addition to his sermons, the two hours were filled with inspirational music, interviews with public figures, and Christian news stories. The show was translated into three languages and broadcast to seven different countries. An eighth would be added next week, if his attorneys were earning their exorbitant salaries.

The walls of his church soared above him but somehow didn't have the effect of making the preacher look small. On the contrary, he seem to be one with the vast complex, woven into the fabric of the concrete and glass. Part of his congregation's growing excitement.

As his voice echoed through the church, amplified by its

state-of-the-art PA system, the pitch of the crowd changed percep-tibly. Sex and drugs were always surefire attention grabbers.

Fifteen years ago, his sermons had been full of God's love and salvation. He had thought that he could change the world from his little chapel in western Maryland with a simple message of hope. How naive.

The years had changed his message. Selections from the Bible had been replaced by quotes from prominent politicians. The concept of universal love and peace had succumbed to an ultra-conservative political agenda.

The cathedral had been completed nearly ten years ago and had cost almost ten million dollars. As his message evolved, he had out-grown the small chapel and loyal congregation that had been so important to him in his youth. He'd gladly given up recognizing the faces looking up at him for the opportunity to command the souls of an entire world.

"The Lord has told me over and over again to save the children—that they're the future." His congregation shouted its agreement.

"He's told me that Satan wants us all, but mostly he wants the little ones. Evil is always plotting, always looking ahead."

He paused, holding himself completely still, scanning the crowd. He stood there for almost a minute, mouth moving in silent prayer. It was one of his favorite dramatic devices, giving the impression that God himself was sending a confidential message—right then and there. The audience responded, as they always did, and their shouts flowed through the cavernous interior of the church, building power, until they hit him like a tidal wave. Blake stood, arms outstretched, feeling the hearts and minds of his con-gregation open to him, waiting to be filled with his wisdom. The wisdom of God.

"Do you know what his weapon is?" Blake said quietly into the microphone. The congregation went silent so quickly that it seemed as if a transparent wall had been suddenly dropped in front of the stage. He repeated himself for the benefit of those who hadn't been able to hear him over the din.

"Do you know what Satan's weapon is?" He answered his own question. "Drugs."

Once again, the crowd shouted its agreement.

Years ago, the growing use of narcotics—especially by the young—had alarmed him. Now it consumed him. Users were everywhere—even in his church. He could feel them. Weekend Warriors, he called them. The men and women who joined his congregation to be entertained and to relieve their guilt. When they left, though, they went home and forgot about God until Sunday once again rolled around. At home, they fornicated, drank, and smoked marijuana. Or worse. These hypocrites would pay for their weakness and burn in the fires of hell for all eternity, he knew; but not before they corrupted others. And the Lord had charged him with putting a stop to it.

Blake marched to his podium, picking up a well-worn Bible that had been given to him years before by his father. He held it over his head.

"The Bible warns us about the evils of strong drink," he continued angrily. "But Satan didn't stop at alcohol. No, he invented more seductive things to enslave mankind. Now we have heroin. We have cocaine. We have marijuana. And don't kid yourselves that it's not in your neighborhood, not in your children's schools. It's everywhere!"

He was shouting into the microphone now. Sweat and spit flew as he ran up and down the stage.

"And don't bother looking to the government to protect you from this plague. The liberals like to say that they are on the side of the working man, but I know the truth." He motioned to the crowd. "We know the truth!"

Blake put the Bible back and waved his free hand in the air frantically.

"They just want to make sure that they don't offend any of the drug pushers." He effected an outrageously deep voice and spoke to an imaginary woman next to him. "Sorry if you got mugged yesterday, Mrs. Smith, but we wouldn't want to punish anyone—that might violate their civil rights."

Blake chuckled into the microphone, shaking his head. The crowd laughed with him. He had always thought of his sermons as a roller coaster ride. Intensity had to be matched occasionally with humor and informality to have maximum effect. Otherwise you just exhausted the poor creatures.

He returned to his confidential tone. "I have something I need to tell you all." He shook his head sadly. "I just need a moment to pull myself together first."

He sat down and once again looked out over the crowd. Through the glare of the lights, he could make out the concerned faces worn by the people in the first few rows. He motioned to the director of the choir, who turned and began "The Old Rugged Cross." As the rest of the choir joined in, Blake allowed a sad smile to cross his lips. It was a song he found particularly inspirational.

When he sat in his chair listening to the choir and surveying his church, he always felt a pang of regret. There was no disputing that the space was functional. It seated thousands, was acoustically perfect, had sufficient parking, and hid television and sound equipment with ruthless efficiency. It was the feel of the structure that bothered him. He had hoped for a more gothic look, a church full of interesting stone work and stained glass. What he had ended up with was a stark tribute to mankind's intellect and not the monument to the human spirit that he'd expected. The harsh angles and blank walls spoke of mathematics, not of soul.

The architects, whom he was still suing, argued that they had shown him the drawings every step of the way and that he had approved them all. But what did he know of blueprints and construction? He was a man of God.

The completion of his cathedral had marked the beginning of Blake's dominance in the highly competitive TV evangelism game. His ministry had expanded quickly, as he knew it would, and his fame had been bolstered by an endless procession of ghostwritten books, a small university in Tennessee, and an ever-growing group of powerful political allies. Blake had discovered early in his career that if the Lord wouldn't provide, there were probably any number of congressmen who would. To ensure his good standing with the men in power, he continually donated substantial funds to various campaigns and gave his allies ringing endorsements through his complex and constantly expanding network.

Of course, these allies were as godless as any man on death row. Hedonistic men who cared only about maximizing their own power and influence. Whores. But the Lord had taught him that it was just those flaws that made these men so painfully simple to manipulate. He ignored the darkness and lust that they nurtured in their black hearts. Their intentions were irrelevant—they were tools. And through him they had unwittingly become God's tools.

As the final stanzas of "The Old Rugged Cross" filled the church, Blake walked back to his podium, head bent forward in defeat. He took a long deep breath that echoed through the church.

"I don't know how to say this, it grieves me so," he began. "One of our congregation's children was murdered last week."

Cries of "No!" and "Lord save us!" floated up and seemed to hang in the still air. Blake held up his hand, calling for silence.

"Bobby McEntyre was sixteen. He was on his high school's varsity football team. He was a good student, and was active in his church." Blake's eyes began to mist, and a tear dripped down his cheek. He ran the sleeve of his dark suit across his face, wiping it away. His congregation shouted its support.

"Bobby and a couple of his friends were driving to a Safeway in East Baltimore." Blake shrugged dramatically. "It was just another Wednesday night—not late—about eight o'clock. It took a few moments for Bobby's friends to grasp what had happened after the windshield shattered." He paused. "The police say that a couple of drug pushers got into an argument, and these good Christian boys were just in the wrong place at the wrong time." Blake turned and looked up at the large sculpture of Jesus crucified in front of the organ pipes at the back of the stage. "The wrong place at the wrong time," he repeated to the Savior. His voice cracked.

His wavering tone was the cue for the technicians in the booth to cut to a video of a laughing Bobby McEntyre tossing a football with his younger brother. When this appeared on the monitors in the church, as well as on the TVs of millions of viewers, a woman in the audience began to cry. He walked to the end of the stage, squinting against the lights.

"Mr. and Mrs. McEntyre, please come up here." He held his hand out to help a heavyset woman in her early forties onto the stage. Her husband followed close behind. Both had tears in their eyes. Blake hugged them and turned them to face the crowd and cameras.

"I wanted to bring the McEntyres up here so that we could all express our sympathy and to tell them that they will be in our prayers." The congregation mumbled its agreement. "I also wanted to tell them that I'm beginning a scholarship to Lord's Baptist University in Bobby's name."

The McEntyres hugged Blake again, tearfully expressing their gratitude and telling him how happy the scholarship would have made their son. A few people in the crowd clapped at the gesture. Blake watched the McEntyres as they were ushered back to their front row seats.

"I know that Bobby is in Paradise now, but he must feel great sadness in his heart at leaving such a wonderful family."

A man at the edge of the stage signaled that there were only five minutes left in the broadcast. Catching him out of the corner of his eye, Blake nodded imperceptibly and walked back to his pulpit. It was important not to let the realities of television interfere with the electricity of the Lord's presence.

"I want everyone in this church and everyone watching from home to join the Lord's mortal battle with drugs. Write your congressman! Write your senator! Write the President! Tell them that we have had enough!" Blake pounded his fist on the podium, creating an exploding sound over the PA system.

"Don't wait until tomorrow—write today," Blake insisted. "We can take back America from the pushers, but it's got to start with us! I don't want any other parents in my congregation to suffer like the McEntyres have."

He pushed himself away from the podium and walked to center stage. He stood there with his arms straight up in the air.

"God bless all of you," he shouted without the aid of his microphone. Thanks to the near-perfect acoustics of the building, his voice made it to all corners of the structure. It was his signature end to the service.

The choir began their final song as Blake disappeared through an inconspicuous door at the back of the stage.

As he walked toward the rear of the church, his chauffeur fell into step next to him. "Straight back to the office, Reverend?"

"Yes. Can we make it there by one-thirty?"

Carl looked at his watch and frowned. "I'll do my best, but it depends on traffic."

Despite its considerable bulk, the black limousine slipped effortlessly through the light afternoon traffic, a tribute to the man behind the wheel. Blake sat in the back sipping a Coke and flipping through the *Washington Post. The New York Times* and *LA Times* sat untouched next to him on the soft leather seat.

The front page of the *Post* was dominated by a picture of a young black boy. It was unmistakably a reproduction of a school photo. The boy mugged uncomfortably, hair and collar neater than they had a right to be on a child that age. The accompanying article caught Blake's eye. He grimaced as he scanned through the first few paragraphs.

They told a story of a young boy living in downtown Washington who had repeatedly refused to get involved with drugs, despite escalating peer pressure. His abstention had irritated the local pushers sufficiently to inspire them to douse him with gasoline and set him alight. Blake flipped the page, finding another picture of the boy. This time he was lying in a hospital wrapped in bandages. The only skin visible was a small patch on his right shoulder. His eyes were covered with large round pads that looked like something used to wax a car. Clear plastic tubes ran from his nose to a complex machine by the bed.

Disgusted, Blake tore out the article and stuffed it into his brief-case. Too bad the boy wasn't white—a story like that could break collection records.

Blake scooted into the corner of the back seat so that he could see his driver's face. "Did you read about the boy in Washington who was set on fire?"

"I sure did, Reverend. Breaks your heart, don't it?"

"Why is this happening? What can we do to keep these kids away from drugs?"

Carl was one of the few black people that Blake knew well. He was under the impression that the black community was com-pletely homogenous and that his chauffeur was its spokesman.

"Don't know, Reverend. Most of the kids I see don't have much of a home life. And even if they did, it wouldn't do any good. The pressure to be cool, do drugs, you know—all that stuff—it's pretty strong. Comes a time when kids don't want to listen to their folks anymore. It's the same old problem, really. Kids want to feel grown up. They want to feel important."

Blake smirked. Carl had a God-given talent for understatement. "I remember being a kid—how important it was to fit in," Blake agreed. "But I don't remember the unpopular kids being set on fire." He scooted back to the middle of the seat and flipped on a small television, signaling that the conversation was over.

The traffic thickened as the highway melded into a two-lane Baltimore city street. Carl continued north, past the new Camden Yards baseball stadium, and took an indirect route to the parking garage under the building that housed the church's main offices. Blake jumped from the car, almost forgetting his briefcase, and walked quickly though the gloom to the elevator. His watch read 1:35, and he knew that John Hobart would have been waiting for precisely five minutes. Tardiness was not one of Hobart's failings.

Blake's organization took up the entire fourteenth floor of a hundred-thousand-square-foot office building that passed for a sky-scraper in Baltimore's Inner Harbor. Anyone accidentally getting off on the floor occupied by the church would probably mistake it for a large law firm. The space was tastefully decorated with plush beige carpet and thick wood paneling. Crystal vases filled with dried flowers sat on antique mahogany tables. Walls were sparsely covered with original artwork, and employees were dressed in dark suits or well-pressed skirts and blouses. Only the light religious music playing over invisible speakers hinted at the true nature of the tenant.

Blake strode purposefully past the reception area near the elevator doors, not returning the greeting of the young woman sitting behind the desk. As he walked into his office suite, his secretary motioned toward his office, indicating that his appointment was waiting. Blake threw his coat on the sofa and walked though the open door of his office.

"Afternoon, John, sorry I'm late."

"No problem, Reverend, I just got here myself," John Hobart replied, looking up from the yellow legal pad resting in his lap.

Blake sat down across from him and pulled a pen from his pocket. He could feel Hobart watching him as he dated the first page of the pad. He didn't immediately meet his gaze. Hobart had a lifeless stare. His eyes had a way of eliciting a nervous laugh from all but the most powerful of men. They seemed to be able to see things that people didn't want seen.

Blake had hired him five years ago as head of church security, a move prompted by his growth into a full-fledged public figure. He hadn't liked Hobart when they'd first met, but the man's qualifications had been undeniable. Hobart had spent two tours of duty in Vietnam attached to a special forces unit, and had been highly decorated. Upon his return, he had gone to work for an accounting firm, getting his CPA less than a year later. Despite his success there, he had joined the Drug Enforcement Administration in the late seventies. He had explained to Blake that the boredom and irrelevance of the accounting business had finally worn him down.

Blake's initial dislike for Hobart—his son would probably say that John gave him the creeps—had prompted him to continue his search for a security manager. He had spent weeks weeding through steroid-enhanced bodyguards, sleazy private investigators, and classless ex-cops. After all of the interviews were finished, he found himself rereading Hobart's resume. Despite the fact that a polite rejection letter had already been sent, he called Hobart back for a second interview. It hadn't changed his opinion of the man; and in fact, his feelings about Hobart still hadn't changed. In the end though, Hobart had seemed to be the smart choice.

There had been no cause to regret his decision. Hobart had created a security force that the Mossad would respect. His less than sunny personality and ambiguous religious leanings were no great hardship when Blake weighed them against his own personal safety and the safety of his family.

In addition to his security expertise, Hobart's accounting knowledge had become indispensable in handling the church's less-than-above-board transactions. While the Reverend liked to see himself as an honest man, he had grown accustomed to the finer things in life. He had also become increasingly addicted to political power, which had a price. His donations to various government officials didn't always meet the current definition of legality, and could be extremely embarrassing to a great number of people if they were to become public. Hobart seemed to have a special genius for setting up shell corporations and foreign accounts that looked completely legitimate, even under heavy scrutiny.

Blake's secretary poked her head into the office. "Sorry to bother you, Reverend, but Senator Haskins is on line one."

Blake stood and marched over to his desk. "Thanks, Terry."

Hobart went silently back to the legal pad sitting in his lap. He spun his chair so that his back was to his boss, and suppressed a smile.

The family-values senator and the family-values preacher.

Blake had spent the last five years throwing money at "return to family values" campaigns. A shameful waste of resources, as far as Hobart was concerned. The Reverend came from a nice, white, middle-class family in western Maryland. Dad was a preacher, and

Mom stayed home making pies and taking care of her 2.5 children. Blake seemed to think that people who wavered from that cosmic norm did so by choice. He thought that he could simply convince them of the superiority of a wholesome and fulfilling home life, and when convinced, they would come around instantly.

Hobart knew better. He'd grown up in a poor, blue-collar family in New York that couldn't have been farther removed from Blake's idyllic childhood.

Young John had been a disappointment to his father, and after a few drinks the mere sight of John would set his father into a violent rage. Like most men, he had hoped that his son would be a younger version of himself. He had wanted an athlete. He'd wanted a boy who would turn into a tough-talking, hard-drinking man. What he'd ended up with was a son who was much smaller than his peers, pale and reed-thin. He seemed to blame John for his small stature, as if the boy had kept himself from growing just to irritate him. Athletics held no interest for John. His first love was chess, a game his father's limited intelligence couldn't grasp.

A few days after Hobart's fifteenth birthday, his mother had been walking up the street with an armload of groceries, as she always did on Tuesdays. When she'd come around the corner, the flashing lights of two police cars parked in front of her home had momentarily blinded her. She hadn't waited to reorient herself, but had dropped the bags and run to the house. The injuries that she and her son had suffered as a result of her husband's binges had been getting worse. She was convinced that her son was dead.

She burst through the door only to find John sitting on a kitchen chair, swinging his legs back and forth, sucking on a popsicle. A large policeman was crouched next to him, talking softly into his ear. He turned when he heard the door slam. There had been an accident, he told her. Her husband had fallen down the stairs. His neck was broken.

She'd gone numb. Not at the sight of her husband's limp body at the bottom of the stairs, but at the look on her son's face. The policeman followed her gaze to John's emotionless expression and explained that they thought he might be in shock. She'd walked over and knelt down in front of him, looking in his eyes. It was there that she found the truth about what had happened that day.

That incident had formed John Hobart's entire philosophy on life. Most of humanity's problems were rooted in centuries of misguided and often contradictory moral teachings. For a man with the intelligence and resolve to rise above this tangle of right and wrong, there was no problem that couldn't be solved simply, quickly, and finally. Despite its simplicity, Hobart had never met anyone besides himself who truly grasped this philosophy and had the inner strength to live by it. There had been a few men in Vietnam who were beginning to understand, but they had all become addicted to the killing—dependent on the brief sensation of ultimate domination to mask their feelings of guilt and horror. Hobart saw killing as nothing more or less than an effective tool, and he used it with the thoughtless precision of a master craftsman.

"Sorry about that," Blake apologized again, replacing the receiver. "What's on our agenda today?"

Hobart stood and quietly closed the office door. "Nothing too interesting, Reverend. I wanted to confirm that we'd funded Senator Haskins the money he requested—but it seems that we did." He pointed to the phone. "Also, I wanted to let you know that I negotiated our own elevator when we renewed our lease. Starting next week, you'll have a key to the far-right elevator downstairs. None of the others will service this floor, except in emergencies. I've been a little concerned about the easy access to your office. As it stands now, some crazy drug addict could waltz right up here and mug your secretary."

Blake nodded. He wasn't thrilled about being imprisoned in his own office, but he deferred to his security chief's expertise. Operational details, necessary as they were, bored him to tears.

"Did you read that article in the *Post* today about that young boy getting set on fire because he wouldn't do drugs? I was looking at it on the way here."

John gave a short laugh, trivializing the incident. "It's a crazy world, Reverend." He flipped a page on his pad. Blake could see the heading at the top of the page. Offshore Investment Accounts. He wasn't yet ready to be immersed in numbers.

"How much does the U.S. spend on trying to stop illegal narcotics?"

Hobart frowned and looked at his watch. Blake had seen that particular phrase of body language a thousand times, and it still irritated him.

"Well?" he prompted, letting his anger seep into his voice.

Hobart dropped his pad onto the table, looking frustrated. "Annually? Somewhere in the fifteen billion dollar neighborhood, I guess."

"And how much of the church's money did I spend supporting law and order politicians last year?"

Hobart thought for a moment. "That's a tough figure to put your finger on, Reverend. We don't break it out anywhere."

"Guess."

"It must be in the two million range. Give me a few days and I'd be happy to pull it off the computer."

Blake waved his hand dismissively. "No thanks."

Hobart reached for his pad again, obviously anxious to finish their meeting and go home. Blake knew he hated working on Sundays.

"So am I wasting my money?"

Hobart released the pad with a sigh, but didn't answer.

Blake repeated the question.

"I don't know, Reverend. Is it a waste of money to try to do something good?"

Blake laughed out loud at his security chief's attempt at Christian philosophy. "I'd appreciate a straight answer, John."

Hobart gave a defeated look. "Okay, Reverend. If you're asking me whether your giving these congressmen a few million every year will stop the spread of narcotics in America, the answer is no. Teen drug use has more than doubled in that last few years—you've seen the surveys. Coke use is up almost two hundred percent. Pot's up a hundred and fifty percent. Heroin's doubled."

Blake leaned back into his chair, taking a passive role in the conversation. An unusual position for the preacher.

"Then what would you suggest? We have considerable resources and will. How should we allocate them to win the war?"

Hobart started slowly. "Look, Reverend, illegal narcotics are a serious problem—and serious problems demand serious answers. That's where things break down. The best way for a politician to get reelected is for him to look like he's doing great things for the country, but not actually do anything at all. That way everybody's happy and nobody's mad enough to mount an effective negative campaign."

"That's a pretty cynical view of the government of the greatest country in the world."

Hobart chuckled. "The greatest country in the world. Why? The Japs have a stronger economy. Man for man, the Israelis are better fighters. The European children test better than ours. And hell, I'd feel safer walking a dark street in Trinidad that I would West Baltimore. Yeah, we were the greatest country in the world once, but now we're on our way out. In the next twenty years the rest of the world's gonna run over us like a steamroller."

A flush had risen from Blake's collar. Insulting the United States of America wasn't much better than insulting the Lord himself. But there was truth in what Hobart was saying. He couldn't deny it.

"So what do we do to stop this slide?"

"Hell if I know, but I think you're right in starting with the drug problem. There are, oh, say, thirteen million regular users in the U.S. About a third of those are heavy users. Quite a bit of the crime and violence that's eating this country up can be directly or indirectly traced back to those addicts."

"So what, then?" Blake said in a frustrated tone. "Should the government just execute anyone caught dealing drugs?"

"Waste of time, Reverend. You'd break the bank, keeping that many people on death row. Not to mention the cost of the appeals. Besides, you're talking about changing the way the judicial branch works to make it an effective policy. Not likely."

"I'm sick of people telling me there's no solution. The Lord had told me that there is a way. And he's charged me with finding it."

"There are a lot of ideas out there, Reverend. One is legalization and regulation." Blake frowned and opened his mouth to give a well-practiced argument to this proposal. Hobart cut him off. "I know you're dead against that option, Reverend, but it's not as bad as you think. It increases tax revenue and takes the criminal element out of the drug game. The effect would probably be something like the repeal of Prohibition back in the twenties. Of course, it wouldn't do anything to decrease drug use. It'd probably increase it a little, actually."

Blake folded his arms across his chest, indicating that he was looking for a better idea.

"Another idea is to have the U.S. buy all of the world's drug output and destroy it. Of course, that doesn't do anything for manufactured drugs like speed, X, or LSD. Also, you'd probably have every country in the world with ten feet of soil growing poppies— and you'd still have black market dealing. Other than that, we just keep on doing what we're doing."

"Which isn't the least bit effective."

Hobart shrugged. "Complete waste of time and money."

"That's it, then. I should just save my money and let my children grow up in a country where they could be shot down in the streets at any moment." Blake was pounding on the conference table. Always the preacher.

"There is a way, actually. It's something we used to bat around late at night back at DEA. It'd put an end to drug use and trafficking almost overnight."

Blake leaned forward in his seat. "How?"

"When you think about it, all you'd have to do is change the mission of the DEA from confiscating drugs and jailing dealers to confiscating drugs, poisoning them, and then putting them back out on the streets."

Blake turned his eyes to the large window overlooking the Inner Harbor and began chewing on his eraser. After almost a minute, he stood and walked to the window. The fall sun reflected off the water. Small sailboats appeared and disappeared in the glare.

In the distance, he could see a stark white Coast Guard cutter heading out to sea. Next week they would probably be chasing a Colombian boat with a cargo hold full of sin and death.

"Think about it, Reverend, it's a win-win proposition. Hard core drug users, who are leeches on society anyway, would either have to clean up their act or die. That would include dealers, who are mostly heavy users. Anyone with half a brain would decide that the risk was too great and would stop using. Remember a few years back when the FDA found a couple of grapes with a little cyanide in them? You couldn't pay people to eat those things. And as I recall, it wasn't even enough to make you sick."

Blake grunted. He himself had sworn off grapes.

"The other plus in this kind of an operation is the cost. After you started it up, it would probably be self-sustaining. The DEA confiscates the drugs—in essence, gets them free—then puts five dollars' worth of poison in them and sells them for one hell of a profit. Besides, after a while you wouldn't have to do much poisoning. Fear would do your work for you."

Carl pressed a button on the remote clipped to his key chain and slowed the limousine to a crawl. The imposing gate guarding the entrance to Blake's estate swung open obediently. As they drove through, Blake caught a glimpse of a man in a dark suit standing partially obscured by a hedge, and recognized him as one of the guards who had been assigned to the house. He had initially resisted having men at the house, but finally acquiesced when Hobart promised to keep them out of sight. As always, Hobart had kept his word. Blake had actually been forced to introduce a couple of them to his young daughter, who became convinced that they were well-dressed ghosts. While he didn't normally tolerate talk of the occult from his children, he really couldn't blame her. Sometimes he thought they were well-dressed ghosts too.

The drive was nearly three quarters of a mile long, and climbed a gentle hill to the main house. The rise of the hill and the carefully calculated placement of trees kept the house completely hidden from the road. Carl stopped the car under the portico growing from the front of the large white Tudor and walked quickly around to open his boss's door.

"Will you be needing the car anymore this evening, Reverend?"

"I don't think so. Be here at seven-thirty."

Carl touched the brim of his hat, climbed back into the car, and pulled slowly away.

"Hello!" Blake called, dropping his shoes on a priceless Oriental carpet centered in the large entry hall. Directly across from him, a black antique screen partially obscured by a potted tree depicted Japanese women washing in a stream.

"Erica! I thought I told you to get rid of this thing!" he shouted.

Blake wasn't crazy about the Oriental theme that his wife had chosen for their home. He considered the inhabitants of the Far East to be a godless people, and had developed a disdain for their culture based on the few business dealings he'd had with them. His wife's last purchase had finally pushed his good nature too far. He'd be damned if the first thing his guests saw when they entered his home was a bunch of half-naked heathens immortalized in lacquer.

No one answered his call, so Blake followed the sound of Beethoven's Ninth Symphony. He padded through the immaculate home in his stockinged feet, his nose latching onto the unmistakable smell of garlic and oregano.

"Did you have a good day?" Erica Blake asked as she stirred a seafood steamer full of spaghetti with a ridiculously long wooden spoon.

"Why is that screen still in the entry?"

Erica turned away from the stove. "I put a tree in front of it, honey. I thought . . ."

Blake cut her off. "I want it gone when I come home tomorrow. I don't mind you collecting these things, but I won't have obscenities at my front door. You can put it in your bedroom if you like."

Erica nodded and silently turned back to her pasta.

Blake sighed and headed for his bedroom to change.

Erica had been the perfect wife when he had still been at his little chapel in western Maryland—reserved, God-fearing, and supportive. The further his star had risen, though, the further she had retreated into her furniture collecting, painting, and childrearing. While her increasingly introverted nature was not really a hindrance to him, he had hoped that she would develop into a formidable ally. He still saw himself as a preacher, but he needed a politician's wife.

Ten minutes later Blake reappeared in loose-fitting khakis and a Polo shirt. His children, Joshua and Mary, were already seated, and Erica was spooning sauce onto plates heaped with pasta.

"Hi, Daddy," Mary said, waiving her little hand. Josh remained unusually quiet and did not meet his father's gaze.

"Hello, Princess. Did you have a fun day today?" She smiled and nodded her head.

Blake turned to his son, who had begun junior high the month before. "How was school today, son?"

A strange look flashed over Joshua's face. Fear? Then it was gone.

"Fine, Dad." He studied his food.

"Something wrong?"

"Huh-uh."

They finished the meal in silence. Blake resisted the urge to have a second helping. His pants were starting to feel a little tight.

"You all finished, honey?" Erica asked her daughter. She smiled and nodded again.

"Why don't you wipe all that sauce off and run off and go watch some TV?"

"Can I?" she dragged a napkin across her face and took off before her mother could change her mind.

Dinner had left Blake a bit confused. Their usual lively conversation had been replaced by the quiet clinking of forks against porcelain. And now Erica had suggested that Mary go watch TV, a device that she could effectively argue was the root of all evil—though she would never dare to do so in front of him.

"Josh has something he wants to talk to you about," Erica said as the sound of their daughter's footsteps faded into the distance. She was talking to her husband but looking directly at Josh, who squirmed uncomfortably.

She prodded again. "Josh?"

"It's about Jimmy," he said, still working to find a comfortable position in his seat.

James Miller was Josh's best friend. They had met in the fourth grade and had been virtually inseparable ever since. Two peas in a pod.

"What about Jimmy?"

Josh looked to his mother for support. She wasn't offering any.

"He, uh, got expelled today."

At first Blake thought that he hadn't heard correctly. "Expelled?"

Josh nodded.

"What? Why? Was he cheating?" Blake couldn't imagine Jimmy doing anything warranting expulsion. There must be some mistake.

"Uh, no."

Josh didn't seem able to continue. He stared at his plate. Blake looked at his wife. "What?"

She was silent for a moment, but finally decided to jump in and help her son. "They found some marijuana in his locker, Simon."

He fell silent, staring dumbly at his wife. Finally he turned back to his son. "Did you know that Jimmy was using drugs?"

"Not really, I . . ."

Blake exploded, slamming his hand down hard on the table. The drinking glasses swayed dangerously as Josh scooted back in his chair, putting some distance between him and his father.

"Don't give me that 'not really' crap! Either you knew or you didn't!" The flames of hell began to glow alarmingly bright around his son's head.

Tears welled up in the boy's eyes. His mouth moved, but at first no sound came out. "He just told me a few days ago."

"Bullshit!" Blake yelled, reaching across the corner of the table and grabbing Josh's arm. "Have you been using drugs? Answer me! Have you been using drugs?"

Josh looked to his mother again, and in that brief moment Blake saw the truth in his son's eyes. He let go of the boy's arm and slumped back into his chair. A wave of nausea hit him violently and then subsided.

"It was nothing Dad. Really, I . . ."

"Get out of my sight," Blake said quietly.

Josh stood and walked slowly from the room wiping at his eyes with his sleeve.

Erica reached across the table to take her husband's hand, but he pulled away.

"We'll talk about this later," Blake said in a slightly threatening tone. He pushed his chair back and began walking slowly to his den.

There wasn't anything Oriental in his den. The cluttered room was dominated by a large desk in the far corner. Books on various aspects of Christianity littered poorly organized book shelves. But it was the overstuffed chair by the fireplace that he was interested in at the moment. He did his best thinking in its embrace.

Blake grabbed some kindling out of a bronze bucket and carefully organized it in the fireplace. When the fire was roaring to his satisfaction, he sat, regretting for one of the few times in his life that he didn't drink.

It was too quiet. He grabbed the TV remote and flipped quickly through the channels, finally deciding on a local newscast. He didn't have much interest in what the well-groomed anchorman was saying, but the background noise was somehow comforting.

". . . young Katerina Washington was found dead in her home in Washington, D.C., this evening." Blake turned his attention from the dancing flames to the television as the scene cut to a shot of a dark D.C. neighborhood. Four police cars were parked haphazardly in front of a small gray house, their blue lights giving a sick swirling effect to the scene. A small lump under a white sheet was being rolled down the sidewalk as a growing crowd looked on. The cameras turned and focused on a young woman sitting in the back of one of the squad cars. The powerful lights glared off of the glass, partially obscuring her tear-streaked face. A man with a microphone stepped into the picture, successfully stopping a policeman who seemed to be walking toward the house.

"Lieutenant, can you tell us what happened here?"

The cop looked bored. His eyes met the camera as the reporter pushed the microphone into his face. "The victim was found by her mother about an hour ago. It looks like a bullet came through an open window and struck her in the head. She was killed instantly."

"Do you have any suspects?"

The cop shook his head. "Nobody seems to have seen anything. There's a lot of drug trafficking in this neighborhood. Seems pretty likely that it was a stray bullet from a gunfight that took place earlier today."

"Shit!" Blake yelled, throwing the remote at the TV. When it hit, the channel changed to an old episode of "Father Knows Best." He turned his attention back to the fire. The television played on, recalling another time. A time when America was on the right track. A time before drugs, before hippies, before Vietnam.

After about ten minutes he rose from his chair, turned off the television, and walked to his desk. Glancing back to make sure that the door to the den was firmly shut, he picked up the phone.

John Hobart was sitting in the small office that he kept above his garage. The room was lit only by the screen of his personal computer and a small halogen desk lamp. For the past two hours he had been reviewing the status of Blake's offshore accounts, a job that was becoming easier and easier with recent advances in technology. And that concerned him. The thought of an overzealous reporter finding an MIT whiz kid to dig up embarrassing information about the church had been bouncing around in his mind for some time. But he had done, and was doing, everything possible to prevent that kind of thing from happening. There was no point in spending time worrying about things that were beyond all control.

His concentration was disrupted by the phone sitting on the credenza behind him. He picked it up on the first ring. Not surprisingly, it was Blake. He gave very few people his home number.

"What can I do for you, Reverend?"

Blake's voice was low and quiet. There was something in his tone that could only be described as despair.

"Remember what we were talking about today? Your simple solution to America's problems?"

"Yes." Hobart was cradling the phone in the crook of his shoulder, half listening, as he punched instructions into his computer.

"I recall you saying that one of the best things about this, uh, operation, was that maintaining it wouldn't take much manpower."

"I don't know if I used those exact words. What are you driving at, Reverend?"

There was a moment of silence on the line. "Could a small organization with substantial financial resources carry out a course of action like we discussed without the involvement of the government?"

Hobart stopped tapping at the keyboard and focused for the first time on the conversation. "That's an interesting question, Reverend." He thought about it for a few moments. "Sure, I don't see why not."

"Would you be interested in being involved in an organization like that?"

Hobart couldn't believe what he was hearing, and for a moment thought he had misunderstood Blake's meaning. Replaying the conversation in his head, he decided that he wasn't mistaken.

"I'm probably the only man for the job," Hobart replied honestly. Other men would crack in the face of mounting casualties, he knew, or would make mistakes that would lead the FBI to their door. Hobart's amoral nature and intimate knowledge of investigative procedure combined to make him perhaps uniquely qualified.

"Let's discuss it tomorrow. Eleven A.M." The phone went dead.

Hobart sat quietly in the semidarkness of his office, still stunned by the conversation. He had seen the Reverend act rashly before, but he usually came to his senses within a few days. Hobart suspected that his boss would regret this conversation in the morning, and by eleven o'clock would have forgotten all about it. He'd seen it before.

He flicked off the computer and the lamp and sat in the dark silence of the office. His mind raced, running endless scenarios for the operation and for his meeting with Blake the next morning. He would have to downplay casualties and cost, but most important, he would have to devise a plan that would insulate Blake from any personal risk.

Hobart pulled his knees to his chest, balancing his heels on the edge of the chair. Until now, he hadn't realized how much of the frustration and resentment he'd suffered at the DEA was still with him. He had spent years trying to compete against the world narcotics machine using conventional legal tactics, and had suffered defeat after defeat at the hands of men of vastly inferior intellect and capability. Now he had a chance to level the playing field, to use methods that would make the most ruthless cartel enforcer cringe. A chance to beat them at their own game.

3

Baltimore, Maryland,
October 16

The Reverend Simon Blake stared silently at the blank piece of paper lying on his desk. He reached for the mug of coffee next to him, but feeling that the cup had gone cold, withdrew his hand and leaned back in his chair.

It was a little after ten o'clock on Monday morning. Sermon-writing morning.

Usually Monday was his favorite day of the week—the day that he created the message that would keep millions of viewers glued to their televisions and on the virtuous path. But today the words wouldn't come.

As soon as he had settled in behind his desk, his thoughts had turned to his son. Pictures of Josh's "innocent" experimentation with marijuana flashed through his mind, gaining mass and speed. Soon the image of his son taking his first hesitant puff on a joint was replaced by that of an older Josh sitting alone in front of a mirror piled high with cocaine. Finally he saw his son, old and emaciated, lying in a garbage-strewn alley with a needle in his arm.

Blake knew that he couldn't let that happen.

A knock at his office door jolted Blake back to reality. He straightened up in his chair and ran a hand through his short hair.

"Come in."

John Hobart strode through the door, closing it firmly behind him. "Good morning, Reverend. You ready to talk?"

Blake stood and walked silently to the conference table near the door. Hobart sat down next to him.

"Have you made a decision, Reverend?"

Blake shook his head slowly. "I'd like to hear some specifics."

Hobart's tone was casual. "What do you want to know?"

"You talk, and I'll tell you if I'm getting bored."

Hobart cleared his throat. He'd hoped to avoid getting into details. They'd just give the Reverend ammunition. He was too close to blow it now.

"Well, at first, we would concentrate on coke and heroin—those drugs, and drugs based on them, seem to be the major problems right now. I would expect that after the first few . . . casualties, the media would saturate the country with the story. Every addict would be on the alert. I think we could expect a substantial drop in use almost immediately."

Blake broke in. "What about the truly addicted? Do you think that they would be capable of just stopping?"

"I think so. There are programs out there to help people like that, they just haven't had much of an incentive to go."

Blake looked satisfied with that answer and signaled for Hobart to continue.

"The fact of the matter is that casual users—not addicts—account for the vast majority of drug consumption in the U.S. I think we can count on them to stop purchasing right away. And that's going to throw a real monkey wrench into the drug dealing and manufacturing machinery. They work just like any other business—credit, cash flow, profitability, inventory—all words you'd hear at a cartel meeting, I guarantee you. Suddenly they can't sell the product they paid so much to produce and ship. The same thing that'd happen to Ford if it suddenly couldn't sell cars, is going to happen to them. In essence, they'll go bankrupt. And without their phenomenal cash flow, they won't be able to pay for the political influence, police protection, and muscle that has kept them in business for so long. I think their infrastructure would collapse faster than anyone expects."

"You mentioned casualties. How many?"

It was a subject Hobart had hoped to stay away from. He lied. "Not many. Drugs are a recreational item; nothing more. I think people would be quick to give them up with that kind of a threat hanging over their heads, don't you?"

He knew Blake's answer to that question. The preacher couldn't understand why people used drugs in the first place.

"Cost?"

"About a million five, total. It should be a self-sustaining operation after the initial start-up." Blake didn't even flinch at the number.

"And my involvement?"

Hobart smiled. "None whatsoever. You give me the okay to drain the money from your accounts, then you fire me. There would be absolutely no way to trace anything back to you. In the unlikely event that anyone ever comes sniffing around, I'll make it look like I embezzled the money."

Blake stood and walked once again to the wall of glass behind his desk. He stood there motionless with his hands clasped behind his back.

"This is it, Reverend. Your chance to smash the cartels and bring America back on course." Hobart felt an excitement he hadn't felt for years. The government, with all its whining bureaucrats and human rights fanatics, had lost its battle with drugs. He wouldn't.

Of course, there were drawbacks that Hobart hadn't elaborated on. Casualties would undoubtedly be significant—but that was all to the better. America needed to have its population thinned. It was like laser surgery. Cut out the cancer and leave the healthy tissue.

And then there was the FBI. They could be counted on to do everything in their considerable power to spoil the party. It would be one hell of a tough investigation, though. No traceable motive, victims who would be reluctant to talk, and an opponent who knew their investigative techniques backwards and forwards.

They might eventually get close enough to make him run, but

by then it would be too late. The users would be gone—one way or another. The memory of the initial casualties would be fading in the minds of the population, but new drug-free neighborhoods would be right out their front door. The pressure would be on for the government to maintain the new status quo.

Hobart suppressed a smile. Someday he might be recognized as one of the most important figures in American history.

"It looks like I've got some thinking to do, John," Blake said from his position by the window. "Let's talk tomorrow."

Simon Blake didn't move from the window as he listened to his security chief walk quietly out of the office.

The moment was at hand. His moment. God had chosen him for a great mission. He was destined to drive Satan from the hearts and minds of America. Until today he had thought that he was to accomplish this through his expanding television ministry and political influence. Now he knew the truth. God didn't want a messenger—it was too late for that. He wanted a soldier.

John Hobart was already waiting when Blake walked into his office the next morning. He was sitting cross-legged with his back to the door, bouncing a pencil impatiently on his knee.

"Early start today, John?"

"You know me, Reverend." He put the pencil down next to his leather-bound legal pad.

"I guess you want my answer on your proposal." His tone was aloof.

Hobart smiled. The Reverend's tone and choice of words spoke volumes. He was already distancing himself from the project. There was no need to distance yourself from something that wasn't going to happen.

Blake sat down behind his desk. "My answer is a conditional yes. But I think that we have some moral obligations here."

Hobart's smile faded. Moral obligations had a way of turning a workable concept into a disastrous operation.

"I feel that you have to warn the public of your intentions. Also,

I don't want marijuana tampered with. There are just too many basically good kids involved."

"I never had any intention of going after pot," Hobart stated. "But could you be more specific about the warning?"

"Large ads in three or four major newspapers ought to do it. Say, three days' notice."

Three days. Hobart wondered if the time frame had a biblical origin.

"No, I don't think that's a good idea. It's going to complicate an already complicated operation and increase my exposure. I strongly advise against it." Hobart leaned forward, punctuating his words by locking eyes with Blake across the office. The Reverend looked unimpressed.

"Nevertheless, that's the way it's going to be, John. If you don't think you can handle the added risk then maybe you're not the right man for the job."

Hobart didn't let his anger show in his expression. Someday he'd take a knife and carve that smug look right off Blake's face.

"I'm going to have to research how much ads like that cost and increase my estimate."

"Just take two million—that ought to cover it. I assume that I can afford it?"

Hobart nodded, knowing that the church could probably afford ten times that amount.

"Is there anything else?" Blake was obviously anxious to end and forget this conversation.

Hobart nodded. "Only one thing—my termination."

4

Washington, D.C.,
November 1

Mark Beamon waved wildly at Tom Sherman, associate director of the FBI. Sherman stood nearly motionless at the entrance of the bar, carefully scanning the crowd. Understandably, he was unable to see Beamon, who had effectively hidden himself behind two half yards of beer balanced precariously on the table. Beamon stood, crossing and uncrossing his arms over his head. Sherman spotted him and began weaving through the tables.

"Nice place, Mark." They shook hands warmly.

"Oh, don't be coy. The bartender tells me they have to roll you out of here most weeknights," Beamon joked, taking his seat and sliding one of the half yards to his friend. "So how was it?"

Sherman had just returned from New Mexico, where he had attended his daughter's college graduation.

"Not so good. She's staying. Sprang it on me just like that. An accounting firm in Santa Fe made her a pretty good offer."

"So what's not so good? Getting a job's tough these days, Tommy. It's not like when you and I were kids. The competition out there's pretty bitter."

Beamon watched his friend take a long pull from the beer. He knew what was bothering him. Sherman doted on his daughter—always had. Having her a thousand miles away for four years was one thing, but having her that far away permanently was another.

"It's a lot of miles, you know."

"Yeah."

Sherman looked like he wanted to say something, but he didn't. He began scanning the bar again, looking at the young faces that surrounded them. "Did you get us any food or are we on the Mark Beamon beer diet?"

"I got some of those mozzarella sticks and a plate of nachos— oh, and buffalo wings." Beamon ignored the pained look on his friend's face. Sherman had been an insufferable health nut ever since he'd quit smoking. "I might've gone a little overboard, but I figured you'd be bringing Leslie. She must be pretty worn out from the trip, though, huh?"

Sherman shook his head. "No. I thought just you and I could have a talk."

Beamon wrestled his glass out of its wooden stand.

"You really did it this time, Mark."

The waitress intruded on their conversation, sliding the platters of junk food onto the table. Beamon assured her that they weren't quite ready for another round of beers as he eyed the food guiltily. The roll of fat around his midsection—popularly known as the Bureau Bulge—was expanding at an alarming rate. Worse yet, the extra weight was spreading to his face, making his eyes look like they were sinking into his thickening brow. But what the hell, too late for a career in modeling anyway. He reached for a wing.

"C'mon, Tommy, the press made half of that stuff up."

"Mark, you called the war on drugs a waste of time right in front of Calahan and two guys from the *Post*. And you did it so loud, half the room heard you."

Beamon grimaced at the name of the current Director of the FBI. He had met William Calahan for the first time at a retirement party for the outgoing Director, and Beamon had taken an instant dislike to him. It had been only three days since the announcement of Calahan's appointment, and the new Director seemed to have already sized up the entire organization and found it wanting. He had talked at Beamon nonstop for fifteen minutes about what he saw as the Bureau's numerous failings, keeping the distance between their noses at less than two inches. Following this discourse, which left Beamon thinking that the new Director was dangerously ignorant and conceited, he had immediately changed the subject to his rebirth as a Christian in the mid-seventies, and the fact that he felt that most of the Bureau's senior staff were alcoholics.

When Calahan had finished his little speech, Beamon had taken one step backward and drained the full bourbon and water he'd been holding. After a quick "nice meeting you," he had turned away and rushed off to find Tom Sherman and a few more drinks.

The Director had never forgotten this inauspicious first meeting, and his initial disdain for Beamon had turned to dislike, then to hatred. It had been hovering in the loathing stage for the past year.

"I can handle Calahan," Beamon said. "Jesus, Tommy, I'm the best investigator the Bureau's got. What's he gonna do? Get rid of me?"

"Goddam right. You pushed him too far this time, Mark. Calahan spent half the morning in my office literally screaming at me."

Beamon reached for another buffalo wing and submerged it in ranch dressing.

"What's the worst job you can imagine, Mark? How would you like to spend the next five years in charge of a task force reviewing the Bureau's filing systems? I'm not making that up—he actually suggested it."

The table next to them broke out into a drunken rendition of Happy Birthday, serenading an embarrassed girl who must have just turned twenty-one. Beamon watched them for a long time as they swayed happily to the tune. Finally he turned back to his friend. "What's the bottom line here?"

"Houston."

"Huh?"

"Houston, Texas."

Beamon stared blankly at him.

"You know. That big state near Mexico."

Beamon broke from his trance. "What's in Houston?"

"Assistant special agent in charge. A slot just opened up. You'd be Steve Garrett's number-two man."

Beamon leaned back in his chair and lit a cigarette. His entire career was flashing before his eyes. He'd been known as a miracle worker. Impossible case? Call Beamon. He'd devoted more of his life than he liked to admit to the Bureau, taking on the cases that most people ran from—investigations that would take years of leg-work to solve. And instead of fading into anonymity toiling on an unsolvable case, he had, with a few notable exceptions, successfully concluded them within six months.

And now his reward. A demotion and banishment to Texas. He'd always known it was coming, but the reality of it, sitting there in the Tibre Creek Inn, was more than he'd bargained for.

"Fuckin' hell, Tommy. An ASAC? You know I don't work and play well with others. Give me a shitty office, but for God's sake put me in charge."

Sherman shook his head sadly. "You know I can't do that Mark. Special agent in charge would make you too high-profile. You've gotta disappear or you just won't survive. You knew this was coming, Mark. You had to. You never gave an inch your whole career. You refused to play the game and now it's time to pay up."

Beamon drained the enormous glass in front of him in under two seconds, eliciting a sincere round of applause from a group of college students sitting at the adjacent table. Beamon smiled and nodded in their direction. He waved at the waitress and held up two fingers. "Right back where I started," he said, turning back to Sherman. "I grew up near there."

"I know."

Beamon took a thoughtful drag on his cigarette. "Houston, huh."

"Houston," Sherman agreed.

"What did Garrett say?"

"He was excited to get you."

Beamon frowned. He didn't know Steve Garrett well, but he knew him better than that. "What did he really say, Tommy?"

Sherman waited for a moment before answering. "He asked if you were as big a prick as your reputation."

"And you said?"

"Bigger."

Beamon laughed. "Oh, thanks, bud. Go ahead and put in a good word for me."

"But then he asked if you were as good as your reputation."

"And you said?"

"Better."

John Hobart brought his new Jeep Cherokee to a stop, and watched a thick knot of people disperse across the road. The sun was shining for the fourth day in a row and the temperature had risen to a near record sixty-two degrees. It was lunch hour, and the Inner Harbor was crawling with local business people, sightseers, and well-dressed conventioneers.

Hobart knew from his former place of employment that a national Baptist conference was in town for the entire week. Thirty thousand holy rollers had descended upon Baltimore, along with their three hundred buses, which were having a disastrous effect on downtown traffic.

The light changed and Hobart stepped lightly on the gas, eliciting dirty looks from the last-minute stragglers hurrying across the street.

He would never get used to the new Inner Harbor. Baltimore had turned its downtown into a gleaming example of urban renewal. The streets were well lit, and the buildings were tall, clean, and modern. Street performers juggled, sang, and joked in front of glass shopping malls and food courts. Across the water, he could see the strangely angled roof of the National Aquarium. A tourist attraction extraordinaire, it was constantly engulfed in a sea of humanity impatiently waiting to get inside.

Fifteen years ago, the Inner Harbor had been infested with rats and old rusting cargo ships. Back then, anyone unfortunate enough to work downtown ate their lunch in their office and left as soon as the bell rang.

The only noticeable holdover from that era was the garbage floating in the murky harbor water, and the hordes of homeless men begging for money from families that hailed from places like Kansas and Iowa.

Hobart couldn't help glancing in the rearview mirror as the building that housed the church's offices disappeared from view. He had spent so much time there over the years that his spacious office had started to feel like home.

It was funny how things worked out. He had taken the job with Blake as a short-term arrangement; the money was good and the security work wasn't particularly demanding. As Blake's focus moved away from pure religion and toward politics, though, the job had become more and more interesting. Using the church's finances to pull the strings of some of the most powerful men in America was a hell of a lot more stimulating than protecting Blake from a bunch of overzealous Bible bashers.

Hobart had spent the first three days after his meeting with Reverend Blake tied to his computer, shifting and manipulating the church's accounts. Money had been deposited across the U.S. and in a number of foreign countries under various individual and corporate names. In all, Hobart had siphoned exactly two million dollars from the church, mostly in the form of payments for phantom services. Unless an accountant was willing to travel across the third world verifying various purchases, construction projects, and donations, the money would never be missed. Hell, even if a Big Six firm was hired specifically to look for wrongdoing, it would take them at least six months and a million miles to sort things out. And when they did, the police would show up at someone else's door, not his.

When he had been completely satisfied with the financial stability of his new organization, tentatively called the Committee for a Drug-Free Society, or CDFS, he had made his way back to the office for the last time.

Blake had been perfect. And why not? He did this type of thing for a living. Hobart had slammed through his office door, "accidentally" not getting it entirely closed. They had argued loudly, Blake making vague accusations, and deriding his attitude. Hobart had constructed an equally vague defense. Finally the Reverend had told him to get out. Hobart had slammed the office door behind him, getting it closed this time, and walked quickly past the four people waiting in Blake's outer office. He had felt their eyes on him as he strode purposefully down the hall.

When the elevator doors opened into the lobby, the front desk guard was standing directly in front of him, blocking his exit.

"Reverend Blake called down and asked me to take your elevator key," he had said nervously. His right hand shook slightly as he held it out in front of him.

Hobart silently complimented his former boss on his thoroughness as he slid the key off its ring and placed it in the guard's outstretched hand. He forced his way around the man and walked through the sunlit lobby. As he opened the first set of glass doors, the guard called after him. "The Reverend told me to tell you that he'd have your personal belongings sent to your house."

Hobart left the building shaking his head. He'd make a covert operative out of Simon Blake yet.

But now that part of his life was over and a new chapter had begun. He gunned the Jeep though a yellow light. He had an appointment in less than two hours, and he had at least an hour's worth of work to do at home first.

Hobart jerked the wheel right, almost missing the narrow side street. He was nearing Canton, about two miles east of the Inner Harbor. Recent years had seen the transformation of this waterfront area from a poorly maintained warehouse district to a yuppie haven. He was a few blocks north of the water, though, and the neighborhood was typical Baltimore. Narrow brick row homes and crowded, potholed, car-lined streets. Elaborate Catholic churches adorned street corners, recalling another time.

Hobart scanned the streets as he drove. It seemed that every other doorstep held a dull-looking chain smoker taking advantage of the unseasonably warm weather. Shouted profanity floated through his open window as women yelled at their children or at the dogs running loose in the street.

He continued on, glancing back and forth from the street to a small Post-it note stuck to his dashboard. Cresting a hill, he could see the blackened metal roofs of the city as they melded together into a black and silver tapestry.

Only a few blocks from the waterfront, he found what he was looking for—a small brick warehouse with a professionally dressed woman in a wheelchair gliding back and forth in front of it. He swung his car into the nearest available space and jogged across the street. Hearing him coming, the woman turned and gave him a practiced smile.

"Mr. Severen, I presume. I'm Karen Styles." She held out her hand, keeping the other one firmly around the chair's left wheel.

He took it. "Please call me John."

In between bouts with the church's various bank accounts, Hobart had managed to contact an old acquaintance who had a talent for forgery. He'd provided four different identities, complete with passports, driver's licenses, birth certificates, and even library cards. The license in the name of John Severen pictured him as having sandy brown hair and a thick mustache. Hobart had made the appropriate changes to his appearance with the help of a well-stocked theatrical makeup shop. He still wasn't used to the change. It was disorienting to look in the mirror and not see his closely cropped black hair and smoothly shaven face. Worse yet, the mustache itched mercilessly.

"Let's take a look," the Realtor suggested, using the key in her hand on the heavy metal door to the warehouse. Hobart reached over to help her. She found the lights and he followed her in.

They entered a small outer office. The walls had been painted yellow sometime in the distant past but had faded to an uneven tan. Hobart walked across the stained carpet and through a door at the back. It led to a nearly identical room. Two large windows had been cut into the wall to the left of him. Judging by their crooked appearance, the work had been done long after the sturdy brick building had been erected.

"If you walk back around here, you can see the bathroom and the entrance to the warehouse section." He followed her, examining her thin neck as she maneuvered the wheelchair through the narrow hall. It would take less than a second to snap it. She'd never know what happened. He frowned. Too dangerous. She was a loose end that he would have to tolerate.

The bathroom was small and basic. A sink, toilet, and mirror. It had the same faded yellow walls but they were stained by mildew, causing wide black streaks that at first glance looked like wallpaper. Karen stopped at another formidable-looking door and tugged at it with all her might. It didn't budge. She looked at Hobart who, finished with his examination of the bathroom, pulled it open. She wheeled through with a grateful smile.

It was just about the right size, close to fifty by fifty feet, with a twenty-five-foot ceiling height. The walls consisted of old brick, occasionally obscured by dirty wooden shelves. At the far end was a tall garage door. It looked large enough to back in a semi. Hobart wandered around aimlessly, stirring up the brightly colored sales flyers littering the floor and ignoring the Realtor's sales pitch.

"Until two weeks ago the warehouse was occupied by a T-shirt company." She reached down and picked up one of the flyers. "That's where all these flyers came from. Obviously, it will be broom clean if you decide to take it."

"And there are apartments above?"

"Two. I confirmed that they're both available, but I hear that they're not that nice."

"You said eight hundred dollars for the warehouse?"

She nodded.

"How much for the entire building?"

She chewed her bottom lip. "Probably double that, sixteen hundred. Keep in mind that there's no access to the upstairs from here."

He took another quick turn through the space. "I'll take it for a year with a one-year option. It'll need some work, though. I assume that the owners wouldn't mind if I made a few improvements—at my own expense, of course."

"What kind of improvements were you considering?"

"Nothing special. A little paint, a new carpet, maybe an alarm system."

She shrugged. "I can't imagine that would be a problem. What kind of business are you in, John?"

"Wholesale antiques."

"Really? That's interesting," she said in a slightly bored tone. "Let me pop out to my car and call the owners. I want to make sure that I quoted you right on the apartments, and ask them about the improvements. If everything's all right, we can go back to my office, fill out a little paperwork, and it's yours."

"Fine."

It was almost five o'clock when Hobart left the realty office in Fells Point, an area known for good seafood and dive bars. The smell of steaming crabs hung in the air, inviting him into the restaurant directly across the street. He glanced at his watch. Dinner would have to wait.

Hobart pulled his car into a narrow space about a block from his final destination. He fished a small scrap of paper out of his pocket and dialed the number written there on his cellular phone. It rang four times before being picked up by a machine.

"Leave a message," was the only greeting, followed by a loud beep. He didn't. Instead he pulled a small black knapsack off the floor of the Jeep and walked across the street, straining to make out the numbers on the houses in the waning light. When he got to 619 he turned and walked into the narrow passageway between it and the house next door. The cracked cement under his feet was under two inches of sudsy water. It smelled like laundry detergent.

The passageway eventually opened into a small backyard separated into two parcels by a short chain-link fence. Hobart entered the gate on the left. He looked around to confirm that no one was watching from the windows of the surrounding houses, and pulled out a large screwdriver. It turned out to be unnecessary. The door swung open when he grabbed the knob. Smiling, he entered the kitchen.

Dishes were stacked everywhere, and judging from the smell, they'd been there for some time. Hobart's gaze fell on a small pile of bones lying on the floor and he froze. He stood perfectly still for almost a minute listening for any sign of a dog. Hearing nothing, he padded quietly into the living room. No self-respecting canine could have missed his less-than-silent entrance.

He made a quick walk through of the house, confirming that no one was home. The other rooms were in a condition similar to the kitchen. Plaster was falling from the ceiling in places and half the lights seemed to be burned out. The furniture—what little there was of it—looked like it had been retrieved from city dumpsters. The single bedroom didn't actually have a bed, only a foul-smelling mattress lying on the floor.

He moved quickly, placing listening devices in the phone, the living room, and bedroom. He was thankful for the surgical gloves covering his hands—he wasn't anxious to touch anything with his bare skin. No telling what you could catch.

When he was finished, he situated himself in a worn out La-Z-Boy next to the front door. It wasn't particularly comfortable. It didn't recline and it looked like most of the foam had rotted and fallen out onto the carpet. Other than that, the chair was ideal. He couldn't be immediately seen from the door, and it was more sanitary than sitting on the floor—though only marginally.

Next to him was a large shelf overflowing with books. He leaned over and scanned the titles. No novels or fiction, just textbooks on subjects like physics and chemistry. Archaeology also had a place, but the thick dust on the covers suggested that the subject had fallen from grace. He was glad to see that his old friend was keeping his mind sharp.

The friend he was waiting for was one Peter Manion. Hobart had flipped through a bootleg file on his ex-informant the day Blake had given him the go-ahead. He hadn't seen Manion for years—not since his DEA days.

Manion had been born on the east side of Baltimore to a working-class family in 1957. He'd shown an early aptitude for math and science and was encouraged by his mother, a particularly strong woman whose interest in education belied her lack of one. His father hadn't shared her convictions and had constantly belittled his son for his shy, quiet demeanor. In the end his mother prevailed, and Manion won a full scholarship to Johns Hopkins. It was there that he became interested in the darker side of chemistry.

One evening in the last half of his sophomore year, Manion had been befriended by a pretty psychology student. After a few weeks, his new friend brought up the possibility of Manion cooking up a batch of LSD. He'd resisted at first, but the promise of quick and easy money finally seduced him. When he finished that first batch, curiosity had overwhelmed him and he tested his handiwork.

That had been the beginning of a drug problem that engulfed his life and ended in his addiction to heroin. He left JHU in 1978, the middle of his junior year, and had been in a drug-induced fog ever since.

They had first met during Hobart's tour as a Baltimore DEA agent in the early eighties. Manion's intelligence, connections, and paranoia had made him an ideal resource for the young John Hobart. While he never actually informed on individuals, Manion had been a fount of information on the manufacture of designer drugs and the refinement of biological intoxicants.

Hobart hadn't seen him in almost ten years, but hadn't had any difficulty in finding the addict. He lived only three blocks from the house that he'd occupied the last time they'd met, and his phone number had been in the book. Drug dealers could only afford so much anonymity.

At six-thirty Hobart heard the unmistakable sound of a key turning in the lock on the front door. He pulled his .45 automatic from its place under his left arm and quietly stood. By the time the door finally swung open, he had flattened himself against the wall about a foot away from the doorjamb.

The man who entered was taller than Hobart, but his body seemed to sag from some unseen weight, bringing his head to eye level. Hobart recognized him immediately, though the years of inactivity and drug use had taken their toll. He maneuvered himself behind the man and pressed the barrel of his gun snugly into the back of his neck.

Peter Manion froze. "Darren, is that you? I told you I'd get you your money next week, man. I got some stuff cooking. I swear you'll get every dime." His voice was thin and Hobart had to strain to hear despite the fact that he was right behind him.

"Have you not been paying your bills, Petey?"

Manion's body snapped straight, forcing Hobart to adjust the barrel of his pistol. Manion obviously recognized his voice.

Hobart slowly circled around to face him, drawing the gun along the slack skin of his neck.

Manion looked straight into Hobart's eyes, ignoring his elaborate disguise. He began unconsciously rubbing the wrist that Hobart had broken so many years before.

"How you doing, Peter? Long time no see." Hobart grabbed the front of Manion's filthy sweater and pushed him onto the La-Z-Boy that had been his home for the last hour.

He sat down on an old army footlocker that passed for a coffee table. "You look like you've lost weight—been working out?" The haggard face across from him continued to stare blankly. Finally it spoke. "I heard they drummed you out of the DEA."

Hobart shook his head at the feeble attempt at bravado. "That's what everybody thinks. Fact is, I just switched organizations."

"Who you working for now? FBI?"

Hobart shook his head.

Manion's eyes widened. "CIA?"

Hobart smiled and nodded almost imperceptibly. Peter Manion had always been a borderline paranoid schizophrenic. Hobart still remembered his fantasies involving the CIA and how they were behind everything from Kennedy's assassination to the closing of the local Seven-Eleven. Manion saw the CIA as a faceless, all-powerful organization with operatives behind every corner. Hobart intended to put that paranoia to good use.

Manion pulled his knees up against his chest and cradled them in his bony arms.

"What do you want, man?"

"Just a little information. Should be right up your alley."

Manion remained silent. He looked like he needed a fix.

"We're getting a little operation together and I need your expertise in chemistry." Manion perked up bit at the word "chemistry."

"The Company's getting fed up with all this narcotics money that's running around. It's keeping some governments afloat that we'd prefer to see sink. You understand what I mean?"

Manion was looking desperately around the room as Hobart spoke. He seemed to not be paying attention.

"We need to cut off their money—so we're going to poison the U.S. narcotics supply."

Manion's hands popped open and his feet fell to the carpet with a thud. "You're crazy!" His eyes continued to dart around the room. Hobart wasn't sure if he was looking for somewhere to run or for CIA agents hiding behind the furniture.

"I have my orders. We'll make it worth your while. Ten thousand dollars and a lifetime supply of top-quality heroin. Poison-free, of course." He punctuated his words by pulling a wad of bills from the bag at his feet and slapping them down on the sofa next to him.

"No way, man. There's no way you can make me help you. I got rights." The last part sounded more like a question than a statement.

"Of course you do," Hobart said soothingly. "This is a great deal, though, if you think about it. We're going to do this with your help or not. So why not make it easy on yourself?"

"No fucking way, man!" The spit that sprayed from his mouth mingled with the dust in the air.

Hobart looked down at his feet, where a can of lighter fluid sat. His old informant didn't seem like the barbecuing type. No doubt the stuff was used to manufacture some kind of high.

He reached down and picked up the greasy can, studying it.

Manion was hugging his knees again, rocking back and forth, mumbling as though in prayer.

"You know, Peter, I was watching an interesting show on PBS last night. It was on those monks in Vietnam who set themselves on fire to protest the war. Remember them? I saw one of 'em do it when I was over there. Nasty." He turned the can and began reading the back. "They said that burning is the most excruciating way to die. They also said that a person's sense of smell is the last thing to go. Do you believe that?"

Manion shook his head miserably, sweat dripping down his forehead. Hobart was starting to enjoy himself.

"Awful smell, burning flesh—must be even worse when it's your own." Hobart picked up a steak knife from a half-empty plate on the floor and put it to Manion's throat. With the other hand he squirted the lighter fluid on his head. Manion buried his face in his knees, protecting his eyes. The knife pressed to his neck kept him from rising.

"Last chance," Hobart advised, tossing the nearly empty can behind him and pulling a lighter out of his pocket. Manion's face came out from behind his knees at the familiar sound of the sparking lighter. He looked like he was about to scream, and Hobart pushed harder with the knife, diminishing the cry into a pathetic whimper. He held the lighter a safe distance from Manion, whose eyes were locked on the quivering flame.

Hobart fully intended to kill him if he didn't agree. He'd be forced to pick a less dramatic method though. A screaming ball of flame running around the house was bound to attract attention.

Manion closed his eyes and began sobbing quietly.

Hobart was getting impatient. "C'mon, Petey, what's it going to be?"

5

Near Cumberland, Maryland, November 1

John Hobart set the cruise control at sixty-six and leaned his seat-back into a more comfortable position. It was a beautiful night. Cool, but not cold, and crystal clear. The new Jeep rode as smoothly as a Rolls-Royce down the empty highway, allowing him to gaze through the glass sunroof at the stars. He occasionally glanced back at the road to confirm that he wasn't straying over any important lines.

He'd left Peter Manion's house just before seven o'clock, maneuvering through the thickening city traffic and onto the highway out of Baltimore. City had turned to suburbs, and finally the suburbs had given way to the grassy hills of rural Maryland. The radio was beginning to fade, erupting in loud static every few minutes. He fed a classical CD into the dash.

It was almost another hour before he saw his exit rushing to meet him. He tapped out the complex rhythm of the last concerto on the CD as he swung his car off the highway. It wasn't an exit ramp in the true sense of the word, more of an ill-kept asphalt road breaking off from the main thoroughfare. The night closed in on the car as he sped away from the interstate. The faded gray asphalt climbed a steep grade into the darkness.

Eventually the road turned to gravel and then to dirt. He switched on the four-wheel drive and struggled through deep ruts, slowing to under ten miles per hour. The road narrowed to the point that tree branches swished against both sides of the car. The air, moistened by the dense trees, had turned into a swirling fog. Hobart leaned closer to the windshield, resting his chin on the steering wheel.

Finally the headlights illuminated a small break in the trees to the right. He turned carefully into it, hearing the bottom of the Jeep scrape as he maneuvered down a steep incline. When he leveled out, a small cedar cabin nestled in the trees became visible about twenty yards away. He cut the engine and coasted to a quiet stop next to its large redwood deck.

His breath came out like steam, illuminated by the light still on in the interior of the car. His boots made a satisfying crunching sound as he walked around to the back of the car and pulled a large black suitcase out of the cargo space.

The cracked and faded exterior of the cabin, illuminated briefly by the Jeep's headlights, didn't fit with the interior. While the furniture had a hand-me-down look common to weekend retreats, the cabin was immaculately maintained inside. Floors were swept and oiled, and the kitchen was well stocked. Flashlight in hand, Hobart weaved his way through the dark living room and lit a propane lamp on the wall. The flame came to life, bathing the inside of the cabin in a soft blue-white glow.

After unpacking his suitcase in one of the cabin's two bedrooms, he went back out to the car and pulled a large cooler out of the back. It was full of perishables that couldn't be kept at the cabin during his long absences. He switched on the refrigerator and loaded in the food, keeping a cold beer on the counter for himself. He started a fire in the wood stove and settled onto the sofa. The sound of the wind blowing through the tall pines that surrounded the cabin lulled him to sleep.

Hobart jerked as the hot grease spattered on his arm. He quickly threw a lid on the pan, hiding the cooking bacon within. Last night's fog was only a memory, and the sun was beginning to filter through the skylights high above him. In the light, the house took on a colder feel. The cabin had the same unlived-in look as his home in Baltimore. The motion in the kitchen and the smell of bacon and eggs seemed out of place in the sterile atmosphere.

He was halfway though eating his breakfast when he heard the unmistakable sound of tires rolling down the steep hill to the cabin. He looked at his watch as he pushed the chair back and wiped his mouth on a napkin. Fifteen minutes early.

Hobart waved he walked out the front door and onto the deck. Robert Swenson returned his greeting by sticking an arm out of the window of his beat-up Cadillac. Pulling to a stop next to the Jeep, he jumped out and slammed the door behind him.

"What the hell's going on, John? A week ago the Reverend comes into my office and tells me he fired you. You don't return any of my calls, then I get that cloak and dagger message from you on my voice mail."

Hobart ignored his question. "You didn't tell anyone you were coming here did you?"

"Hell, no, your message was pretty clear on that subject. So what's going on?"

"Come on in," Hobart said, turning and starting back into the house. "I'll tell you all about it."

Once inside, Hobart repositioned himself in front of his breakfast and started in on it again. "Can I get you something?" he asked, watching Swenson drag a chair in from the living room.

"Nah, I grabbed an Egg McMuffin on the way. So what happened?"

"Nothing all that interesting, Bob. Just got sick of that prima donna, you know? We had it out and he fired me."

Swenson shook his head knowingly.

Hobart had first met Robert Swenson in Vietnam when their Special Forces units had been temporarily combined. After the war was over, their lives had continued on similar paths. Hobart had joined the DEA, and Swenson, the L.A. Police Department's narcotics division. Later, when Hobart had taken the security chief post at the church, he'd brought his old friend in as his right-hand man.

"Shit, John, he'll probably change his mind next week."

"Not that big an issue, really. There's some stuff I've been want-ing to do and this'll give me a chance to do it."

Swenson snatched an untouched piece of bacon from Hobart's plate. "What do you have going? Starting a private contracting business?"

"In a way. Actually, I asked you to come here 'cause I want you to come and work for me. I think I've got something for you that you'll find more fulfilling than chasing Simon Blake around."

Swenson looked interested, as Hobart knew he would be.

Swenson had been married for almost six years when his wife had been killed in a car accident. They seemed to have had a per-fect marriage—she was one of the few women able to adjust to the life of a cop's wife. Between that and Swenson's rare talent for sepa-rating his personal life from the job, it looked like a relationship that was going to last. Hobart couldn't remember exactly when she had died, but it was sometime in the mid-eighties—maybe '84.

As he recalled the story, it had been a clear night in Chicago and Helen had been returning from a college where she was taking classes. The stretch of road where she died was perfectly straight. Inexplicably, a car coming the other direction ran off the road, through a grass median, and head-on into her Volkswagen Rabbit. The other driver survived, protected by his one-ton pickup. Helen had been decapitated. Later it was discovered that the driver had been hopped up on some drug or another.

"So?" Swenson prompted.

Hobart had spent most of the drive to the cabin trying to figure out a way to hedge on his offer to Swenson. Not to give too much away. He hadn't been able to come up with anything practical. There seemed to be no alternative to jumping in with both feet.

"I intend to stop the illegal narcotics trade in the U.S."

Swenson laughed and gnawed on the piece of bacon. "Don't tell me the DEA's taking you back."

"I'm serious, Bob. America's being torn apart by drugs—you ought to know that better than anyone. I've decided to put a stop to it."

"Never knew you were such a patriot, John."

"I think of it more as an interesting challenge." He wasn't joking, and from Swenson's expression, it looked like that was beginning to sink in.

"Hey, I'm with you in theory, John, but let's face it, the war on drugs is a joke. You and I devoted some of the best years of our lives to chasing our tails."

Hobart put his fork down and took a deep breath. "That's true, we did. But now I think I've found a way to make up for that lost time."

"Planning on running for President? I don't see you as the baby-kissing type."

"I'm going to poison the drug supply."

Swenson dropped what was left of the strip of bacon onto the table and stood. He walked back into the kitchen and poured himself a cup of coffee. Hobart went back to his breakfast.

"You're serious," Swenson said from the kitchen. It was a statement and not a question. He came back around and took his seat, sipping at the steaming mug. A deep crease appeared in his forehead as he mulled over what he'd just heard.

"Why not? I assume you agree that it would take care of the problem."

Swenson nodded. "Yeah. It'd work. Given the right scale."

Hobart had expected a more enthusiastic response than the blank stare he was getting. Had it not been for Swenson's wife being killed by a narcotics user and his subsequent bitterness, Hobart wouldn't have dreamed of trying to recruit him for this operation. If Helen were still alive, Swenson undoubtedly would have marched into the nearest FBI office and turned him in. She wasn't alive though, she was lying in a coffin in two pieces somewhere in Chicago. And that made all the difference.

Hobart reached discreetly under the table and closed his hand around a hard piece of wood. That morning he had sawed off a baseball bat to a two-foot length and taped it under the table. Robert Swenson was the closest thing to a friend that he had, but his friend either had to get on board or disappear.

It wouldn't be difficult. He would put Swenson's body back into the Cadillac and run it off the edge of one of the winding mountain roads that crisscrossed the area. It was risky, but the local cops weren't rocket scientists. And it was less of a hazard than having someone not involved in the operation running around knowing who was behind it.

Swenson was silent for almost five minutes and Hobart's hand began to sweat, making the handle of the bat damp and slippery.

"I'm in," he said finally. Hobart's hand loosened on the handle. "But we're gonna have to put together a decent amount of money to get something like this off the ground."

Hobart's hand dropped completely from the handle at the word "we." He wiped his wet palm on his slacks. "Already taken care of."

"Blake's in on it, then?"

"No." Hobart's tone and expression made it clear that Blake's name should never be mentioned again. Swenson took the hint and changed the subject.

"How many people do you figure we need?"

"About eight more. I've already scheduled meetings with them here. The first one arrives at three."

"People you've known for a long time?"

"For the most part," he replied vaguely, beginning to clear the dishes off the table.

"What if you ask them and they aren't interested?"

"That's my problem, I'll take care of the recruiting. You go tie up any loose ends you have in Baltimore."

"Just tell me one thing before I leave."

"Sure. What?"

"How the hell are we gonna pull this off?"

Three o'clock rolled around quickly. Swenson had gone less than an hour ago. They'd spent a productive day going over operational details. It was surprising how much it helped to have someone to bounce ideas off of. Things that seemed brilliant alone in front of the fire could sound stupid out loud.

"Johnny! How you fuckin' doing!"

Hobart's second recruit had arrived and was making his way to the house.

Bill Karns had been a narcotics cop in Chicago when they'd first met. Since then he had quit the force and become a private investigator. His wife died a few years back, leaving him without any surviving family. Given the pick of the litter, Hobart probably wouldn't have chosen him. In his opinion, the man was brainless and undisciplined. On the other hand, he knew that Karns would go for this plan in a big way. His bigotry ran deep. Almost as deep as Hobart's own.

"Looks like you put on a little weight since I was last in L.A.," Hobart observed sternly, slapping the roll of fat adorning Karns' waist.

"You know how it is, Johnny." Karns was the only person in the world who called him Johnny. He'd forgotten how irritating it was.

"Come on in."

Karns was sweating profusely despite the damp cold of the woods. Hobart maneuvered him to the chair that Swenson had occupied earlier that day and got them both beers. Karns grunted his thanks and twisted the top off.

"Good to see you, Johnny. It's been too goddam long."

"You didn't tell anybody you were coming up here, did you?"

"Shit, no. In my business you understand the word 'confidential.' He took a pull from the bottle, almost emptying it. "You needin' a good private investigator?"

"No. But I do have a job for you. Good pay, but you'd probably do it for free."

Karns looked interested, but not so interested that he didn't finish the beer in one large gulp and begin looking woefully at the one across from him. Hobart got the hint and pushed it toward the still-perspiring man. Then he smoothly slipped his hand under the table and around the bat.

"I'm putting together an organization that's going to stop the use of illegal drugs in the U.S.," he said simply.

Karns laughed. "My ass. How the fuck you gonna do that?" He lifted the beer bottle.

"I'm going to poison the narcotics supply."

The beer stopped about four inches from Karns' mouth. "The fuck you are."

"The fuck I am." He could see the wheels in Karns' head slowly turning. It was their only speed.

Karns scooted his chair back and slapped his knee, laughing. "Shit! That oughtta just about piss off the niggers and the spics!"

Hobart smiled. "I expect it will. So you're in?"

Karns banged his beer bottle down on the table. "You're really serious?"

Hobart pulled a briefcase from the floor next to him and laid it on the table. He opened it, exposing neatly bundled stacks of hundred-dollar bills. "That's fifty thousand dollars. Your advance."

Karns' eyes were glued to the briefcase. He reached blindly for the bottle of beer, almost knocking it over.

"So are you in?"

"Fuck, yeah!" He reached out and caressed the bundles, pulling one out and flipping the edge like a deck of cards. He looked up at Hobart. "You're right, you know."

"About what?"

"I would have done it for free."

He'd been luckier than he deserved. The bat was still taped to the bottom of the kitchen table at his cabin, unused. The remaining six recruits had come and gone over the last week. They had taken quite a bit more work than Karns, whose life could be summed up on a postcard. Hobart had served meals, hiked, boated, and hunted with the rest. He'd probed deeply into their lives, looking for serious girlfriends, jobs, homes that they were attached to, sick relatives, set-in-stone future plans. Only when he was completely satisfied with their answers did he wrap his hand around the bat and pop the question.

There had been a few tense moments of indecision and varying degrees of enthusiasm, but in the end they had all agreed. Hobart had counted on at least one of them having to disappear. Two was probably more likely. He had been dreading the added exposure.

The remaining recruits were all of better quality than Karns, though they lacked his blind loyalty and single-mindedness. Karns would stay with him to the end, no matter what the circumstances. The rest would be wary of the FBI and dealers, and would get out when it got too hot. While they lacked Karns' simple predictability, they made up for it with intelligence and experience. Every one of them was capable of running a top-notch undercover operation.

Hobart slowed his car to match the speed limit as he closed in on Baltimore. He hoped to avoid the police completely over the next year.

"Peter! Good to see you!" Hobart was sitting in his favorite chair by the door as Peter Manion walked into the dimly lit room. His .45 rested next to him on what passed for a table. Intimidation value.

"Hi, John," Manion mumbled. He squinted his glassy eyes to see his guest more clearly. His speech was a bit slurred.

The fact that Manion hadn't been startled by his presence confirmed in Hobart's mind that he probably had fortified himself with a healthy dose of heroin in honor of their meeting. The ten thousand dollars that he had left behind on his first visit had been put to good use.

"What have you got for me?"

Manion walked over to a large pile of books that hadn't been there the last time they had spoken. The jackets were free of the dust and drink rings that covered everything else in the house.

"Orellanin," Manion said, holding a book up as though Hobart could read it through the cover.

"Come again?"

"Orellanin. That's what you've got to use, man." Manion was starting to warm up to his subject. The combination of drugs and his fanatical interest in science appeared to have made him forget the real reason that they were speaking. To him, it had become nothing more than a conceptual exercise in biochemistry.

"Never heard of it."

"I'm not surprised, man. It's distilled from a mushroom that grows mostly in Poland. The *Cortinarius orellanus.*"

Hobart was shocked. Manion was yanking his chain. For a moment he wondered if the police were standing right outside the door, but quickly dismissed the idea. He'd reviewed the tapes from the bugs he'd planted and gone over the house with a fine-tooth comb before its owner had arrived. He picked up the .45 and aimed it at a surprised Peter Manion.

"I'm not in a joking mood today, Petey my boy. Not at all."

Manion dropped the book and backed slowly into a corner, his hands out in front of him. "Don't shoot, man. I *am* serious. This stuff's perfect."

Hobart lowered the gun slightly. "I'm listening. But you damn well better dazzle me with your genius."

Manion moved slowly around to the ragged sofa, keeping his back against the wall the entire way. When he sat down, a cloud of dust rose around him. "Listen. The problem with poisoning coke and heroin when it's being processed isn't getting it into the drugs—that's easy. The problems are in distribution."

Hobart leaned back and pulled a small pad from his jacket. He fished around for a pen. "Go on."

Manion, looking more comfortable, continued. "Let's say you just dump a bunch of, say, arsenic into a vat of coke while it's being refined. No problem, you're done, right?"

Hobart nodded.

"But it wouldn't get you anywhere. Distribution would totally fuck you up. Most times, when the stuff is sold, some dealer or another tries it, right? If not, they could just be getting twenty keys of baby powder. So, they try it and drop dead. Who's gonna buy it then?"

Hobart shrugged. It was a good point. "So what's the answer?"

"I already told you, man. Orellanin." Manion picked up the book that he had dropped while looking down the barrel of Hobart's .45, and held it to his chest. Hobart could just make out the picture of a mushroom on the front.

"The beauty of this stuff is that it has like a two-week delayed reaction. Say you shoot it," he pantomimed using a syringe on his arm. "You feel great, while the poison's making its way to your liver and kidneys. By the time you start feeling shitty, you're fucked. Your major organs are toast. The only way their gonna save you is a transplant—and there isn't gonna be time for that."

"What if a doctor found out early? Could he give the patient an antidote then?"

"Is none, man. I think a few people who've eaten the mushrooms have been saved by getting their stomachs pumped, like, right away. That wouldn't really apply here, since you don't eat coke and horse. Of course, a full blood transfusion might do it—totally change out the guy's blood right after he's been poisoned. I'm only guessing on that, though."

"So I need to crush up a bunch of mushrooms?"

"Not exactly. The poison has to be extracted. It's pretty much a no-brainer, though."

Hobart smiled. "I'm sure you won't have any trouble at all."

"Hey man, I didn't mean . . ."

"I've got a nice warehouse," Hobart cut in. "We'll set you up with whatever you need. Hell, we'll put together a lab that'll put Hopkins to shame."

Manion perked up at that. The thought of being surrounded by steaming beakers, Bunsen burners, and microscopes seemed to agree with him. It had been a long time.

"Okay, Peter, how many of these mushrooms do we need?"

"Depends on how much stuff you want to hit."

"Say fifty keys."

Manion tapped his chin and did some quick calculations. "That's gonna take a lot of 'shrooms, man. You're in the neighborhood of a ton there."

Hobart took a deep breath and let it out loudly. "About a ton. Shit. Is there anything else I can use?" This was becoming more complicated than he'd bargained for. As was often the case, the concept had looked better without the details.

"As far as hitting the stuff at the manufacturer, probably not. You need that delay, man. That's what makes it all work. You could get a shorter delay out of paraquat."

That one rang a bell with Hobart. The DEA had used it back in the seventies. "The defoliant?"

"Yeah, it's a herbicide. Two-day delay—easy to get. I think they call it StarFire or something, now. Two days isn't gonna get you far, though."

Hobart's mind was racing. Manion was right, it wasn't enough. It had to be the orellanin. "What about downstream stuff, Peter? The stuff we hit right before it makes it to the street?"

"No need to get fancy on that. Go to Safeway and buy rat poison with cyanide in it."

Hobart nodded. "So how do I hit the stuff at the refinery?"

Manion picked up a potato chip from a plate full of molding food and began munching on it. "Oh, shit, getting it into the stuff—that's the easy part."

6

Warsaw, Poland,
November 21

The Krolikarnia was considered a moderately nice hotel, though through the dirty glass of the car window it looked more like a Harlem boxing gym. Hobart eased himself out of the cramped interior of the cab and straightened his body out for the first time in what seemed like ages. He took a deep breath, cleansing his memory of the knuckle-whitening landing at the Okecie Airport, and even more nervewracking ride from airport to hotel.

Hobart doled out twenty American dollars to the cabby and walked around to pull his bags from the trunk. The ex-communist cabbies hadn't yet warmed to performing this service. He had barely begun to pull at his suitcase when, with an unintelligible shout, the driver merged the cab back into the heavy afternoon traffic. His sudden acceleration almost slammed the trunk shut on Hobart's hand.

An atmosphere of lawlessness pervaded Warsaw, and nowhere was it more evident than in the traffic patterns. It seemed the Poles felt that their newfound freedom extended to a considerable amount of artistic license on the road.

The fumes expelled by the cars racing by were beginning to choke him, so Hobart hefted his bags and entered the hotel. A bored-looking woman sitting at the front desk watched him approach. Except for her, the small lobby was empty. She smiled wearily as he approached, but remained silent.

"Hi, I'm Dr. John Stapleton," Hobart said with a thick Southern drawl that was obviously lost on the desk clerk. "I think y'all have a reservation for me."

Still not uttering a sound, she flipped though a well-worn leather book lying on the equally worn desktop. Computers hadn't found their way to the Krolikarnia yet.

"I have it," she said in a thickly accented voice. "Please, you sign your name here."

He obliged and she handed him a key attached to a six-inch-long piece of wood. The number 414 was burned into it.

"Thank you," she said, sitting back down and turning her eyes to the front door. Hobart got the feeling that he'd heard her entire repertoire of English.

No eager bellhop materialized, so he hefted his luggage and walked into an old iron-gated elevator directly opposite the desk.

The sun streamed through an open window in his room, illuminating the sheer white curtains blowing in the breeze. The space was so small that it was difficult to walk around the single twin bed in the middle of the room.

Hobart pushed a Kleenex into the ancient keyhole from the inside and lay down on the lumpy bed. International travel always sapped his energy, and the effect was getting worse as the years passed.

The room looked like something out of a 1950s gangster movie. It was a simple small cube. A sink stood in the corner with a large painted pitcher teetering on its edge. There was no television; the furniture consisted only of the bed, a lamp resting on a nightstand, and a broken wooden chair sitting next to the window.

Glancing at his watch, Hobart saw that he had a few hours before his meeting. He hated to take a nap—it always seemed to prolong jet lag—but he decided that he should stay sharp. It would probably be impossible to sleep anyway. The disguise he was wearing had been driving him crazy since he put it on. Effective, though. It was getting so he didn't even recognize himself anymore.

A gray wig of nearly shoulder-length hair adorned his head and was tied back in a neat ponytail. The full beard was a bit darker. The proprietor of the costume store had insisted that no one ever had a perfectly matched beard.

He wore wire-rimmed glasses with clear glass, and beneath them his eyes were tinted green by contacts. Having perfect vision, he'd never had to deal with contacts before. So far they had been more trouble than they were probably worth.

The disguise was completed by a tan corduroy jacket covering a reddish wool sweater and well-worn jeans. It was a bit stereotypical, but he doubted that his new associate would notice. It seemed that the Europeans looked at Americans as one stereotype or another anyway. They seemed disappointed when they saw one that didn't fit their categories.

Hobart awoke to the sound of knocking on his door accompanied by a comically accented voice. "Yoo hoo. Professor Stapleton—are you asleeping?"

He had never actually spoken with Lech Orloski on the phone, but the voice was exactly what he had expected.

Hobart had located the man on the Internet through a loosely knit group devoted to exotic mushrooms. The strange and elaborate subcultures that inhabited the world never ceased to amaze him. There seemed to be a club, organization, or magazine built around every subject imaginable.

When Manion had first suggested using orellanin, Hobart had been concerned about the complexity of gathering the mushrooms. In the end it had been simple. His Internet search had no potential to expose his true identity, and all communications, until now, had been carried out by computer.

Hobart had simply e-mailed Orloski as to the type of mushroom that he was interested in and the fact that he needed about a ton. This had produced more than a few questions, but he had managed to answer them to the Pole's satisfaction.

Orloski had, of course, been familiar with this particular type of fungus and had e-mailed Hobart that it would be a simple matter to collect them. He had even arranged for a shipping method that would bypass U.S. customs. That last little service had cost plenty.

Hobart swung his stockinged feet off the bed and walked quickly to the door, effecting a scholarly stoop in his shoulders. He opened it to find Orloski just as he had pictured him—tall, round, and with an enormous beard spilling across his chest.

"Professor!" the Pole cried as the door opened. "It is so good to finally see your face!" He grabbed Hobart's shoulders and kissed him hard on both cheeks.

Hobart took a step backward when the Pole released him, still trying to shake the gauze out of his brain. "It's good to finally meet you, too, Mr. Orloski."

"Please, call me Lech. My car awaits. Are you ready?"

Hobart grabbed his shoes and coat off the floor and motioned toward the door.

The wind was blowing with surprising force, making it necessary for Orloski to put his full weight behind opening the front door of the hotel. He held it long enough for Hobart to slip through, and then made for a tiny European car illegally parked in front of the hotel. Hobart watched the man pour himself into the car and expand into the limited space inside. When Orloski was down to one leg outside the vehicle, Hobart jogged around to the passenger side. His diminutive stature benefited him occasionally, and this was definitely one of those times. Orloski's bulk spilled over the console between the seats, and Hobart found himself sandwiched between the Pole's fleshy shoulder and the car door, the handle of which had settled uncomfortably into his ribs.

"Are you comfortable?" Orloski's tone suggested that the car was a Rolls. The pained look on his passenger's face seemed to escape him.

"Oh, sure, Lech. Just fine."

"Wonderful!"

Armed with the knowledge that his client was happy, Orloski

jumped on the gas and sent the small car hurtling into traffic. He took the long route through the city, detouring around endless traffic circles and pointing out historically significant sights by the dozens. He would get halfway through a dissertation on one landmark when another would appear. The prior story was instantly forgotten as he began a half lecture on the next. This went on for about an hour before they broke out of the city and into the rolling countryside.

The wind that had been blowing in Warsaw grew stronger, unhampered by the narrow streets and sturdy stone buildings. The gentle rocking of the car and Orloski's habit of racing up behind other vehicles and slamming on his brakes was making Hobart queasy. He concentrated on the mist-covered landscape and ignored his host's dissertation on Polish family life and the sad history of his ancestors.

After about forty-five minutes, they passed a large group of peasants collected on the top of a windy knoll to their right. They walked bent at the waist, reaping phantom crops from the scrub that blanketed this part of Poland. Orloski changed subjects without taking a breath.

"There are your mushrooms." A fat finger pointed to the slowly circling peasants, almost touching the glass of the passenger-side window. He swung the car carefully onto a muddy side road and stopped. Throwing the door open, he began the laborious project of getting out. He had to hurry to catch Hobart, who had started immediately up the road toward the center of activity. Orloski was breathing heavily as he pulled alongside.

"I found this place a few days after we spoke," he said between gasps. "The man who owns the land allowed us to pick the mushrooms for a small fee. In fact, I believe that I hired some of his family to help." Orloski scanned the distant men and women intently, trying to pick out one of the owner's family members. Not interested in meeting anyone else in Poland, Hobart changed the subject.

"How many people do you have working here?"

"Oh, quite a few. I would guess around fifty. You needed the mushrooms so quickly, you know. I think I am employing nearly every person over ten and under seventy from Takestek.

"Takestek?"

"A nearby village. The citizens are very happy to work for the fair wage I pay them."

Hobart wondered what he considered a fair wage. A dollar a day? Less?

As they crested the hill, Hobart could clearly see the workers' path. In front of the brightly dressed peasants, the mushrooms grew surprisingly thick. Behind them lay a smooth brown-green carpet of grass. About fifty yards ahead, an old flatbed truck was parked in the middle of the muddy road. A young man in jeans and knee-high rubber boots was picking through a pile of mushrooms at his feet.

He looked up from his task briefly, catching a glimpse of Orloski. He waved and stepped carefully around the pile. They met halfway and the boy, who looked much younger close-up, kissed the Pole on both cheeks and then offered his hand to Hobart.

"This is my eldest son, Paul. Paul, I'd like you to meet Dr. Stapleton."

"A pleasure to meet you, Doctor." His English was only lightly accented.

They walked side by side back to the truck, listening intently to Paul's status report.

"I believe that we have about the amount you asked for in the truck, but we have paid the workers until three o'clock, so I thought we'd keep going until then. I assume that you won't mind a few extra kilos?" He looked at Hobart, obviously expecting a show of gratitude for his extra work. Going above and beyond for a customer wasn't a concept that had taken Poland by storm.

"That would be fantastic," Hobart gushed. "The more of these I can get, the more people I can help."

Hobart had told Orloski that the mushrooms were part of a research project at the University of North Carolina Medical

School. The mushrooms, he had said, contained a chemical that could be helpful in treating cancer.

"How much longer?" Orloski asked.

"It's two-fifteen now—forty-five minutes."

"Would you like to inspect them now or wait until Paul is done?"

"Oh, I don't think that I want to inspect them at all," Hobart said. "I'm a chemist, not a botanist. That's why I hired the foremost expert in Eastern Europe."

Orloski swelled with pride. "Let's return to my car, then. I have a bottle there that will help keep this damp chill away."

Hobart's second drink, and Orloski's fifth, was interrupted by a shout from Paul. The large pile of mushrooms in front of him had dwindled to nothing, and the workers had straightened up and were walking slowly across the field. Back to their village, Hobart assumed. The two men walked quickly up to Paul and the truck.

"All ready," he announced. The mushrooms had been sealed into six large wooden crates that were tied securely to the back of the truck.

"Wonderful! Dr. Stapleton and I will be taking the truck to the docks so that they can be shipped out immediately. Very perishable, must hurry."

Paul nodded knowingly, and took the keys offered by his father. After a short good-bye, he ran down the hill and sped off in the little car that had brought them there.

Lech pointed to the open door of the driver's side. "After you." Hobart looked at him with a confused expression. "The passenger's side door doesn't open, I'm afraid," Orloski explained.

Hobart surveyed the truck skeptically. It looked as if it had been welded together from spare parts. Rust had eaten away the bottom of the body, which now seemed to float magically above the chassis. All in all, though, it looked a hell of a lot safer than the go-cart they had arrived in, so he climbed aboard. Orloski followed, having some trouble getting himself into the elevated cab. The whiskey hadn't improved his limited mobility.

With a loud grinding noise, they were off. The truck swayed down the mud and gravel road and onto the highway. Orloski pressed the accelerator to the floor, increasing their speed to the truck's maximum of forty. It seemed too fast.

"There haven't been any problems with the shipping arrangements, I hope," Hobart said.

"Of course not. Everything has been taken care of."

Hobart nodded gravely. "Normally, I would never ask your help on something like this. It's just that U.S. Customs can be so unreasonable sometimes. I'm afraid that your mushrooms might sit in quarantine forever before they release them. If they begin to rot and lose their potency, my experiment will be ruined."

The first indication that they were approaching their destination was the smell. The fragrant dampness of the Polish countryside began to fade, replaced by the stench of industry. A cloud of smog on the horizon closely followed the noxious odor, and Orloski started into an animated history about the small river port that was their destination.

The city lacked the hustle of Warsaw. It also lacked the architecture and recent renovation. It was a town of abandoned houses, cracked concrete, and most of all a pervading stink that seeped into every crevice of the old truck. Occasionally a small child could be seen playing in a large pile of bricks or rolling an old tire. Mostly, though, the streets were empty. Orloski pointed the truck down a desolate road leading to the docks. His speech on the history of the area had ended somewhere in the 1600s. He seemed to have no interest in the city as it existed in the present. Hobart was thankful for the silence.

"Here we are," Orloski announced, parking the truck next to a group of wooden crates with large red lettering on all sides. Docked at the end of the pier was a smallish gray-and-white freighter. Rust began at the decks and sprayed out over the sides as though someone had dumped brown paint from the edge.

"Please wait here, I'll be back in a moment," Orloski said, sliding out of the cab and hurrying across the dock to a small knot of men huddled near the ship. He disappeared into the middle of the group. About five minutes later, he reemerged with one of the men in tow and hurried back to the car.

His companion was enormous—well over six feet tall, with heavily tattooed forearms that looked as thick as telephone poles.

Hobart jumped out of the cab, relieved to be nearly be done with this phase of the operation.

"John, I'd like you to meet Mikhail. He is the man I told you about."

Hobart offered his hand, but Mikhail just stared down at him. It appeared that he was waiting for Hobart to speak.

"It's nice to meet you, Mikhail. I understand that you can help expedite my shipment's arrival in the U.S." Orloski translated as he spoke. Mikhail listened intently and replied in Polish.

"Mikhail would like to know where you would like your shipment delivered."

"Norfolk, Virginia."

This needed no translation. The man nodded slowly and spoke directly to Orloski.

"He says that there is quite a bit of Naval activity in that area, making his job more difficult. It will cost you another five thousand dollars." Orloski looked apologetic.

Hobart knew that he was being played. Aircraft carriers were not in the business of stopping freighters to look for illegal produce shipments. If there was any additional expense, it was the result of his translator taking a healthy cut of the proceeds.

He was not inclined to generate any ill will by haggling over insignificant amounts of money. It was critical that the product reach the U.S. More important, Hobart wanted Orloski happy. The FBI would undoubtedly be speaking with him in the coming months, and the happier he was now, the more forgetful he might be then.

"That seems fair, Lech, but there is something I need to know," Hobart said in a serious tone.

"What's that?"

"Your friend here is reliable, right? You know how important my research is."

Orloski looked insulted. "Of course he is! I personally guarantee their safe arrival."

Hobart considered himself a good judge of character—a near prodigy, in fact. Orloski would skim as much as he could, but he would deliver. In fact, if he had it to do over again, he would have never made a physical appearance in Poland.

The shipping arrangements had been a difficult decision. Hobart had originally considered taking the mushrooms into the U.S. legally. In the end, though, he had decided that the added scrutiny was a risk he'd rather not take. His passport was good, but he wasn't anxious to subject himself to any undue attention from customs or any other government agency. While smuggling carried its own risks, they weren't resting on his shoulders.

"When can I expect my crates to arrive in Norfolk?"

As Lech translated, Mikhail produced a full-sized clipboard from behind his back. His brow creased with concentration as he silently ran a finger down the grease-streaked papers.

"December fifth," Orloski translated.

"Fine. I have traveler's checks amounting to three thousand dollars with me. I'll give him the other two upon delivery." Lech looked doubtful, but translated as Hobart spoke.

Mikhail shook his head furiously. He and Orloski argued for almost five minutes in Polish. Mikhail seemed to be winning.

"Lech," Hobart broke in. "Tell him that he gets an additional three thousand if they're on time."

Orloski smiled and started in on their heated conversation again, every once in a while shooting a glance in Hobart's direction. Finally the debate ended and Mikhail yelled something to the group of men behind him. For a moment Hobart thought that they were going to be physically thrown off the dock.

"He has agreed to your terms," Orloski said happily. "It wasn't easy, but I finally convinced him that you are an upstanding member of the American academic community. You would be surprised at Mikhail's respect for higher learning."

The group of men hurried past them and began pulling the crates off the truck.

"Mikhail would like to know where he can reach you."

"He can't. I'm going to be on the road for the next month," Hobart lied, leaning against the truck. "I was hoping that I could stay in touch with you, and you could let me know when my assistant should meet the ship."

"I'm sure that can be arranged," Orloski replied. "We'll discuss it on the ride home. And you can describe to me what it is like to live in North Carolina—I hear it is a wonderful place."

Hobart walked toward the truck, glancing back one last time at the crates being moved across the dock. Leaving them there with no receipts, not even a handshake, was tying his stomach in knots.

Hobart snatched his last suitcase off the conveyor and headed toward the glass facade of the Baltimore-Washington International Airport. He started to jog as he passed through the automatic doors, his heavy luggage throwing him slightly off balance. The plane had been almost an hour late arriving, having sat on the runway in New York for what seemed like a lifetime. Bob Swenson was expecting to meet him in ten minutes.

He gunned his Jeep up 295, and in fifteen minutes was only a few miles from the warehouse. It had been nearly two weeks and five thousand miles since he'd left his hunting cabin. It felt like two years.

As he pulled up to the rented warehouse in Canton, little had changed. The only noticeable difference in the building was the new front and loading dock doors, and the tasteful but sturdy-looking bars on the first-floor windows. Venetian blinds had been installed inside, and were closed.

He jumped out of the car and walked up to the new front door. A small metal box, painted the color of brick, was discreetly bolted to the door frame. He rapped on the door. Swenson let him in almost immediately.

The outer office had been completely renovated. A fresh coat of white paint covered the walls. Two antique sofas sat on plush beige carpeting. A small tree grew in the corner, enjoying the light filtering through the blinds.

"How was your trip?"

"Productive."

"Good. You ready for a tour?"

Hobart checked the bottom of his suitcase for dirt, then laid it on one of the sofas. "Sure."

Swenson led him into the back office. It was furnished in the same style as the reception area, though a large desk stood in the place of the sofas. A new-looking computer took up most of the top. A map of the United States was framed over a small love seat opposite the desk. Colored pins were stuck in New York, Chicago, Washington, D.C., Los Angeles, and Baltimore. A plaque on the desk was engraved with the words John Severen, President, Clipper City Antiques and Oddities. A crystal tray held business cards with the same inscription.

"Looks pretty good."

"Yeah, they just finished. I'd rather deal with ten pissed-off coke dealers than one Baltimore contractor." He sat down behind the desk. "I've barred all the windows and replaced the doors with steel. We've got motion detectors in the reception area, the office, and the warehouse. All the windows and doors are wired." He threw Hobart a key chain. "The small key opens the panel on the keypad out front—you probably noticed it as you came in the door." Hobart nodded.

"The large gold one opens the front door. You can't open the loading dock from the outside. The two silver keys are to the apartments upstairs. You've got the one on the second floor. The boxes you wanted me to pick up at your house are in the bedroom."

Hobart fished his keys out of his pocket and added the new ones to the ring.

"So when do we get the mushrooms?"

"They tell me December fifth." Hobart took a piece of paper out of his wallet and tossed on the desk. "Give this guy a call and tell him you're working for Professor Stapleton. He'll let you know if the shipment's going to be on time. It'll be coming into Norfolk."

"Where're you gonna be?"

"Bogota. I'm flying out in a couple of days."

Swenson's eyes moved across the piece of paper. "No problem, I'll take care of it."

"How're our guys doing?"

"Better than we expected, actually. I got them all their IDs within a couple of days and they're all on location. The guy in New York has a lead on a warehouse owned by Anthony DiPrizzio. Word on the street is that he ships a lot of stuff through there. He's trying to get hooked up with a job. Miami's actually set up a bogus trucking company and is putting the word out that they don't much care what they ship. They seem pretty sharp."

"They are," Hobart replied. "I figured we'd send our best two guys to Miami. Should be some opportunities to hit big ship-ments."

Swenson nodded his agreement and continued. "Let's see . . . The guy in D.C. has set himself up as a supplier to street dealers. Not a real sexy operation but he says he's done some deals already. Chicago set up a lab and is making designer stuff—speed and acid mostly. They say they'll probably start doing deals in about a week. The guys in L.A. are setting themselves up as midlevel operators. They say things are moving along but that it could be a couple of months before they get things really rolling."

"How are the finances holding up?"

"Pretty good so far. The warehouse cost us a few bucks, and your last-minute plane tickets are a hell of a lot more expensive than I thought, but we should be okay. Look, I've got a full report for you on the computer. Let me reel it off the printer and you can go through it tonight. The shredder's out in the warehouse."

Hobart sat quietly as his associate punched at the keyboard. Swenson gave a sharp push on the front of the desk, sending him and his chair rolling to the printer which had just come alive. "Oh, I almost forgot, the security code on the door is HEAT. The one on the computer is TIME. I think words are easier to remember than numbers. He pulled the pages off the printer and handed them across the desk. "Why don't you go check out your apartment and get some sleep."

The apartments hadn't been renovated to the degree that the office had. The carpet was clearly new, and there was a new coat of paint on the walls, but the appliances, cabinets, and bathrooms were vintage 1970s Baltimore. On the positive side, the rooms were spacious and well lit, and the furniture was comfortable, if not luxurious. Even better, his partner had stocked the refrigerator with food and beer. Hobart screwed the top off of a Budweiser and settled onto the sofa. The TV remote was on the coffee table and he used it to flip to CNN. Settling back, he scanned the report in his hand. It was headed CCAO, Clipper City Antiques and Oddities.

Swenson had used clever euphemisms for their operation, and the report ended in a cash flow statement and balance sheet. Hobart had no difficulty understanding the real contents of the pages, but anyone picking it up would read a rather confusing antique company financial report. Clever. He was lucky to have Swenson on board.

He took a last gulp of beer and headed for the shower. It was early, but he knew that he should get sleep when he could. Things were going to start moving pretty fast.

"Howdy, ma'am," Mark Beamon said with a deep Southern drawl.

The young woman sitting at the desk in front of him leaned forward to get a better look at the ornate silver plates adorning the toes of his boots. Then she leaned back, taking in the enormous ten gallon hat perched on his head.

"Can I help you, sir?"

"I'm the new deputy marshal in town. Marshal Beamon."

"You're Mark Beamon?" She jerked to her feet.

Beamon pulled a long piece of hay from his pocket and began chewing it. "I shorly am. And you're Christie—my new secretary, right?"

She stuck out her hand. "Welcome to Houston, Mr. Beamon."

"Mark, please." He pointed behind her.

"So is this my office?"

"Yes, sir. Let me give you the tour." He followed her into the small office. She stood in the center of it and spread her arms wide. "Here it is."

Beamon tossed his hat at a picture of the President, attempting to hook it on the edge of the frame. Both the picture and the hat fell to the carpet.

"Great tour, Chris. Have a seat." He tested his chair like a bather trying to sit in water that is too hot. Finally he settled into it, satisfied. He looked across the tidy desk at his new secretary. He had checked her out before he came. Top scores from all polled.

"So do I have anything to do today, Chris?"

"Yes, sir. Steve said he wanted to see you as soon as you got in. He should be in his office. Straight down the hall. Last door on the left."

"How's his mood?" Beamon asked out of habit. Director Calahan's emotional state was always in question. Realizing he wasn't in Washington anymore, he held up his hand. "Never mind. Do I have lunch plans?"

"Not that I know of."

"Do you?"

"No, sir."

"Inexplicably, I was passed over by the Queen for a knighthood. Just Mark, please."

She smiled. "Okay, Mark."

"Better." He rose from his chair and headed for the door. "What say you and I do lunch around noon?"

Beamon peeked his head around the doorjamb of his new boss's office. "Steve! How you doin'?"

Steve Garrett stood up from behind his desk and walked across the room. They shook hands warmly.

"It's been a long time, Mark."

"Five years?"

"It's gotta be."

Beamon headed for a sofa in the corner. Garrett closed the office door and sat down on the love seat across from his new ASAC.

"So how's your first day so far, Mark?"

"Good. I just met Chris—she seems great."

"Yeah, you lucked out. She's one of the best."

There was an awkward lull in the conversation. Beamon wanted a cigarette but resisted. Garrett's move.

"So where do we stand, Mark?"

Garrett wasn't going to get off that easy. "Whatever do you mean, Steve?"

Garrett looked down at this thumb and began cleaning imaginary dirt from under the nail. "A high flyer like you can't be too happy about being banished to Houston to work for a . . . conservative guy like me."

Beamon shrugged. "I'm not gonna bullshit you, Steve. Was this my first choice? Nope. I thought I was due an SAC slot. But Tom Sherman disagreed. Probably for good reason—he's a lot smarter about stuff like that than me. So here I am."

Garrett nodded thoughtfully. "And how are you gonna play it?"

Beamon smiled. "Any way you want me to, boss."

"I'm serious, Mark. Tom tells me you live up to your reputation as the best investigator in the Bureau. But I also hear you can be . . ."

"Go ahead and say it, Steve."

"I don't need a lot of problems, Mark. I'm getting old."

Beamon's tone turned serious. "You're not gonna have any, Steve. Look, I need some latitude to do my best work, I'm not gonna deny that. The whole solemn dignity thing never worked for me. But give me a little rope and I can be a hell of an asset to you. I'm looking forward to working here. I really am. Calahan's a thousand miles away, and I get to help a bunch of young energetic FBI agents turn into top-notch investigators."

Garrett frowned. "Try to impart the skills and not the attitude. I can live with one Mark Beamon, but fifty'd be a bit much."

Beamon laughed and pantomimed spitting in his right palm. He stuck out his hand. "That'd be too many even for me. Friends?"

Garrett stared at his hand with mock suspicion for a few seconds, then reached out and grabbed it.

7

Above Bogota, Colombia,
November 26

At the request of a pretty Hispanic stewardess, John Hobart put his seat in the upright position for the final approach into Bogota's Eldorado Airport. He watched with mild interest as her ample bottom swayed gracefully through the narrow aisle, jiggling seductively as the plane shuddered through the Andean turbulence.

He hated flying. It wasn't that he was afraid of crashing—irrational fear was not one of his failings. It was the inactivity that put knots in his stomach. Most people could put their flying time to good use, but there was something in the white noise that wouldn't let him think. He could only wait until the wheels touched the ground and the dull hum of the engines faded into the rustling of the passengers reaching for their belongings.

He looked out the window for the thousandth time. There wasn't a cloud in the sky. The captain promised a temperature of sixty degrees and a light westerly breeze.

Hobart hadn't been to Colombia in almost fifteen years, but little had changed. A cabby dropped him in front of his hotel, still trying to convince him that he knew of places more suitable. It could have been the same man who had chauffeured him around the city in the early eighties.

Hobart stood for a moment on the sidewalk and ran his hand through his newly colored jet-black hair. A combination of sunlamps and dyes had darkened his skin considerably. Contacts turned his eyes brown.

The effect was marginal. Between his European features and accented Spanish, he would pass as a half-breed at best.

His two large black bags had sailed through a disinterested Colombian customs checkpoint without so much as a glance from the officers on duty. He hated leaving things to chance, but sometimes it was unavoidable. Had he been unfortunate enough to have been stopped, the officials would have undoubtedly been very interested in their contents. Fortunately, people were not generally in the practice of smuggling things into Columbia.

The hotel was far worse than the one in Warsaw. Buildings on the Continent aged more gracefully than their counterparts in other parts of the world. Cracked plaster and broken tiles just seemed to add character—a reminder of Europe's colorful past. In South America, run-down was just that, run-down. The hotel looked like it had been built ready to fall down.

The room was about what he'd expected. A filthy cubicle with no furniture other than a twin bed with a single blanket and a folding chair. A mirror hung across from the bed. Judging from the discoloration on the wall, it had at one time adorned the top of a bureau.

Hobart shoved his suitcases under the bed and pulled a crumpled street map out of his back pocket. As near as he could tell, the bar that his friend had suggested for their meeting was about twenty blocks from the hotel. He had two hours before they were to meet, so he decided to walk. It would give him a chance to acclimate to his surroundings. The air and exercise would do him good. Bogota's eighty-seven-hundred-foot altitude was giving him a splitting headache.

It was almost four o'clock by the time he left the hotel, but the winter sun was still powerful. It heated his black T-shirt, making the jacket he was carrying unnecessary. Pulling a pair of sunglasses out of his pocket, he began his hike across town.

Bogota seemed to be trapped in time. The feeling that he had stepped back to the early eighties grew in him as he walked. The streets were bursting with people in clothes that hadn't been in style for years. The small houses that lined his route were painted with little thought to the color of the houses next door. Garbage was piled high in the yards of many of the homes that would have looked abandoned had it not been for the people sitting on the porches.

Every few blocks or so a group of dirty children surrounded him, begging for pesos. He noticed that he was one of the few people being mobbed, making him feel self-conscious about his disguise.

Slowly the houses became more and more scarce, appearing only occasionally, sandwiched between colorful shops and bars. Music blared from the small cantinas, replacing the squeals of children playing in the streets and the cautioning shouts of their mothers. Despite the early hour, drunk patrons stood elbow to elbow in the cramped cantinas, swaying maniacally to the volume-distorted Spanish rhythms. An old man stumbled out of an open door, nearly knocking Hobart over, and finally landing on his back in a pile of bulging garbage bags. He sank deeply into their soft contents, and that, combined with his altered equilibrium, was making it impossible for him to get up. He apparently found his predicament hysterically funny and began a drunken, coughing laugh that could be heard clearly over the noise of the bar ten feet away. Eventually a woman stumbled out of the same door and pulled him to his feet. They walked off, clutching each other for support.

Hobart jogged across to the quieter side of the street, continuing his search for the place where his friend had promised to meet him.

The man that he was in Bogota to see was Reed Corey. They had been attached to the same Special Forces team in Vietnam, and a far as Hobart was concerned, Corey was one of the finest jungle fighters in the history of the U.S. Army. Since his discharge after the war, Corey had wandered aimlessly through Asia and South America. He seemed unable to assimilate back into polite society.

Hobart understood his predicament. After three tours in Vietnam where his team had made its own law, returning to the U.S. had been strangely confining. While Hobart had forced his own personal transition, Cory had resigned himself to living in the less genteel countries of the world.

Corey was prone to excesses. He always had been. Drinking, fighting, sex. One thing Corey could not abide, though, was drugs. Hobart remembered sitting idly one time in a small village not thirty miles from Saigon, watching Corey beat one of his men nearly to death—something that he couldn't do as an officer. Corey had discovered a stash of heroin in the man's duffel. He'd never understood other men's need to occasionally escape the grim reality of the war. The things that drove other men to the edge— the heat, bugs, rain, brutality—all seemed to go unnoticed by him.

Why rot your brain when you could be blowing some gooks out? he used to ask. All in all, a perfect recruit for this operation.

On his second pass down the street, Hobart found what he was looking for. He turned off the sidewalk and hurried through the thickening traffic. The entrance to the Piñata Verde was doorless, basically a hole cut in a galvanized metal wall. He stepped through and scanned the room. It was nearly empty. A few tired-looking patrons sat alone at tables with lines of empty shot glasses extending in front of them. The bartender sat on a stool behind a plywood bar, concentrating on an American game show dubbed in Spanish—Hobart couldn't place which one. No one acknowledged his arrival. The only sound in the room came from the television and the bartender trying to beat the game show contestants to their answers.

Hobart padded quietly to the back of the bar, keeping his eyes on the booths to his left as he passed them. He slid into the last booth, and began reading the graffiti carved into the cheap wood table. It looked like Corey would be a little late.

A lone figure at the bar came to life. Ordering two drinks, he jumped unsteadily off his bar stool and started to make his way to the corner booth where Hobart sat. The man was clearly not native. His matted light brown hair came down straight onto his shoulders, framing a tangled full beard. The tie-dyed shirt, baggy shorts, and Birkenstocks completed the effect of a hippie-era throwback. Hobart studied him as he approached.

The man slid into the booth and pushed a full shot glass across the table to Hobart. His ample belly brushed the table.

"Almost didn't recognize you, John. You look like a fucking spic." Reed Corey lit a cigarette, cupping his hand needlessly in the stagnant air. As the flame briefly illuminated his face, Hobart recognized his eyes. They were watery and red-rimmed, where they had once been clear and sharp, but there was no mistaking them. He stared quietly at what was left of his old army buddy, and Corey stared back. "It's good to see you, John. Been a long time." He wiped at his nose with the back of his hand and sniffed loudly.

"It's good to see you too, Reed. . . . You've changed."

Corey laughed at the comment, patting his round stomach. "Yeah, a little too much of the good life." He went through his nose-wiping ritual again.

It was clearly time to switch to plan B. Hobart had come to Colombia expecting to convince Corey to hit the drugs. His training, talent, and knowledge of the area made him the perfect candidate for the operation. Or so he had thought. The man in front of him looked like he'd have a hard time getting up two flights of stairs. Hobart hoped Corey had enough of his faculties left to at least provide some information.

"So what are you doing in Bogota? And why the getup?" Corey asked, turning sideways and putting his feet up on the bench. He sniffed deeply.

"Working on a little operation," Hobart replied hesitantly. His old friend could no longer be trusted. Corey's condition screamed drug habit, and while that could work in his favor for getting information, it would work against him in trying to coerce Corey to keep his mouth shut. Addicts tended to quickly forget past promises and fears in their eagerness for their next fix.

On the other hand, he was the only game in town.

"I could use a little information and you came to mind."

"What kind of information?"

Hobart scooted closer and lowered his voice. "Information on cocaine manufacturing."

Corey looked surprised. He took a long drag on his cigarette. "I heard you got booted out of the DEA. They decide to take you back?"

"Nope. Working for myself."

Corey scooted even closer and craned his neck unnaturally. His position obscured his mouth from the other people in the bar. Hobart wondered if lip-reading eavesdroppers were common in Bogota's seedier bars.

"So what do you want to know exactly?"

"I'm looking for a large coke manufacturing plant that supplies the U.S. I need to know its exact location, who runs it, and where they get the chemicals they use for processing."

"Which one?"

Hobart shrugged. "Doesn't really matter."

Corey laughed quietly and scooted back to his side of the booth. "What're you up to?" He lit a new cigarette with the waning embers of the old one.

"What's the difference?"

"None, I guess."

"I could use a .22 pistol, too."

"Jesus, John. Anything else? Maybe a fucking invitation to Luis Colombar's birthday party?"

Hobart recognized the name. Colombar was the most powerful of Colombia's cartel leaders. "I don't think that will be necessary."

"Pretty tall order—and it's gonna cost me to fill it. I don't have to tell you that asking those kinds of questions can get you killed. You know what I mean?" His expression was vaguely hopeful.

Hobart looked on with a bored expression. He was being buttered up for the price tag. He knew damn well that the information he needed was already locked in Corey's coke-addled brain. He decided to move things along.

"How much?"

Corey made a show of calculating the amount. "I can probably get you the information for, say, five thousand dollars. The gun will cost you another thousand. That's cost, John. I'm not making anything on the deal."

"I can trust your information, right?"

He looked insulted. "Have I ever steered you wrong?"

He hadn't. Hobart hoped that the drugs and years had left just a fraction of the unfailing reliability that he'd counted on in Vietnam.

"Six thousand it is. When?"

Corey thought for a moment. "Wednesday. I'll meet you at the bar directly across the street at eleven-thirty."

Hobart scowled. He wasn't looking forward to spending nearly a week idle in Bogota.

Changing the subject, Corey held up his shot glass. "To old times."

Hobart picked up the glass in front of him and gulped back the cheap tequila.

Corey stumbled out of the Piñata Verde at two-thirty A.M. Hobart watched him from the garbage-strewn alley where he'd been standing motionless for the last six and a half hours. He let the drunken man get a fifty-yard lead, and walked quietly out onto the street after him. Corey took him straight north for almost a half an hour, though his weaving gait didn't get them very far in that time. Finally he turned east though a narrow alley, exiting onto an empty four-lane road. About half a block from the alley, he turned again and made his way up a set of stairs to a white house with a sagging roof. It took him almost a minute to find the lock with the key.

Hobart watched until he disappeared into the house. Shivering slightly, he turned and walked back the way he came. Five minutes of vigorous waving found him a cab that took him back to his hotel.

He lay awake on the hard mattress until the sun appeared in his window and the light began inching across the stained vinyl floor.

Unexpected changes in plans always made him nervous. There were so many angles to consider. But he had five days until their next meeting and nothing to do but think.

Hobart paced slowly across the small room that had been his home for almost a week. It was ten o'clock Wednesday night. Almost time.

The week hadn't been wasted. He had had time to explore Bogota and many of the surrounding mountain roads. Talking with everyone who would listen, he had also managed to put a little polish on his rusty Spanish. On the whole, though, he had felt like a horse stuck in the starting gate of a race. But the gun was finally about to go off.

With his newly acquired knowledge of the city, Hobart maneuvered his rented car though the back streets and alleys of Bogota, ending up in a parking space three blocks from his final destination. It was 11:28. He hurried up the well-lit street and entered the bar across from the one he and Corey had met in almost a week ago. There was no name on it, only a hand-painted sign welcoming its patrons. The bar was wall to wall with sweat-drenched revelers, grinding and shaking to an ear-splitting disco song. Hobart couldn't remember the artist, but he remembered the year: 1977.

He paused in the doorway. There was no way to easily circle the crowd. All of the tables had been moved to the sides of the large room, and patrons had spilled from the dance floor and were gyrating in every open space they could find. Light was supplied almost exclusively by a spotlighted disco ball.

Hobart took his last gulp of fresh air and began pushing his way methodically through the crowd. He started at the left. When he hit the back wall, he moved a few feet to his right and plunged in again. Wet bodies ground against him, and disgruntled dancers mouthed silent insults as he pushed by. An elbow, inadvertently thrown by a large man with a gold tooth, dazed him. Hobart wondered angrily why Corey would choose this place to meet. It seemed that anonymity could be found in more convenient locales.

Finally, a lone brown head bobbed up in the sea of black. It was less than ten feet away, and Hobart adjusted his trajectory accordingly. It took a full five minutes, but he finally found himself standing alongside his old friend. He felt conspicuous when he stopped and began swaying to the rhythms in an effort not to stand out. Corey glanced at him and twirled around. For a moment he thought that his old friend hadn't recognized him, and pulled a hand back to give him a sharp jab in the ribs. Before he could, though, he felt a large padded envelope being pressed into his stomach. He grabbed the heavy package, and pulled an envelope with six thousand dollars in cash from his waistband. Corey took it and disappeared, deftly swinging a rather overweight woman between them. By the time Hobart was able to work his way around her, Corey was gone.

Back in his rental car, Hobart ripped open the package with his teeth and pulled out of his space and into traffic. He didn't have much time if Corey had left right after their meeting.

He had driven the route between the bar district and Corey's home a number of times during his exploration of Bogota.

The late-night traffic was making it unnecessary to concentrate very hard on driving. He dumped the envelope out on the seat next to him and began sorting through the contents with his free hand, occasionally glancing up at the road.

They consisted of a .22 caliber semiautomatic pistol, twenty or so shells—which were now bouncing all over the passenger seat—a folded topographical map, and an empty envelope with handwriting on it. The envelope had the names of various chemicals used in the processing of cocaine, with company names and addresses next to them. The map had a small circle near the center with something scrawled next to it. The light in the car was too dim to read the blue pen against the blue-green of the map.

Hobart stuffed everything back in the envelope as he approached Corey's neighborhood. Pulling over into an empty spot about three blocks away, he collected the remaining shells off the floor and threw the repacked envelope into the trunk of the car.

After double-checking that the trunk was locked, he walked briskly across the street and into the alley that Corey had led him through a week before.

Hobart found a comfortable spot between a dumpster and some garbage cans, and settled in. From that position he could just see Corey's front door around the corner of the alley, but would be invisible to anyone walking by. He pulled a long thin knife out of the sheath taped to his calf, and laid it on his lap. The black blade didn't reflect the light from the street.

Hobart checked his watch for the twentieth time—he could just make out the hands. They read four-thirty A.M. He had been sitting motionless, surrounded by garbage, for almost four and a half hours. In that time only three people had walked through the alley. None had seen him, or at least none had acknowledged his presence. People sleeping in alleys were hardly a novelty in that part of Bogota. The only attention he got was from the rats, upon whose turf he seemed to be intruding. Every fifteen minutes or so another cat-sized rodent would stroll within five feet of him, stop, and stare. He stared back, occasionally he considered throwing something, but knew that the minute he did, Corey would come around the corner. Murphy's Law.

His legs were starting to cramp from his partially crouched position, and that worried him. Corey might be a fat drug addict now, but his days as a killing machine were still fresh in Hobart's mind. It had to be over in a few seconds. He didn't want to give Corey's body the chance to produce enough adrenaline to bring him out of his stupor. A fight with Corey, even at half of his former capacity, could prove lethal.

To the degree that Hobart felt emotional pain, this had been the most painful decision he had ever made. Seeing his old friend brought back memories that he thought were dead and buried. Memories of Corey on point, gliding silently through the jungles of Asia. He had always taken the point and Hobart had always been a few feet behind him, following his footsteps through thick mud or tangled living carpet. Corey's instincts and sharp eyes had kept him and his team from getting their asses shot off more times than he could remember.

Corporal Reed Corey was gone though, and in his place stood a drug-soaked impostor. An insult. To Hobart, Corey was already dead—he was just going to make it official. The regret wasn't for the act of sliding the knife into the back of his head—it was for the memories of Corey that would be forever overshadowed by this last meeting.

There was no alternative, Hobart had decided, though he'd made little effort to find one. Corey was now completely unreliable. Should he put two and two together and figure out that it was Hobart behind the drug poisonings, he would undoubtedly sell that information to the highest bidder. The thought of dodging cartel enforcers as well as the FBI didn't sit well with him. This was the most effective solution to the problem.

At about seven, Hobart noticed shadows beginning to appear. The light of the coming dawn was turning him from an invisible stalker to a derelict bum sleeping in an alley. It was time to move on. Corey was a no-show and he was bone tired.

It was difficult getting up initially, but the blood started flowing back into his legs as he walked up to the house that he had seen Corey go into a week before. As he passed by, he noticed an envelope taped to the door. It was almost invisible against the peeling white paint. Hobart jogged casually up the steps and grabbed the envelope, hoping that it might give some indication as to Corey's whereabouts. To his surprise, it was addressed to him. The letter inside was in the same precise lettering as the list of chemical wholesalers in his trunk.

John,

I don't know what's going on, but knowing you, it's something heavy. If I were you, I wouldn't want some small-time coke dealer running around with too much information. I know you hate loose ends even more than me—remember Pyon Te? So I thought I'd take your money and go on a little vacation.

I want you to know that the info I gave you is totally accurate and that I'll take our conversation to my grave.

Good luck with whatever the hell it is you're doing.

It was unsigned.

Outsmarted by a coke addict. He tore the note up into small pieces as he walked back to his car, throwing the pieces on the ground with frustrated snaps of the wrist.

Pyon Te.

He vaguely remembered the name. Just another nothing village somewhere in southeast Vietnam. His team had been sent there toward the end of the rainy season in what—1969? It had been a routine operation. Round up the occupants of the village and question them regarding reports of VC activity in the area. What had happened there that rated a mention twenty-odd years later?

It came to him as his key hit the lock of the rental car.

The rain had been coming down in sheets all day. It had slowed them down sufficiently to put Hobart and his team more than two hours late in arriving at the village. The light had been waning as they surrounded the small group of huts and began creeping through the mud toward them. Corey had taken the lead, as he always did, and by the time Hobart arrived in the center of the village, almost all of the twenty or so inhabitants were kneeling in a deep puddle at the edge of the swollen river that wound its way through the region.

Hobart had been questioning a particularly stubborn villager when he'd caught a hint of movement through the rain about fifteen meters south. The downpour had quieted enough for him to recognize the figure as a child of ten or eleven. He had calmly raised his pistol and squeezed off a single shot. The bullet hit the child squarely in the ear.

Inexplicably, Corey had been shaken by the incident. He had stood over the small body for some time. For a moment Hobart had thought he was going to cry. In Hobart's mind there had been no choice. The girl could have made it to any number of adjoining villages in less than an hour, and if the village was indeed VC-controlled, his team could have ended up with more than they could handle. Corey hadn't seen it that way.

No loose ends.

Back at the hotel, Hobart spread the contents of the envelope onto the bed. He picked up the .22, loaded the magazine, and stuck the rest of the shells in his pocket. The gun looked like it had been well maintained, but he regretted forgetting to ask for a holster. Next he smoothed the map out on the bedspread. A small blue circle was drawn on a mountainous area about fifty miles from Bogota. Next to it was printed an exact latitude and longitude that ought to get him within a hundred feet of the refinery. He smiled. Where Corey had found precise coordinates escaped him. Still a miracle worker.

He put the gun and map under his mattress and focused his attention on a small white envelope. Running a finger down the list written on the back of it, he saw what he was looking for.

KEROSENE: GARCIA QUÍMICO: 12 ROHO

8

Bogota, Colombia,
December 2

Hobart spent almost the entire next day looking for a Global Positioning System. These units were relatively new on the American market, having become more reliable following the recent launch of additional navigational satellites. The concept was simple: The small handheld unit tracked as many synchronous satellites as possible and triangulated its position to within a few feet. Hobart had assumed that Corey would give him a general area on a map and that he would have to search that general area for the plant—necessitating the use of his rusty orienteering skills. He had to admit that Corey had come through. That is, if the refinery was at the coordinates scribbled onto the map.

He finally located a GPS at a high-end electronics store in one of Bogota's ritzier sections. He paid probably double what it was worth and started the long drive into the mountains.

It was almost ten P.M. when he reached the outskirts of Bogota. Another thirty miles of highway driving brought him to a gravel road that wound its way into the mountains. The night was clear, though the moon was only a sliver. The waning moon, in combination with the thickening jungle canopy and narrowing road, gave the illusion that the world ended at the edge of his headlights.

Almost an hour into the mountains, he was forced to reduce his speed to a slow crawl. He cursed himself for opting for an economy car instead of a more sturdy four-wheel drive. Pressing a button on the front of his GPS, he watched it light up and read out his coordinates. He punched another series of buttons and the unit calculated the direction and distance to his preprogrammed objective. It read just over six miles and the directional arrow pointed northeast. He had been heading roughly north for the last hour, and hoped he could cover the rest of distance in another hour.

In the end, it took him almost ninety minutes to cover four miles. The road never seemed to go straight for more than ten feet and in many places deep ruts had been carved by the heavy Andean rains. When the GPS read out two miles to his objective and the arrow had moved to point more or less west, Hobart eased into a small clearing in the jungle. He could get the car only about five feet from the edge of the road—any farther and he would risk getting stuck.

The smell was somehow different from Asia, he noted as he jumped out of the car and retrieved his bag from the trunk, but the sights and sounds were enough to cause an uncomfortable sense of deja vu. Pushing it away, he laid his bag on the ground and pulled out a pair of night vision goggles, which he strapped to his face and turned on. The jungle around him was bathed in an eerie green light. Despite the goggles' ability to amplify existing light ten thousand times, his vision was still murky. The weak mix of moon- and starlight was being diffused by the thick canopy of the jungle.

He quickly changed into fatigues and military boots and stuffed the bag under a dense bush. He rose, walking quickly to the car, and let the air out of the driver's side front tire. Anyone noticing it would assume that the driver was out looking for help. A necessary trade-off. The flat would slow his getaway if things got hairy.

Hobart stuffed the .22 into the thigh pocket of his pants, took one last reading on the GPS, and started out at a slow pace. The foliage was dense, impassable in places, and he made poor time. He used the GPS sparingly, stopping every fifteen minutes or so to correct his direction. The unit was having some difficulty tracking satellite through the trees and mountainous terrain, but in the end he was able to get the fixes he needed.

Hobart had been in the jungle for a little over two hours when he checked his position for the last time. He was sweating profusely despite the cool temperatures—every step had been an adventure of bogs, tangled vines, and jagged rocks.

He was pushing the GPS back into his pocket when he heard the unmistakable sound of a human voice—startlingly out of place amidst the white noise of rustling trees and a billion insects. The jungle seemed to change instantly with the presence of another human being. Hobart slowed his pace to a crawl, working his way toward the voice. In less than a minute, the sensitive photo cells of his goggles began to pick up a green glow through the trees. In another minute, the world began to look like an overexposed photograph, and he pulled the goggles off. Dropping to his belly, he crawled toward the light and activity. His progress was slow, every motion setting off a chain reaction of rustling foliage. He was forced to match his speed to that of the weak breeze. Another one hundred yards and he could see his objective. Corey hadn't let him down.

It was less impressive than he had expected—just an old shack. Constructed out of native trees and woven with large leaves, it could easily be mistaken for the residence of a poor farmer. The tip-off was the four dirty-looking men with rifles, sitting with their backs pressed against the hut, warming their hands around a small fire.

Next to the structure was a grouping of metal barrels, each about three feet high and two feet across—he counted six. While he could see them clearly from his position in the dirt, they would be completely invisible from the air. The tops had been covered with a thin layer of leaves and vines. The barrels were what he was looking for. The only chemical needed in quantity to process coke was kerosene.

He watched the four men pass a bottle between them, laughing loudly. He was close enough to see the rotting teeth of the one on the right before the man hid them with the bottle.

Hobart lay there quietly watching for nearly two hours. Two things struck him. The first was the incompetence of the guards leaning against the hut. He guessed that not one of them could hit the broad side of a barn with their rifles dead sober—which they certainly were not. He also doubted that they had a combined IQ over ninety. Their conversation seemed limited to the sizes of women's breasts and the sizes of their respective penises. Their laughter came on cue just before the punch line, suggesting that the dialog was the same every night.

Hobart calculated fair odds that he could walk up, kill all four with a knife while singing the "Ave Maria" at the top of his lungs. Not that he faulted Luis Colombar's choice in manpower. The Colombian police weren't any kind of real threat to the most powerful organizations—cops were too easily dissuaded. And at the moment, the different local factions seemed to be enjoying an uneasy peace. The guards were more for show than anything else.

The only thing that made the "Ave Maria" plan unworkable was the second thing that struck him. Since he had arrived, at least twenty people had come out of the hut for a smoke or a quick stroll around the clearing. He seriously doubted that the ten-by-ten structure could hold such a crowd, so the actual refining must be going on underground. It was impossible to estimate how many people were beneath him. Fifty? A hundred?

Hobart didn't hear the rumble of the Toyota Land Cruiser's engine until after its headlights had washed over the dense foliage that he had hidden himself in. He buried his face in the soft earth, presenting his newly dyed black hair to the light. He lay perfectly still, straining to hear what he could no longer see. The vehicle skidded to a stop with a deep gravelly sound. He heard the engine die and two doors open. When the lights blinked off, he slowly raised his head.

He was safe. The guards crowded respectfully around a heavy-set Hispanic man as an impeccably dressed Japanese man in his mid-fifties walked around the back of the truck.

*   *   *

"Quit hovering around me," Luis Colombar shouted, giving the man closest to him a hard shove. He was in a particularly dark mood. Since he had broken the back of the Cali Cartel and become the most powerful narcotics manufacturer in Bogota, he had gotten used to doing whatever he wanted to do, whenever he wanted to do it. And what he didn't want was to be touring one of his refineries in the middle of the night when he should be at home in bed with his beautiful young wife.

It was his assistant's doing. Perez had been insisting for years that Japan's youth were getting restless. The thought of working eighteen-hour days and living in a one-bedroom apartment in a smog-filled city wasn't as satisfying as it had been to their parents. And where there was discontent, there was business opportunity.

Colombar turned, acknowledging his guest's presence for the first time in an hour. He hated the Japanese. All business and no fun. He'd personally picked up the little yellow bastard from the airport not two hours ago. He had a big evening planned. Some of the finest women, food, and liquor in Colombia were waiting for his guest at Colombar's estate.

Despite his protests, his guest—reportedly the most powerful organized crime boss in Japan—had insisted on coming straight to one of Colombar's refineries. He wanted to see how it was all done. Fucking nips.

"This way, Yakashiro," Colombar said in English. The Japanese man walked past him, eyes focused on the door of the small hut in the center of the clearing. Colombar followed him through the door and opened a trapdoor under the mats on the floor. They descended a ladder to a dirt floor twenty feet below.

The room at the base of the ladder was the exact same size as the hut and gave the impression of an Old West mine. The crumbling dirt walls were held at bay with rotting timbers, and light was provided by a single rusty oil lamp. At one end of the room was a metal door. It too was covered in dust and mud, making it look less out of place than would be expected. It opened, as if by magic, when Colombar approached.

The underground structure took on a much different look as they passed through the door. Timbers were replaced by cinderblocks painted a uniform white. Light was provided by overhead fluorescent fixtures. This room was only slightly larger than the first and was lined with wooden benches. Four serious-looking men sat on them, eyeing the Japanese visitor suspiciously.

Colombar pulled two respirators off a hook at the door and handed one to Yakashiro. They silently affixed them to their faces. One of the guards pulled another heavy door open and the two men entered, still adjusting the straps on the sides of their masks. Colombar paused halfway through the door. "You don't have a lighter or anything that could produce sparks on you—do you?" The Japanese shook his head gravely. Colombar wondered if his guest really understood anything he was saying.

The room was long and narrow. Large open vats were lined up along the walls, three to a side. Two men paced up and down the length of the room trailing thick black air hoses attached to elaborate masks similar to those worn by firemen. Colombar began to explain the scene as his potential associate pulled up alongside of him.

"The first stage of the refining process takes place in this area." He spoke slowly. Yakashiro's English was poor, and he was obviously having trouble understanding Colombar's accent. The masks didn't help, either.

"The vats are full of coca leaves. First we cover the leaves with potash and let them sit for a while." Colombar walked to the first vat and motioned Yakashiro over. The Japanese man looked into the vat with a look of mild interest.

"The ash begins to separate the alkaloids from the leaf. At that time the mix is doused with kerosene—explaining why we have to wear these masks."

He pointed to the men at the far end of the room and the hoses trailing behind them. "Actually, we found that these masks are only safe for temporary exposure to this room. We had to install those hoses that vent to the outside for the people that work here regularly." The truth was that he had resisted the expense of installing that particular amenity as long as he had been able to. After the death of the sixth worker, though, it had become difficult to find replacements.

They walked to the next vat, which was filled with kerosene almost to the rim. Colombar grabbed a large stick leaning against the wall and gave the leaves a quick stir. "As the leaves soak, the alkaloids begin to float in the kerosene. We squeeze the kerosene from the leaves and put it into drums—they're stored in the next room."

They passed quickly through the door at the other end of the room. Colombar hung his respirator on a nail and motioned for his guest to do the same.

He pointed to a group of metal drums neatly lined up against the wall. "Sulfuric acid and water are then mixed with the kerosene-alkaloid solution. The acid helps to transfer the alkaloids to the water, which sinks to the bottom. The kerosene is then removed, leaving a mixture of water and cocaine, which is then dried into a paste."

They walked past the drums to a bank of tables guarded by no less than five dim-looking men. They stood as Colombar approached. He ignored them and broke off a baseball-sized chunk of what looked like off-white Play-Doh. He handed it to Yakashiro. "We call this *pasta*. It is cocaine in its most raw form."

Yakashiro squeezed and rolled the cocaine paste through his fingers, remaining silent.

"The process to transform the *pasta* into cocaine's final form is even more complicated. Let me show you. Right through here."

Hobart slid his body straight back, putting fifteen feet or so between him and the clearing. Rotating to the right, he began a slow crawl around the perimeter. Occasionally he caught a glimpse of the hut from a different angle through the trees. It took him almost two hours to make a three-quarter turn, but he finally found what he was looking for. A rusting flatbed truck sat idle in a narrow slot cut into the trees. The canopy of the forest hung low over it, shielding it from flying eyes. Poor farmers didn't keep trucks any more than they did barrels of kerosene.

He crawled closer, the faint smell of kerosene reaching his nose when he was less than four feet from the rear of the truck. The license plate was barely readable at this distance, and he committed it to memory.

Peter Manion had devised a simple, yet elegant, plan for the actual poisoning. Hobart had envisioned a risky commando-style operation in which Corey—now he—would have to actually infiltrate the factory and dump poison into the product before it was packaged. The final plan was a hell of a lot simpler.

As it turned out, orellanin had properties not entirely unlike cocaine. In essence they were both biological toxins, only with very different effects. All he had to do was poison the kerosene. As the alkaloids melted from the coca leaves and were transferred to the kerosene and water, the orellanin would combine with the cocaine molecules and transfer smoothly and evenly into the final product.

It looked like the act of actually poisoning the kerosene was going to be even more simple than he had imagined, as well. The open flatbed would allow him to hit the shipment as it went from the supplier to the refinery. He had originally planned to infiltrate the warehouse in Colombia—adding the local police and security guards as a complicating factor. Not to mention the problem of deciding which barrels to hit.

Having found all he had come for, Hobart crawled directly away from the clearing until the light from the guard's kerosene lamp faded to a faint glow. Switching on his night vision goggles, he stood and walked briskly back to the car, the coordinates of which he had programmed into the GPS before leaving the road. He stuffed his fatigues and gear into the bag and changed back into the dirty jeans and T-shirt that he'd been wearing for a week. Pulling a can of Fix a Flat out of the bag, he filled up the tire and began the slow journey back into town.

*　　*　　*

Hobart couldn't remember feeling this good in years. He adjusted the air vent above him and took a sip of ice cold Jim Beam from the plastic cup in his hand. His hatred of flying was overcome by the joy of being freshly showered and in clean clothes. He'd spent just under four weeks in Bogota. With no intervening baths, his disguise had improved dramatically. Something he'd have to remember.

It had been an exhausting trip. He'd spent nearly every night on his belly near the clearing that housed Colombar's refinery and every day tossing and turning on the uncomfortable mattress in his filthy hotel room.

The refinery seemed to be a very professional operation, and that worked to his advantage. They had a production schedule, and they stuck to it. He imagined that the penalties for falling behind were more severe than a light Christmas bonus.

They used two barrels of kerosene a night, without fail. Two of the guards took the old truck up to the chemical plant specified in Corey's note and purchased fourteen barrels every Wednesday. Production went on around the clock, seven days a week.

Hobart took the pillow offered by the stewardess and propped it against the window. He fell asleep with his drink still in his hand.

9

Baltimore, Maryland,
December 26

John! How'd it go?"

Hobart fell onto the sofa in the reception area of the office. It wasn't as comfortable as it was stylish. "Good and bad, I guess. Reed's . . . unreliable."

Swenson frowned and sat down on the sofa across from him. "So what did you do?"

"I paid him for the information I needed and reconned the refinery myself."

"How'd that go?"

"That's the good part. They run on a tighter schedule than Du Pont. Unless something weird happens in the next couple of weeks, getting to the kerosene shouldn't be a problem."

The frown on Swenson's face melted into a relaxed smile. He stood and disappeared into the next room, reappearing a moment later with two beers in his hand. He gave one to Hobart. "Things have been shaping up around here, too."

"I saw the new addition." Hobart pointed through the door behind him to a large TV suspended near the ceiling.

"Yeah, I figured that when things start popping, CNN'll probably have some interesting programming."

Hobart nodded his agreement and rubbed his eyes. He'd put off the subject long enough. "Did the mushrooms arrive?"

"Yup. Two days early in fact. I picked 'em up in Norfolk last week. You wanna see 'em?"

Hobart sighed with relief. The shipping arrangements that he'd been forced into had been gnawing at him since Poland. He stood and waited for his partner to lead the way.

They walked back through a narrow hall leading to a heavy metal door. Next to the door, two respirators and two pairs of goggles hung on a long nail. Swenson took one of each for himself and handed Hobart the others. "Potent stuff," he explained.

Hobart took him at his word. When they had secured the goggles and masks to their faces, Swenson pushed the heavy door open and walked through.

The warehouse had changed dramatically since Hobart had last seen it. Cheap antiques and dirty wooden crates were stacked everywhere. Old metal signs advertising long-defunct household products hung thick on the walls. Rolled-up rugs were stacked between the legs of overturned chairs.

"Follow me."

They began what seemed like a random route though the stacks of furniture that had looked completely impassable a moment before. The haphazard mess had obviously been created by careful design. Someone coming into the warehouse through the office wouldn't even consider trying to cross to the opposite side. But following Swenson, a well-hidden path appeared as if by magic.

About fifteen feet from the back of the warehouse, a wall of furniture that rose almost halfway to the ceiling stood in front of them.

"How much did all this shit cost?" Hobart asked, jabbing a tattered armchair with his finger. His voice sounded artificial through the respirator.

"About ten thousand. It's all junk—I just needed volume. I'd say we look like antique dealers now, though."

"I'd say," Hobart agreed.

Swenson pushed aside an Oriental rug and ducked under a large dining room table. Hobart followed him, noting that some of the pieces in the furniture wall had actually been nailed together.

As they emerged from under the table, a fifteen-by-forty-foot space opened up in front of them. It was dominated by five large wooden crates stacked against the wall and a long folding table that would have looked at home in a grade school cafeteria. Three empty crates sat in the far corner next to their splintered tops.

A thin figure in a white coat, thick rubber gloves, and an apron was stooped over an iron bathtub throwing in handfuls of mushrooms. The smell of alcohol was strong, even through the respirators.

"Peter! Look who's here," Swenson called.

Peter Manion glanced back, and seeing Hobart, snapped upright. He was wearing the same goggles and respirator.

"Quite a setup you've put together here, Peter," Hobart said, walking the length of the table. It was piled with glass beakers and a mystifying array of other equipment. Hobart wondered how much of it was really necessary and how much was for Manion's personal enjoyment. No point in dwelling on it, he barely knew a test tube from a Bunsen burner.

"So what are you up to?"

"Uh, I'm converting the active agent in the mushrooms to a concentrated powder form. You see . . ."

Hobart cut him off. Despite his nap on the plane, his eyes were burning from lack of sleep. The last thing he needed was a two-hour blow-by-blow on the chemical processes involved in distilling poison. "How much have you gotten done?"

"Oh, I'd say about of fifth of it. I've got another week or so to finish."

Hobart walked over to a large metal drum much like the ones that he'd seen full of kerosene in Colombia. Out of the top grew a transparent rubber tube capped by a cork stopper. "So you're putting it in here?"

"Yeah. As soon as it's dried into a powder I pour it in there. It's a slow process—you don't want to get any powder in the air. It's real concentrated."

"So how much of this stuff am I gonna need?" Hobart sat down on a rickety chair next to Swenson.

"Depends. Are the drums the same size as this one?" He pointed a shaky finger at the barrel with the tube in the top.

"Yeah."

"I'll have to do some calculations, but probably a half a pound per drum—something like that."

As Manion turned, the reflection fell away from his goggles and Hobart got a good look at his eyes. He was flying. No doubt this was the reason for his enthusiastic cooperation. Hobart wondered if he even remembered why he was working with the mushrooms, or if he'd just pushed it to an unused part of his brain. In any event, he seemed happy, and Hobart wanted to make sure he stayed that way until the job was done.

"How you fixed for money, Pete?"

Manion looked at the ground. "Well, you know, okay, I guess."

"Bob, see that Peter gets a thousand bucks before he goes home tonight." He stood and turned toward the exit, letting Swenson go ahead of him. He wasn't sure if he could make it back through the maze.

"Keep up the good work, Peter."

Back in the office Swenson popped the top off another beer. "So when are we leaving?"

"We'll let Peter finish what he's doing—get that all tied up. Then we'll go. How're our guys in the field doing?"

"Things are getting set up pretty quickly. They all seem to have their covers set. Most of them have made at least one clean transaction."

Gaining a reputation for dealing good drugs at a fair price would deflect blame to other parts of the distribution chain when they began introducing the orellanin into the mix. At least that was the theory.

Out of the top drawer of his desk Swenson took a few sheets of paper held together by a paper clip, and handed them to Hobart. "Here's a full report. It's pretty current, I did it a couple of days ago. You were a little later getting back than I thought."

"Yeah, me too." Hobart rose slowly from his chair. "Hopefully Peter won't go too fast, I need the week off."

*   *   *

A well-rested John Hobart sat behind his desk punching numbers into a LOTUS spreadsheet. CNN was providing background noise.

The figures represented a one-year financial projection for Clipper City Antiques and Oddities. Things looked like they'd get a little tight in about twelve months, but it wasn't worth worrying about. Who knew what the next year would bring?

He had been in Baltimore for a little over a week—plenty of time to slow down and focus on the details. He was completely up to speed on his four undercover teams and had spent some time thinking about the future of the project. So far he was happy with the plan that he'd originally devised. A few holes had appeared, but they were easily filled.

Swenson peeked his head around the corner of the office door. "He's done."

Hobart saved the file he was working on and walked slowly back to the warehouse. Swenson was standing next to the entrance, waiting for him, when he walked up and pulled a respirator off the wall.

"You won't be needing that, actually. The lab's clean. I'm getting rid of all the waste this afternoon."

Hobart hung the respirator back on the nail and followed his partner into the warehouse, weaving his way through the furniture with practiced ease. They found Manion tying up a large Hefty bag. All of the lab equipment was gone, and the floor and walls looked as though they'd been freshly scrubbed. There was still a puddle of water near a drain in the floor that Hobart had never noticed before. Near the loading dock door, a pile of garbage bags sat next to the remnants of the wooden crates that had protected the deadly mushrooms on their voyage from Eastern Europe. In the corner opposite the refuse, a stack of Tupperware containers sat, each sealed in its own Ziploc bag.

Swenson pointed to the containers. "I had Peter break the orellanin into smaller containers. The ones marked with red tape are for you. He figured out the exact amount you need."

"That's it," Manion said, tossing the last bag onto the stack. "It's ready to haul away." He was breathing hard, unaccustomed to the physical demands of cleaning.

Swenson put his arm around Manion's narrow shoulders. "We really appreciate your help, Peter."

He really knew how to play the addict. Hobart noticed that Manion actually seemed to have taken a liking to his partner, who was pulling a wad of bills from his pocket. Swenson pressed them into Manion's trembling hand and began walking back out to the office with him, leaving Hobart alone. He walked over and ran his hand across the innocent-looking Tupperware, remembering that his mother had used similar containers to store leftovers.

It was almost time to find his place in the history books.

Hobart settled into the ragged easy chair for the last time and surveyed the dark room around him. Very little had changed. The same dishes sat on the coffee table, the food on them perhaps slightly more petrified than it had been a month before. The same books were stacked on the floor, though they seemed to have collected quite a bit of dust in his absence. The same closed-up smell assaulted his nostrils. He found all these things comforting in a way. He hated surprises.

Most of the money that he had given Manion he found stuffed in an envelope between his mattress and the filthy carpet. For all his brains, Manion just wasn't very sneaky—something Hobart appreciated in a flunky. His usefulness was waning, though. Swenson had stayed close to him throughout the distillation process, asking questions constantly. Manion, who loved to talk endlessly about physics and chemical reactions, would have made a great college professor in another life. The reward for teaching Swenson everything there was to know about the distilling process wasn't tenure, though.

Hobart had almost dozed off when he heard a key hit the lock. Looking at his watch, he registered that he'd been there for almost three hours. He watched Manion's unmistakable figure come through the door, leaving it open behind him. A moment later a young girl walked through and pulled the door shut behind her.

She was just a waif, really. All skin and bones beneath a billowing, full-length chiffon dress. She shared Manion's pale complexion and red-rimmed eyes, though she was much younger. Eighteen at the most.

"Who's your friend, Peter?"

They both spun around, startled. The waif almost fell over.

"John! What are you doing here? I'm finished!" He backed himself against the wall. The waif was over her initial fright but wasn't sure what to do. She stood in the middle of the room nervously shifting her weight from one foot to another.

"Just one more thing, actually." Hobart rose from his chair, stuffing his hands in his pockets. They were covered with surgical gloves and he didn't want Manion to panic. He walked up to the young girl and looked her over carefully. His first impression had been correct, she was definitely no older than eighteen. A closer inspection revealed that she was really quite pretty, in a sort of fragile way. Also, she didn't seem to share Manion's shoddy personal hygiene habits.

"You didn't answer my question," Hobart said, not taking his eyes off the girl.

"Tracy. Her name is Tracy."

"She looks a little young for you."

Tracy was squirming beneath his gaze but hadn't mustered the will to move yet.

Hobart bent and picked up a black satchel lying on the floor. He continued to focus on the girl's face. There were no lights on, and it seemed to glow in the semidarkness of the room.

"Come here a sec, Peter."

Manion did as he was told and took a place next to Tracy.

"Who is he, Peter?" She seemed even younger when she spoke. Her voice came out a high-pitched whisper.

"It's okay, Tracy. He'll leave soon, I promise."

"He's right Tracy, with any luck at all, I'll be out of here in five minutes, tops."

With that, he drew his .45 and pointed it in their general direction. Tracy let out a squeal and Manion put his arms straight up in the air, like a train robbery victim in a bad western. Hobart put his index finger to his lips, silencing them both. Reaching into his bag, he pulled out a couple of handkerchiefs and handed one to each of them.

"If you would be so kind as to stuff these in your mouths?"

They stared blankly at him.

"C'mon, start stuffing," he prompted, leveling the gun at Tracy's nose. That seemed to be enough incentive for her, and she began pushing the cloth into her mouth. Manion followed suit.

"Get all of it . . . good. Now please turn around. Hobart pulled two bandannas out of the satchel and blindfolded both of them.

"Now, why don't you both lie down on the floor and relax." They both sank awkwardly to the floor.

Digging around in the satchel, he pulled a full syringe and a two-foot length of rubber tubing. He reached in again, fishing around the bottom of the bag until he found another syringe, brought along for just such a situation.

He wrapped the tube tightly around Manion's upper right arm and unbuttoned his sleeve. The vein was adorned with an endless trail of holes and bruises—the result of fifteen years of daily injections.

Manion began grunting and wiggling until Hobart pressed the .45 up under his chin. The cold metal froze him. When he'd calmed down, Hobart plunged the syringe into a vein and depressed the plunger. Manion jerked with the initial prick and then relaxed deeply as the heroin flooded him.

Hobart turned his attention to Tracy, who seemed to be straining to hear what was going on. He unbuttoned her sleeve, but found no tracks. The other arm was also clean. He sat confused for a moment. She had the look of an addict and was hanging around with Manion . . .

He grabbed the hem of her skirt and began pulling it up. Her hands came to life, grabbing her thighs to stop the progression.

The barrel of the gun under her chin was just as effective on her as it had been on Manion. She went limp and began sobbing quietly through the handkerchief in her mouth.

He pulled her dress the rest of the way up, exposing her pale thighs and a pair of faded pink panties. Pulling her legs apart, he found what he was looking for—track marks scrawled across her inner right thigh.

He drew his glove-covered finger up the soft, cotton covered cleft between her legs and then back down the edge of her panties, where wispy blond pubic hairs peeked out from behind the fabric. Her sobbing grew louder, and she began choking on the handkerchief in her mouth.

He moved quickly, repeating the procedure performed on Manion. He felt his fingers dig deeply into her thigh as the heroin relaxed her muscles, and he let go abruptly. A hand-shaped bruise on the girl's thigh would probably go unnoticed by the overworked Baltimore coroner, but it didn't pay to be careless.

Hobart pulled the handkerchiefs out of their mouths, removed their blindfolds, and stood up, stretching his back. As he was throwing his things into the satchel he looked carefully around the room, making sure that he hadn't left anything but the syringes with the appropriate fingerprints pressed onto them. Manion's breathing was becoming increasingly labored as Hobart padded silently out of the living room and through the back door. Each of the syringes had contained enough heroin to kill two, maybe three people.

The dampness of the soil had finally managed to soak through Tek Markus's jeans, making it impossible to sit still any longer. He lifted himself up a few inches and scooted farther back into the bushes, showering himself with droplets of icy water in the process.

It was too cold to wait any longer. Rico Washington's mother had left for her night job more than ten minutes ago and Tek was starting to lose the feeling in his hands. He cupped them to his mouth and blew. The gray smoke of his breath slithered through his fingers and disappeared with no effect.

Tek kicked his friend's leg gently, being careful not to bring down another waterfall. "Put that forty down and let's get busy, man."

'Twan finished peeling the label off a half-empty beer bottle and then smoothed it back on with his palm.

"Wake up, man. What's wrong with you?" Tek said.

'Twan finally looked up. "This is bullshit, man. Rico ain't gonna do nothin'. He's okay, you know?"

"That's easy for you, man. He ain't been dissin' you all over the 'hood."

'Twan renewed his attack on the label in silence, but Tek could read his friend's expression in the twilight. He was in. He might not be happy about it, but he was in.

Rico had started shooting his mouth off about getting revenge a few days after his sister's funeral. At first, Tek had just ignored it. After all, he hadn't shot her on purpose; it had been an accident. Besides, Rico was a nobody—by all reports, he didn't even own a gun.

But now almost two months had gone by and the verbal attacks just kept on coming. If anything, they had become more frequent and bitter. People were starting to ask Tek what he was waiting for. Starting to speculate that he was scared.

Tek grabbed a small tree with his left hand and 'Twan's arm with his right, and hoisted both of them to their feet.

'Twan mumbled something unintelligible, but followed solemnly as Tek made his way to the front door of the small gray house. Tek stopped at the door and looked over at his friend, who was shifting his weight nervously from one foot to the other and chewing desperately at his lower lip. Frowning deeply, he knocked on the door and stepped back two paces.

When the door began to open, Tek used the added distance to build up momentum. He drove his left shoulder hard into the door and managed to wedge a foot inside the house. Grabbing the thin bronze chain stretched tight in the narrow gap between the door and the jamb, he used his foot as a lever until the chain broke free and he was able to slip gracefully into the house. He pulled a machine pistol from his waistband as 'Twan closed the door behind them and circled to the back of the room.

Rico Washington stood three feet in front of him, wide-eyed and wearing only a pair of red boxer shorts and a Georgetown Basketball sweatshirt. At seventeen, he was two years Tek's senior and a full foot taller. He had started shaving recently and it had raised an uncomfortable-looking rash on his cheeks.

"Whassup, Rico?" Tek said, leveling his machine pistol at the boy's chest.

Rico backed up a step and looked past Tek. "'Twan—what's going on, man?"

Tek held the gun steady, but looked back at his friend. 'Twan had both hands thrust into his pockets and had squeezed his body between an empty bookcase and the wall. He was looking at his shoes as though it was the first time he'd ever seen them.

Tek knew now that bringing him along had been a mistake. 'Twan and Rico had grown up two doors from each other. They had been fast friends until about the fifth grade, when 'Twan's interests had turned to the streets that Rico wanted so much to escape. They hadn't spoken a full sentence to one another in years, but the memory of their friendship hadn't completely faded, either.

Tek turned his attention back to Rico, satisfied that 'Twan was not going to interfere one way or the other. "What you thinkin', dissing me around the 'hood? You lookin' to die?"

Rico straightened his shoulders and thrust out his chest, trying to use his considerably superior size to psychological advantage. Tek wasn't impressed. He was used to killing men older and larger than himself. Nobody was bullet-proof.

"I asked you a question, Rico."

"You killed my sister, man. You fucking shot her in the head."

"You're nothin', man. Look at you—I kill your sister and you don't do shit," Tek yelled back, his voice dripping with hatred and contempt that he didn't really feel.

Rico stared back at Tek, eyes burning with rage and frustration.

"What's your sister think of you now, huh? Now that she knows her brother's too much of a pussy to take out the guy who killed her and just runs on at the mouth instead?"

Rico's eyes softened perceptibly and he looked away.

It was useless. The spark of anger that Tek had been carefully fanning since breaking through the door just wouldn't burn. Shooting a boy he hardly knew just for being pissed about the death of his sister was harder than Tek had planned. But it had to be done. Without his reputation, he was nothing.

Tek looked at his right hand. It was still numb from the cold. He couldn't feel the rough grip of the gun on his palm, or the cold steel of the trigger under his index finger. The only sensation was a vague burning as the heat of the room seeped into his skin.

He moved his eyes back to Rico and pretended that the finger on the trigger belonged to someone else. The gun jerked twice as the ghost hand tightened and Rico sank to his knees, then pitched forward. Tek jumped to the side, barely avoiding being knocked over by the falling body.

"Oh, fuck man, you killed him," a very young-sounding voice behind him said.

Tek twirled around on his heels, gun stretched out before him, but it was only 'Twan.

"No shit. Let's get out of here."

10

Western Maryland,
January 5

Hobart was starting to feel as if all he did was travel. He was looking forward to the day the preliminaries would be over.

The sun was rising directly behind him and though it was still low in the sky, he reached for his sunglasses. He had been driving for almost an hour, heading west to Saint Louis. His back was already starting to ache—probably due to the anticipation of being in the same position for the next thirteen hours. Leaning the seat back helped, though it put his arms in an uncomfortable position. Switching back and forth was probably the answer.

This was the part of the operation that put him on edge. Full-page ads explaining the CDFS's actions would only save those who would be better off dead, and give the FBI another thread to pull on. The Reverend had made his decision, however, and Hobart had given his word.

He had originally thought to just shove cash into three FedEx envelopes and mail them off with the ad. After some research into the costs of the ads, though, he had reconsidered. It wouldn't be wise to send the better part of two hundred thousand dollars accompanied only by an anonymous letter. Three ad clerks would most likely be driving Corvettes the next day.

After some thought he had decided that the best bet would be to have cashier's checks issued and to enclose them with the ad.

The problem was that he would have to walk into a bank to get the checks, and that it would take the FBI less than a day to swarm all over the issuing branch. Not a thrilling prospect, but there seemed to be no alternative.

It was almost four o'clock by the time the Gateway Arch began to emerge from the haze. Hobart maneuvered his car through the light traffic for about ten minutes before exiting the freeway. He slowed and swung the Jeep right for no particular reason and continued on until he spotted a small branch bank on his right. He drove for almost another fifteen minutes, finally turning into a strip mall and parking in the sparsely populated lot.

He looked in the rearview mirror and examined his disguise for flaws. He wore a gray wig of slightly long but well-groomed hair, and a closely cropped gray beard. His eyes were tinted blue by contacts and partially hidden by wire-rimmed glasses.

He had darkened his skin somewhat with a foundation and accentuated the wrinkles around his mouth and eyes. This, combined with a slightly stooped walk perfected in Warsaw, made him look much older than he actually was. Looking in the mirror with a dispassionate eye, he guessed mid-fifties. He hoped everyone else would too.

After putting on a pair of blue leather gloves and a matching topcoat, he grabbed the black satchel lying next to him on the passenger seat and walked quickly back to the main street. It took another fifteen minutes to hail a cab, but mercifully one pulled over just as it began to rain.

"Where to?"

"First Missouri. The one on the corner of Pine."

The cabby nodded and eased the car back out into traffic.

"What can I do for you, sir?"

The thin young man behind the teller window didn't look like a bank employee. His long blond hair was tied back in a ponytail that seemed to go quite a way down his back. Despite his youth, his skin had a ruddy complexion, suggesting that he spent most of his spare time outdoors. The nameplate next to him introduced him as Lance.

"Hi, Lance," Hobart said, hoisting the satchel into the teller window. "I'd like to get a couple of cashier's checks made."

"Oh, I'm sorry sir, you don't do that here. Our customer service representatives are the ones that take care of cashier's checks. That lady right there can help you." He pointed to a graying woman sitting at a neat desk near the front of the building.

"Thanks." Hobart dragged the satchel off the counter and maneuvered back through the line of people waiting behind him.

"Hi, may I help you?"

"I hope so. Lance over there told me that you were the person to see about having cashier's checks made."

"That's me. My name's Jennifer. Have a seat."

"Actually, I have a lot of cash in this bag. Is there an office we might use?"

Jennifer frowned with concentration for a moment. "Maybe. I think that my boss might have taken an early lunch. Why don't you wait here and let me check." She dashed around her desk and disappeared around the corner. She reappeared in less than a minute.

"We're all set. Could you just follow me?" Hobart trailed her around a corner and into a small office alongside the teller line. Jennifer sat behind the desk and motioned to one of the two chairs in front of her.

"If you could tell me the amount of the checks you'd like made, and who they're to, I can get them going. Did you say that you were going to pay cash for the checks?"

"Yes, if that's not a problem."

"Oh no, no problem at all. Now, what do you need?"

"Let's see. I need one made out to *USA Today*." Jennifer scribbled on a legal pad. "That one should be in the amount of $57,500."

She looked up. "You said that you were going pay for these checks with cash?"

"If it's not a problem," Hobart repeated.

She shrugged. "No, I guess not."

"The second one is to the *Washington Post* in the amount of $53,565. And the last one is to the *LA Times* in the amount of $72,000 even."

She added the numbers on a calculator on the desk, ripping the tape off when she was done. "Including fees, that will be $183,072.50."

Hobart tugged at the straps on his bag and began pulling out neatly bound stacks of hundred-dollar bills. Jennifer looked on in amazement.

"There you go. I think it's all there."

Jennifer looked around her and picked up an empty cloth bag with the bank's logo on it. She slid the money off the desk and into the bag and struggled for the door.

"I'll go get your checks. Would you like a cup of coffee? It might take a few minutes."

"No, thank you, I'll just wait."

She paused at the door. "Oh, could you please get out your driver's license and Social Security card. The bank is required by law to keep track of large cash transactions."

"Sure, I'd be happy to."

When she reappeared she was holding three cashier's checks. Hobart looked them over while she copied information from his forged driver's license.

"Look okay?"

"Perfect. Thanks a lot for your help."

She slid the license back over to him. "Now, Mr. Harrison, if you could just look over the information on this form and sign at the bottom if everything looks accurate."

He glanced briefly at the form and signed, using his left hand. The signature was completely illegible.

Jennifer stood up and offered her hand. "It was nice to meet you, Mr. Harrison. Let us know if we can be of any more help to you."

"Thanks, I will."

Back out in the parking lot, the rain had slowed to a drizzle. Hobart hurried down the street in the opposite direction of his car, the empty satchel hanging from his shoulder by its long center strap. When he was well out of sight of the bank, he began looking for a cab. It only took about five minutes to get one this time.

The cab driver watched his rearview mirror silently as Hobart piled into the back seat.

"I'm going to the Safeway up a few miles on the right, but I think I'd like to see the Arch first." The cabby started the meter and made a U-turn in the middle of the street, heading back to the freeway. Hobart relaxed and began going through a mental checklist, distracted only by the sound of western music and the overpowering scent of car air freshener.

His tour around the Arch killed about forty-five minutes, and it was almost five thirty when the cab driver let him off at the Safeway where he had parked his truck. He went in and did a little food shopping, stuffing a cooler full of ice, Pepsi, and deli sandwiches. The shopping trip took fifteen minutes—plenty of time for the cab driver to move on.

Hobart grunted as he hefted the cooler into the back seat of his car, centering it for easy access from the driver's seat. Pointing the Jeep back toward the freeway, he glanced at his watch. He wanted to get in at least five hours of driving tonight.

"How'd the bank thing go, John?" It was eight o'clock and Robert Swenson was already staring intently at his computer screen.

Hobart tossed three cashier's checks on the desk. "Went okay. File these, would you?"

Swenson took them and walked to the filing cabinet in the back corner of the office.

"You're working on the ad?" Hobart asked, motioning to the computer, though his partner's head was still stuck in a file drawer.

"Nah, playing solitaire. I finished the ad yesterday. Hang on and I'll print it out." He slammed the file drawer shut and sat down at the computer. When the whirring sound of the printer stopped, he pulled a single sheet off the top and laid it on the desk in front of him.

*****ATTENTION NARCOTICS USERS*****

In light of the seriousness of the drug problem in America and the government's inability to stem the tide of illegal narcotics, the COMMITTEE FOR A DRUG-FREE SOCIETY has voted to act unilaterally to end this threat.

Let it be known that on [date] the CDFS will begin a SYSTEMATIC POISONING OF NARCOTICS IN THE U.S.

To include all organic and manufactured illegal . recreational drugs.

Anyone using narcotics after that date will run a SERIOUS RISK OF DEATH or permanent disability.

We at the CDFS regret that such drastic measures must be taken and any casualties that may result from our actions. It is our belief that the countless lives saved from drug-related health problems and violence will eclipse those lost as a result of our decision.

*****ATTENTION NARCOTICS USERS*****

"I went out and bought this software package called CorelDraw—it's like a desktop publishing thing—does graphics. But I haven't had time to figure it out. So I ended up just doing it on Word."

"Shit, looks okay to me. It gets the point across. I like what you did with making us look remorseful. It plays well."

"Hey, John, if I didn't believe that this would save lives in the end, I wouldn't be here."

Hobart backpedaled. "I know, Bob. I wouldn't, either. Hey, I talked with my friend in Mexico. You're set for next week. He offered to let you stay at the house—but I told him the hotel would be fine."

"You haven't had time to tell me anything about this guy, John. How about a little background. I'm about to bet my ass on the reliability of his information."

"His name's Richard Penna—call him Rick. We met years ago when we were both with DEA. Actually, I haven't seen him in almost ten years, but I still get a Christmas card every December. Hell, I'll bet there's one at my house now."

Hobart settled himself into the chair more comfortably and put his feet on the desk. "Could I get a Pepsi, Bob?"

Swenson dug through the small refrigerator at his feet.

"Anyway, back in '83, Rick and I were on a four-man detail to apprehend some dealers in D.C. To make a long story short, these guys somehow got tipped off and they were ready for us. Things got ugly real fast, and Rick got hit in the leg while he was in these guys' backyard. He managed to get behind a tree and stop the bleeding in his leg, but he was pretty much pinned down. I went in and dragged him out."

Hobart took the can of Pepsi offered him and continued. "The whole thing really got to him, and he ended up taking an early retirement—got some disability pay—a pretty good deal, if I remember right. But he credits me with saving his life."

"Sounds like you did."

Hobart smirked. "Not really. Like I said, he was behind a tree and he'd stopped the bleeding. The guys out front took care of the perps in about ten minutes. Truth be told, he'd have been better off sitting it out behind that tree than getting dragged across an open yard by me. Stupid move on my part, but shit, we all do stupid things when we're young."

Swenson nodded.

"So Rick retires and gets hooked up with some investors in an up-and-coming resort area in Mexico. I understand that he got in on the ground floor there and he's done really well. Word is that he's still pretty plugged into what's going on, though—kind of as a hobby. I suppose it's also helpful to be able to get whatever your customers need."

Swenson looked skeptical. "And you think Rick will let me in on what's going on with the heroin trade down there. C'mon, man, I've never met him and you haven't seen him in years."

"Rick's a guy who likes to drink a lot and talk big. And he trusts me. You're not gonna have a very hard time maneuvering him into telling you anything you want to know. Shit, you'll probably just have to sit there and take notes."

11

Near Houston, Texas,
January 15

Steve Garrett smiled mischievously. "So fess up, Mark. Deep down, you're missing all that high-powered headquarters stuff, aren't you?"

Mark Beamon sighed and adjusted his seat belt to rest more comfortably across his chest. "Oh, yeah. It's been tough, but the opportunity to work for a man of your stature doesn't come along every day."

Garrett laughed. "No, seriously, Mark. You're not getting bored are you?"

"Not a chance," he replied honestly.

Beamon had been at his new job as the number two agent in Houston for only a couple of months, but he already felt like a new man. To him, the field agents *were* the FBI and Washington was just there to make their lives easier. Unfortunately, his view wasn't a popular one with management.

The fierce loyalty and sense of belonging that had made the Bureau special was quickly fading in Washington. It was becoming just another nine-to-five government organization, run by typical social-climbing bureaucrats.

He had been overjoyed to find that his cynicism wasn't shared by the agents on the street. They were out there chasing the bad guys with the same dedication that he remembered as a young man. He felt he was back where he belonged.

"I was beginning to think those guys at headquarters just kept me around for target practice."

His new boss chuckled. "Well, you sure as hell gave them enough ammunition."

"You know how it is."

Beamon turned and stared blankly out the window, surveying the hard earth and stones as they flashed into view and then just as quickly disappeared. His mind wandered back thirty years to the last days of summer after his graduation from high school. The small concrete schoolhouse where he had spent a good deal of his childhood had long since been torn down, but it hadn't been far from where they were now.

His family had been so proud when he was accepted to Yale on a full academic scholarship. Like many of his friends from that period, he had been the first of his family to go to college. The fact that he was accepted to the Ivy League was completely lost on his father, who saw all colleges as equally regal and mysterious institutions. Until the day he died, he would brag to anyone who would listen that his son had gone to college. When they asked which one, he'd reply that it was a place "back east." Beamon never quite understood that particular mental block.

On the day before he left, he finished packing and drove out to the desert with his girlfriend. Driving the obscure desert roads with a case of warm beer had been a favorite pastime in an era of quickly disappearing drive-ins and skating rinks.

He had never seen her again. Her parents moved to Dallas about halfway through his freshman year at Yale. They had written at first but the time between letters grew longer and longer as the months passed. He could still see the way she looked with the desert sun setting behind her. Strange what the mind grabs and holds on to. It had seemed at the time to be a pivotal moment in his life, but had turned out to be nothing.

The harsh ring of a cellular phone interrupted Beamon's daydreams, and he turned his head away from the side window, not yet ready to be pulled back into reality. They still had an hour of driving before they reached their destination and what would undoubtedly be a very long and very dull meeting.

Garrett punched the button on the side of the phone, turning it to Speaker. "Steve Garrett," he announced.

"Mr. Garrett, this is Bill Michaels. We just had a report of a branch of Houston National being robbed and a guard there being killed. A single marked unit is in high-speed pursuit on Limestone Road about forty miles west of Houston, heading north. We've dispatched agents to the scene."

Beamon sat upright and looked behind him out of the back window of the car, then scanned the landscape all around.

"Keep me posted, Bill, I've got my portable with me."

"Yes, sir."

Garret punched the button one more time and the phone went silent.

"Did you know that I grew up around here, Steve?" Beamon asked.

Garrett looked at him strangely. "I think someone mentioned that to me once. It might have been you, actually."

Beamon wasn't listening. "I spent about six years here as a street agent, too." His voice was rising in volume.

"So?" Garrett replied, dragging the single syllable out longer than he needed to.

"Well, I'd swear that if we take a left onto an old dirt road about a mile up here," Beamon pointed through the windshield, "we'd get to Limestone. It's not a very long road, as I recall."

Garrett looked at him blankly.

"Are you suggesting that I get us involved in a high-speed chase on a dirt road in my wife's car?"

Beamon looked around him in disgust. "Jesus, Steve, I thought this was a Bureau car. Couldn't you have gotten her something a little more sporty?"

Garrett frowned. "You got a gun?"

"Nope. You?"

"Huh-uh."

Beamon shrugged. "Shit, Steve, they gotta be most of the way up Limestone by now. We'll just take a leisurely drive up there, pull in way behind the cops, and show up after they've got the whole thing sewn up. You know how the Director's always harping on our relationship with the locals. Lots of PR points to be had here, you know? Besides it'll be fun."

Garrett mumbled something under his breath that Beamon didn't catch. Then he spoke up in a defeated tone. "Okay, where's the turn?"

Beamon smiled broadly. "You should be able to see it up on the left in a minute or two."

A narrow dirt road appeared as they came over a rise, and Garrett swung the car onto it, slowing to under forty miles per hour. He simultaneously grabbed the phone and hit a speed-dial number.

"Bill Michaels, please."

"Bill? It's Garrett. Please advise the police that Mark Beamon and I are heading up . . ." he paused and looked to his new ASAC for help. He didn't get any.

"Shit, I don't know. Some road that goes to Limestone."

Beamon strained to hear what was being said on the other side of the phone, but it was impossible over the noise of the car. It wasn't used to being off the asphalt.

"That's right. We should hit Limestone in—" he looked at Beamon, who held up six fingers, "—six minutes. I'm driving a blue '92 Ford Taurus. Tell 'em not to shoot at me."

He hung up the receiver.

The Ford's suspension did an admirable job on the old road, though the low-slung bottom scraped the ground every few minutes. Each time metal scraped rock, Garrett winced as if he could feel the car's pain.

Beamon knew that he wasn't making points by shaming his new boss into this chase. The thought of a couple of young kids in a squad car coming up against a proven killer didn't sit well with him, though. And as an added bonus, they'd almost surely miss their meeting.

"We should be coming up on it pretty soon, so stay sharp. If I remember right, this road's gonna dead-end into it."

Garrett leaned forward slightly, squinting through the dust kicked up by the car's tires. A low ridge bobbed up and down on their left like a buoy in the ocean. The wail of a siren became barely audible from the north.

"Shit, it looks like we may be closer than we thought." Garrett touched the brakes, slowing the car to a little over thirty miles per hour.

"Sound travels funny out here—that squad car could be anywhere," Beamon said, trying to sound casual.

The crossroads appeared in front of them, following a natural gully, and marking the end of the ridge to their left. Garrett pulled the car as far to the left as he could without getting into the rocky soil that guarded the road's edge, and set up for a hard right turn.

Just as his hands tightened on the wheel, a dark green car rocketed into their field of vision, heading at a speed that was going to put the front grill of Garrett's wife's car into its passenger side door. Beamon's hands flew instinctively to the dashboard, bracing himself for an impact, as Garrett slammed on the brakes and spun the wheel hard to the right. The tires didn't bite into the loose dirt and gravel, and the car's forward momentum continued, back wheels drifting left in a lazy arc.

It turned out to be just enough to avoid a major collision, and their front bumper only lightly tapped the back of the car in front of them. The impact was enough to send the other car into an exaggerated fishtail, finally slamming its front end into a sturdy rock outcropping along the left side of the road.

The siren that had seemed to be in front of them turned out to be emanating from a police cruiser coming up quickly behind them. Beamon had been right about sound in the desert—the siren had been reflecting off the low ridge to their left, making it impossible to accurately pinpoint.

Both men jumped out as the squad car skidded to a stop behind them. Garrett had his FBI credentials held high in the air and was yelling "FBI" at the top of his lungs just in case the police hadn't gotten the message. He dropped them when a gunshot shattered his wife's front windshield.

Beamon jumped for the ditch alongside the road and began crawling toward the police cruiser.

"Mark, you okay?"

It was Garrett, yelling through a barrage of gunfire that seemed to be coming solely from the car that they'd just run off the road. Beamon hoped that it was just another acoustic trick, and that the cops hadn't forgotten their guns too.

"Yeah. You?" he shouted back.

"Yeah."

By now Beamon was directly below and to the left of the squad car. He could just see the top of its lights from the four-foot-deep ditch that he was lying in.

"Hey guys," he shouted to the men above him. "It's Mark Beamon with the FBI. You got a call telling you we were coming, right?"

"Yes, sir, Mr. Beamon," a young voice replied. "You should be okay to come up here."

Beamon noted that the shooting had stopped. He struggled to his knees and peeked over the edge of the ditch. As luck would have it, the squad car was turned sideways in the road, and its front fender was only about five feet from his position. The shooter was nowhere in sight, probably huddled behind his car, reloading.

Beamon jumped out of the ditch and rolled to the squad car, noting sadly that it wasn't as smooth a ride as it had once been. His headquarters-bred gut caused him to bounce up once every revolution.

He ended up on his back behind the front wheel of the squad car, looking up into a frightened face.

"Are you all right, sir?"

"So far." Beamon dragged himself to his knees and began brushing himself off.

A slightly older cop was peering around the back bumper of the squad car. Beamon's eyes moved from him to the young cop's gun.

The young man followed Beamon's gaze to his right hand. "Is there something wrong, sir?"

"Three-fifty-seven with a four-inch barrel," Beamon observed in a conversational tone that sounded out of place in the eerie silence that had followed the suspect's initial barrage.

The young cop didn't seem to know how to respond to the comment.

"You know, I only brought an old .38 snubnose with me," Beamon lied. "I don't suppose you'd consider lending me yours, and using the shotgun."

"No problem, sir," he said, handing the pistol over.

Beamon eyed carefully down the sights as the young cop slithered into the car for the shotgun. Early in his career Beamon had been a firearms instructor and one of the best shots in the Bureau. It had been years since he'd spent any meaningful amount of time practicing, but shooting was like riding a bicycle. He figured he'd probably still rank in the top five percent.

Beamon turned to the cop at the rear bumper. "Can you see anything?"

"Not really, sir. The suspect's car is sideways to us with its back wheels in a ditch. It's about thirty-five yards from us and about fifteen from your car. He must just be sitting behind it. Can't really go anywhere without walking right out into the open." The cop moved back to let Beamon take a look. The name tag on his uniform read O'Rourke.

Peering around the back bumper, Beamon could see Garrett about forty feet in front of him, back pressed against a rock outcropping. He didn't look happy as he stared back, arms crossed in front of him.

"You okay there, Steve?"

His boss replied with an obscene gesture.

Beamon leaned back against the tire of the car and took a deep breath. The two police officers looked hopefully at him, obviously grateful to relinquish command of the situation.

"What're you hearing about backup, guys?"

"Ten or fifteen minutes," O'Rourke replied.

Beamon grimaced. The smart move, he knew, would be to just wait for the troops. That plan of action had one rather serious flaw, though. He wasn't looking forward to being found covered in dirt and hiding behind the tire of a squad car. All in all, that would be only marginally better than being shot in the ass.

"Look, Bud," he yelled in the general direction of the suspect's car, "it's four against one now and the odds aren't gonna get any better for you. Why don't you just come out from behind the car with your hands on your head, and we'll put an end to this before they bring in those fucking SWAT prima donnas."

He peeked back around the bumper to see if his speech had any effect. For a moment there was nothing. Then a single shot rang out. Beamon whipped his head back behind the car. The two cops looked disappointed.

When his heart slowed down enough for his brain to start functioning again, Beamon realized that the suspect had never appeared from behind the car. What was he shooting at? He let that compute for a minute.

"I do believe that man just shot himself," he said finally, mostly to himself. Expressions of disappointment were replaced by expressions of hope on the faces in front of him.

"Why don't one of you guys go check it out."

O'Rourke adjusted his gun in his hand and began to make his way toward the back of the car. Beamon stuck a foot out, blocking his path.

"That was a joke, son. Geez, you guys need to lighten up."

"I'd be happy to go, sir."

Beamon believed him.

"Nah, it was my play. I'll go. You guys cover me."

He poked his head out one last time, and seeing that it was clear, ran to Garrett's position behind the rock.

"What do you think?" Garrett asked, arms still folded. He looked like he was getting ready for a siesta.

"I think the guy might have shot himself, actually."

"Great! When's our backup getting here?"

"Ten minutes or something. I think I'm gonna go around and take a look, though."

Garrett didn't seem excited about that strategy. "You really think that's smart, Mark?"

The truth was that he didn't, but he'd never let that stop him before. "No fucking way I'm gonna be found hiding from a corpse."

With that, he began moving slowly away from the rock, eyes focused intently on the car in front of him. In his peripheral vision, he could see that the two policemen had their guns out over the hood of their car.

He gave the suspect's Buick a wide berth, moving silently around it. When the area behind the car started to come into view, he wanted to have at least thirty yards between him and the shooter. He may be a touch rusty, but there still weren't that many people who could outshoot him at that distance.

The dirt road behind the suspect's car slowly came into view as Beamon continued circling to the left. He concentrated on staying relaxed and breathing evenly.

A motionless foot appeared and Beamon froze. He waited for a couple of minutes, watching for movement. Satisfied that there was none, he began edging left again, keeping his eyes locked on the leg that was slowly appearing. Even from this distance, it was obvious that the dirt next to the man was discolored and slightly reflective. Beamon quickened his pace, bringing the man into full view. He was dead.

He relaxed his grip on the .357 and walked up to the car. The top of the suspect's head was missing, and a 9mm pistol had been dropped in the dust next to a still-smoking crack pipe. Beamon ignored the pistol, focusing on the man's right leg. Everything below the knee was missing.

"He's dead!"

Garrett appeared from behind his rock. O'Rourke and his partner stood up from behind the car, still pointing their guns in the general direction of the Buick.

Beamon continued to stare at the suspect's stump of a right leg. "Uh, was there anything unusual about the description of this guy when it came over the radio?"

They two policemen looked at each other as they followed Garrett toward the car. "Not really. Male Caucasian, mid-thirties, about six feet."

"Is that it?" The front page of a newspaper appeared suddenly in Beamon's mind, complete with a large unflattering picture of his face. The headline read:

FBI CHASE CAUSES INNOCENT MAN TO COMMIT SUICIDE

"No, wait a minute. They did say he had a real bad limp."

Beamon rushed to the car and dove into the open passenger side door. The front seat was empty. He crawled in, leaning over the seat into the back. He exhaled violently enough to blow the thin layer of dust off the seat in front of him. A paper bag full of cash had been knocked onto the floor between the seats. On top of it sat a prosthetic leg.

It had been long over a week since Swenson left for Mexico. To relieve the boredom, Hobart had set to updating his financial records and reestablishing contact with his operatives. Unfortunately, after three solid days of work he'd run out of things to do. After that, the days seemed to last forever.

The fact that he couldn't go home, and felt uncomfortable going to places he had regularly frequented before, magnified his idleness. The tastefully decorated walls were beginning to close in on him as he sat in the office, watching CNN and playing chess against the computer.

When his mind wasn't fully occupied, he tended to worry. Every day, his thoughts worked through what had occurred thus far. He began with his individual operatives spread out across the U.S. Would they get caught? If they did, would they give him up? It was true that none of them knew where he was or how to contact him, but the loss of his anonymity would sure as hell give the FBI an edge. And what about the FBI? He had worked with them long enough to foster a grudging respect for their tenacity and intelligence.

Finally his thoughts would turn to Reed Corey. He was finding it difficult not to replay Corey's escape over and over again in his head. How could he have made such a stupid mistake? He'd gone to Colombia specifically to recruit one of the best military men he'd ever known, and then after meeting with him, had dismissed him as some kind of brain-dead coke fiend.

What was the old saying? Hindsight is twenty/twenty.

On the other hand, Hobart didn't have much respect for the intelligence or professionalism of drug dealers—even the top men sitting in their fortresses in the mountains of Colombia. As far as he was concerned, they were just a bunch of children. Having said that, though, he wasn't anxious to have them gunning for him.

And then there was the future. An operation of this scale was bound to have screwups. What would they be?

Hobart turned back to the chess game glowing on the computer screen. He knew better than to sit around and run endless dooms-day scenarios. Pretty soon there would be FBI agents and cartel thugs behind every telephone pole. He tried to focus on his game, but it was becoming more and more difficult.

It was almost three o'clock when the sound of the telephone broke through the drone of CNN. He snatched it off the desk before the first ring faded. "Clipper City Antiques and Oddities."

Swenson's voice cut through the static of a marginal connection. "How are things going?"

Hobart glanced at a VU meter next to the phone. It indicated that the line was free of bugs. "Question is, how are things going with you? Did you find what you were looking for?"

"I think so."

Hobart frowned deeply. "What do you mean, you think so?"

"Well, actually I'm ninety-nine percent sure, but it's all based on circumstantial evidence. Penna gave me a general location for the refinery and told me it was disguised as a private airfield. I found the strip pretty much where he said it'd be, but I can't get very close 'cause it's clear-cut. I'm working from about a hundred and fifty yards with a spotting scope—can't hear any conversations. There's a pretty big hangar on the property, bigger than they need. No planes ever go into it. Every couple of days, a plane lands. They load it up with a few boxes and off it goes again."

"Sound like what we're looking for."

"Yeah, I'm sure it is. They also bring a lot of supplies into the hangar, though they don't seem to be on as tight a schedule as your friends in South America. Also, I can't tell how much stuff they've got stockpiled 'cause it's all stored inside."

"So are we a go?"

"Absolutely. I've tracked the, uh, items in question to their suppliers, and shouldn't have a whole lot of problem with access. Their security just doesn't anticipate this kind of thing. You'd need an army to steal a fucking peso from these bastards, though."

That was one of the things they had working for them this early in the game. Drug dealer security was set up to prevent someone from stealing finished product—not to stop someone from introducing something new into the production line.

"The problem I'm gonna have down here is with timing. I can, uh, do what we proposed within, say, four days of your go-ahead. But I don't know when it will affect America, if you know what I mean."

Hobart smiled. The doomsday scenarios that he'd been creating over the last week didn't seem to have materialized. At least not yet.

"That's not a problem. I should be able to get my timing down to somewhere between five and ten days, so we'll make the notification coincide with that. You just do the best you can to work within that time frame. If your product is a few weeks late, it's a few weeks late. Where can I reach you?"

Swenson gave him the number.

"I'll call you on the twenty-second, at three o'clock your time. Stay on top of what's going on down there."

"Don't worry," Swenson replied. "Talk to you next week."

12

Bogota, Colombia,
January 22

Hobart tempered his need for anonymity with his need for sleep and compromised on a slightly nicer hotel this time through Bogota. While the employees were less forgetful when it came to faces, the bed was a lump-free queen, and the bathroom wasn't down the hall. Correcting another mistake, he rented a sturdy four-wheel drive at about five times the cost of the puny economy car he had subjected himself to the month before.

It was 3:55 P.M. Bogota time, and would be approaching three o'clock in Mexico. He picked up the phone next to the bed—another amenity he was grateful for—and dialed the number Swenson had given him. It was picked up on the second ring.

"Hello."

The combination of street noise floating though his open window and the static on the line made it difficult to hear. "How are things going over there?" he asked in a loud voice.

"Real good. Just waiting for the go-ahead."

"You've got it. I'm going tomorrow night. I should be back home sometime the day after."

It was difficult to tell if the sound coming through the line was a heavy sigh or just another wave of static.

"It'll be good to get this over with and get home. I'll see you in a couple of days."

There was a loud click as Swenson replaced the receiver.

His final words struck a chord. The tension was building in Hobart too. The preliminaries of a mission always tied him in knots. Too much planning and not enough action.

Hobart maneuvered the powerful Range Rover through the mid-morning traffic, cutting across the heart of the city. Ahead of him, the mountains seemed to float in a haze of exhaust fumes. He sucked in a deep breath of the foul-smelling air and exhaled loudly. The adrenaline pumped evenly through him as he approached the point of no return. He had almost forgotten what it felt like during his uneventful years with the church. It was a little like dying, he imagined.

The traffic eased as he moved farther from the city center toward the suburbs. By the time he turned off on the old mountain road, his was the only vehicle in sight.

The ride wasn't much more comfortable than it had been the first time, but he was covering terrain at least three times faster. He worked through the gears slowly, keeping in mind that a road like the one he was on could cripple even the Range Rover. This was not the time to get careless.

About halfway to the pullout that had been so useful on his reconnaissance missions, a cloud of dust became visible high on one of the switchbacks in front of him. A moment later, the source of the cloud appeared. He instantly recognized it as the truck used by the refinery. Right on time.

The decrepit old truck slowed to a crawl, its right tires dipping out of sight on the steeply angled shoulder of the road. Despite the distance still between them, Hobart could see the look of concentration on the driver's face as he stared intently forward. The expression was almost too intense. Happy hour must have already started.

Hobart's suspicion was confirmed when the man in the passenger seat put a clear, unlabeled bottle to his mouth and took a healthy slug. The driver maintained his focus on the road as they passed within a foot of each another. His passenger stared intently at Hobart through glassy eyes. It wasn't a look of suspicion—more one of mild interest. Not very many cars traveled this road. In fact, this was the first time Hobart had seen one, despite his frequent trips to study the refinery.

It was almost another half an hour before he found the pullout. He took a deep breath and backed the truck down the steep slope and into the jungle. At the bottom he came to a full stop for a moment, shifted into first gear, and gunned the engine. The truck came to life, shooting up the steep incline like a rocket. Satisfied that he wouldn't have any trouble getting out, he backed down again.

Hobart jumped out of the truck, and struggled back up the hill on foot. From the road, the Range Rover was completely invisible. The only problem was the tree branches that had been bent from its entry. They all pointed to the truck's position. Fifteen minutes of sweaty work in the waning light returned the branches to a more or less natural position. He walked along the road one last time, satisfying himself that everything looked as it had before his arrival.

He opened the hatch on the back of the Range Rover, and changed into the torn jeans and T-shirt that had served him so well on his first trip. A grimy poncho and weathered felt hat completed his costume. Scooping up a handful of dust from beneath his feet, he splashed it on himself and brushed it in vigorously. Finally he pulled a full bottle of tequila out of his bag, and dabbed the clear liquid on his poncho. Walking around to the passenger-side mirror, he examined the result.

It wasn't great. A close inspection would undoubtedly reveal him to be a gringo. Of course, a close inspection wouldn't be necessary if he was forced to speak. His Spanish was still weak.

The good news was that he was completely unrecognizable as the well-groomed, bespectacled man who had passed by the guard's truck only an hour ago. Not that Hobart anticipated being seen, but it paid to be cautious. Secreting the .22 in his waistband, he began backtracking on the road until he found the other feature that had prompted him to pick this as an ambush site. A little over one hundred yards from where he had pulled off, a sharp turn in the road combined with a deep horizontal rut. It had been necessary to slow his Range Rover to a crawl to negotiate these obstacles, and he imagined that the old truck the guards were driving would have to nearly stop.

Walking down the slope to the south of the road, Hobart picked out a comfortable-looking tree and sat down, leaning his back against it. He estimated another two hours before the truck came lumbering back up the mountain.

The change in temperature as warm day turned to cool night dispersed the clouds, and he could see the stars twinkling through the canopy of the forest. Other than that, it was completely black.

His estimate had been optimistic. It was almost three hours before he heard the unmistakable sound of the old engine struggling in the thin mountain air. He stood, stretching his legs. The truck's headlights weren't visible yet, and he had to feel his way up the slope and into a thick stand of grass. The natural sounds of the jungle stopped. The only things that existed were the coughing of the motor and the soft grass beneath him.

He shielded his eyes as the truck's light arced through the night, searching for his fully dilated pupils. Slowly he lifted his hands away from his face, adjusting to the sudden explosion of color around him. The smell of exhaust fumes replaced the comforting perfume of decaying leaves.

As expected, the truck slowed with a shudder as the washed-out groove in the road became visible to the driver. The front tires dropped in gingerly. Once in, the driver gunned the engine and the tires obediently popped out the other side. The drums of kerosene in the back pulled apart and clanged back together, despite the ropes securing them to the bed.

When the back wheels had fully cleared the wash and the driver had peeled his eyes from his sideview mirror, Hobart jumped to his feet and circled behind the truck. The gears ground as it slowly gained speed, held back by the weight of the drums.

Hobart jogged up behind the struggling vehicle and sat down on the foot or so of empty space remaining on the back of the makeshift plywood bed. Taking a deep breath, he relaxed for a moment, knowing that the large metal drums completely hid him from view. After he had collected himself, he grabbed the rim of the drum directly behind him, using it to steady himself as he peeked over the cargo.

During his reconnaissance of the refinery, he had noted that the back window of the cab had been replaced by an old metal sign. It was still there, further blocking him from the eyes of the men up front.

The truck swayed violently as it made its way up the road, forcing Hobart to keep both hands on the barrels in front of him to keep from falling off—something he hadn't anticipated. He was going to need his hands.

Climbing carefully onto the swaying barrels, he noticed a gap where three of them hadn't been pushed completely together. He crawled over and wedged his right leg down into it, then rocked back and forth, confirming the stability of his position. The truck hit a bump, and drums shifted, biting painfully into his thigh.

With both hands now free, he pulled a pair of pliers out of his back pocket and began twisting the tops off of the drums. The smell of kerosene, combined with the rocking of the truck and the loud laughter coming from the cab, were causing the nervous lump in his stomach to evolve into full-fledged queasiness.

It took him almost ten minutes to get the tops off all of the drums and to stash them in a cloth pouch brought along for the purpose. He stuffed the pouch partially into the hole that his leg was wedged into and pulled a bundle from under his poncho. It consisted of seven lengths of white PVC pipe, each about eight inches long. One end of each pipe had been sealed with a white plastic disk, making them look like candles on a stand. The other end was sealed with only a condom stretched tightly across the opening.

Half listening to the loud conversation coming from the cab, he slid them, condom first, into the holes in the tops of the drums. The large bases kept the pipes from falling in.

The pain in his leg was becoming excruciating as the weight of the drums shifted rhythmically back and forth. The constant rubbing had torn through his jeans and was working on his skin. He could feel blood beginning to slide down his leg.

After a few more minutes of agony, Hobart began pulling each pipe back out in the same order that he'd put them in. The condoms had been dissolved by the kerosene, and the deadly powder emptied into the drums with anticlimactic silence. He threw the pipes one by one into the trees behind the truck, holding his breath against any particles that might escape into the air.

By the time he had the seventh of ten tops screwed back on, kerosene had sloshed onto the tops of the barrels and was being held in quivering pools by their raised edges. He had managed to avoid most of it, but he could feel it beginning to drip down the hole next to his leg. He shifted violently to keep the poisonous kerosene away from his widening wound.

One more.

He tightened the second to the last top with his pliers. As he pulled the last one out of the cloth pouch, the conversation that he had been half monitoring took a turn for the worse.

"Pull over here, I've got to piss," the passenger in the cab said in Spanish thick with alcohol.

Hobart began working his leg from between the barrels, cursing quietly. It came out in painful inches as the truck slowed to a stop. He threw the last stopper into the trees and positioned himself so that he could use his free leg to push against the drums. As the passenger nearly fell from the truck, Hobart's foot cleared the hole, and he dropped on his back onto the kerosene pooled on the tops of the barrels.

The quiet splash startled the man stumbling toward the trees. Hobart watched through half-closed eyes as the man spun clumsily, moving his hand from his fly to his side. It took him a few seconds, but he finally managed to get his gun clear of its holster and level it in the truck's general direction.

Hobart lay perfectly still. His body tensed as the barrel of the gun leveled at him, praying that the man wasn't stupid or drunk enough to fire a gun at fourteen barrels of kerosene from five feet away. Apparently, he was. His hand jerked on the trigger, and Hobart's teeth clenched involuntarily as he waited for death. Nothing happened.

The safety was on.

Hobart continued to watch through half-closed eyes as the man tried to comprehend what had happened. It didn't take long. He flipped the safety off the revolver and leveled it at the back of the truck again.

"You on the truck. Get down from there!"

Hobart stirred. He sat up slowly, as though in a drunken stupor.

"What the fuck is going on out there, Carlos?" The driver yelled, opening his door.

"It looks like we have a passenger!" Carlos was speaking confidently now, but was still swaying slightly from the tequila that he'd been nursing on the drive.

Hobart jumped off the truck, falling to the ground. The fall wasn't pantomimed; his leg was completely numb. He lay there motionless on the dirt road, thankful to be off the top of the barrels. The poisoned kerosene had been soaking through his clothes.

From his position on the ground, Hobart could see the flicker of the headlights as the driver passed in front of them.

"What the fuck were you doing up there?" Carlos screamed, pushing the gun into Hobart's face as he got unsteadily to his feet. The driver stopped a few feet away and leveled a rifle at his head.

"Ceratibo," Hobart replied quietly, keeping his head down in a submissive pose. Ceratibo was a small village about twenty miles past the refinery that was the truck's destination.

Carlos pushed his .357 harder into Hobart's cheek, pressing him back against the truck. He used the barrel of the gun to force his head to the right.

"Does this look like a fucking bus to you?"

"No, señor," Hobart replied, trying to keep his answers to simple phrases that were easy to pronounce.

"Smells like one of the tops came off the kerosene, and this ass-hole's been sleeping in it," Carlos said to the driver, looking disgusted. "Hey, I got an idea."

He grabbed the front of Hobart's poncho and swung him away from the truck, almost falling himself. Digging in his pocket with his free hand, he produced a lighter and flicked the flame to life.

"I'll bet this prick would make a nice torch!"

The driver laughed and Hobart almost joined him. It seemed ironic that he was replaying his recent visit with Peter Manion, but on the other side of the lighter. If there was an afterlife, Manion was loving this.

Hobart fell back against the hill behind him, sliding a hand innocently under his poncho and releasing the safety on the .22 tucked into his waistband. It wasn't ideal, but if he had to he could shoot both men, take their guns and money, and the kerosene would still end up at the refinery by tomorrow night.

The driver chimed in as Hobart began to slowly pull the gun free.

"Carlos, you fucking moron. You light that asshole up, and he's gonna run right over to the truck and blow us all to Kingdom Come."

Carlos looked disappointed, but seemed to see the wisdom in his friend's words. He put the lighter back in his pocket.

"Now let's get the hell out of here—we're late as it is." The driver's tone suggested that he was Carlos's superior.

"What do you want me to do with this piece of shit?"

"You shoot off that gun an' we're gonna have trouble," he warned. "They'll be able to hear it from here." The driver walked back around the truck and began surveying the drums. Finding the one without a top, he stuffed a rag into the opening.

Carlos grunted in frustration as Hobart continued to slowly free his pistol.

When the driver's door slammed shut, Carlos finally made a decision and gave Hobart a vicious kick to the face. He could have avoided it easily, but there was no sense in pissing the man off anymore.

Through watering eyes, he watched Carlos pull out his penis and begin to relieve himself on his chest. As he felt the warm fluid seep into his clothes, he briefly considered pulling the gun. The thought passed quickly, though, and he just lay there quietly as Carlos zipped his pants up and walked back to the truck, cackling.

The moment the truck disappeared from view, Hobart jumped up and jogged slowly across the road. He managed to make it down to the forest bed before the light from the receding truck completely disappeared. He stripped off all of his clothes and strapped on his night vision goggles. He headed quickly away from the road, remembering a stream that ran fairly straight north to south. It took him about ten minutes to reach it, and he walked into its center and began scrubbing. The mountain water took his breath away at first, but no more than the mingling smells of kerosene and urine. The water stung the open wound in his leg, drowning out the throbbing coming from his blood-spattered nose. Finally he put his goggles on a rock at the side of the stream and washed the blood from his face, carefully feeling the bridge of his nose. Broken. Another battle scar to add to his collection.

The trip back to his truck went much faster than he had anticipated. Visibility was poor, even with the goggles, though it was sufficient to avoid large objects such as trees. They did manage to pick up one of the pipes that he had thrown from the back of the truck, giving it an eerie greenish white glow. He gave it a wide berth.

Back at the Range Rover, he quickly dressed and pulled out onto the road. The smell of kerosene hadn't been completely eradicated, so he rolled down the window to circulate the air.

He tried unsuccessfully to push the thought of the poison from his mind. It hadn't made it to the gash worn into his leg, but had it penetrated his skin? Had the poison mixed well enough to cause the fumes to be dangerous, or had it been forced to the bottom when it was dumped in?

He wished that Peter Manion were still alive. Even if the news was bad, he'd rather know now. Wondering for the next two weeks was going to be a hell of a lot worse.

13

Baltimore, Maryland,
January 30

The good news was that it had been a week since his kerosene bath in Colombia, and he felt fine except for the dull throbbing in his nose. Of course, that didn't prove anything. Manion had warned him that the effects of the mushrooms would be negligible for almost two weeks. And then you'd be dead.

The bad news was that he hadn't heard a word from Robert Swenson since he had given him the go-ahead. Hobart was struggling to keep his mind from running endless worst-case scenarios. Its current favorite was that his partner had been captured and was at this moment giving him up. He had briefly considered moving from the warehouse, but where to? Better to just sit it out and keep his eyes open. In the interim, a bullet-proof vest and extra clips for his .45 had found their way under his jacket.

He had planned to have a ballpark time frame on the arrival of the tainted heroin before putting the ads in the paper, but it didn't look like he was going to have that luxury. In the scenario currently branded into his mind, the heroin didn't even get poisoned—Swenson was caught going in. In any event, his best guess was that the first wave of bad coke was going to hit the American shore in about four days. His estimate wasn't based on scientific study or statistics—it was really just a guess. There were too many variables to get a reliable estimate. Shipping schedules, modes of transportation, Coast Guard activity, final destination. The list went on.

Grabbing a handful of tissues from a box off the desk, he walked to the open filing cabinet behind him and pulled out three Federal Express envelopes, careful to keep the tissues between his fingertips and the flimsy cardboard. He tossed them on the desk and sat down. It wasn't quite the elevating moment that he had hoped for, but the ads had to go today. He had probably already waited too long.

The climax to all of the preparation seemed to dissolve in light of Swenson's disappearance. All Hobart could do was hope that his partner hadn't been caught until he had finished what he was there to do. Or better yet, that he had been shot leaving the refinery area.

Hobart switched on the computer in front of him, and pulled up Word.

Dear Sir or Madam:

I have enclosed an ad that I would like placed on a full page in Section A on February 3. I have also enclosed a cashier's check for the amount quoted to me by your advertising department.

The amount of the check should, I hope, be enough to convince you that this is not a hoax.

Sincerely,
CDFS

He stuffed each envelope with a copy of his letter and a copy of the ad, careful not to touch the paper with his fingers. He mentally thanked FedEx for its self-sealing envelope—the FBI was doing amazing things with saliva these days.

He opened the front door carefully, scanning the street. Fortunately, this section of Baltimore housed almost no Hispanics. A Mexican drug enforcer would stand out like a man in a tuxedo. Not spotting anyone who looked like they were from much farther south than D.C., he stepped out onto the street and set the alarm. His eyes continued their slow sweeps of the neighborhood. The fact that no one had tried to knock down the warehouse with machine guns was a good sign. Maybe Swenson was killed after all. The thought of his old friend's bullet-riddled corpse lying on a dilapidated airstrip in Mexico was sad, but not as sad as the thought of his own bullet-ridden corpse lying next to a dilapidated warehouse in Baltimore.

He glanced at his watch as he pulled his truck out into the quiet street.

Four thirty. Just in time for the fucking rush hour. Maybe the aggravation of the Beltway would be enough to get his mind off Mexico.

The traffic had been even worse than he expected because of a fender bender that left two middle-aged men fistfighting in an overgrown grass median.

Instead of getting his mind off his problems, the cramped confines of the truck and mindlessness of driving had focused his thoughts into an ever-changing and increasingly morbid collage.

It was almost eight o'clock when Hobart pulled back into his parking space in front of the warehouse. The three FedEx packages were now irretrievable, locked in a drop-off box near the Capitol building.

The street was as he had left it. The group of children playing ball in the alley alongside the warehouse were still there, though the bright winter sun had been replaced by shadowy streetlights.

The warehouse wasn't as he had left it.

The perimeter security was on, but the interior systems had been disabled. Hobart shut down the door alarm and moved quickly inside, pushing the door shut with his foot, and drawing his gun out of sight of the people on the street. Something else had changed. What was it?

He had left the lights on, as they were now. The furniture all looked untouched. Then it hit him—there was a quiet, almost imperceptible, hum coming from the office. He vividly remembered shutting off the computer after using it.

Hobart moved silently across the floor and darted into the office, his .45 held out directly in front of him and his finger already squeezing gently on the trigger. No one. He walked quickly around the desk. The computer screen glowed a soft gray.

THE PASSWORD IS INCORRECT. WORD CANNOT
OPEN THE DOCUMENT
C:\WINWORD\ADLET.DOC

Someone had been trying to access the letter that he had just written to the newspapers. Hobart flipped the switch on the computer's side and walked back to the door of the office. The outer room was still empty and quiet. He slipped through it and down the hall toward the warehouse, peering into the empty bathroom as he passed. The door to the warehouse was open, and he heard the unmistakable scraping of furniture being moved—as though someone was searching for something.

He stood motionless for a moment, back pressed firmly to the decaying brick wall beside the open door. It couldn't be the cops— no way—he hadn't done anything yet. The Mexicans? How could they have bypassed his security?

No point speculating when the answer was fifteen feet away. He jumped through the doorway and leveled his pistol at the head of a man wearing dark sunglasses and carrying a large box. The man dropped the box while Hobart was still in motion. The sound of breaking glass was followed by the strong smell of beer.

"Jesus, John. Don't shoot," the man cried. He sounded like he had cotton balls in his mouth.

Hobart didn't instantly recognize the soft, round face before him, but the voice was unmistakable. "What the hell happened to you?" he asked, sliding the gun back into its holster under his arm.

Robert Swenson pulled off his sunglasses, revealing black circles around red eyes. His cheeks bulged comically. "Pretty nice, huh?" He bent and collected a few unbroken beer bottles from the open top of the box. "You haven't been keeping the 'fridge stocked."

"Did you do it?" Hobart said, ignoring Swenson's comment.

"Why yes, I'm fine. Thanks for asking. Yeah, it's done. Shit should hit the streets in a week or two."

Hobart sighed heavily, feeling the week's anxieties melt away and the burning in his stomach fade with them. He took the beers from his partner's hand and walked back to the office, sitting in the chair in front of the desk. Swenson took his usual place behind it.

"Doesn't look like things went too great for you, either," Swenson said, pointing to Hobart's swollen nose. "Did you get the job done?"

"Yup. And the ads went out in FedEx today."

"I figured that's what the file ADLET was." He pointed to the blank computer screen. "Couldn't get in though—didn't know what your password was."

Hobart pointed to the beers on the desk. Swenson grabbed them and put them in the refrigerator, pulling out the last two cold ones and handing one across the desk.

"So where the hell have you been?" Hobart asked.

"Fucking bad luck's all. I was too close to the airstrip and got spotted. Some guy taking a piss where he shouldn't have been, you know. Anyway, they kicked my ass good—thought I was DEA." He took a pull on his beer, shaking his head at the memory. "They kept me in a back room in the hangar I told you about for a few days. To make a long story short, they were waiting for their boss to give the okay to put a hole in my head."

"Did he?"

Swenson smiled mischievously. "You're gonna love this. So the boss shows up. We talk for a couple of minutes and I stick with my story about wanting to charter a plane. By the end of our conversation, I'm pretty sure I'm a goner. Then he quotes a Bible passage to me—kind of out of the blue, you know. I guess that was supposed to be my Christian burial. Anyway, I recognize the quote from one of Blake's sermons—you know how good my memory is for useless shit—and I cite it. So that leads to a big conversation about God and the Bible. Turns out this guy's some kind of combination murderer/dealer/Christian soldier. So we talk Jesus for about another hour and he just lets me go. Actually, he didn't only let me go, he made his soldiers apologize to me and take me back to my hotel."

His story finished, Swenson leaned back in his chair and put his feet on the desk. "So what's with the nose?"

Hobart related his adventure with the drunk guards on the truck, leaving out the part about lying in the tainted kerosene.

Swenson laughed loudly, seeming to take perverse pleasure in the image of his ever-serious partner getting pissed on. "We're a couple of sorry old farts, aren't we? All we have to do is fool a bunch of drunk dumbshits with second grade educations, and we both get caught and beat up." His laughter faded into a quiet giggle. "Thank God, it's over."

"You said it," Hobart replied, holding his beer up. His partner leaned forward, and the bottles clinked quietly as they touched together.

The Reverend Simon Blake padded down the stairs in the new slippers that his daughter had bought him for Christmas. They were a bit small, but he could never bear the thought of taking back anything she bought him. As soon as she forgot about them, they would be relegated to the box at the top of his closet. They would make a nice addition to the ugly ties, useless electronic gadgets, and one very large belt buckle stored there. Erica insisted that the children pick out his gifts themselves.

A cold blast of air tried to blow his robe apart as he opened the front door, but the belt tied across his ample belly managed to hold. He trotted out onto the frost-covered porch, retrieved two newspapers, and rushed back to the house. The sun was peeking up over the trees at the end of his property, quickly turning the frost into gently quivering dew.

Back in the kitchen, Blake poured a healthy slug of skim milk into a bowl of low-fat granola. A look of distaste spread across his lips as he watched the individual grains bob up and down in the white liquid. This was the substitute for bacon and eggs that his wife had devised to halt the progression of his waistline. No way to start the day, as far as he was concerned.

The *Baltimore Sun* and *Washington Post* lay in front of him on the table, wrapped in damp plastic bags. The house was dead silent. He'd had the same ritual for years. Getting up a half an hour before the rest of the family to read always seemed to put his day into perspective. He knew that there wasn't much time before pandemonium struck, so he pulled the *Post* out of its bag and carefully stripped it of its rubber band.

As he smoothed the paper out on the damp table next to him, his hand passed over the boldface type announcing the top story of the day.

ORGANIZATION THREATENS U.S. NARCOTICS SUPPLY.

His emotions ran away from him for a moment, starting with excitement and ending, inexplicably, in despair. He had managed to put the entire situation out of his mind over the last few months and now it all came flooding back. Seeing it in black and white, sprawled across the front page of the *Post*, made the whole thing uncomfortably real. He smoothed out the paper one last time and began reading.

Toward the end of the article, he was feeling a little better. It seemed that the press hadn't gotten ahold of any information that his ex-security chief didn't want them to have. Blake nurtured a healthy fear of the tenacity of the press, as did all television evangelists. The story had also described how serious the drug problem was, and that this may be an effective way to correct it. Overall, a more balanced piece than he had expected.

Blake's reflections were interrupted by the sound of small feet pounding down the stairs on their way to the kitchen. He quickly folded the paper back up and pushed it to the center of the table, as if it were some girlie magazine that he was hiding from his parents. Realizing what he had just done, he shook his head silently. He just wasn't cut out for this kind of work.

14

Washington, D.C.,
February 7

Thomas Sherman gathered up a stack of folders from his desk and tucked them securely under his arm. He paused on his way out to catch the tail end of a news report on the television nestled in a bookcase next to his desk. The channel was perpetually tuned to CNN—a station that was becoming more and more a staple in the diet of FBI and CIA. When they weren't caught up in something trivial, CNN had its nose in everything. More evidence of the superiority of free enterprise over government agencies, as far as he was concerned. Profit, it seemed, was the great motivator of man.

When the screen faded into a commercial for Teflon pans, he clicked the TV off and continued for the door. He should have been running a tape on the report—it dealt directly with his top priority of the day. The problem was that he had never learned to record on the complex VCR built into the TV—despite his daughter's diligent tutelage.

Sherman rushed down the drab hall, taking a hard right into the last office suite. He smiled at the Director's secretary as he charged through the outer office. She smiled back. "They're all in there, Tom."

Punctuality was not what had propelled his meteoric rise through the ranks of the Bureau to become its second in command. Sometimes he wondered what had propelled it. His soft voice and grandfatherly demeanor didn't fit the image of the take-charge FBI man. Mark Beamon delighted in introducing him as a hat maker, insisting that Sherman had became the associate director only by some bizarre twist of fate.

He closed the door quietly behind him, confirming uncomfortably that he indeed was the last to arrive. Director Calahan sat behind his large desk, framed by two American flags. Across from him sat Frank Richter, associate deputy director in charge of investigations, and Eric Toleman, ADD in charge of administration. The chair between them was empty, and Sherman rushed across the thick carpet to take it.

"Sorry I'm late," he said, narrowly averting dropping all of his papers on the floor as he sat.

"No problem, Tom, we know you're a busy man," the Director replied with a sarcastic edge to his voice. It was well known that he didn't like to be kept waiting.

Sherman had learned to dread these meetings. Calahan had become Director almost two years ago and liked to have his hands in everything. That, in and of itself, was not a problem. Sherman had been critical of the previous Director for his lack of involvement in day-to-day administration. The problem arose when Calahan had decided on his first day that his fifteen years on the appellate bench, and subsequent appointment to the FBI, made him the country's number one law enforcement expert. But he had never bothered to learn the first thing about the operation of the organization he now commanded. That, combined with his comically overinflated ego, made him a dangerous man. It was common for him to ask questions that a first-year agent could answer; but if any of his executives appeared pedantic in their reply, he would throw one of the tantrums that had become legend at the Bureau.

Sherman stretched his long legs out as far as they would go without hitting the desk in front of him. The three executive agents were seated in a straight line in front of the Director's desk, like schoolboys in the principal's office—a position that they had become accustomed to over that last couple of years, and one that was obviously designed to give Calahan the psychological edge.

"I didn't call this meeting, Frank did," Calahan announced. "You wanted to talk about this drug poisoning business?"

"Uh, yes, sir. I was going to call a meeting last night, but I thought it would be better to come in with a few more facts." He shuffled the papers on his lap until he was comfortable that they were in the proper order.

"It looks like the CDFS is going to make good on its threat. We have reports of three suspected poisonings from hospitals across the country. Let me stress that these aren't confirmed victims. They do have symptoms that are consistent with poisoning, though, and the hospital staff has established that they are drug users. None have died yet, but all three are terminal and not expected to live through the week." He paused to see if anyone had comments.

"That's why I was late," said Sherman. "I was watching a report on this on CNN."

"Yeah, it looks like the press has picked up on one of the three, and they're all over the TV with it. It's been a slow news month."

"Do we know anything about the people poisoned?" Sherman asked.

"Not yet, I've got our guys running them down. We really just got the word last night. I should have a hell of a lot more tomorrow."

Calahan cut in. He seemed to have a formula to calculate how long he would allow a conversation to go on without his input. "Where are they from?"

Richter shuffled through his well-ordered notes. "Two from Miami, one from New York."

"And the cashier's checks?"

"We're working on it, but nothing so far," Richter replied vaguely. It had been irrefutably proven that giving Calahan too many details would set him to suggesting endless, and painfully obvious, investigative avenues.

"So have you done anything but sit around with your thumb up your ass, Frank?" Calahan's voice rose a notch.

Sherman cut in, rescuing his subordinate. "Director Calahan, there really wasn't anything to investigate until last night. Frank's as on top of it as anyone could be."

Calahan looked as though he was going to lash out, but then seemed to think better of it.

Richter continued, effectively veiling his anger. "Sir, this is pretty high-profile and it crosses the jurisdictions between us, DEA, and the local police. I suggest that we form an interdepartmental task force to handle it."

Calahan thought for a moment, playing absently with the handle on the front drawer of his desk. "And who would you suggest that we put in charge of this task force?"

"I was thinking of Dave Schupman—he's a hell of a good investigator."

Tom Sherman squirmed in his chair and suppressed a laugh. It came out sounding like he was trying to clear his sinuses. Calahan's eyes moved to him. "I take it you disagree, Tom?"

"Uh, yes, sir." He turned to face Richter, feeling a little guilty about his lack of self-control. "Look, Frank, Dave's a great investigator but he comes off like an MIT computer nerd. Christ, last time I saw him he was wearing a pocket protector."

"Actually, I think Dave *is* an MIT computer nerd," Toleman said, speaking for the first time in the meeting. He looked around him for confirmation.

Sherman ignored the comment and continued. "I think we all understand why Frank suggested Dave. I think we also know who we should put in charge of the investigation."

Richter's eyes narrowed. "Good thinking, Tom. Maybe he can just beat the information out of a few dying junkies."

"That charge was bullshit, Frank, and you know it," Sherman snapped back.

The Director broke in again. "Who are we talking about?"

Sherman and Richter had locked eyes and looked like they were in telepathic communication. Toleman answered the question. "Uh, I think they're talking about Mark Beamon, sir."

A look of disbelief crept across Calahan's face. Sherman winced.

He would have liked to have introduced the idea a little more gently.

"Is that true, Tom? Is that what you're suggesting?"

Sherman nodded, getting ready to speak, but Richter cut in before he could open his mouth.

"Sir, Beamon's uncontrollable—he's only been in Houston for a few weeks and he's already gotten the SAC there involved in a gunfight. A goddam gunfight! I can't be responsible for his actions if we bring him back."

"Relax, Frank, I agree with you," Calahan said smoothly. His distaste for Mark Beamon was no secret. "But I also agree that Dave is a bad choice. We need someone who plays better to the press." He turned back to his deputy. His shocked expression had melted into one of disappointment. "I'm surprised that you would bring up Beamon, Tom. Give me another recommendation."

Sherman stood abruptly and turned to the men beside him. "Could you excuse us for a few minutes?"

Toleman looked relieved and headed for the door before Calahan could change his mind. Richter rose more slowly, his body language suggesting suspicion. Sherman's powers of quiet persuasion were well documented. Even Calahan had been known to succumb.

The associate director followed them out as far as the door and closed it behind them.

"So what's so important, Tom?" There was a hint of nervousness in Calahan's voice.

"I would like to reiterate my recommendation that we put Mark in as head of this investigation," Sherman replied, taking his seat again.

Calahan laughed maliciously. "Just dying to get your old buddy back to D.C., aren't you, Tom. Having to spend too much time with your wife?"

Sherman ignored the insult. He knew that he had the power to intimidate the Director and that this was just his feeble attempt at keeping the upper hand.

Sherman stood, walking around behind his chair and grabbing the back of it to support his weight. "I sent Mark to Houston so that he could finish his career in peace. If I was really a good friend to him, I'd leave him there."

"Then leave him there. The Bureau's got to have one other guy who can handle this case. Find him." It was a direct order, but the conviction had drained from Calahan's voice.

"No, I don't think there is." Sherman walked over to a wall virtually covered in photographs. Almost all depicted Calahan with a well-connected government official.

"The recent criticism of you in the press has given us a black eye."

Sherman was referring to the widespread speculation that Calahan had been using Bureau resources for personal benefit. An allegation that everyone in the FBI knew was absolutely true.

He continued scanning the photographs but in his mind's eye he could see a flush coming over Calahan's face. The Director's inability to conjure up a good poker face when backed into a corner had been the subject of more than a little concern at the FBI.

"Go on," Calahan said coolly.

"The press loves Mark. Hell, they damn near deified him after the Coleman kidnapping. And whether it's true or not, they think he's our best man." Sherman moved to his right and began trying to find Calahan's young face in a photograph of his law school graduation.

"I've got a bad feeling that we've only seen the tip of the iceberg with these first three poisonings. If I'm right, the press is going to latch onto this thing and not let go. We'll be performing this investigation under a microscope." He turned and looked directly at his boss to drive the point home. "We damn well better look like we're pulling out all the stops to get these guys. And if this whole thing turns out to be nothing, we just send Mark back to Texas. And you know what the media says? They say that you pulled out the big guns to ensure the safety of a bunch of drug users. What a guy."

Sherman crossed his arms, signaling that he was done with his pitch. Calahan turned and looked out the window while his deputy stared intently at the back of the wide leather chair. Finally he swiveled it back, and they were once again face to face.

"Have it your way, Tom, but keep him away from me."

Sherman nodded. "I'd also like to suggest that Mark report directly to me and not Frank. I don't think that their relationship is particularly constructive."

Calahan was already shuffling through his "In" box with feigned interest, indicating that the meeting was over. "Whatever. It's your show."

As he walked out of the Director's office, Sherman wondered whether or not he should be happy with his victory. Mark Beamon and he had been friends for almost fifteen years, and he knew that taking this job would be a risky move for Beamon. He suspected that one of the reasons Calahan had agreed so quickly was that he was looking forward to making Beamon a scapegoat for anything that went wrong.

Mark Beamon pushed an old lamp off his sofa and twisted the top of his beer. The house was a goddam disaster. He'd been in Houston for three months and had unpacked the sum total of three boxes and two hanging bags. It was the same story every move, putting off unpacking, and buying whatever he needed to survive. It was this procrastination that was responsible for his owning three ironing boards and no less than six electric razors.

The phone range just as he was cutting into the top of box number four and cursing himself for never marrying. He gratefully tossed the old utility knife on the couch and waded through the packing material strewn across the floor. He got to the phone just before the machine picked up.

"Hello."

"Hi, Mark. How you doing?" Tom Sherman's voice.

"Still trying to settle in. What's going on with you."

"Well, I'm knee-deep in it, I guess. Things are nuts around here."

Beamon pushed himself up onto the counter. "I'll bet. I've been watching the news. This drug thing must have the Director taking oxygen." He paused for a moment to savor that mental image.

"Any chance you and I could get together, tomorrow?" Sherman asked.

Beamon remained silent.

"You still there, Mark?"

"Yeah, but I'm thinking about hanging up. Tell me you're not about to get me involved in this fiasco."

"The media doesn't have the whole story yet, Mark. I think we could have a serious problem here."

Beamon knew better than to ask for details. This kind of case was just too tempting. "Geez, Tommy, I'd love to help you guys out, but I'm just the ASAC Houston. I don't think I'm really qualified to take on something like this."

"Don't bust my ass over that, Mark. You know I did the best I could for you."

"Yeah, I know. Besides, I kind of like it here. It's sort of a politics-free zone."

There was a long pause over the line. "The Bureau's going to get one hell of a black eye over this if we don't wrap it up quick, Mark."

Beamon tried unsuccessfully to keep the anger and frustration out of his voice. "You know what? Standing here in the middle of some piece of shit Houston suburb, demoted, with my entire life in boxes, I'm having a hard time giving a rat's ass. I think I'll let Calahan and Richter take this one."

"I thought you might say something like that, Mark. So let me put it another way. Do it for me."

Beamon sighed and jumped down to the kitchen floor, gritting his teeth. Tom Sherman was the best friend he'd ever had. "I fucking hate you."

"Oh, it's not gonna be that bad. I've gotten you pretty much a free hand here. You'll be reporting directly to me—Frank's out of the loop."

"That must have taken some doing," Beamon said, genuinely impressed.

"I think the fact that they're bringing you back tells you exactly how important this investigation is to the Director. He tells me he's already taking a lot of heat from the White House. You come out here and put an end to this thing fast, and I expect that the Director will let you have his wife".

Beamon laughed. The Director's fanatical devotion to his rather unattractive and bitchy wife was a topic of some speculation at the Bureau. Most of it was pointedly unflattering.

"Want to hear the rest of the good news?" Sherman asked.

"I don't know if I can take any more."

"I've been having trouble renting my town house on Capitol Hill, so it's yours as long as you're here. You'll clean up on per diem."

Mark nodded into the phone and smiled. Sherman's trouble in renting his vast D.C. real estate holdings stemmed from the fact that he never listed any of them. His father had owned a number of department stores when he died, and Sherman had inherited them. Apparently he had wanted to be an FBI man since he was six, and as soon as he got in, he turned the operation of the stores over to a close family friend. No one knew exactly how wealthy he was, though popular theories put his net worth in the fifteen million dollar range. Sherman's willingness to put up needy agents and their families in any number of half-million-dollar town houses across D.C. hadn't hurt his popularity.

"You owe me big for this, Tommy. I mean it. Paybacks are going to involve half-naked women, palm fronds, and grapes."

"Uh huh. You're flying TWA tomorrow at 10:06 A.M., flight 324. Your ticket's at the desk. I'll have someone pick you up at National."

"Yeah, fine."

Beamon hung up the phone and sat quietly on the counter for a moment, looking out across the sea of boxes filling his living room. It was a no-win situation, he knew. If he wrapped the case up quickly, Calahan would take as much credit as he possibly could and send his ass back to Houston on the first plane available. And if he blew it, Calahan'd hang him out to dry.

On the bright side, though, it could be one hell of a case.

*   *   *

"Thanks for the ride, Todd," Beamon said, tugging mightily on a large suitcase wedged in the trunk of the Ford Taurus. The muscular young agent standing next to him grabbed a loop on the side of the bag and freed it effortlessly. Beamon frowned and took it from him, hoping that the moment Todd let go it wouldn't drop to the ground. He managed to arrest it with an inch to go.

"It's been a real honor to meet you, sir," the young man said.

"Good meeting you too, Todd. I imagine I'll be seeing you around."

They were standing in the middle of the narrow breezeway that ran under the J. Edgar Hoover Building. The dismal gray facade of what was often referred to as the ugliest building in D.C. wrapped around them, but failed to block the cold wind. Beamon looked around as the car that had brought him pulled slowly away, heading toward the heavy traffic of Ninth Street. He had always liked the building. If it was supposed to be a monument to the man whose name was carved on the front, it was a triumph. Hoover had embodied grace and beauty about as much as a rusty jackhammer. The squat, monochrome bunker really did him justice.

He turned and hurried to the glass doors. It didn't take long to realize that the thin suit that had been serving him so well in Houston was transparent to the damp midwinter cold of the nation's capital.

"Mark!" squealed a plump black woman sitting behind the reception desk on the other side of the doors. Beamon insisted that everyone call him by his first name. "Mr. Beamon" had always made him think that his father was standing behind him. Inexplicably, he'd never grown out of the feeling.

"Victoria!" He dropped his heavy bag and leaned over the desk to give her a peck on the cheek. "So how's your son, darlin'? Is he graduating this year?"

"One more year," she answered, taking a cursory glance at the credentials that he was holding.

"Does he know what he wants to do when he gets out?"

"He tells me he wants to be a G-man."

Beamon shook his head and pulled the bag back to his shoulder. Victoria clipped a gold pass to his lapel. "Hopefully he'll grow out of it."

Beamon tiptoed into Tom Sherman's office, putting his finger to his lips when the secretary spotted his approach. Sherman was sitting with the back of his chair to them, looking out the window and dictating a letter in slow, purposeful sentences. Beamon took the pad from her hands and motioned for her to get up. She rose and gave him a quick hug, then padded quietly out of the office. Beamon had been a constant source of entertainment to the executive office staff when he had been stationed in D.C. She looked happy to have him back.

"Please feel free to call me if you have any questions or comments. Cut a copy to Calahan on this one please, Billie."

Sherman swiveled his chair back around as Beamon furiously scribbled on the pad in his lap.

"Jesus!" He slammed his feet down on the floor, bringing the chair to an abrupt halt.

"Yours Truly, or Sincerely?" Beamon grinned.

"Sincerely, you asshole." He got up from the desk and grabbed his friend's hand. Sherman's secretary reappeared with a couple of cups of coffee, trading Beamon for her note pad. He tested it and shot her an approving look. Billie made the best coffee in the Bureau. Always something exotic.

"I got your fax, Tom. Thanks. The information was kind of sketchy, though. You have anything new?"

"We'll find out in a few minutes. Frank's gathering together everything we've got. He's giving a presentation for us and the Director in about five minutes." Beamon followed him to a group of sofas set up for conversation. Unlike Calahan, Sherman rarely discussed business from behind his desk.

"So how's Houston treating you—no more gunfights, I hope."

Beamon laughed. "You know how it is, Tommy. Stuff like that just seems to happen to me. Bad luck."

"Yeah, right."

"So you guys got time for dinner tonight—I feel like I haven't seen Leslie forever."

"Way ahead of you. She's promised to make you an Indian feast."

Beamon licked his lips in an exaggerated motion. Houston hadn't turned out to be a hotbed of fine Indian cuisine.

A familiar voice behind him shattered the image of shrimp vindaloo and dal that had constructed itself in his mind.

"So, I see he's arrived."

Beamon didn't stand, but twisted around in his seat.

"How you been, Frank?"

Richter took the chair next to him and extended his hand. "Not bad, Mark. I hear you're tearing up Houston."

Out of the corner of his eye, Beamon saw Tom Sherman look up and begin to rise. He took a deep breath and did the same.

"Good to see you, Mark," Bill Calahan lied, taking a seat on the sofa against the wall and putting his feet on the coffee table. He didn't offer his hand. "So what do you have for us, Frank. I hope it's more than yesterday."

Richter flushed, and Beamon remembered why he liked Houston so much.

"Yes, sir." He handed out an identical blue folder to each of them, keeping one for himself. Clearing his throat quietly, he began.

"Of the three people identified as possible poisoning victims yesterday, one died early this morning and the other two are not expected to survive another forty-eight hours. We've sent our best people out to examine the corpses but we don't have any data back yet. Reports from the hospitals suggest that the victims all have severe liver and kidney damage. The three victims are Jason Scott of New York, Randall Sanchez, and Steve Platt—both from Miami. I'll run through what we know about them in that order.

"Scott was an attorney at a large law firm in Atlanta. He informed the doctors at the hospital that he was a heavy cocaine user when he was admitted. Prior liver damage from a childhood illness apparently contributed to his rapid decline. He's the one that's already dead—and he died before he could give us the name of his supplier."

He flipped the page. "According to DEA, both Sanchez and Platt are involved in the cocaine trade in Miami—call 'em midlevel managers. I expect a full report this afternoon. Our guys have tried to interview them, but they're pretty sick. Neither one is talking about where they got the drugs."

Richter closed the blue folder in front of him and watched the other men page through theirs. For the most part, the folders contained what he had told them, though the illness was described in more detail and each victim had a limited biography and photo. Beamon was the first to speak.

"So we're sure that we're dealing with poisoned drugs here, and not coincidental illnesses, or some other poisoned product."

"Pretty much," Richter replied. "Apparently this kind of organ damage isn't very common. It's definitely the result of some toxic substance. The fact that all three were confirmed coke users implies a connection."

Beamon looked skeptical.

"Those three aren't the whole story, though. What I didn't lay out in writing is that there have been more reports of similar terminal illnesses since I wrote this. When I left my office, there were twenty-two reported cases virtually identical to these. Of course, they're all unconfirmed."

Beamon let out a low whistle and tossed his folder onto the coffee table. His aim was dead on, and it bounced off the Director's feet.

"So what's happening from the cashier's check angle?"

"We've interviewed everyone working at the bank that day, except one teller who quit and we haven't been able to locate. No prints—the guy wore gloves. The woman who did the checks for him gave us a pretty good description, but it sounds kind of suspicious. Five foot eight or less, long gray hair, bright blue eyes, beard, dark tan. Except for the height, probably a good indication of what he doesn't look like. We also have his signature and driver's license number. The driver's license is from California and it's in the name of someone who died as an infant. Whoever he is, he's covered his tracks pretty well."

"I assume that they'd rotated through all their surveillance tapes?" Beamon said.

"Yeah, no pictures. We're also expecting to run into a dead end on the FedEx packages. No prints or fibers on the letters or ad copy that we can't identify. We're still tracking down the prints on the outside of the envelope, but I'm not hopeful."

Beamon leaned back in his chair and put his feet up on the coffee table in front of him, knowing full well that it would irritate the hell out of Calahan.

"So what do you think, Mark?" Sherman asked.

"I think we've got problems," he replied quietly.

"Would you care to elaborate?" Calahan didn't bother to mask his annoyance.

"Sure." He pulled his feet off the table and sat in a more upright position. "Okay, how is coke distributed? Say it gets manufactured in Colombia. It's shipped to the U.S., in this case, probably into Miami. Then it gets passed down through the chain, from the big organized crime guys to the street dealers and users. So let's say this stuff gets passed down to some middleman somewhere who's actually one of our friends from the CDFS. He drops in a little poison and sends the shipment on through the chain. Now, depending on how much the people further down on the chain trust each other, they may or may not try the stuff. If they do, they're gonna die. If they don't they just keep passing it along. Frank said two of our victims were midlevel dealers—that tells me that someone hit a shipment fairly high in the chain, and these two unlucky bastards were the suspicious types who like to try the stuff."

The group was silent for a moment, letting his words sink in.

"So what you're saying is that we may have a large quantity of coke, possibly distributed all across the States by now, that is going to kill everyone who uses it," Sherman said.

Beamon turned to Richter. "Have we confirmed that it's only coke?"

"Not really. Three people isn't much of a basis for a good statistic." He turned back to Sherman. "Yeah. Best case."

"And you agree with him, Frank?" Calahan asked.

"Yes, sir."

"Recommendations?"

"I recommend that I get to work catching these guys before things get out of hand," Beamon answered. "I'll need to put together a few people to help me out. Are there any empty offices around? Maybe something with a decent-sized conference room?" Beamon stood up and jammed his hands in his pockets.

"Why don't we just give Mark the SIOC," Richter suggested, using the acronym for the FBI's Strategic Information Operations Center. "He's gonna need the communications equipment and computer anyway."

"Fine." Sherman began to rise. "Mark—this is top priority—you can have anyone you want, unless they're undercover." He turned to Calahan. "The most important thing now is to get a press conference together to announce Mark's appointment and to warn people about the scope of the threat. Do you agree?"

"Absolutely," the Director replied. It was well known that he loved to see himself on television. "Perhaps we can set something up for tomorrow?"

15

Mark Beamon walked unsteadily along the center line of the street. The sun was blinding him as it reflected off the windshield of a van stopped in the middle of the road about twenty yards away. He turned slowly in circles, watching brightly colored cars skid to abrupt stops and well-dressed young men and women jump out and take cover behind their open doors.

Beamon's slow turning eventually brought him face to face with a haggard group of men peeking out from behind the van. They were further distinguished by the old gray Thompson submachine guns gripped tightly in their hands.

He was vaguely aware that he was dreaming, but he dropped to his knee and pulled his pistol anyway. He was completely exposed, standing alone in the middle of the street. At least he had backup.

The men behind the van started firing, filling the air around him with bullets. He could see individual rounds as they whipped past him and as they left the barrel of his .357. He looked behind him. The young agents crouched behind their car doors, reached into their jackets in unison, and pulled out laptop computers. As they powered up, a beeping sound drowned out the gunfire.

He swung his arm wildly at the alarm clock as the beeping turned to ringing. He hit the snooze button dead center, and silence once again reigned in the dark bedroom, though the smell of gunpowder in his nostrils was slower to dissipate as the dream slipped away. When the ringing started again only moments later, he realized that the phone, and not the alarm, was the culprit. The bright red numbers on the clock hovered in the darkness, announcing that it was just after four A.M.

Beamon fumbled for the phone, keeping his body flat on the bed. Finally finding the receiver, he pulled it to his ear.

"Beamon," he announced sleepily.

"Turn on CNN." Tom Sherman's voice.

Beamon pushed the phone back onto the nightstand and sat up. In his youth, he had loved these late-night calls—they promised an interesting morning and made him feel important. Now they just made him feel tired.

He piled his two pillows behind him and fumbled for the remote. After a moment of searching, he found it, and the room was bathed in the unsteady gray light of an old black-and-white movie. Humphrey Bogart was lighting a cigarette in the lobby of an obscenely ornate hotel.

The light in the room flickered again as Bogart disappeared and a thin young woman with a microphone took his place.

The woman's green coat glowed in the harsh light of the TV cameras, contrasting her pale skin and quickly moving red lips. Behind her the light faded, leaving about forty feet of dead space ending in a white building with heavy-looking double glass doors. As his eyes adjusted, Beamon began to focus on the dead space. Upon further examination, it appeared to be full of people at different levels of activity. Along the bottom of the television, the caption "JOHNS HOPKINS HOSPITAL" was spelled out in capital letters. Slightly larger was the word "MUTE." Beamon had always like TV better with no sound.

"So what the hell's going on, Tommy?"

He pressed the volume control, and the woman's voice went from a timid whisper to a self-assured shout: ". . . what you're seeing is happening at hospitals all over the country."

Beamon focused on the screen as the camera panned away from the reporter and splashed light on the activity behind her.

He had never been in a war but was a fan of war movies. What he saw reminded him of triage after a battle. The soldiers were always strewn out in the dirt, some lying quietly, others writhing and bleeding. Heroic doctors and nurses would run from litter to litter, hunched over against sniper fire and helicopter wash.

Every once in a while, a light from another source flooded the scene, bringing a new perspective. He punched the volume button one last time.

". . . it's impossible to tell how many patients there are here, because they keep moving them in and out of the hospital—I lost count at seventy-eight. Obviously the doctors have begun examining people out here in the parking lot. From where I'm standing I can see in through the glass doors of the building. It looks like the floor is covered with patients. I'm not sure how they're getting stretchers in and out—it looks impossible to walk in there." Steam billowed from her mouth as she spoke.

The camera panned right, illuminating the face of a blond man in a leather bomber jacket, lying on the ground amidst the turmoil. His face was stark white. Beads of water clung to his cheeks, shining like diamonds under the harsh camera light. He didn't acknowledge the attention, he only stared up through the rain, chewing on his lower lip with a jerky mechanical precision. Blood had begun to flow from it, mixing with the light rain to run pink down his chin.

Beamon sat silently in his bed, vaguely aware of Sherman's breathing on the other end of the phone. The reporter turned away from the camera and tried to stop a quickly moving young doctor. He shrugged her off without looking up. Her second attempt, involving actually grabbing a man's arm, met with more success. He was much older, apparently wiser about good publicity's role in saving lives.

"Could you tell us what's going on here, Dr. . . . ?"

"Mason," he replied looking into the camera with a practiced calm. "We're not entirely sure. The symptoms seem to be consistent with the victims of the suspected drug poisonings that have been getting so much press lately, but yesterday we only had six patients with those symptoms. Today . . ." His voice trailed off as he pointed to the chaos behind him.

"Doctor, the prior victims of these tainted drugs were all diagnosed as terminal. Are you saying that none of these people are going to survive?" Her professional poise began to crack as it sank in that she might be standing in the middle of a graveyard.

"I really couldn't say." He fingered the stethoscope hanging around his neck. "What I can tell you is that they're at the best hospital in the world and we're doing everything we can—now you'll have to excuse me."

Beamon hit the Mute button as the reporter began to summarize the few words that she'd been able to get.

"Shit, Tommy," he said quietly into the phone. As he spoke, the screen darkened for a moment, switching to a man standing in front of a similar scene. The caption placed it as a hospital in Phoenix.

"I sent a car for you, Mark. It should be there in less than fifteen minutes. See you at the office." There was an audible click.

Beamon sat for a moment in silence, cradling the receiver in his lap. He'd had a gut feeling that this case was going to be uglier than anyone expected. But he hadn't planned on this.

The doorbell rang just as Beamon finished the right sleeve on the shirt he was ironing. He laid the iron upright on the board and jogged to the door, wearing only a pair of gray slacks.

"Mr. Beamon, I'm Steve Adams. I was sent to pick you up." Beamon examined him carefully. He looked impossibly young.

"Come on in, Steve." Beamon eyed the crisp white collar poking up from the young man's navy topcoat. "Agent Adams—I do believe that you look like a man who knows his way around an iron."

A puzzled look came over the smooth face.

Beamon led him to the ironing board and offered him a position behind it.

"I owe you one," he called, racing up the stairs of the town house to shave.

Less than five minutes later he reappeared, still bare-chested, but now wearing shoes and holding a jacket, coat, and tie. He found his shirt hanging neatly on the end of the ironing board, and the young agent flipping through a six-month-old copy of *Newsweek.*

"I knew you wouldn't let me down . . . what's your name again?"

"Steve Adams."

"Sorry, it's early," Beamon explained, as he finished buttoning his collar and began tying his tie. "Okay, let's go."

Beamon stretched wildly as the Bureau sedan cruised slowly past Union Station. He glanced at his watch. No wonder his mind was still foggy, it had been less than twenty minutes since Sherman's call.

"Hey, Steve, you know if you take a right at this light, there's a little twenty-four-hour donut shop up about a mile on the left."

Adams looked at him incredulously. "Sir, I don't know if you've been briefed, but there are hundreds of people dying. Mr. Sherman told me to get you to headquarters as soon as possible."

"Shit, son. I'm not a doctor—there's nothing that I can do for these people now that I can't do in ten minutes. Take a right."

Adams went silent and swung the car onto a narrow side street. Beamon's memory for pastry was photographic and it was less than three minutes before a Dunkin' Donuts appeared.

He jumped out of the car before it had made a full stop, and walked briskly toward the shop. The perfume of brewing coffee masked the smell of the city.

"Here, I got you some coffee," Beamon said sliding two steaming cups into the drink holders between the seats, and dumping a handful of sugars and creams between them. "I forgot to ask how you took it."

As they pulled away, he searched through the grocery-sized bag on his lap. "Bear claw?"

"No, thank you."

Beamon could barely keep from laughing out loud. Young agents could be so unbelievably stiff. It was the academy that did it, he knew. Pumped them full of patriotic images of saving the world, and built up their confidence with constant reminders that they were the best America had to offer. He had been the same way after graduation.

"You sure? Donuts are the cornerstone of good police work— especially the creme-filled ones."

"I'm sure."

This one was a tough nut, and Beamon decided that he was too tired to crack him. Settling back into the comfortable seat, he nibbled on an eclair and lit a cigarette. He ignored the young agent as he made a show of rolling down his window.

Beamon had quit smoking the day that he arrived in Houston. Back in D.C., though, the willpower had drained from him. He hoped to have this thing wrapped up before lung cancer set in.

Perry Trent peeked around the doorjamb of the open door to the Oval Office. "Mr. President?"

Daniel Jameson sat in jeans and a red work shirt on the leather sofa centered in the office.

"Morning, Perry. Come on in. Coffee?"

"Yes, thank you." It always made Trent uncomfortable to have the President of the United States pour his coffee. He nodded a greeting to Michael Bryce, the White House chief of staff, who had taken his customary seat in a soft tapestry chair directly across from the President. As attorney general, Trent rated a less comfortable spot a few feet farther from the power.

"So what the hell's going on, Perry. Yesterday you told me some crazy had dropped rat poison in a few drugs, and this morning I get woken up out of a sound sleep and told that hospitals all across the country are filling up with dying dopers." Jameson plunked two sugars into the cup and held it out.

Trent reddened slightly. The President was already suffering from a serious ulcer and dangerously high blood pressure, though those facts had been effectively kept from the press. When he had asked for a briefing on the first victims, Trent had downplayed the situation. At the time there had been no reason to think that it was anything more than some right-wing fanatic running around with a household chemical. No reason to start the President's ulcer bleeding.

"I was wrong," he explained simply.

Trent had spent almost the entire drive to the White House on the phone with Tom Sherman at the FBI. Now that he was sitting across from the President, he wondered what they'd talked about for so long. The information he had didn't amount to much.

"It would appear that a shipment of cocaine has been tainted with an extremely deadly poison that attacks the liver and kidneys. It looks like the shipment was hit somewhere pretty far upstream—and now it's been cut up and distributed all over the country."

The President let out a sound like a leaky tire and leaned back into the sofa. Trent paused, thinking that the President was going to ask a question. When he didn't, Trent continued. "The FBI began their investigation the moment the ads appeared in the paper and are tracking a number of leads. So far none has panned out. Obviously they have made this investigation their top priority."

"And you think Bill Calahan is competent to run an investigation of this magnitude?" Bryce asked.

"No, but Tom Sherman can. And he's brought in Mark Beamon to head up the investigation."

"Isn't he the guy that found that Coleman kid?"

Trent nodded.

"Good choice," Bryce said. "The press loved him—not a lot of political savvy, though."

The President seemed deep in thought for a moment. The two men watched his expression carefully. "So what's your recommendation, Perry?" he asked finally.

Trent's brow furrowed slightly. "I don't think that there is anything you or I can do, really. The Bureau's got its teeth into this thing, and I've directed them to use every method available to get these guys—fast. I told Sherman confidentially that if he had any ideas that might be unconventional, I wanted to hear them. And if they had any merit, I'd bring them to you."

Trent took a sip of his coffee. "I know that neither of you much cares for Bill Calahan, but I don't think he's particularly relevant to the investigation. In my opinion, we can trust Tom to get this investigation off the ground pretty quickly."

"Calahan's having a press conference tomorrow at ten, isn't he?" Jameson asked.

"Yes, sir."

"Okay, Perry. Thanks. I want to be kept up on everything that happens in this investigation. Daily reports. Nothing's insignificant, right?"

"Yes, sir."

Trent promised himself that he wouldn't make the same mistake twice. Jameson would get more detail than he could handle. Trent was painfully aware that he was getting off easy. Too easy. It gave him a queasy feeling.

"Thank you, sir," he said, putting down the nearly full cup of coffee and heading for the door.

"Close it behind you, please," Bryce called.

"So what do you think?" The President didn't look at his chief of staff, but concentrated on the stained glass lampshade next to him.

Bryce slid his feet onto the table in front of him, pushing himself farther back into the chair. "It's a difficult situation. The press is going to come out firmly against the poisoners and are going to be more and more critical of us every day these guys aren't caught. On the other hand, the public perceives your administration to be soft on crime."

The President opened his mouth to protest, but Bryce cut him off.

"I'm not saying that it's true—but you're a Democrat and you've stressed rehabilitation over punishment. The fact is that crime's gotten worse with every administration since Lincoln—you just happen to have the chair now."

"So what are you getting at, Mike?" Jameson respected Bryce's ability to see all angles of an issue, but God knew he liked to hear himself talk.

"I'm not sure that these guys—what do they call themselves? The CDFS? Are going to be all that unpopular."

"I'm not following you."

"Look, Dan, you go talk to some guy working forty hours a week in a factory in Sheridan, Wyoming, and you ask him what he thinks about the whole thing. You know what he'll say? He'll say that the druggies got what was coming to them. That it's about time someone cleaned up the cities."

Jameson flushed. "So what are you suggesting? That we tell the media that I think it's okay to go out and kill as many people as you want—just as long as they're narcotics users?"

Bryce straightened up in his chair. "No. That's what's so difficult. You have to go out there and say that the government is going to do everything in its power to stop these guys—but you have do it in a way that doesn't make our friend in Wyoming mad. The media's on your side. They'll focus on the most horrible and unjustified deaths. You know, high school track stars with straight A's, cute twelve-year-olds from the projects—that kind of thing. You're not gonna see the guy with a murder rap and six aggravated assaults. I'll guarantee you that."

Jameson stood up and walked past his desk to face the large window behind it.

Bryce continued. "You'll have to be at that press conference tomorrow, Dan. We've got to make sure that the media sees you getting personally involved in this."

Jameson was only half listening. "Is it our fault, Mike?"

"Excuse me?"

"I don't just mean you and me. I mean the government in general. In the last, say, fifteen years, what has the U.S. government done that has really made a difference to its citizens?" He turned around and looked at Bryce. "Now things have gotten so bad, the public is forced to take action to correct the country's problems."

"This isn't the public taking action, Dan. This is some nut running around murdering people."

"Yeah, you're probably right," Jameson said, but he wasn't as certain as he made himself sound.

Bryce stood. "Of course I'm right. You've got a good record of trying to get a handle on crime. We just have to make sure we keep that in front of the public during this thing."

16

Washington, D.C.,
February 9

Beamon punched in the combination to the door guarding the
FBI's Strategic Information Operations Center, or SIOC, and pulled
the heavy door open. Inside, the space was broken into a number
of soundproof rooms. The interior walls were glass, and he could
see straight through to the back.

The suite was almost empty. Beamon nodded to a young agent
manning the phones as he refilled his Styrofoam cup with coffee.
Calls coming into the JEH Building after hours were fielded in
SIOC. It was this kid's unlucky week.

To Beamon's left was the largest of the four rooms and the space
reserved for his team. Through the glass wall he could see that
Laura Vilechi was already hard at work. She sat at the conference
table that dominated the room, framed by a large blackboard. Her
nose was stuck in a blue file folder.

On the blackboard she had written a chart.

INVESTIGATION

DRUGS	CHECKS	POISON
Tracing to Source	Bank	Identifying
?????	Description (Disguise)	
	Handwriting Sample	
	Alias/Driver's License Number	
	Lance Richardson?	
	Physical Evidence (Fed Ex)	

Beamon shook his head and wondered for the fiftieth time if he'd made a mistake in hiring Laura as his right-hand man—as he intended to introduce her.

They had met almost five years ago on an embezzlement case and discovered quickly that they couldn't agree on anything. Beamon was the absentminded professor—prone to flashes of brilliance that left everyone shaking their heads in amazement. Between those flashes, though, he had to struggle to keep up with the mundane details of the nuts and bolts investigation.

Laura had a completely different style—and the chalkboard told him that it hadn't changed. She had a photographic memory for details, and fanaticism for process. She left no stone unturned, and never, never made mistakes.

Their first meeting had been less than pleasant. She had already decided how she wanted the investigation run, and she wasn't about to let anyone screw it up. Beamon had his own ideas about how to get things done. She had stood there, hands on hips, staring coldly at him as he ranted and raved about her inexperience and uninspired approach to investigation. She hadn't backed down, and he respected that.

"How you doin', Laura," Beamon said, slipping through the door and closing it quietly behind him. He couldn't believe it, but he was actually a little nervous.

She looked up at him with mild suspicion. "I'm good, Mark."

Beamon examined the blackboard more closely, finally pointing to it. "I see you haven't changed."

She pointed to the large bag of donuts dangling from his right hand. "I see you haven't, either."

Beamon laughed and set them on the table.

"I didn't know what you liked, so I got an assortment."

She opened the bag and pulled out a chocolate-covered. The topping stuck to her fingers. "Well, I'm here, but I sure can't figure out why."

"My doctor told me I didn't have enough stress in my life. Naturally, you came to mind." Beamon flashed a wide grin and reached into the bag to find another bear claw. "I think you took our last run-in too seriously, Laura. I defended my methods and you defended yours. Shit, if anybody came off that case worse for the wear it was me."

"Come on, Mark. You obviously don't agree with my methods. Why did you bring me in on this?"

Beamon frowned. "If I gave you the impression that I didn't agree with your methods, I'm sorry. The fact that you and I approach a problem from opposite sides is precisely why you're here. I'm willing to admit that my weakness is detail and procedure. And as I see it, yours is being too rigid." Laura bristled slightly at the criticism, but he ignored it. "Put both of us together, you get the perfect investigator."

"And you think we can work together?"

Beamon turned serious. "Yup. Our problem last time was that neither one of us was really in charge. This time I'm the boss."

They stared straight at each other for almost ten seconds. Laura finally averted her eyes and reached for her donut. "Maybe next time it'll be me."

He laughed. "The thought keeps me awake at night. So when did you fly in? You look tired." Her blue skirt and white blouse looked like they had come directly from a suitcase, and her strawberry blond hair wasn't pulled back as tightly as he remembered it. It didn't matter, though, she would have been striking in old blue jeans and a dirty sweatshirt.

"I got in tonight at ten. I was up watching TV when CNN started reporting on the hospitals, and I figured I might as well come in before the phone started ringing."

Beamon nodded toward the blue folder lying next to her on the conference table.

"So what have we got?"

"Not a whole lot," she said quietly. "The Saint Louis office has interviewed everyone at the bank where the suspect got the cashier's checks—except one guy who apparently quit and is on a rock-climbing trip in parts unknown. We should be able to find him in a few days, but he didn't really have much in the way of direct contact with our guy. Anyway, not much there." She flipped the page.

"We and DEA are interviewing the victims who are still able to talk and getting the names of their suppliers. DEA's working on tracing the poisoned drugs back to where they got hit—but it's too soon to see if that'll go anywhere." She flipped another page.

"Our forensics guys haven't had much luck in figuring out what the poison is, but they're working on it round the clock. Apparently they've brought in one of the world's leading experts on toxicology. He's from Harvard, or something." Laura tossed the folder on the table, sending it spinning to the far edge.

"What about the envelope? Anything there?"

"Zip."

"So I'm safe in saying we don't have dick," Beamon said.

"An unfortunate choice of words, but that's what it boils down to."

"Any estimates on casualties?"

"Last time I looked, we were moving into four digits."

Beamon crossed his arms and stared at the blackboard. "This should be one hell of an interesting case. It's the only crime I've ever investigated that the victims won't want to talk. We're gonna hit a brick wall trying to get information out of the narcotics community."

Beamon considered his next move. No brilliant strategies flashed into his mind, and he knew from experience that he couldn't force them. They would probably have to wait for the CDFS's next move to get anything concrete. That is, if there was a next move.

The piercing ring of a phone cut off his train of thought. He looked around, spotting it on a credenza against the wall. He strolled slowly over and picked it up: "Mark Beamon."

"Mark! It's Trace."

Trace Fontain was the head of the Bureau's laboratory science group, and in charge of filtering through the blood of the victims and confiscated narcotics to isolate the poison. Beamon didn't know him well, but they had been running into each other every now and again for the last fifteen years.

"What's the good word, Trace?" Beamon found a remote control and was trying to figure out how to turn on the television anchored to the wall above him.

"Afraid there is none, Mark. Your choices are bad news and worse news."

"Jesus, I just can't seem to get a break around here. Bad news first."

"We haven't been able to figure out what they're using yet. We know it attacks the vital organs, but it's nothing we've ever seen before."

"Fuckin' hell, Trace. All you have to do is put the shit under one of those mass spectron microscope doodads and the goddam computer does your job for you."

Laura frowned deeply and stared up at him. He'd forgotten how much he hated that look.

She was right, of course. Trace had enough academic plaques to side a house. The Bureau was lucky to have him.

"Sorry, Trace. It's early, you know? Hit me with the worse news."

"You're really not gonna like this one."

"I'll try not to kill the messenger."

"We've been interviewing the victims that are still lucid, and examining the organs of the dead ones, and there is evidence that the poison has a, uh, bit of a delayed reaction."

Beamon considered that for a moment. "So, like, if I snort some coke today, I might not show symptoms till tomorrow? They have stuff like that?"

"Uh, no. It's a little worse than that. It works on kind of a bell curve. Depending on how much you take and your body chemistry, reaction times are different."

"Get to the point, Trace."

"Well, a pretty good average would be, uh, right around a week and a half for the first symptoms. Death three days after they start appearing."

Beamon started pounding his head slowly on the wall in front of him. "No more bad news today, okay?"

"You all right, Mark?" Laura asked as Beamon slammed down the phone.

"Did you know that some poisons have delayed reactions?"

"Sure, I guess. I never really thought about it."

"And how long do you think the longest delayed reaction would be?"

"Dunno. One or two days?"

"Try one or two weeks."

She was silent for a moment. "Is this another one of your dumb jokes?"

"You're not feeling any better, are you, honey?"

Erica pulled the gray and brown afghan up around her husband's shoulders and looked into his red-rimmed eyes. The Reverend Simon Blake didn't reply.

"I can't imagine that this is helping any," she said, looking at the TV where a CNN anchor was discussing casualty estimates. In the upper right-hand corner of the screen a black-and-red graphic depicted a needle and vial with the simple caption "THE DRUG CRISIS." The media's ability to attractively package a tragedy like a bar of bath soap never ceased to disgust her. She took the remote control off the arm of her husband's chair to try to find something a little more upbeat. He snatched it back before she could aim it, slamming it back down on the arm of the chair.

Erica eyed him strangely. She couldn't ever remember him grabbing something from her that. She had also expected him to have something to say about what was happening in the news, but he hadn't uttered a word on the subject. He just watched the reports, keeping any feelings about them bottled up inside. It was probably just the flu, she reasoned, as she walked angrily out of the room.

"Close the door," her husband yelled. She wanted to leave it open—he hadn't showered and it was getting a little close in his den. But she didn't want to argue, and did as he asked.

As the door clicked shut, Blake increased the volume on the TV until the sound penetrated every corner of his mind. He sat there, staring blankly at the screen in the dim light of the den.

He had stopped sleeping after the first few victims died. It had turned out that two of the first few had been drug dealers—scum of the earth, as far as he was concerned. But he'd been responsible for their deaths and that was a sensation he wasn't familiar with, and as it turned out, wasn't fond of.

Then the sky had fallen. CNN was estimating four hundred deaths and another six hundred terminally ill. A thousand people. Hobart and he had discussed the possibility of casualties, but never in his wildest dreams had he thought anything like this could happen. Why hadn't people stopped using? The ad had been clear enough—had they not read it? No, that was impossible. The media had saturated the airwaves with the story. Everyone knew, he told himself. Everyone.

Blake coughed loudly, leaning over the arm of his chair until the spasms subsided. Waves of nausea came over him, combining with the burning in his stomach. For a moment he thought he was going to throw up, but he managed to fight it off.

Mark Beamon pressed his back against the wall, narrowly avoiding a collision with a Secret Service man hustling to the other side of the room. He didn't know how those guys did it. There must have been thirty people moving frantically back and forth waiting for the President to appear; all dressed the same, all with nearly the same haircut, and all talking in the same medium-loud monotone. And these guys had to keep it all straight. No thanks.

Beamon slid a few feet to his left, giving himself a partially obstructed view of the curtain leading to the small auditorium where the President held his press conferences. He could detect movement behind the curtain, but couldn't really see anything.

He wished they'd get this show on the road. The makeup that had been slathered onto his face in preparation for the television cameras was beginning to dry in the corners of his eyes, and it was driving him crazy. He reached up to scratch at it.

"Don't do that, Mark."

Beamon turned his head toward the familiar voice and watched Laura Vilechi weaving effortlessly through the crowd.

"Laura! What are you doing here?"

"I brought you a present."

"A present? Really? What is it?"

Laura pulled a deep maroon tie with subtle blue dots from her bag and pressed it against the frayed lapel of his jacket. She nodded approvingly. "I didn't have time to do anything about the suit, but this tie should help."

"I take it you don't like the one I have on."

Laura pursed her lips and ran her tongue across the front of her teeth. "If you're going to be on TV, you need a tie that says 'trust me, I know what I'm doing. I've got everything under control.'"

Beamon grabbed Laura by the shoulders and moved her a couple of feet to her right. A boom mike just missed her head.

"I know I'm going to regret asking this, but just what is it that *my* tie says?"

She pulled it out of his jacket and held the tip like it was the tail of a dead mouse. "Meet me at my trailer later, I've got a cooler full of brewskis."

"I brought a six-pack. It's a little early, but I thought we might need it," Robert Swenson said, slamming the door to the apartment and making a beeline to the refrigerator. It was 9:58 A.M., and Hobart was sitting on the sofa, watching the lead-in to the President's press conference. The subject today was near and dear to his heart.

Swenson plopped down on the sofa and put two beers on the coffee table in front of them, unopened. The scene on the television changed from a reporter framed by the White House to a crowded room with an empty podium at its focal point. An unintelligible rumbling came from the reporters fidgeting in neatly organized chairs.

A few moments later President Daniel Jameson strode purposefully out onto the stage, followed closely by two conservatively dressed men. He took his place behind the podium and shuffled papers for a moment, a look of deep concern on his face.

"Shit," Hobart said, no louder than a whisper.

Swenson looked over at him. "They haven't said anything yet."

"See that ugly son of a bitch next to Calahan."

"Yeah."

"That's Mark Beamon."

"Beamon. Why do I know that name?"

"He's the asshole that got me thrown out of the DEA," Hobart replied, twisting the top of a beer. Swenson was about to ask for more details, but the President began to speak.

"As all of you know, a group known as the Committee for a Drug-Free Society threatened, through advertisements in a number of major newspapers, to poison the U.S. narcotics supply. It would appear that they have made good on that threat. I understand that current estimates of dead and injured are nearing a thousand people." He paused for a moment to accentuate the point. The reporters struggled to contain themselves.

"I have directed the FBI to take the lead in this investigation, and to make it their top priority. I have further directed that all other law enforcement agencies give the FBI their full cooperation. With that, I would like to introduce Bill Calahan and Mark Beamon from the FBI."

Jameson began to turn away from the podium but was prompted back by the shouted questions of the press.

"We'll take questions at the end of the conference," he said into the microphone, and turned away again, shaking hands with the two men moving toward the podium.

Calahan spoke first, with Beamon flanking him a few feet behind.

"At the request of the President, I've formed a task force to investigate this most serious crime, and have told my people to make it their top priority. I've also appointed Mark Beamon, whom many of you know, as head of the task force. Mark should be able to bring you up to speed on where we are in the investigation. Mark?" Calahan gave up the podium and took a place alongside the

President. Beamon moved forward and adjusted the mike, wondering how he was going to stretch what little he knew into a reasonable speech. There was nothing he hated more than coming out on national TV and saying he didn't know what the fuck was going on, but that he'd do his best to find out.

"Obviously the Bureau's been investigating this case since the ad requests were first made. We have a number of leads that we're aggressively pursuing, though we don't have any suspects yet."

Christ, this sounds lame.

"We haven't been able to isolate the poison used, but we have been able to get a feel for how it works. I think you guys have already done a pretty good job of describing its effects." There was a hint of sarcasm in his voice. The press seemed to be in a bitter contest to see which network could be the most graphic.

"What we just found out this morning, though, regards the, uh, reaction time." He paused, knowing that his next words were going to send a panic through the narcotics community. He felt a little bit like he was about to yell fire in a crowded theater.

"Apparently, symptoms will not appear for between one and a half and two weeks following contact with the poison. Death can be expected within three days of the appearance of symptoms. There appears to be no antidote."

Beamon stepped back involuntarily at the force of the shouted questions from the men and women in front of him. Gathering his composure, he raised his hand, effectively quieting them.

"To date, it would appear that only cocaine has been contaminated, but let me stress that the ads did not limit their threat to coke. At this time, all illegal narcotics should be considered suspect."

Beamon leaned against the podium and, for the first time, looked directly at the camera. "If you're using illegal drugs, stop. Go to a rehab clinic, see your priest, start drinking, take up knitting—whatever it takes. Even if we catch these guys tomorrow, there's no telling how much of this stuff is floating around on the streets."

He turned his head and called to Calahan and the President to join him. The two men approached the podium, looking reluctant.

"Uh, I guess we have time for a few questions." Every hand in the hall shot up.

Neither of the men flanking him made a move, so Beamon pointed. "Stacey."

A woman who seemed too elegantly dressed to be a reporter stood up. Beamon remembered her having a little more class than most of her peers.

"If there is a two-week delay on the reaction time on this poison, is it possible that these first thousand casualties are only the tip of the iceberg? Does the FBI have an estimate of how many deaths are expected?"

Calahan didn't seem to want to get anywhere near that question, so Beamon answered it himself. "Could the first thousand only be the tip of the iceberg? Maybe, but there are way too many variables to make an accurate estimate."

All hands went from scribbling to reaching for the ceiling.

"Gill." He was quickly running out of reporters that he knew to have even a small spark of decency.

"Mr. Beamon, there have been a lot of rumors flying around that this is a covert government operation to stop the illegal narcotics trade in the U.S. Would you care to comment on that?"

"Not really. But we've got the number one expert on government operations right here. Mr. President?"

Jameson stepped up to the podium, looking angry. "That's ridiculous. If anything, my administration has been criticized for not being heavy-handed enough with the punishment of criminals, and of being too reform-oriented. These kind of rumors are bound to start when something like this happens—they are completely unfounded."

Jameson stepped back, whispering in Beamon's ear to wrap things up.

Beamon leaned into the mike. "We've got time for one more. Kim?"

"You said that you're following up a number of leads. Would you care to comment on those leads, and give us a feel for how long you expect it'll take to resolve this case?"

Beamon smiled. "No, and I don't know. But you can rest assured that we're doing everything humanly possible to find these guys. Thank you."

Hobart flipped off the TV and finished his beer.

"They don't have shit," he observed.

Swenson looked concerned. "But there's some history between you and that Beamon guy?"

"Yeah," Hobart admitted. "Must have been ten years ago—we were working on a joint investigation. Peter Manion was one of my snitches back then. He was stonewalling me and I was pushing him around a little bit. To make a long story short, Peter fell over a table and broke his arm. Beamon walks in a few minutes later and goes ballistic. Takes Manion to the hospital and comes back and presses charges against me."

"So what happened?"

Hobart smiled. "I fought back—got Peter to testify that Beamon was in on the whole thing. Goddam hearings went on for a year with both of us on unpaid leave. In the end, I got canned and he got demoted and sent to . . . Montana, I think."

Swenson nodded thoughtfully. "Is he good?"

"Sure. But not as good as he thinks he is. He doesn't have much support with management, either. Getting an official reprimand for beating up an informant is pretty tough to live down."

Hobart laughed as he stood and walked across the room to a strangely configured chess board and pulled a black king off the television. He placed it ceremoniously on the board.

"I'd been meaning to ask you about that, John," Swenson said, walking quietly up behind him. "I don't think you've got it set up quite right."

Hobart surveyed the board. "It's set up exactly right." He pointed to the right side of the board where a white king and queen sat in the first rank. Eight white pawns were spread out over the board. There were no more white pieces. "We're the white. You and I are symbolized by the king and queen. The eight pawns represent our men in the field."

He shifted his focus to the left side of the board, where two full rows of pawns stood, one blue and one black. On the first rank stood a king and queen of each color. "The black pieces represent the FBI. Beamon's the king. Tom Sherman, the associate director, and Beamon's strongest ally, is the queen."

"And the blue?"

Hobart scowled. The answer was obvious. Maybe his partner wasn't as bright as he had thought. "The narcotics cartel. I don't know who the king and queen represent yet, but my guess is that it will be Luis Colombar and his advisor—Alejandro something. Colombar's the most powerful man in Colombia now—and it was his refinery that I hit. Of course, nothing stays the same for long in that business."

17

Near Bogota, Colombia,
February 12

Luis Colombar walked briskly through the spacious entryway of his home listening to the complex chime of his doorbell fade away.

"Roberto! How have you been?" Colombar said to the tanklike man standing on the other side of the door. The two men shook hands warmly, effectively disguising their hatred for each other. Roberto Ortega wiped his feet carefully on the mat in front of the door and entered. Colombar noticed a complex sweat stain in his white cotton shirt that accurately traced a shoulder holster. This was the first time he had seen Ortega unarmed.

It had been a difficult call. On one hand, these were all businessmen—the most powerful drug lords in Colombia—and should be able to be trusted not to start a gunfight in his living room. On the other hand, the bad blood between many of his guests was old and strong. In the end, he had personally guaranteed everyone's safety, and politely insisted that no firearms be brought into his home. A few of them had offered token resistance, but deep down they had been relieved by the directive. Colombar was a killer, drug dealer, and thief, but he was a man of his word.

"You are the last guest to arrive, Roberto," Colombar said, scanning his front yard as he slowly closed the door. The one hundred yards between the front of his house and the formidable white stucco perimeter wall was thick with carefully laid out native plants. Secreted in this foliage were no fewer than twenty men with meaningful bulges under their arms. Their dark suits looked out of place next to the explosions of color supplied by the flowering plants.

Colombar followed Ortega closely as they wound through the wide halls of his home. Light was provided solely by the endless skylights dotting the terra-cotta roof.

Colombar had hired the finest architect in Colombia to design his home, and had brought in an interior designer from New York to furnish it. It was obvious to anyone who knew him that the house didn't reflect the man. The sophistication and class that he had hoped would spring from the art-encrusted walls had only served to highlight his poor upbringing and crass sense of humor.

The hall eventually opened to an expansive room with a high, clear-glass roof supported by imported Canadian logs. Each log was draped with a large antique tapestry, their well-worn ends dangling down into space.

No less than fifteen men stood in small clusters, sat on well-coordinated leather sofas, and huddled around various tables covered with sterling silver chafing dishes. Occasionally a burst of laughter would come from one of the groups. It sounded strained.

Colombar stopped at the top of the steps leading to the sunken floor of the room, and watched Ortega stride bull-like through the men, straight to the table covered with dripping beer bottles.

He looked down over the crowd. "Gentlemen! I believe that with Mr. Ortega's arrival, we are all here. Shall we begin?" His accent had improved significantly over the last year, thanks to a voice coach who had a talent for transforming wealthy South Americans into sophisticated Europeans. All eyes turned to him as he strolled across the room, trying to look calm and in control. The men followed him to a conversation pit that had been set up specifically for this meeting. At the focal point of the grouping of furniture was a large-screen TV.

Colombar sat on a sofa directly across from the television. The other drug lords followed his example, looking less collected as they jockeyed at the last minute to sit next to an ally and not a dreaded enemy.

Unbeckoned, a young man walked quickly from a door at the side of the room and slipped a tape into the VCR under the TV. At thirty-three, he was ten years Colombar's junior, and seemed to exude the sophistication that the drug lord would never achieve. His gray Armani suit fit as if he'd been born in it. He flashed a practiced smile at the group. His teeth were white and straight.

"I think some of you know my attorney, Alejandro Perez," Colombar said. "I've asked him to give us a little presentation on this situation." With a wave of his hand he gave the floor to Perez.

"Gracias, Luis."

Perez scanned the crowd as he spoke, using all of the public-speaking skills that he had learned at Georgetown Law. "As they say, a picture is worth a thousand words, so I have prepared this videotape. It includes what I feel are significant media reports relating to this, uh, situation. It will only take a few moments to view, and I think you will find it interesting. My understanding is that all of you speak English. If not, please let me know now and I will translate as the tape runs." Perez made a show of looking from face to face. No one spoke, though he knew that at least three of the men would have a hard time ordering a hamburger in English.

"Okay, then." He pushed a button and the television came to life.

His tape began with Beamon's press conference and then ran smoothly into various CNN reports from hospitals across the country. It ended with an interview of a cocaine addict. His face was in shadows and his voice disguised, but he was clearly an educated man—probably around Perez's age.

The addict told the reporter between sobs that he had taken a leave of absence from work to put himself in a rehab clinic. He also related that he had last snorted coke five days earlier and was waiting to see if he had been poisoned. He had sworn to himself that if he survived he would never do another line.

The television faded artistically to black, and Perez punched the stop button on the VCR.

"If I can take up just a few more moments of your time, I'd like to make a few comments about what you have just seen." He paused. No objections were raised.

"Mark Beamon, the gentleman speaking at the press conference, my sources say is probably the FBI's top investigator. I have also heard that he and the Director are mortal enemies and that he had recently been demoted and sent to a field office in Texas. I think that Mr. Calahan's willingness to bring him back to head this investigation shows the American government's commitment to putting a stop to the CDFS's actions."

Perez pushed one hand in his pocket, adjusting the hang of his suit into yet another well-thought-out configuration. "Having said this, my sources, whom I consider very reliable, tell me that the FBI has no significant leads in the case. The narcotics manufacturers' and dealers' unwillingness to cooperate with the authorities is working against them. In addition, it seems reasonable to hypothesize that the individuals involved in this drug poisoning operation are quite sophisticated and probably have some knowledge of investigative procedures." Perez pulled a folder from the top of the television next to him.

"Current estimates put deaths at twenty-eight hundred, with an additional seventeen hundred showing symptoms that would suggest that death is inevitable within the week." He tossed the folder back where he'd found it. "I think that the last segment on the tape really drives home what we're seeing on the demand front. Only five days from the first death, we are already experiencing a substantial downward trend in cocaine purchases by casual users, who, as I'm sure you know, consume the lion's share of the cocaine supplied annually to the U.S."

There was a general grumbling from his audience. Perez knew that many of them wouldn't have known that. The demand for their product had always been a given—it was manufacture and transport that demanded the concentration of the men in this room.

Perez started pacing back and forth as he spoke, and all eyes in the room followed him closely. "It's impossible to tell at this early a date exactly what kind of a demand reduction we're going to see, but I performed an informal poll of some of our associates in the States this morning, and I think the problem is even more serious than we had thought. Apparently, street-level dealers' phones are silent. Some have been put in the unusual position of calling their customers and cutting prices to cost. Reports suggest that their calls have been mostly unsuccessful and that purchasers are insisting that the dealers use some of the product at the sale as an act of good faith. Many of them are unwilling to do this, unless they have a supply that was purchased well before the ads came out."

An impossibly fat man sitting next to Colombar interrupted him. "So what does that translate into in numbers."

"It's difficult to say at this point, but my survey suggests that we can expect around a sixty-five percent reduction in the casual use of cocaine in the next couple of weeks, if this threat continues. That translates into, say, a fifty-percent reduction in overall demand."

With that statistic hanging in the air like a noose, the room broke into loud conversation. The men turned back and forth to one another, pointing and gesturing wildly, voices fighting to be heard.

Colombar stood.

"Gentlemen . . . *Gentlemen!*" The din faltered and went silent.

"I believe that Alejandro is almost finished. We have the rest of the day for discussion." He motioned to Perez and took his seat.

"Thank you. In the habitual users, I think it is safe to surmise that we will see a less significant drop in use. I have no estimate of what that will be."

"Maybe it is a government plot." The fat, loud one again.

"I don't think so. The U.S. government has never shown any real commitment to stopping the demand for drugs in their country. No, the U.S. has always concentrated on stemming supply—despite the fact that this approach has proven to be woefully ineffective."

The room was silent. Colombar looked around to see if any

more questions were forthcoming, but the men seemed deep in thought.

"Thank you, Alejandro."

Perez pulled the tape from the VCR and walked briskly out of the room, nodding to the group as he went. The sound of Italian shoe leather against stone seemed very loud in the silence following his speech.

"Any comments?" Colombar asked, to get the conversation rolling. Roberto Ortega was the first to speak.

"Your assistant is very smart, Luis, but as with others of his kind, he told us our problems but didn't offer any solution." He fairly spat out the words. Ortega hated the new generation of criminal—slick and well educated. Despite this well-known bias, his comments got a few nods from the group.

"Alejandro is here to provide information, Roberto, not to run our business for us," Colombar chided. "It is our job to find a solution."

The fat man to Colombar's left spoke again. Sweat glistened on his upper lip despite the air-conditioning. "And what do you suggest, Luis?"

Colombar felt the attention of the room focus on him. It was a position that he was finding more and more comfortable.

"As we speak, my men are tracing the tainted coke back to its source, looking for the moment that it was poisoned—information that will be very difficult for the authorities to obtain. We'll catch these people ourselves and cut their fucking heads off." Colombar stood and walked through the conversation pit, aiming himself at the elaborate wet bar in the corner of the room. He regretted the profanity at the end of his last sentence. It didn't fit with his new image.

He dropped an olive in the martini he was preparing. Grimacing slightly, he took a sip. Tequila was his drink, but it lacked a certain sophistication. He turned back to face the group.

"I would appreciate you gentlemen using your resources to do the same. If we can pinpoint exactly where the poison was put into our product, we will be quite a bit closer to finding our quarry." He returned to his seat.

"And what if Pedro is right, and this is the work of the U.S. authorities?" a thin man sitting on the edge of the sofa asked.

Colombar smiled. "Then we simply find proof of that and leak it to the press. I'm sure that they would be very interested in a story like that. I must agree with Alejandro, though. I don't believe that the U.S. government would ever take such drastic action within their own borders. They are much more decisive in other people's countries." There was a general grumble of agreement.

Colombar spotted his butler standing motionless at the entrance to the living room.

"Gentlemen," Colombar said, standing in a single quick jerk and startling a few of the guests with whom he was not on the best terms. "I believe our luncheon is ready." He weaved through the group, hoping that none of them noticed that he had left his nearly untouched drink on the table. He decided that his image could survive a couple of beers at lunch. They were imported from England, after all.

Scott Dresden carefully placed the white cuff links in the mahogany and glass display case across from his desk. The pounding in his head was beginning to subside, succumbing to the three extra-strength Tylenols he'd chewed up fifteen minutes ago. The cuff links were a gift from the secretary general of Interpol, and took a place of honor next to various other items commemorating police forces from across Europe and Asia.

It had been almost a year since Dresden had given up his post as the ASAC in the FBI's Portland, Oregon, office, and had accepted a transfer to Germany. He had spent the last twelve months in Bonn as the assistant legal attaché. The title called forth images of bureaucratic attorneys reviewing endless documents. Nothing could be further from the truth. In 1940, J. Edgar Hoover had decided that crime, along with the rest of the world's big business, was going international. Shortly after coming to that realization, agents known as Legats began cropping up in major embassies across the world. The plan met with some success and the program had gone through a number of expansions, adding offices to more far-flung countries across the globe.

Dresden's gift for languages and interest in European cultures made him perfect for the position. It had been a difficult call—conventional wisdom was that becoming a Legat significantly reduced one's visibility and, therefore, promotability. In the end, he'd decided that it was worth it to spend a few years in Europe and to give his children an opportunity to see the world.

He carefully closed the glass door to the case and walked back to his desk, plopping down in the tall leather chair and leaning as far back as possible. He had removed a spring from the base of the chair, making it possible to go almost horizontal. Running his fingers through his thick, dark hair, he closed his eyes and concentrated on relaxing. His headache's grip on the back of his head loosened a little more.

The morning had started as a typical one. He had been running late, practically pulling his pants on as he ran out the door. A few New York driving tricks had put him at the office one minute before eight o'clock. At eight-fifteen he was quietly reviewing the leather Franklin Day Planner at the top of his desk.

At eight-twenty Mark Beamon had called from Washington.

Beamon had related that Trace Fontain, Harvard University and the Centers for Disease Control, had finally isolated the poison used to taint the U.S. coke supply. It came from a mushroom indigenous to Eastern Europe—Poland mostly. Smack dab in the middle of Dresden's territory.

One of the things he liked best about running a Legat was the fact that you were given as free a hand as could be had in the Bureau. For the most part, headquarters just wasn't watching. They preferred to defer many decisions to the individual legal attachés, based on their contacts and knowledge of the culture. Now, though, Dresden felt freedom leak away as he was drawn into one of the most visible cases the FBI had ever been involved in.

He'd spent the last five hours on the phone with every law enforcement officer he knew in Eastern Europe, calling in a number of favors that he had hoped to save for a cushy consulting job after retirement. Dresden's network in the former Soviet Union was impressive, and the wheels of the investigation were turning. The problem was coordinating with the myriad local law enforcement groups—the people who might have noticed an American running around the woods piling mushrooms into a pickup truck.

Dresden's secretary slipped into the room, her mouth already forming the beginnings of a sentence. Recognizing his position, she caught herself and instead padded silently across the carpet and set a cup of tea down on the coaster on his desk. The man on her heels wasn't as considerate.

"Wake up, Scott—I just got off the phone with Customs," Kip Spence said, taking a seat in front of his desk.

Dresden righted himself slowly, reaching for the steaming cup on his desk.

"What did they have to say?" The pounding in his head notched higher.

"Nothing. You know Customs. Said they'd check their records and fax us any significant shipments of mushrooms over the last six months. It'll take 'em a few days, though."

Dresden frowned. His opinion of that particular government organization had never been very high. "Well, I think I've talked to damn near every person I know this morning." He touched his right ear unconsciously. It was bright red.

Spence grimaced. "Cryin' shame that Europe doesn't have *America's Most Wanted*. Why the hell don't we just commandeer a little cash from headquarters and put an ad in every local rag from here to Moscow?" He held up his hands, framing an imaginary advertisement: "If you have any information regarding an American picking a bunch of poisonous mushrooms in the last couple of months call the number below. A thousand dollar reward for information leading to the apprehension of this suspect."

Dresden took another sip of the scalding tea. "Precisely what I suggested. Mark Beamon told me that they'd kinda lucked in to isolating the poison as fast as they did, though. Some guy at the CDC is a fungus-ologist or some such thing. He's hoping that these guys are counting on us taking a few more weeks to nail down the source. Wants to see if we can catch 'em napping."

"Long shot," Spence observed.

His boss nodded in agreement. "The scary thing is, I think it's the best we got."

The Toyota Land Cruiser slammed headlong into a deep puddle, sending thick, muddy water splashing across the windshield and drenching the men in the open Jeep a few feet in front. Luis Colombar whooped with joy and punched at the CD player that was skipping wildly as the truck's tires bounced along the rutted dirt road. Glancing in his rearview mirror, he saw another Jeep full of men approach the same mud puddle cautiously, finally forging reluctantly ahead.

"Fucking pussies!" he shouted over the engine noise and intermittent sound of Madonna coming through the vehicle's hidden speakers. He stomped on the gas one more time, nudging the Jeep in front of him. One of the men sitting in the back almost toppled out, caught at the last second by a companion. Colombar felt a slight pang of disappointment. He was curious as to how his new truck's suspension would handle a body. Probably wouldn't feel a thing.

Life had been good since the meeting with his associates. Quite a few had called later that evening to thank him for his cool head and diligent work in solving what had become known simply as "The Problem." Colombar had always felt that it was counterproductive to have so many lords and no king—as long as that king was him.

This was the perfect opportunity to show that he could rise above the petty infighting between the different Colombian factions and move into a de facto leadership position. When he had gained their trust, he would kill them. With the heads of the major families gone, Colombia's vast narcotics machine would be looking for new leadership. He would slip in as savior and give everyone raises. He suspected that most of them wouldn't mourn their prior bosses' passing for very long.

Colombar glanced again in the rearview mirror. His chase car had fallen even further behind. The Jeep in front of him was maintaining its speed only out of fear that he would ram them again if they slowed. With a flurry of expletives, he let up on the gas slightly and allowed his men to catch up. He was at the height of his popularity with Colombia's nouveau riche, but it never paid to get too far from one's more tangible protection. He had never seen good will stop a bullet.

Every week, Colombar left his fortresslike home and traveled to one of his refineries or plantations. Perez refused to join him on these field trips, insisting that it was stupid—though he didn't have the balls to actually use that word—to get physically close to any illegal operation. Colombar had berated his advisor repeatedly for his unwillingness to get his hands dirty. Perez would be surprised to know that the day he agreed to go on one of Colombar's outings would be his last day on earth. Though he would never admit it, Colombar feared Perez and those like him. Their education, level heads, and ability to hobnob with senior government officials worried him. Perez's fear of dealing one-on-one with the production and smuggling end of the business made him, in Colombar's opinion, unsuited to leading a major drug organization. But it made him the perfect second in command.

Colombar jerked the wheel right, driving by memory through the dust kicked up by the vehicle in front of him. As he came out of the thick cloud, the forest became more dense, forming a solid living wall less than a foot from the sides of his truck. He slowed further, carefully staying in the middle of the road so as to minimize any paint damage that might be caused by an errant branch scraping against his new toy. In less than five minutes he was in a clearing dominated by a small, dilapidated hut. The men in the vehicle behind him had managed to catch up, being less concerned about their paint job.

Colombar pulled slowly into a man-made hollow in the forest and set the emergency brake. The beat-up flatbed that was normally parked there had been moved out into the open and covered with camouflage netting in anticipation of his arrival.

"Buenos dias, Señor Colombar," one of the refinery's dust- and sweat-encrusted guards said, opening his car door for him. The guard's smile suggested a disdain for toothpaste.

Colombar ignored him and started for the hut. The cotton of his shirt was already starting to cling to him. The day wasn't particularly hot but a recent rain had doused the forest, and was now evaporating, filling the air with a visible cloud of unbearable humidity.

Colombar's personal guards had already taken up positions at each end of the clearing and in front of the hut, displacing the two men who had been standing stiffly at the entrance, awaiting his arrival. They now stood in a new, less-prized station, nervously straightening their fatigues.

"What was that?" Colombar asked no one in particular, stopping short ten feet from the entrance to the hut.

One of the refinery guards fingered the strap on his rifle nervously. "What?"

Colombar stood perfectly still, his head cocked slightly, scanning the tree line.

"I heard someone in the woods—there." He pointed.

The guard sighed with relief and a sadistic smile crossed his lips. "Oh, that's just Manuel. You know him, he works with us." The man pointed to one of the rotting front teeth that he still had. "Gold tooth."

Colombar nodded, prompting the man to continue.

"He's real sick, kept throwing up all over himself. Smelled fucking awful—so we threw him out in the woods." The guard smiled again. "You can still smell him when the wind is right." His final words were met with snickers from his healthier companions.

"Motherfucker drinks too much tequila," Colombar replied angrily. "You go get him—I'm not paying him to sleep in the woods."

The man shook his head gravely, stepping back as Colombar poked him hard in the chest. "It's not the tequila, Señor Colombar—I swear. He's real sick. Think he's gonna die."

Fucking peasants. He paid off half of the law enforcement officials in Colombia to stay away from this place. All these assholes had to do is sit around and suck on bottles.

He waved to the four men who had been in the Jeep in front of him, and three of them trotted off into the jungle. The one who had almost been pulled under Colombar's tires stayed behind. He still looked a little shaky.

A few moments later the men reappeared, crashing through the jungle wall. They were dragging what looked like a corpse by its legs. It clutched a thick wool blanket in one hand, leaving most of it sliding along behind. As they broke into the clearing, the blanket caught on a tree and was pulled from the stiff hand. Only then did the body show signs of life, making a mournful sound deep in its throat. They dropped the sick man's feet onto the hard dirt surface in front of the hut.

Colombar pushed at the man's ribs with the toe of his cowboy boot. He leaned over slightly and squinted, bringing the man's face into sharp focus. His mouth was caked with dirt and vomit, and a fist-sized leaf was stuck to the side of his mouth. His skin had gone an eerie greenish white—an unusual color for a Latino who spent his days in the heavy Colombian sun. The guards were right about the smell.

"What the hell's wrong with him?" Colombar gave the man another nudge with his boot, then moved to a safer distance. "And what happened to his foot?" He pointed to the man's right foot. It was wrapped tightly in a rag heavily stained with dirt and blood. It smelled faintly of kerosene.

"I don't know what is wrong with him, señor. He was fine until a couple of days ago. Then he started puking all the time and couldn't pee. When he finally did, he pissed blood." The guard glanced nervously at Manuel. "He cut his foot week before last. We cleaned it with kerosene to keep the infection away—but I guess it didn't work."

Colombar's mouth curled into a snarl. His teeth gritted almost audibly. He spun quickly on his heel, simultaneously pulling the .45 holstered in the small of his back. The young guard moved back instinctively, catching his heel on his sick companion's torso. As he fell, the butt of Colombar's pistol slammed into his teeth, knocking out most of the top row. Colombar grabbed a handful of the man's hair. He dragged the man off of Manuel, who had begun vomiting again, and pulled him to the center of the clearing. His guards had perked up and were moving toward him, but were unsure what was happening.

Colombar stuck the barrel of his pistol in the man's face. "He's been into my coke!" he screamed.

Blood and spit gurgled from the man's mouth, forming clusters of red-hued bubbles that were beginning to flow down his cheek. He tried to speak, but his voice was muffled by the flowing blood and his inexperience at talking with no front teeth. He shook his head vigorously instead.

"Get Juan!" Colombar shouted at the men now encircling him, delighted by the interesting turn of events on what was usually a tedious day. Two of them ran to the hut and disappeared through the door.

Colombar dropped to his knees, landing one squarely on the man's stomach. Blood and detached teeth flew from his mouth.

"Don't lie to me, you fucking cockroach," he yelled, pressing the barrel of his gun into the man's cheek.

The guard shook his head again, a look of terror spreading across his swelling face.

Colombar stood and turned his attention to the two remaining refinery guards. He stared at them through his gunsight. They were completely frozen, except for their eyes, which darted from side to side looking for an escape. There was none.

"Manuel here's been into my coke." It was a statement, not a question. "And you let him have it."

"No, señor! There is no way he could have gotten to it without one of us seeing him! No way!"

The barrel of the gun moved slowly from one man to another as if it had a mind of its own and was deciding which one to shoot.

"Let go!" Juan Cortegna screamed at the guard who was pushing him roughly out of the hut. Cortegna's hand had slammed into the deceptively sturdy door on the way out, and he was squeezing it between his thighs when he saw Colombar holding two guards motionless with his pistol.

"Señor Colombar! What is going on?"

"That!" Colombar pointed in the general direction of Manuel without taking his eyes off the guards in front of him.

Cortegna looked unsure how to respond for a moment. "Manuel? He is very sick, I am told. An infection."

"He's been into my coke," Colombar repeated for the fourth time.

A look of horror swept across Cortegna's face for a moment, followed by a look of deep thought. After a moment he spoke. His voice had calmed somewhat. "No, that is quite impossible. You know the safeguards that we use. Manuel has no access to the final product."

Colombar did understand the security measures that Cortegna had in place, but the evidence, and more important, his gut, told him that Manuel had been poisoned. The fact that he couldn't figure out how it had happened made him that much madder. Outsmarted by some piece-of-shit guard.

"Your fucking safeguards don't work then . . . unless you were involved." He turned the gun on Cortegna, who began to shrink away. The sturdy frame of one of Colombar's men blocked his retreat.

"You know I would never do that, señor. You know!"

Columbar did know. Cortegna had been with him for years—he was one of his most loyal employees.

"What makes you think that Manuel has been stealing your product, señor? He does not even like coke—says it doesn't agree with him."

Colombar began pacing the length of the clearing, the pistol hanging loosely in his right hand as it swung back and forth. The guard who had greeted him when he arrived had managed to rise to his hands and knees and was crawling around aimlessly, as though he was looking for his teeth. As Colombar passed by him, his hand tightened almost imperceptibly on the gun. The man once again fell flat. This time with a baseball-sized hole in the back of his neck.

Finally Colombar spoke. "Juan, have all of the kerosene loaded on the flatbed and brought to my house. Immediately. You," he pointed to the driver of his chase car and then the two terrified men standing with their backs to the hut. "You're going to take those two to the house."

"And him . . ." Colombar looked down at Manuel, who was now breathing in shallow gasps from all the excitement. "Tie him to my luggage rack."

The Jeeps were both overloaded, and he sure as hell didn't want this filthy piece of shit stinking up the interior of his new truck.

"Doctor! So good of you to come on such short notice." Colombar strolled across his living room and shook the soft, plump hand of the elderly man standing at the entrance. Dr. Santez, a tiny, white-haired man in his late sixties, had been Colombar's personal physician for almost seven years. Santez came when beckoned, treating his wealthy patient mainly for hangovers. And for that, Colombar paid him five times his normal fee.

The doctor looked at him strangely. Usually when he arrived, Colombar was laid out on his couch, stinking of tequila. The man in front of him was the picture of health.

"You look well, Luis," he observed suspiciously.

"Oh, I am, Doctor, I am. Actually, it's one of my men who is seriously ill, and I want you to take a look at him."

The doctor looked mildly relieved. Colombar's violent mood swings had always made him nervous. Generally, if you were invited to Colombar's home for unknown reasons, there was a good chance that you had done something to irritate him and that you were going to end up as plant food for his orchids.

"I'd be happy to, Luis," he said, starting for the back of the house, where he knew that there was a wing for the employees who worked in the compound.

Colombar held his arm out, blocking the doctor's path. "No, no. This way." He pointed to the front door.

It was growing dark as they walked through Colombar's gardens toward a detached three-car garage next to the main house. Black clouds swirled wildly, driven by the unpredictable Andean winds. The rain was light, a mist that was imperceptible until it built up enough to trickle from hairline to chin.

As they approached the garage, Colombar slipped his hand into his pocket and activated the garage door opener. One of the three doors began creeping up.

This section of the garage was used by the full-time gardener. The walls were neatly lined with various exotic lawn tools. Heavy-looking plastic sacks of fertilizer were stacked in discrete piles according to brand and type.

At the base of a riding lawnmower that verged on being a trac-tor, a figure in stained green fatigues raised his head weakly.

A gust of wind blew into the garage and was blasted back into the doctor's face as he stood near the entrance. It carried with it an odor that he was very familiar with. Impending death.

Colombar motioned the doctor in. "Here is your patient." He sat down on a stack of mulch bags, careful to wipe the dust off them first.

"What is his name?"

"Manuel." Colombar replied impatiently.

Santez walked hesitantly to the side of the man and crouched. A weak smile of recognition crossed Manuel's lips.

After pulling on a pair of thin rubber gloves fished from his black leather bag, Santez went about a quick examination of the man. He looked into his eyes and mouth, took his pulse and blood pressure, and carefully unbound his injured foot. Finally he stood, looking down at his patient's chest. It was moving quickly as he took in short shallow breaths.

"Well?" Colombar hopped from his place on the mulch.

"I do not know, Luis—he is very ill. Do you know when he contracted this sickness?"

"I'm told that he was feeling fine until about two days ago and that he deteriorated rapidly."

The doctor nodded thoughtfully. "Could he have come into contact with some toxic substance? Perhaps some pesticide you use in your garden?"

Colombar shook his head. "What I am about to tell you is highly confidential, Doctor. Do you understand?"

There was a clearly implied threat in Colombar's words. Santez nodded. "I believe that Manuel may have been deliberately poisoned . . . like the Americans."

"Are we speaking of the poison secreted in cocaine?"

"Yes."

"But how . . . ?"

Colombar cut him off. "You let me worry about that. All I need from you is to tell me whether or not I'm right."

"I cannot tell you for certain, Luis, though the symptoms seem to be similar. We must get the patient back to Bogota—to the hospital there. I will let you know what we discover tomorrow, though if it is a similar poison to the one in the U.S., I doubt those tests will be conclusive. We will have to examine the vital organs—it is my understanding that this particular toxin attacks the liver and kidneys. This could probably be done by next week.

Colombar stared at the doctor as if he were a retarded child. "I'm sorry. Perhaps I didn't make myself clear." Colombar's politeness was well practiced, but lacked even a hint of sincerity. It was as though he was reading from a cue card. "I need to know tomorrow whether Manuel was poisoned. Please take him to Bogota and do whatever is necessary."

A confused expression crept across the doctor's face. "I can't perform those kinds of tests on his vital organs right away, Luis."

Colombar was becoming visibly irritated. "Why not?"

"He's, uh, using them, Luis."

Colombar took a deep breath and expelled it loudly. Pushing past Santez, he reached up under the back of his thick Irish wool sweater and closed his fingers around the .45 resting in the small of his back. He aimed the pistol at Manuel's chest, and then changed his mind. The concrete floor under him could cause a dangerous ricochet.

Looking around him, his eyes fell on a nearly empty bag of mulch at the base of the stack that he had just been sitting on. He brushed past the baffled physician again and grabbed the bottom of the bag. As he walked back over to Manuel, the upended bag spilled what was left of its contents, leaving a thick brown trail behind him.

In one swift motion, Colombar grabbed the front of Manuel's fatigue shirt, jerking him upright, and pulled the bag over his head. Briefly, the dying guard came back life. His pale hands clawed at the bag, legs kicking wildly. Concerned that Manuel would manage to rip a hole in the plastic, Colombar flipped his victim onto his stomach. Placing a knee firmly in his back, he pulled with all his might, arching Manuel's back and neck into an unnaturally bowed position.

Santez had backed all of the way out of the garage by the time Manuel's struggles had faded. Colombar kept the pressure on for another minute, just to be sure. "Doctor," he exclaimed, looking behind him. "Why, you're getting soaked! Come under the roof."

Santez did as he was told.

Colombar released the bag, and Manuel's lifeless body fell to the floor. There was a hollow smack when his head hit the concrete. "I will expect a complete report tomorrow afternoon, Doctor."

18

Washington, D.C.,
February 14

Laura Vilechi climbed up on a chair and stretched to reach the Volume button on the television anchored to the wall of SIOC. As usual, the remote was nowhere to be found. Not surprising with no fewer than fifteen men coming and going at all hours of the day and night. What was it about men and remotes?

She pushed the Up button, repeatedly watching the word-fragment "VOL" appear in green at the bottom of the screen. The television responded obediently, and CNN went from background noise to a more conversational tone. She climbed down and took a seat at the conference table, shushing two agents talking loudly on the other side of the room.

The camera was panning what seemed like endless rows of dogs in small cages set into austere concrete walls. In the right-hand corner of the screen was the telltale syringe symbol that labeled this as a report on "The Drug Crisis." The dramatic theme music that CNN had composed for the biggest story of the decade filled the room. Laura's interest was piqued. The news media had splashed this unfortunate situation over every publication, radio broadcast, and television station in the country. They had covered it from every intelligent angle, finally slipping into the absurd. She was curious whether the casually dressed young man with the microphone was going to try to interview the house pet of a poisoning victim.

"This is the Seventeenth Street Animal Shelter in Chicago, Illinois," he started, beginning to walk the length of the narrow corridor between the individual cages. The camera panned back and forth, focusing on some of the more adorable animals. He stopped next to a cage containing a small border collie. The cameraman gave each of them half the frame.

"Until yesterday, you might have seen a young family walking through this corridor, looking for a faithful companion for a small child."

He turned and tapped the front of the cage behind him. The collie jumped excitedly at his hand, thankful for the attention. When the young reporter turned back to the camera, his face was grave. "This is Darby." The dog yipped happily when he spoke its name. "Darby is scheduled to be destroyed in three days. Until yesterday, he had a chance. It's easy to imagine a little girl coming in here with her family and falling in love with him." Darby barked in agreement.

The reporter walked away from the cage, and the collie's hopeful face slipped from the frame. It was replaced by the face of a tall, serious-looking woman.

"Yesterday," the reporter continued, "this shelter, and all other shelters in the Chicago metropolitan area, suspended their animal adoption programs." As he turned to the woman, a caption flashed identifying her as the director of the Chicago-area animal shelters.

"Ms. Kelly, may I ask you how you arrived at your decision to stop allowing animal adoptions?"

"Uh, yes." She was clearly unaccustomed to the camera. "Over the past few weeks, we had just over a thirty percent increase in people wanting to adopt dogs—and my research indicates that most animal shelters have seen about the same jump. We didn't know what was causing it at first, but later we started hearing rumors that people were using them to test their narcotics on." Her voice wavered. "At first we didn't think it was true. We couldn't believe that anyone could do something so cruel. But when we thought back on it, we knew it was true. A lot of the people coming in didn't seem to show as much interest in which dog they got. They just wanted a dog." She paused for a moment, a sad expression crossing her face. "Then yesterday we found out for sure. A vet that we work with treated a dog for massive liver and kidney failure. He confirmed that the dog had been poisoned, and that it had traces of cocaine in its blood . . ."

Laura jumped back onto the chair and slapped the On/Off button. She'd bought a yellow Lab after her divorce a couple of years ago and she didn't know what she would do if someone poisoned it.

"Pretty grim, huh?"

She hadn't noticed Beamon standing directly behind her throughout the broadcast. She spun to face him.

"Are we sure we know what we're doing? Working our butts off to save people like that?" She jerked her thumb at the now silent television. "What kind of scum gives poisoned coke to a dog?"

"They're desperate, Laura," he said, taking a chair at the conference table. "You and I will never have any idea what it's like to be addicted to something like that." Beamon's voice didn't have its usual dead-sure ring.

Laura nodded sadly. "I know you're right. Seeing stuff like that makes you wonder, though, doesn't it?" She pointed through the glass wall at the room next to them. "Looks like they're all here. You ready for our first staff meeting?"

He grimaced.

"Good afternoon, gentlemen." Beamon admired Laura as she walked through the door ahead of him. "And lady."

The small table was crowded. Dick Trevor, Laura's counterpart at DEA, sat directly across from Beamon's chair. Tom Sherman was on his right and Trace Fontain his left. There wasn't a smiling face in the room. Laura's mood seemed to be catching.

"So how goes the war?" Beamon asked hopefully.

No one seemed to want to start. Fontain actually looked away, like a kid who didn't know the answer to a question in class.

"Have you seen this, Mark?" Trevor pulled two copies of

Newsweek out of his briefcase and slid one each to Beamon and Tom Sherman. "Just came out today."

Beamon looked at the cover. It contained a graphic picture of a corpse lying on a sofa in a cluttered apartment. It looked like the man had been dead for a few days.

"Thirty-four, Mark."

Beamon flipped through, finding the page. A slightly overexposed picture of him standing at a podium, flanked by the President and Director filled an entire page.

"Do you think this makes me look fat?" He held the picture up to Laura. She smiled and relaxed a little.

"Read the poll," Trevor prompted.

Beamon looked at the facing page as Laura stood up and leaned over his shoulder. A yellow box housed a *Newsweek*/Gallup poll. It asked whether the respondents were for or against the CDFS. Thirty-one percent were showing pro-CDFS, with another seventeen percent undecided.

Beamon closed the magazine and held it up over his head. Laura took it, returned to her seat, and began casually flipping the pages.

"What else you got, Dick?" Beamon asked pleasantly.

Trevor shrugged. "Not a whole lot to report, Mark. We've penetrated a few more layers since our last meeting, but nothing yet. Looks like these guys hit the shipment way up the line. We're talking to some pretty high level distributors now. Sorry."

Beamon knew that Trevor had a bad habit of taking every failure personally, spending nights second-guessing himself. Not a healthy trait in a DEA agent.

"I do have some interesting stats, but they're a little off the subject," Trevor added.

"Go ahead, I'm not in a hurry."

"We've compiled data from our street agents all over the country and washed it through the computer. You'll be interested to know that, as best we can tell, cocaine use is down about sixty percent."

Laura's looked up from her magazine, and an involuntary "Jesus!" escaped her lips before she could stifle it.

Sherman looked at her reproachfully and then turned back to Trevor. "Who told you to take that poll?"

"Uh, Director Calahan said he would be interested in any information we had on what effect the CDFS was having on drug use."

"Well, stop," Sherman said

"Excuse me?"

"Stop. Under no circumstances are you to ever gather that kind of information again. You saw the poll," he tapped his copy of *Newsweek*. "If your stats leak, we'll be fighting public opinion even more than we are now."

Trevor obviously saw his point, but looked uncomfortable.

"I'll talk to Calahan," Sherman promised.

That seemed to satisfy Trevor, and he leaned back in his chair, indicating that his report was completed.

Sherman kept control of the meeting. "Laura, what's happening in your world?"

"Hang on a second," Beamon interjected. "I think Dick's math bears a little conversation."

"And what exactly would you like to discuss?"

"Hell, I don't know. I think we could start with the observation that the CDFS, with a few guys and less money than the U.S. spends on studying the mating habits of the duck-billed platypus, has accomplished something that the entire law enforcement community will never get done."

"So what's your recommendation, Mark? Do we just stop looking for these guys? Let them kill off our problem citizens?"

Beamon looked at his shoes uncomfortably. He felt like a child being reprimanded by his teacher. "No."

"Look, Mark, I understand what you're saying. I've been hearing rumblings about the decline in drug use for a couple of days now, but our job is to catch these guys. Not to make moral judgments."

Beamon turned back to Trevor. "How many people die from drug-related causes every year?"

"Dunno. Lots."

"Stop right there, Mark," Sherman cautioned. "I don't want to hear it. It's easy to punch numbers into a computer and come out with the quantitative benefits of poisoning our narcotics users, and ignore the qualitative issues. But what if it's your kid dead?"

Beamon remained silent and let Sherman change the subject. "Okay, then. Laura, I believe that you were about to report on your end of the investigation."

"Right. Well, we're still groping for solid leads at this point. The check angle has really come to nothing. The suspect bought the checks with cash and then disappeared. We're still doing some follow-up there, but I'm not hopeful." She juggled the papers in front of her and started back in. "The hotline we set up has pretty much turned into a forum for public comment—mostly people applauding the CDFS and telling us to back off. At Mark's suggestion, we've changed it from an 800 number to a toll call. Hopefully that'll cut down on the traffic. As you know, we've publicized a five hundred thousand dollar reward for information."

She stood and walked to the corner of the conference room. A large piece of posterboard leaned against the wall. She picked it up. "We're up to roughly fifteen thousand eight hundred casualties." She placed the edge of the posterboard on the table, giving the rest of the agents a closer look. It depicted a roughly bell-shaped graph. Next to it was a much smaller red bar.

"This blue curve charts the daily deaths from cocaine poisonings since the beginning of the outbreak." Her finger traced the length of the graph. "As you can see, the first section, depicting the first week, is quite steep. That's because of the unexpected delayed reaction in the drugs. Lots of people were using them thinking they were safe. It's starting to level out now for a few reasons. One, because the poisoned coke seems to be getting used up. Two, as Dick pointed out, people are using less. And three, quite a few users are, well, dead. The last one doesn't really have that much of a statistical impact, though."

Sherman pointed to the center of the graph. "And what does it mean when the line goes from blue to black?"

Beamon rolled his eyes. It wasn't enough that Laura spent half her life drawing graphs and charts. Now Tom was actually going to prolong the discussion of them.

"The black line represents our projection of remaining deaths. You can see along the bottom that the color change corresponds with today's date."

Sherman nodded. "You're assuming that no more cocaine is poisoned, though, right?"

"That's right. It's hard to say what would happen if they got to some more drugs. It depends on how comfortable people are feeling that the poisoned stuff is dwindling."

"So what's the other one?" Sherman pointed to the red bar.

"Oh, that's just deaths to date. Fifteen thousand eight hundred."

Laura leaned the posterboard against the wall and took her seat as Sherman turned back to Beamon. "What's happening in your world, Mark?"

"Turns out Customs doesn't have a record of anyone bringing in a shipment of mushrooms that couldn't be traced to a legitimate source—grocery stores, restaurants, whatever. Scott Dresden, out of Bonn, is running down the mushroom angle—where they got 'em and how they got 'em here. No luck yet—he's a good man, though."

"Pretty tall order," Laura observed sympathetically, "finding some guy running around the woods picking mushrooms in Poland."

"And he's got to do it without a single graph," Beamon added.

She kicked him hard under the table.

Beamon turned to Fontain, rubbing his shin with the top of his foot. "Trace—you want to tell everyone what you told me?"

Fontain didn't like meetings, and had protested when Beamon had asked him to come. He spoke reluctantly. "You know that we've been trying to get around and interview just about everyone who's been poisoned. We've been trying to track where people got the bad coke, to help the DEA pinpoint its origin." He shifted uncomfortably in his chair. "Well, we interviewed a young man yesterday who swears that he hasn't done a line of coke in six years.

We did some tests this morning and confirmed that he was telling the truth. He's a heroin addict."

"Goddammit," Sherman exclaimed in a rare use of profanity. "Where'd he get it?"

"L.A."

Beamon jumped in to divert Sherman's attention from the frail-looking scientist. "I typed up a press release a couple of hours ago, Tom. The press should be running a story within the hour."

"Goddammit," Sherman repeated for good measure. "How many people are they gonna get this time?"

Beamon shrugged. The number of deaths was just noise to him—irrelevant to the investigation, and a subject that he found particularly depressing. The last thing he needed was a constant reminder of the lives being lost because he hadn't caught these guys yet.

Sherman's gaze turned to Laura.

"I don't know, Tom. There are so many factors . . ."

"Well, speculate then," he shot back impatiently.

"I can't. We have no idea how much product they hit—in the end, that's the most important variable."

Beamon agreed. "Yeah, but I think we can count on all the poisoned stuff getting used up. There's nothing quite as desperate as a heroin addict in need of a fix. They're gonna take a hell of a lot more chances than some guy who likes to do a few lines before he hits the clubs on Friday night."

"So good of you to come personally to give me the news!" Luis Colombar crossed his expansive living room and gave his physician a firm handshake.

Colombar was dressed impeccably in an off-white linen suit and maroon silk shirt. He showed off the thousands of dollars worth of ongoing dental work correcting years of youthful neglect.

Santez followed him to the bar, where Colombar poured him a Stolichnaya and tonic. Even there, in his beautiful home, in his expensive suit, with his practiced accent, the drug lord was surrounded by an aura of violent insanity. It wasn't just the memory of his recent experience with Colombar—it was something in the drug lord's gait. Something around his eyes.

The doctor accepted the drink gratefully, downing a good portion of it in the first gulp. It burned its way down but didn't kill the butterflies below.

"And so what news?" Colombar asked.

Santez didn't understand what he was involved in, but his churning stomach told him that it was big. Regret coursed through him—regret for the greed that had prompted him to take the job as Colombar's physician and had entangled him in the invisible web of the cocaine trade that blanketed his country.

"We have not been able to fully complete our tests on Ma—the subject's—organs." Somehow speaking Colombar's victim's name out loud seemed impossibly dangerous. "However, based on information provided by Johns Hopkins Hospital in the States and our initial review of the damaged liver, I believe that there is a ninety-five percent probability that the subject was poisoned by the same substance that is being used to poison drug users in the USA."

There, he'd said it. He watched Colombar's face carefully.

To his relief, the drug lord appeared to be unaffected by the news. He just stood there and sipped his drink. Finally he laid down his glass and clapped Santez on the shoulder.

"I really appreciate your help on this, Doctor." He took the drink from Santez's slightly trembling hand and began leading the old man out.

"Drive carefully!" he called as Santez slid behind the wheel of the Blazer that he always rented when he came into the mountains. Santez held his breath as he turned the key—sure that the car would explode into a ball of fire. The engine roared innocently to life.

"You heard?"

Alejandro Perez had appeared like magic and sunk into one of the large chairs by the entertainment center. He wore white shorts and a white Polo shirt. A tennis racquet was propped next to him.

"I heard. I think I know how it was done, too."

Colombar dropped into the chair across from him. His jaw was clenched tightly.

"One of the men you brought back goes with the truck to pick up kerosene every week. He tells me that a few weeks ago, they stopped to relieve themselves and found an old drunk hitching a ride on top of the barrels on the back of the truck."

Colombar's expression changed from sullen to hopeful.

"They let him go."

"Fuck!"

"I've doubled our guards on the refineries and told them that one man is to ride on the back of the trucks with the kerosene. We're also going to start using different suppliers on a random basis."

Colombar was still seething at the thought of just barely missing the man who'd done this to him. He took a deep breath, quelling the rage that was building up inside him. "I want the motherfucker who let this happen dead! Send the other son of a bitch back to the refinery—but give him something to remember me by." Guards weren't that easy to come by, and he seemed to be losing them fast.

Perez looked embarrassed. "He, uh, passed away during his conversation with Rico."

"Oh." Colombar stood and paced behind the sofa, a habit his interior designer had complained about on numerous occasions. A light-colored swath was becoming visible on the hand-tied Oriental.

"When do we get the analysis back on the kerosene sample that we sent out?"

"Probably not for another two weeks."

"No matter. I know what it will say." Colombar stopped pacing and leaned against the couch. "Somebody must know something— this guy must have been going around town asking questions." He stopped and turned to face Perez. "Put the word out, Alejandro. I'll pay two hundred and fifty thousand dollars for information on this son of a bitch."

*   *   *

The thick clouds that almost delayed his flight into Denver International had miraculously disappeared. Mark Beamon squinted his eyes almost shut as he swung his car onto a steep gravel road and headed directly into the sun.

At the crest of the hill, he slipped the gearshift into neutral and let the car's momentum fade and then reverse itself. After rolling back ten feet or so, he reluctantly yanked on the emergency brake and brought the car to a skidding stop.

Beamon hated Colorado. He hated the shining mountains, the clean air, and the annoying bicyclists who waved as he passed them in his rented subcompact. Funerals deserved more somber settings. And the funeral of a family member—a child—should, at the very least, rate a good steady rain.

Beamon put the car in gear and forced it forward without releasing the emergency brake. He stopped again when he reached his previous high mark, and surveyed the scene below.

To the left of the cemetery's imposing front gate were no fewer than four white vans, each adorned with a satellite dish and elaborate logo. The logos were illegible from this distance, but it was a safe bet that the vans represented local affiliates of national news organizations. Beamon didn't even bother to count the cars nosed up to the fence, or the people perched on their roofs, peering though camera lenses as long as his arm.

Releasing the brake, he started down the hill. On the drive from Denver, he had started to feel a little guilty about the scene he had made in the rental car agency when they had told him that they didn't stock cars with tinted windows. As he watched the enormous lenses of the press swivel toward him, though, he made a mental note to find out who ran the rental car agency and have someone shoot out his porch light.

Beamon slowed to a stop ten feet from the cemetery's gate and rolled down his window. The camera flashes went wild, but finally dissipated when a large man in dark glasses positioned himself directly in front of the car window.

"Sorry to hear about your nephew, Mark."

"They're not," Beamon said, jerking his head in the general direction of the press. "It's good to see you, Frank. I really appreciate you helping out."

Frank grunted and looked at the ground. "No problem. I just can't believe these vultures have the balls to come out here like this."

"Are you kidding? When my nephew dies from snorting bad coke, they clear their calendars."

Frank shrugged and rose to his full six and a half feet. "It's already started. You'd better get going."

Beamon pulled the car forward, keeping his bumper within two feet of another somberly dressed man slowly pushing the gate open.

Frank had always been a good friend. He hadn't offered a word of protest when Beamon called and asked him to take on the distasteful and only marginally legal job of bouncer at his nephew's funeral. Frank was the only man for the job, though. One look at his heavily pockmarked face and solid two hundred and fifty plus pounds would make even the most obnoxious reporter think twice before spouting off about the public's right to know.

Beamon pulled in too close to a blue Toyota pickup, purposefully blocking it to give himself an excuse to make a run for it at the end of the service. With some effort, he separated himself from the tiny car and weaved his way, alone, through the snowdrifts and headstones toward a small knot of black-clad mourners clinging to each other for support.

He was thankful that no one looked back as he found a strategic position behind a man whose head blocked Beamon's view of the coffin. He peered around the man's shoulder for a moment, looking briefly at his sister. Her head was lowered and her stare was fixed on the thing he couldn't bring himself to look at.

The service went on forever.

The priest alternatively mumbled and shouted, but said nothing about the guest of honor. He talked only of the pervading godlessness that had led to the boy's death. Beamon's mind wandered, and he looked around at the small group of people gathered around him. He recognized almost no one in his sister's life. That wasn't surprising though—they had never made any kind of real connection when they were children. They spoke now only on holidays, and the conversations consisted of the self-conscious prattle of complete strangers.

Beamon was interrupted from his daydreaming by the sudden silence of the priest and the brief crush of people as they moved past him. He looked up and watched his sister moving purposefully toward him. The tear in the corner of her right eye was quickly lost in her cold stare.

"You've never been much of a brother to me, Mark."

He didn't see much point in denying it and remained silent.

"Now's the time to make up for it. Find out who did this to Kevin. Find out and kill him." She brushed past him and headed for the cars.

Kevin.

Hearing his name and looking at the dirty snow around his grave brought back the few fleeting memories Beamon had of the boy. He'd been impossibly bright and completely out of control for most of his life, much like Beamon himself had been. Fortunately, the stifling atmosphere of the early sixties had kept the young Mark Beamon from straying too far from the straight and narrow. The nineties had offered no such barriers. Until now.

"Franz—nein," Scott Dresden pleaded, performing his best tired look from behind the large desk.

Franz Gullich looked down his long straight nose at him, continuing to screw the top off of a fifth of Jack Daniels. When the cap was freed, he followed a tradition that Dresden had come to dread. He threw it in the trash can.

Gullich hadn't become the head of the German police based on sobriety. In fact, his ability to perform magical feats of deduction while half-cocked was the marvel of two continents. He and Dresden had become fast friends during Dresden's tour as assistant legal attaché Bonn—a friendship based on mutual respect.

Gullich's lack of political ambition made him a joy to work with. He'd started as the German equivalent of a beat cop almost twenty years ago on the streets of Munich. Today he was still just a cop. Dresden had come to miss the company of cops in his current position as FBI agent/diplomat.

Gullich pulled two large commemorative mugs from their display case and blew the dust out of them.

The glasses cleaned to his satisfaction, the German worked himself into the sofa at the opposite end of the office and placed the bottle ominously next to him. Dresden hit the intercom button on the complex-looking phone on his desk.

"Hello, Kip? Kip?"

"Hi, Scott. Finally figured out how to use the intercom, huh?"

"Yeah. Hey—Franz is here, why don't you come over for a drink?" Dresden knew that the bottle would be empty by the end of the night and figured to spread out the pain a little.

"I'd love to, Scott, but I've got an appointment that I'm already late for. Tell him I'll catch him when he gets back. I'm anxious to hear what he has to say about Quantico."

Dresden flicked off the intercom and came out from around his desk. His mind wandered to how he was going to get back at his assistant for that little white lie.

Gullich was already pouring healthy slugs of the brown liquid into the mugs, emptying almost a third of the bottle. He slipped his shoes off and put his feet on the coffee table in front of the sofa. The table top wasn't attached and it tipped wildly, almost upsetting the bottle. He didn't seem to notice.

"Cheers," he said holding up his mug.

"Cheers." Dresden settled into a love seat positioned perpendicular to the sofa.

The Austrian took a long pull from the glass. The corners of his eyes scrunched up a bit as he swallowed, accentuating the deep crow's-feet that were a relic of his years walking the streets in the harsh German winters.

The conversation moved smoothly from subject to subject,

starting with general politics and economics and becoming more and more personal as the liquor took effect. An hour later they were having a heartfelt discussion of the perils of in-laws. Dresden's head felt light as a feather, a sensation that he was becoming used to, and one that he knew guaranteed a tough morning. Gullich was less affected, though his English was becoming worse and worse. Dresden was indistinguishable from a native in German and French, but Gullich's English needed work, so he insisted that all conversations between them be in that language.

Tiring of the in-law issue, Gullich fell silent and held up the nearly empty bottle. Dresden offered his cup to be topped off. The Austrian looked mildly disappointed as he tipped a splash into the nearly full mug.

"So how goes the mushroom-hunter hunting?"

Dresden scowled clumsily. His facial muscles were a bit more relaxed than he'd thought. "It's hopeless. They've got me trying to find one lone American, running around the woods somewhere in Eastern Europe, stuffing mushrooms into a garbage bag." He put his glass to his lips, shaking his head. "I might have gotten lucky in Western Europe, but you know the condition of law enforcement in the East."

Gullich swung his feet up on the sofa and leaned his head against a pillow. Dresden thought he was preparing to pass out and watched him carefully during the long silence that ensued. Finally his friend came back to life. "I think you're approaching this whole thing wrong," Gullich said, switching to German.

Dresden leaned forward slightly. He'd known Franz long enough to know not to dismiss his drunken musings out of hand. "Care to elaborate?"

"You grew up here, didn't you?"

"Not here—Berlin," Dresden answered. "My father was in the army. But you know that."

A smile spread across Gullich's face. "It always makes me laugh— how out of touch you are with your countrymen. Let me ask you a question. What do you see when you bump into an American tourist in Bonn?"

They were getting way off the subject here, and Dresden relaxed. His friend must have had a few drinks before he had arrived. He was rambling.

Getting no response, the German answered his own question. "You see a fat, poorly dressed person with no understanding of our culture or language. Without their tour guides, most of them wouldn't be able to find their hotels and would die of starvation in the streets."

Dresden opened his mouth to defend his countrymen but closed it again when he came to the realization that his friend was ninety percent right.

"And that's Western Europe. I expect they're even more lost in the East."

Dresden waited for his friend's eyes to focus elsewhere, and dumped a good portion of his drink into the unhealthy-looking tree next to the sofa. His secretary, who prided herself on her green thumb, could never understand why the tree always looked like it was about to die.

"Okay, so we're a little ethnocentric."

"Put yourself in the shoes—sneakers—of your right-wing friend. You've been to Europe, say, three times. You've toured, oh, London, Paris, and Rome. You speak no foreign languages and have never been to the former Soviet Union. So you've got a problem—you need a bunch of mushrooms from—Poland, is it?"

"That's where they grow, primarily," Dresden confirmed.

"Okay, Poland. You've never been there, don't speak the language, and probably don't know a shiitake mushroom from a portobello. What do you do?"

Gullich drained his glass and turned his head, looking ruefully at the empty bottle on the table. Dresden reached over and poured some of his into his friend's glass.

"You," he pointed at Dresden, "get a book on mushrooms and take your four languages and intimate knowledge of Europe and pick them yourself. You wouldn't have any problem figuring out where you were going and blending in. Like you said—it would be damn near impossible to track a person like you. Joe American, though, couldn't. He'd draw lots of unwanted attention getting lost, trying to find places to eat, trying to figure out where the mushrooms grow—whatever."

"So what's he do?"

"He hires it done. He calls some farmer or something and gets him to pick the mushrooms. He sends the guy some money and has him mail the lot to him in America."

Dresden cursed under his breath, dumping what little was left in his glass into the tree. Franz was right. He had spent so much time ignoring his countrymen's embarrassing attitudes that he had missed the obvious.

Gullich reached an arm up toward the ceiling and swung it around drunkenly. The glass in his hand sloshed and the bourbon dripped down his arm. He switched to heavily accented English again. He had been working on his slang for the past few months, concentrating on the worst that American TV had to offer. "So what do you think, paesan? Am I right or am I right?"

19

Washington, D.C.,
February 18

Bill Karns scanned the street carefully as he walked back to the house he had rented in Southeast Washington. It was almost four blocks from the house to the Korean-owned grocery store that he had come to rely on over the last couple of months.

The day was cold, with a driving wind whipping through the tightly packed rows of decaying houses. The neighborhood had once housed some of Washington's wealthier families, but the last shards of its dignity had been stolen by neglect and young men with spray cans.

The stone homes on his block were distinguished by their round turrets, topped with almost Russian-looking roofs. Their large windows were now covered with boards, which were in turn covered with paint and an infinite number of peeling flyers. The flyers made a loud chattering noise as the wind tore across them. Every couple of minutes a chunk of paper would break loose and go cartwheeling down the street.

Karns turned abruptly right, glancing behind him at the empty street.

Pulling a set of keys out of his pocket with his free hand, he slipped one into the dead bolt. The door popped open and he pushed through, slamming it behind him.

Inside, the house was even less impressive. The hardwood floor had long since been ripped up and moved to a neighborhood more suitable. The artfully rounded walls were covered with graffiti and topped with a discolored strip where an expensive crown molding had been removed.

He walked to the kitchen and laid his groceries down next to a small refrigerator that shared a bright orange extension cord with an even smaller hot plate. Karns's groceries consisted of a twelve-pack of National Bohemian beer, three cans of Hormel Chili, a box of Velveeta, and two bags of generic tortilla chips. He closed the refrigerator door tightly on eleven of the twelve beers, keeping one out for himself.

He had been living in this place since John Hobart assigned him to D.C. at their meeting in his hunting lodge. The house was in a "disputed" area. To the north, the neighborhood was one hundred percent black. To the near south it was Hispanic. Farther south, it was an "up and coming" neighborhood, where Caucasian yuppies were buying relatively inexpensive homes and renovating them with window bars and high-tech security systems.

His first month had been slow. Neither the blacks nor the Hispanics were prepared to accept a fifty-year-old white man with a slight Southern accent into their respective folds. He'd worked his way in slowly—differentiating himself with top-notch product at below-market prices. He was always fair and always had merchandise to sell. Eventually many of the small-time local dealers grudgingly came around. Economic concerns, it seemed, transcended racial bigotry.

There had been problems, of course. Mainly with the dealers that he had usurped. The most vocal of these, and ostensibly the most violent, had met with an unfortunate accident at the wrong end of Karns's twelve gauge. That had quieted down the market resistance temporarily, as his competitors moved in on the dead man's turf. They were better off with Karns than their unpredictable friend. They seemed to realize this, and an uneasy truce was born.

He hadn't heard a word out of Hobart for weeks and he was

getting impatient. Right now he was just another drug dealer, adding to the problem that he had hired on to eradicate.

He sat down on the floor and opened a can of Hormel, dumping it into the dirty pan sitting next to the hot plate. He cut a healthy chunk of Velveeta with his pocket knife and tossed it in with the chili. Stirring occasionally when the sides began to bubble, he polished off his beer and reached into the refrigerator for a new one.

A loud buzzing startled him as he peered into the pan to see if the cheese had completely melted. It was the doorbell that he had installed when he moved in. It was loud enough to be heard anywhere in the house.

Karns pulled his 9mm out of its holster and chambered a bullet before replacing the gun in the holster under his arm. He walked quietly to the front door and peeked through a peephole drilled in the wall. There was a much more obvious hole in the door, but it was just there as a decoy. Looking through it was a good way to get a bullet in the eye.

It took him a moment to recognize the young black boy fidgeting on the porch. Reeling through the file of local dealers in his head, he finally placed him. His street name was Tek, and he was pretty far from home, by drug dealer standards. Karns glanced out the window and spotted another fidgety youth keeping lookout on the sidewalk. He had heard that his counterpart in Tek's territory had been picked up a few nights ago, and that Tek had been having a hard time finding a new supplier. He also heard that there were some other "businessmen" interested in Tek's territory.

Karns opened the door slightly and moved away from it, being careful to stay out of sight of the young man on the sidewalk. Tek took the open door as an invitation and stepped in.

"Close the door behind you. Pretty far from home, aren't you, Tek?"

The young man looked around him, trying to see into the kitchen. He looked nervous. "Yeah."

"I hear you're having a hard time finding product—that some people are moving in on you."

Tek's attention turned from the kitchen to Karns. A sneer passed his lips.

Karns calmly registered the anger on Tek's face. His experience with the local dealers was that they couldn't hit the broad side of a barn at ten paces with a howitzer. He was confident that with his 9 mil and a few extra clips he could walk down the middle of the street and kill every dealer in Southeast without getting a scratch. Hell, they'd probably end up popping each other in crossfires. If this little nigger wanted to pull down, he'd have a bullet in his head before his hand hit his pistol grip.

"Thought you might have something to sell."

Karns nodded thoughtfully. His calm demeanor belied a racing mind. "I might. What do you need?"

"Some rock, man."

Karns nodded again, recognizing the street name for crack cocaine.

"I don't want to get pulled into this shit between you and DJ. Anybody know you're here—other than your backup?"

Tek shook his head, and Karns believed him. If he found a new supplier, he sure as hell wouldn't want his competitors finding out who it was. Besides, Tek and his friend—'Twan was the name, if he remembered correctly—were both heavy users. The opportunity was just too good, Hobart or no Hobart.

"How much you need?"

"I got a grand."

"Let's see it."

Tek's hand moved slowly to his pocket. Karns tensed imperceptibly, though he knew that the jacket pocket was too small to house a Tec-9—the only weapon the young man was reputed to use. A moment later Tek produce a healthy-looking wad of bills.

Karns smiled approvingly. "Have a seat." He pointed to an old vinyl chair sitting in the corner of the room. "I'll be right back."

He rushed through the kitchen, stopping for a moment to turn off the chili that was beginning to boil over. At the back of the kitchen was a new, sturdy-looking metal door leading to a windowless basement. A perfect place to store merchandise, and a nearly impregnable fortress to retreat to, if things ever came to that.

The basement room was mostly in shadow, lighted only by a desk lamp on a small table. Along one wall, mired in gloom, stood a shelf fastened to the brick with long rusty nails. On it were at least twenty shoe boxes. Karns crouched down, his knees cracking loudly.

Pulling out three of the boxes in front, he reached back through barely perceptible cobwebs until his fingers hit crumbling brick. Moving his hand right, it fell on another box. This one was almost indistinguishable from the others, except that the masking tape label on top was printed in red, instead of the uniform blue on all the others.

Taking the top off, Karns began piling small vials into the dusty gym bag lying at his feet. He picked up the bag, weighing it, and tossed in a few more vials. He zipped it up as he walked back up the stairs.

"Here you go," he said, handing the bag to Tek, who'd just jumped up from his seat, startled by Karn's abrupt reappearance. Tek unzipped it and looked inside. His suspicious expression changed to one of approval.

Tek handed him the wad of bills and zipped up the bag. Karns decided to hedge a bit. It seemed safe to assume that Tek would rush off to his customers, supply them, and then retreat to his house to sample the product. There was no way to be sure, though. "I gave you a deal, 'cause I haven't tried that stuff yet. I'm working with a new supplier."

Tek looked up from the bag.

"It should be at least as good as what I had before—you let me know what you think."

Tek hefted the bag to his shoulder, but made no move for the door. Karns faced him silently. Tek looked like he was about to say something.

Karns knew exactly what was going on. Washington, D.C., hadn't been hit with poisoned narcotics as hard as some might have expected—or indeed, many apparently had hoped. Death was still there, though. It flooded their living rooms twenty hours a day, in full color and stereo sound.

He would have never pegged the blacks in the neighborhood's reaction to the poisoning. The popular theory on the street, and in the minds of the more conspiracy-minded black leaders, was that this whole thing was the white government's doing. That it was a plot to wipe out black Americans. The rational reaction, then, would have been to stop using, and to foil the government's plot. Just the opposite had happened. The false bravado that had so often been the undoing of young urban blacks had twisted their logic. They thought that to stop using coke was to admit fear and defeat to the white hierarchy that they had grown to hate. As far as he could tell, the use of cocaine hadn't slowed in Southeast D.C.'s black community. In fact, he knew of at least one gang that had made a group of its inductees smoke crack that they alleged was poisoned. It hadn't been, as it turned out, but they hadn't known for sure.

"What—you worried that it might be mickey?" Karns said, using the slang term that had become popular for poisoned product. Tek's reaction was predictable.

"Hey, fuck you. I ain't afraid of none of that shit." He reached for the door and backed out, keeping his eyes on Karns, who stood motionless, arms crossed.

He watched as Tek joined his friend and half walked, half jogged up the street. They swatted and slapped at each other playfully, oblivious to the driving wind. Karns marveled at how alive they looked. An image of their corpses lying face down on a dirty carpet next to a smoking crack pipe superimposed itself in his mind, and made him smile.

"You sure were in there long enough," 'Twan said haltingly. All this running was getting him out of breath. "You sucking on his dick?" A devious smile.

"Fuck you," Tek replied with mock severity, barely missing his friend's head with a vicious open-handed slap.

As they ran, the bag bounced along under Tek's shoulder. The vials within made a seductive rattling sound.

"Let's stop off at my place and do a little smoke," 'Twan suggested. He had run through his supply two days earlier, and the embargo by Tek's competitors was wearing him down.

"No way—business first." They slowed to a walk. 'Twan was holding his side uncomfortably.

Their first stop was a three-story brick apartment complex, sitting like a large brick box amidst the curving architecture of the rest of the neighborhood. In the mid-seventies, the brightly painted building had been a flagship of urban renewal. The mayor himself had stood barefoot in the grass and cut a wide ceremonial ribbon. He had spoken briefly of a new day for the city's underprivileged, before rushing off to more pressing matters.

The colors had faded over the years, falling victim to pollution and neglect. Hope had faded with them. In the early eighties, a young girl had managed to work her way through the metal guard rails protecting the building's open-air hallways. Her life, like her body, had been abruptly halted by the asphalt below.

Following that incident, the city had covered the entire front of the building with chain-link fencing. People had joked that the cops weren't satisfied with putting the residents in jail, they wanted to imprison the building too. In the end it had just added to the despair that quietly engulfed the neighborhood.

The two young men walked quickly through the asphalt-covered playground spread out in front of the building.

Two heavy wood doors protected the main entrance to the apartment building. One had a weblike crack emanating from its top hinge, keeping it from closing all the way. Tek pulled it open.

The air inside wasn't much different from the outside because of the broken door. As they climbed the stairwell, though, the atmosphere grew heavier. The sounds of civilization replaced the whistle of wind through the buildings. A baby's cry, a shout, a television turned up loud enough for an old lady to hear.

The numbers had long since been torn from the doors of the

individual apartments—an obvious target for budding vandals. Tek knew the building well enough to make his rounds in the dark. It was a prerequisite for his job—lightbulbs were an easy target too.

He rapped authoritatively at his first customer's door. 'Twan was a few feet behind him, looking back down the gloomy stairwell. His right hand rested casually under his sweatshirt.

Mark Beamon leaned back and listened for the cigarette lighter to pop. The street outside his window seemed unusually silent and dark by inner-city standards. He scanned the gray-and-black landscape as if it were an old photograph. The only movement was his faded reflection in the windshield.

God damn Tom Sherman, he thought, tapping the cigarette lighter as though it would speed the heating process. Right now he should have been half-sauced, sitting in front of the TV at his borrowed Capitol Hill town house. Instead, he was here. In the middle of D.C.'s no-man's land, hiding in his car.

A comforting popping sound came from the dashboard, promising a quick nicotine fix. As he raised the lighter to his mouth, the red glow lit his face slightly, momentarily stealing his anonymity. The smoke was barely visible as it twisted through the confines of the car, obliterating its new smell. He concentrated on it anyway, blocking out the dim scene outside of his steel-and-glass cocoon and feeling the nicotine flow through him.

Reports of a serious poisoning incident, the epicenter of which was only a few miles from the J. Edgar Hoover Building, had come flooding into the switchboard less than an hour ago. Sherman had stormed into SIOC only a few moments later.

Beamon had argued vehemently. He had insisted that he was buried with paperwork and subtly implied that there were important leads that he needed to follow up on. In the end it had all been a waste of time. Sherman had listened sympathetically, as he always did. Then he had told Beamon in no uncertain terms to get his ass to the housing project that had been hit. It wouldn't look good for no one from the Bureau to show up when this kind of thing happened in their backyard.

The cigarette had burned down almost to his fingers. Beamon took one last hard drag and tossed the butt out a narrow crack in the driver's side window. A quick turn of the key brought the car to life. He swung it out onto the narrow road.

Turning the corner was like jumping off a cliff. The quiet monotony of the side street gave way to a kaleidoscope of lights and activity. As he drew slowly closer, he could see that yellow-and-black striped barriers blocked the streets leading to an ugly box of a building. Crowds of people milled around the perimeter, many wearing robes pulled hastily over pajamas. The flashing blue and red of the police cars and fire trucks was drowned out by large spotlights—the kind used to advertised circuses and auto dealership sales. They had been set up on an asphalt playground in front of the apartments. They were aimed at the top of the building, and the glare lit the area sufficiently for rescue workers to rush from victim to victim, without the risk of tripping.

The lights gave the building a malevolent feel. The chain-link fence covering its facade became teeth, and the reflective windows, lifeless eyes.

Beamon's car pushed forward. People milled lazily in the streets, knots of conversation formed and dispersed at random. They looked mildly annoyed as they moved unhurriedly from the path of his car. About fifty feet from the barricades, the crowd of haphazardly dressed spectators became too dense to drive through. Beamon pulled the car over onto the sidewalk and continued on foot. He was carefully examined as he proceeded to the barricades.

"I'm sorry, sir. There's no admittance to this area," a haggard-looking cop said. He was moving back and forth in the ten-foot gap in the barricades that allowed emergency vehicles to get in and out. The crowd carefully tested his defenses, anxious to get a closer look.

Beamon reached into his jacket, producing his credentials. When the officer's pacing brought him back, he flashed them inconspicuously. The cop waved him through.

The crowd was even worse inside the barricades. Same number

of people, but instead of milling around in bathrobes, they were moving at a speed between a jog and a sprint, and carrying all kinds of gear. Children—newly orphaned—were herded like sheep toward the fire trucks.

He walked less than purposefully through the rescue workers, feeling stupider and stupider. There was nothing for him to do here except be seen. Out of the corner of his eye he saw another, more energetic, group of people than the one he had just driven through. Three more cops looked like they were barely holding the line. The Press.

Beamon altered his trajectory slightly, taking a path to the building that would get him within fifteen feet of the rabid reporters. That should make Sherman happy.

He was still almost thirty feet out when one of the reporters recognized him and shouted a question, slapping at his cameraman. The others jumped on the bandwagon and the question became an unintelligible roar.

Close enough.

He aimed his best "no comment" wave in their general direction and resumed slowly walking toward the apartment building. He felt alone and detached.

Ahead of him he saw a reporter who had managed to get through the barricades. He was interviewing a child of no more than twelve, holding her arm tightly. Probably asking her how she felt about her parents being dead. Beamon considered helping the kid out, but thought better of it. This wasn't his show.

The scene grew considerably more gruesome as he drew closer. Rushing rescue workers were replaced with grotesquely contorted victims. Directly in front of him was a man lying on a white stretcher. He was wearing only a pair of heart-covered boxer shorts. His face looked lined and old at first, but as Beamon drew closer, he realized that it was only the effect of the harsh spotlights. The man's body was smooth and well muscled.

What was remarkable, and what cemented Beamon's feet to the ground, was what was happening to the man. He had been lying relatively quietly a moment before. Then, without warning, his back began to arch.

Beamon didn't pay much attention at first, anxious to make his obligatory turn through the building and then head back home. But the quiet figure started to scream. His back continued to arch, soon coming fully off the ground. His only points of contact now were his head and heels, which were bunching up the white sheet under him as his stomach continued to rise skyward.

Just when he reached a point where Beamon was sure that he could crawl under him, the man flopped over onto the pavement. His screams died for lack of air, though his mouth still worked silently. The progression continued. Beamon had been awakened from his trance when the man had tipped, but he had no idea what to do. As the man's head and heels continued to close on one another, Beamon's body tensed. He waited to hear the inevitable crack of bone as the man's vertebrae shattered.

It didn't happen. The progression slowed, then finally reversed itself. The man's fluttering eyelids closed as he slipped into unconsciousness.

The show over, Beamon reached out and grabbed a paramedic unfortunate enough to be within his reach. "What the fuck's going on here?" He knew the symptoms of the drug poisonings backwards and forwards. He had never heard of anything like this.

The young paramedic looked at him blankly and pulled away. He was about to rush off, when the unmistakable look of recognition registered on his face. Over the last couple of weeks, Beamon had unwittingly become the most photographed man in America.

"Looks like a different poison," he said simply.

"What kind?"

He shrugged. "Dunno. Heard somebody say strychnine—but I don't know that much about poison, you know?"

Beamon watched him hurry away, then turned and continued toward the building. Looking up, he saw that the windows had been either opened or broken out. The malevolent eyes had turned into empty sockets.

At the bottom of the steps someone caught his arm. A fireman. He looked like he was in charge.

"Mr. Beamon? I'm Shannon Calloway." He extended his hand. "Sorry to hear about your nephew."

"Call me Mark, and thanks." Beamon reached out to take the fireman's hand.

"You can't go in there without one of these." Calloway thumbed at the tank on his back. A hose attached it to a full face mask pushed up onto the top of his head.

"Is there a fire?" Beamon looked for signs of smoke.

"Oh, no—no fire. It looks like the poison was in crack cocaine. There were quite a few smoking pipes lying around. Don't want to take any chances."

Beamon backed away from the building as a burly-looking fireman ran down the stairs with another victim. There was no way in hell he was putting on a respirator and running around this brick graveyard just to please the press.

"I can get you a . . ." Calloway started. A man standing on the steps shouted at him, interrupting his train of thought.

"We're clear in here, Shannon—fully ventilated." The man jogged down the steps, pulling the heavy tank off his back with practiced ease.

"I stand corrected," Calloway said, holding his hand out toward the dark opening where the front doors had once been. "Be my guest."

It took a few moments for Beamon's eyes to adjust to the gloom of the hallway. The shouts of rescue workers and the crash of ax on door echoed through the building. He paused at the base of the steps and forced himself to take a deep breath. He had been holding it since he passed through the shattered doorjamb that was the front entrance to the building. The image of the dying contortionist seemed to superimpose itself on everything he saw.

Feeling a little more collected, he started up the stairs, idly trying to decipher the stylized graffiti adorning the walls. He was on the first landing when the shout "coming through" bounced off the walls, followed by heavy footsteps. Between two firemen was a stretcher with a heavy-looking man strapped firmly to it. The fireman on the low side had to hold the stretcher almost above his head to keep it level. Under normal circumstances, he looked more than up to the task. These weren't normal circumstances. The man on the stretcher was convulsing violently, straining against the heavy straps holding him in place. The motion was throwing the two back and forth, slamming them into the sides of the narrow staircase. Beamon flattened himself against a wall, but it was too late. The hard edge of the stretcher, backed by the full weight of the three men, slammed into his chest. They didn't seem to notice, or at least didn't acknowledge the collision. Beamon stood on the steps, slightly stooped for a moment, catching his breath. When the pain in his chest subsided to a dull throb, he continued up.

He reached the first-floor landing and began walking slowly down an interior hallway. It reminded him of a house of horrors at a cheap traveling carnival. As he walked past open doors, it seemed that the scenes behind them were being acted out for his benefit. Corpses, people in the throes of violent convulsions, crying children. Above them all hovered busy men and women in various uniforms identifying them as fire fighter, paramedic, ambulance driver, police.

Beamon felt the weight of the situation come crashing down on him. The feeling came on suddenly, adding to the pain in his chest. He came upon a closed door—the first he had seen. A large red X had been spray painted on it. Somehow the mark didn't blend with the graffiti blanketing the dank walls, and Beamon reached out and touched it. Still wet.

Two more firemen appeared from a door at the end of the hall and began rushing toward him. Beamon could see something squirming under the clean white sheet covering the stretcher between them. He pushed mightily on the door in front of him. It opened with the sound of cracking wood. He made it through just as they passed and slammed the door behind him.

Shouts could still be heard through the thin walls, and through the open window to his right, but he was grateful for the calm motionlessness of the room.

The only light was provided by the spotlights on the asphalt below, creating a rectangular beam that cut through the room. He could see dust floating lazily in the light, but the more tangible occupants of the room were obscured in shadow. They came slowly into focus.

The room was only about twenty feet square. At the far end was an open kitchen. Dishes were piled high in the sink and on the counters. In the center of a chrome and Formica table sat a box of breakfast cereal and a bowl. The living room consisted of a sofa and a couple of old chairs arranged around a high-tech–looking TV.

On the floor behind the sofa lay a woman in a floral patterned dress. She was on her side, her back arched unnaturally. Beamon walked quietly across the room and stood over the body. Her eyes stared up at him.

Next to the woman was a clear plastic crack pipe. It was lying in a puddle of water that was undoubtedly the work of the firemen who had been trying to clear the poisonous fumes from the building. Beamon looked back at the woman. Something in her expression had become accusing. He walked to the kitchen and began rifling through the drawers. It was hard to make out their contents in the semidarkness, but he didn't want to turn on the lights. The woman on the floor belonged in the dark.

Finally finding what he was looking for—a pair of scissors, he went to the table and sat, pushing the half-full bowl of Lucky Charms off to the side. He pulled a cigarette from his pocket and cut the filter off, lighting it with a cheap plastic lighter. The smoke attacked his lungs, giving him another much-needed rush of nicotine.

He had been working well with the casualty numbers that Laura put on his desk every morning. Numbers agreed with him. They could be added, subtracted, and multiplied, but they couldn't bleed or cry out in pain. Even the television reports, while certainly more graphic than Laura's charts and graphs, were only pictures. Little pixels scanned across an electronic screen at the speed of thought.

He took another drag on his modified cigarette, feeling the eyes of the woman on his back.

The ambiguities of the CDFS's actions, and their long-term effects, had disappeared from his mind. They were killing people. Real people. The obvious conclusions about lives saved in the future by lower levels of drug use, and the other coldly logical arguments for the CDFS's actions, seemed ludicrous as he looked down on the woman's frozen form.

The front door to the apartment began to open, and Beamon waved in its general direction. "FBI. It's all clear in here."

"Mark?"

"Laura?"

She moved through the door and closed it quietly behind her. Through the shadows he could just make out her slim figure and perpetually tied-back hair, as she walked across the room and sat down next to him. "Tom told me you were here." She reach out for his hand. "Are you okay?"

He remained silent and took another deep drag on his cigarette.

"I thought you didn't take cases personally." She looked around the room. "This is just noise to you. Isn't that what you told me?"

Beamon pointed to the woman lying on the floor. "They don't sound like noise this close up."

Laura walked over to the woman, took a quilt off the sofa, and covered the body with it. She looked down at the lump under the blanket for a moment and then took a seat in the chair directly in front of Beamon.

"You know, Laura, I took this case just to feed my ego. Calahan burned me, so I came back to show him and the world just how smart I am. Thousands of people are dead, and I was just playing a game."

"Come on, Mark. You had no idea that this case was going to blow up like it has. No one did." She plucked the cigarette from his mouth and tossed it in the sink. "You know, they put the filters on these things for a reason."

"Yeah, I know."

*   *   *

"You sure you want to do this, Tony? It makes me nervous having you this close to a buy."

Anthony DiPrizzio, head of the DiPrizzio crime family, nodded and calmly straightened his tie. He didn't like to be this close, either, but times were changing, and he needed to be there. This was no time for the hands-off management style professed by his favorite instructor at Wharton. It was time to get personally involved.

It was eleven-thirty P.M., and DiPrizzio was sitting in the small office on the second floor of one of his many New York waterfront warehouses. Across from him was Chris Panetti, an old and trusted enforcer who had worked for his father before Tony had taken over the helm. At the other end of the room sat three more men, each with a shoulder holster wrapped around his thick torso. He knew all of them too. All were men who had been with the Family for years. They were transfixed by a football game playing on a tiny black-and-white television. DiPrizzio watched the game from his side of the office with mild interest. He had never understood the appeal.

The unmistakable rolling sound of the warehouse's cargo doors going up floated up to the office. The men watching the game stood and turned off the television. Panetti stood too, touching the holster under his arm. "I don't suppose I can convince you to watch from up here, eh, Tony?"

DiPrizzio shook his head as he listened to the sound of the door going down again. "Let's go."

"Juan! It's good to see you."

The man standing in front of the rusting ice cream truck parked in the middle of the warehouse looked confused and a bit worried. He stood flanked by two of his own men, who were wearing the same surprised looks on their faces.

"Mr. DiPrizzio. What are you doing here?"

DiPrizzio stopped a few feet in front of the three, careful not to let his eyes wander to the men who were quietly positioning themselves around the truck. "Oh, you know how it is, Juan. Every once in a while they let me out of the office."

Juan's expression didn't change, and he stayed rooted to the floor.

"Why don't you show me what you've got?" DiPrizzio asked.

"Sure, Mr. DiPrizzio, sure."

Juan and his companions walked to the side door of the truck and opened it, producing a wooden crate that looked something like an old army footlocker. They carried it with some difficulty to the front of the truck.

Juan took a key from around his neck and unlocked the box. He opened it, revealing that it was completely filled with one-kilo bricks of cocaine, each individually wrapped in plastic and duct tape.

DiPrizzio bent over the box. He reached out a gloved hand and grabbed a brick, closed the trunk, and placed it on top.

"Chris?"

Panetti leaned over and handed him a pocket knife, which he used to put a small slit in the top of the package.

Juan smiled. "It's top quality stuff, Mr. DiPrizzio, you got my word on that."

DiPrizzio continued to stare at the brick, focusing on the white powder oozing out of it. "I appreciate that, Juan, but I'll tell you what would make me feel even better."

Juan was starting to look nervous again, as were his companions. They were surrounded by no less than twenty of DiPrizzio's men.

"Sure, Mr. DiPrizzio. Anything you need," Juan said.

"Why don't you just try a little." He pointed to the brick.

A look of horror flashed across the young Hispanic's face and then disappeared.

"I'd like to, Mr. DiPrizzio, but you know, I gave it up. It was fucking with me." He pinched the bridge of his nose and winced to illustrate the point.

"Do it for me, Juan. Just this one time."

Juan and his two companions began slowly backing away.

DiPrizzio's easy smile disappeared. "I insist." The last syllable of the word "insist" was drowned out by the clatter of rounds being chambered.

The three men looked around them. DiPrizzio's enforcers, who had been standing so casually a moment before, now each had a gun trained on them.

"This stuff's good, Mr. DiPrizzio. I swear. I wouldn't try to sell you no product that was mickey."

"I know you wouldn't, Juan. This is just for my peace of mind." He nudged the open bag toward him. Juan looked around. He seemed uncertain about what to do for a moment. His companions were frozen.

Finally he walked up to the brick and dug a tiny amount of coke from the slit with his finger.

"No, no, don't be bashful. Get some on there," DiPrizzio said.

Juan reached back down, pulling out some more of the powder. He brought his hand to his nose and inhaled deeply.

"Get it all . . . good."

DiPrizzio put his arm around the quivering man. "Thanks Juan. I'll be able to sleep well tonight."

Juan didn't reply, he just wiped hard at his nose.

DiPrizzio turned and headed toward the office. "We'll hold on to this stuff for a while, Juan. I want you to come back here at the same time in two weeks. I'll have the money for you then. Don't send a messenger. I'll only give it to you."

One of Juan's companion's spoke up for the first time. "Hey! We delivered. We don't work on credit."

DiPrizzio stopped and turned around. "There's been a change in the way we do business. Is there a problem with that?"

The man looked around him and down the barrels of the guns trained on him. He grabbed Juan, who was still standing next to the footlocker looking dazed, and pushed him toward the truck.

20

Baltimore, Maryland,
February 19

Robert Swenson burst through the apartment door without knocking. "You watching this?"

Hobart sat silently on the sofa, fixated on the television. The muscles in his jaw rippled as he slowly ground his teeth back and forth.

Swenson took an indirect route across the room—keeping himself from getting between Hobart and the television. He sat in a chair to the right of the sofa and turned his attention to the screen.

CNN was replaying the events of last night. Mark Beamon's sad face was supernaturally pale as he walked by the cameras. He looked like the eye of the storm as he strode slowly toward a large brick building in the background. The camera pulled back and panned right, focusing on the victims splayed out across an asphalt playground. Swenson ignored the voice-over, focusing on the eerie scene captured on the screen.

Finally the images faded, replaced by a well-dressed anchorwoman. Hobart punched the Mute button on the remote in disgust. For a moment neither of the men spoke.

"What the hell happened?"

"Karns," Hobart answered simply.

"You gave him the okay for this?"

"Fuck, no. Piece of shit did it himself. I knew he was a loose cannon—but I sure as hell didn't think he'd go off and do something like this." Hobart was rubbing his temples now. "Shit, shit, shit," he whispered. Finally he raised his head and looked squarely at his partner.

"We've gotta pull him out. The FBI'll trace that stuff back to him eventually."

With operations like the one that Karns had set up, it was a one-shot deal. Then you pulled up stakes and set up somewhere else. Unfortunately, this wasn't the one shot that he hadn't planned on.

Swenson arched his back slightly, imitating what they had just seen on the television. "What was the deal with those reactions?"

Hobart shook his head miserably. "You know how we figured we'd use cyanide-based rat poison on the downstream stuff—save what's left of the orellanin for big hits?" Swenson nodded.

"Well, it looks like that stupid son of a bitch used the wrong thing. I did a little reading on my own when I was researching this operation. That," he pointed at the now soundless television, "was strychnine poisoning."

"Should be good for our image," Swenson said sarcastically. They had been enjoying the positive public reaction to their activities. The heart-wrenching suffering of the people on the playground was bound to turn people away from their cause.

Hobart grunted and began dialing Bill Karns's number on the small cellular that was resting on the sofa next to him.

Luis Colombar wasn't known for his punctuality. Reed Corey had been waiting for almost fifteen minutes. He began playing nervously with his hair, twisting it back and forth and pulling until it hurt. He pulled harder, using the pain in his scalp to clear his head and to try to return to a mindset he hadn't had in years. The man who had fought bravely in Vietnam seemed to slip further away every year, the memory obscured by drugs and liquor and time.

Corey felt only fear and anticipation, sitting in the expansive living room. The guilt that he expected to wash over him never came.

John Hobart had cold eyes—like a shark in a National Geographic special. They were less windows to his soul than cameras taking in everything around him. Despite this, Corey had come to know his old friend better than anyone. And looking into his eyes the last time they had met, Corey knew that Hobart intended to kill him.

He had made the right decision, leaving the house and spending the last few weeks taking a tour of the sofas of Bogota. He had first heard of Colombar's offer three days ago in a run-down bar not far from where he and Hobart had met. He had been in unfamiliar territory and unsure whether or not to believe the people he was sitting with. The next day he confirmed the story. Luis Colombar had put up a two hundred and fifty thousand dollar reward for information leading to the capture of the person or persons inquiring about certain aspects of his cocaine refining activities.

The memory of his first meeting with Hobart was a bit clouded, but his questions regarding refinery locations and chemical suppliers stood out in Corey's mind. He wasn't sure what this was all about, but he suspected that Hobart was the man Colombar was looking for.

Though he had been expecting them, he was startled by the footsteps coming up behind him. He turned quickly to face the sound, pulling his hand quickly away from his hair and wiping it absently on his dirty trousers. Two men appeared at the far end of the room and walked down the wide steps. Both were impeccably dressed, but the younger one was much more formal. He walked silently behind the older man in a calculated expression of his subordinate status. The older man walked around Corey, not looking at him. The younger one moved toward him.

"Mr. Corey, my name is Alejandro." He didn't offer his hand.

"Hello," Corey stammered. The act of speaking dislodged the sweat that had been collecting on his upper lip, sending a few small drops into his mouth. They tasted salty.

"We appreciate you coming here so quickly. You have information for us?" His smile was warm and calm.

"Uh, yes, sir." Corey hadn't heard the other man coming up behind him but he knew he was there from the gentle tinkling of ice in a glass. Alejandro raised his eyebrows, signaling that he wanted Corey to continue.

"Um, a couple of months ago, a guy that I fought in 'Nam with came to town. Hadn't seen him in years. Anyway, he and I met in a bar and did a little drinking and he starts asking questions about drugs and stuff. I knew he used to be DEA but got kicked out, so I'm thinking he's just interested in talking about the old times. So we talked for a while about coke in general. You know, how big a business it's gettin' to be. That type of stuff." Corey paused and patted his forehead with his sleeve.

"Can I get you something cold?" Alejandro asked. His smile was still warm but there was something in his eyes that told Corey it was a rhetorical question.

"Uh, no thanks." The hairs on the back of his neck stood up at the sound of tinkling ice as the man behind him, who he assumed was Colombar, took another drink.

"So we're gettin' pretty drunk, and we do a little blow, and he starts asking some pretty specific questions."

"What kind of questions?"

"Well, he starts asking about where stuff is getting refined exactly. This is what I thought was weird—he asked about the chemicals that go into making coke and where you get 'em. Like he was kinda specific about that. He wanted to know names of companies that distribute stuff like kerosene."

Something flashed across his inquisitor's face at the word "kerosene" but Corey wasn't sure what it was.

"And you told him?"

"Hey, no way, man," Corey replied too loudly. His voice echoed off the walls.

"You know, he and I are old buds and I didn't mind talking with him about the general state of things, you know, but I didn't want to get into talking about any specifics. I know when to keep my mouth shut, you know."

Alejandro nodded. "I'm sure you do. Please go on."

"So, anyway, I pretty much told him that, you know, I wasn't gonna tell him anything like that. Lot of the stuff I didn't know, anyway. He got pretty pissed off and, you know, just kinda blew outta the bar. Didn't see him again, but I heard he was around for a while longer, you know, a couple of weeks or something."

More jingling ice.

"Now, who might this old friend of yours be?"

Corey was silent as he looked around the room and then finally back into Alejandro's eyes.

"Don't worry, my friend, we'll get you the money. I think you know we are good for it." His hand waved about the room, putting forth the lavish surroundings as proof of their wealth. "I hope you understand, though, we don't keep two hundred and fifty thousand dollars in cash lying around. We can either have it delivered to you in cash or deposit it into a bank account. Of course, we want to check your story out first."

Corey let this sink in, finally deciding that it seemed reasonable. He mopped his brow again.

"His name's John Hobart."

Alejandro pulled an expensive gold pen out of his breast pocket. He wrote down the name.

"And where might we find this Mr. Hobart?"

Corey was silent for a moment. As sure as the sun rose tomorrow, he knew that Hobart had intended to kill him before he left Colombia. Despite that, an inexplicable twinge of guilt grabbed him in the stomach. Memories of their time together flashed jungle-green across his mind. There was no going back now, though. Besides, he wasn't so sure that his old commander wouldn't come out on top in the end, anyway. Son of a bitch could probably teach Colombar a thing or two about cold-blooded killing.

"Last I heard, he was in Baltimore, Maryland, working for some TV evangelist. Blake, I think, is his name. Hell, he's probably in the phone book."

Alejandro smiled and scribbled into his notebook. He looked up and past Corey, nodding conspiratorially. Corey stiffened. He tried to see the man behind him through sheer force of will.

Instead of a knife in his back, he got a grateful smile. "We appreciate your help on this. I hope you understand, we don't want anyone knowing about our conversation or about the information you've given us. I assume that you haven't told anybody?" Corey shook his head.

"Well, as I said, we want to check out your story. I assume that we can contact you at the same number?" Corey nodded.

The butler appeared like magic at the far end of the room. Alejandro stepped aside and motioned toward him. Corey mumbled a good-bye and headed for the door. His gait was unnatural. His entire being was focused on his back, still expecting to be attacked.

He felt a great sense of relief as he passed through the front door and into the hard Colombian sun. He decided that he had made the right decision. Two hundred and fifty thousand easy dollars. And Alejandro didn't seem like such a bad guy.

"Well, what do you think?" Colombar took another sip of his drink.

"It's our man, it must be. Did you notice that he mentioned the kerosene by name, and this guy's ex-DEA. It fits too perfectly."

Colombar walked over to one of the thick sofas and sat down, putting his feet on the table in front of him. Alejandro Perez followed, perching himself on the arm of the opposing sofa.

"And the others?" Colombar asked. Corey was the fourth man to try to claim the reward.

"I think we should start with this one. It seems to be the most promising."

"I agree," Colombar said finally. "Send some guys out to find this John Hobart, and bring him back to me."

"I don't think we should do that, Luis. Kidnapping American citizens and transporting them across the border can be . . . complicated. Actually, I would suggest simply notifying the FBI. They'll find him in short order, and things will quickly return to normal."

Colombar bared his teeth. "I don't want this motherfucker to get caught—I want him dead! Since when do we work with the fucking FBI, Alejandro? Since when?"

"We don't, Luis. I only thought that in this situation . . ."

"In this situation you're going to do what I say—just like always."

Perez took a deep breath to calm himself. He wasn't going to win this battle. He took another approach. "Perhaps you're right, Luis. Better to get this over with quickly. Let me send Renaldo to Maryland. He can take care of the problem there. No need for you to get directly involved."

Colombar thought for a moment. "Okay, do it." He stood and started for the bar at the opposite end of the room. "That piece of shit was lying to us about not helping this guy. Little fucker'd do anything for an ounce of blow and fifty bucks. No, he gave him the information all right. Son of a bitch has cost me twenty million dollars! Call whoever's driving him back to town and tell him to dump that fucker's body by the road somewhere."

Perez had already enjoyed one minor victory in the conversation. Two was going to be pushing his luck. "I don't think we should do that, Luis."

Colombar turned away from his ice bucket and stared at him, dumbfounded.

"You're telling me that I can't kill some cockroach street addict that cost us God knows how many millions?"

"We asked for information out on the street and offered a reward. I'm concerned that if it gets out that we killed the man who brought it to us, no matter how justified, we may have a hard time collecting intelligence in the future."

Colombar slammed his drink down on the table, spilling most of it. "This isn't open for discussion. Kill him."

21

New York City,
February 23

Anthony DiPrizzio put his finger to his lips and motioned to the television, prompting his consigliere to move quietly to the sofa next to his desk. DiPrizzio leaned back in his chair and turned his attention back to the screen where Jake Crenshaw, America's voice of conservatism, was beginning his show.

The audience was on its feet—most clapping loudly, the others punching the air with balled fists. The occasional loud whistle or catcall mixed into the thunderous applause.

Crenshaw quieted the crowd, using the same gesture as a professional football player in a stadium.

Crenshaw snapped the paper in his hands loudly, signifying that he was about to speak.

"I'm a little depressed today," he told the cameras. "Oh, you probably think you know why. You think it's because I had to sit through three hours of Democratic drivel last night—geez, and I thought *I* liked to hear myself talk."

The audience giggled.

"But that's not it, ladies and gentlemen. Why am I depressed? It's because tonight's the last night of college week." He indicated to the cameraman to pan across the crowd full of young people, most advertising their respective universities in bold letters across their chests.

"As you probably know, we've flown in youngsters from different universities to sit in the audience every day this week." He turned to his producer. "Who do we have today?"

"Princeton and Yale," came the unmiked voice.

"Princeton and Yale . . . a couple of fine community colleges," Crenshaw boomed.

The audience laughed again.

He turned and struck a pose reminiscent of the Heisman Trophy. The crowd cheered in anticipation. He walked over to a large easel near his desk and flipped back the sheet covering it. On it was a vertical red bar with numbers going up one side in increments of one thousand.

He took a red indelible marker from the tray on the front of the easel and made a show of reading from the paper in his right hand.

"Says here that the death toll's reached twenty-four thousand five hundred." He drew a corresponding square on top of the red bar and colored it in.

He turned back to the audience. "It also says things are tapering off. You think these people are finally wising up?" An uncertain grumble came from the crowd. "No? Me neither."

Crenshaw walked to the end of the stage, still holding the marker. "Y'know, I'm getting a lot of garbage for our little chart. You wouldn't believe the mail I get." He affected a whining voice. "How can you condone murder, Jake? How can you condone the killing of the people in society that need our help most?" He grimaced. "Ladies and gentlemen I want to be perfectly clear on this point. I DO NOT condone murder . . . but this just ain't murder."

The crowd cheered again—more fists in the air. This time he let them go, pacing the stage. "Look, the CDFS gave the druggies plenty of warning. Geez, the liberal press had this story plastered across every TV and newspaper in the country. Look at this . . ." A newspaper article popped up on the screen. The headline was "Vigilante Group Threatens to Poison U.S. Narcotics."

"This was clipped from a local newspaper from a town of less than two thousand people in South Dakota—not exactly a hotbed of narcotics trafficking. My point is this: Everyone knew what was going to happen. It's like putting a gun in front of somebody and then warning them over and over that it's loaded. If they shoot themselves, is it murder?"

The crowd was on its feet.

"And now Jameson gets on the TV and says that this is a crisis that compares to WW II." Crenshaw looked straight into the camera. "I'll tell you what the crisis is, Danny Boy, it's that you liberal Democrats let these druggies take over our cities in the first place." He jogged back to his desk and picked up a copy of *Newsweek*.

"I guess the White House doesn't actually subscribe to this, but it has an interesting statistic this week." He flipped through the magazine, stopping at a page marked with a paper clip. He held it up.

"I don't know if the cameras can pull in on this . . ." The camera closed in on the article.

"If you can't read this, it says that forty percent of the U.S. public is behind what the CDFS is doing and that fourteen percent are undecided. If you were to read further in the article you'd find that it says that the undecideds are moving to pro-CDFS positions, and that quite a few of the people who were arguing against what they're doing are changing their minds."

Crenshaw turned and nodded almost imperceptibly. "Looks like it's time for a break." He mopped his brow with a pudgy hand. "It'll give me some time to cool off."

The television screen faded into a pizza commercial as Anthony DiPrizzio pulled himself upright and hit the Mute button on the remote in front of him. "It would seem that the tide of public opinion continues to turn, eh, Randy?"

"And that ain't the worst of it," Randall Matlin said, tossing a manila folder onto DiPrizzio's desk.

DiPrizzio slid the folder toward him and began flipping through the pages it contained. "The numbers are worse than we thought."

"Yeah, I didn't expect demand to drop off as fast as it did. It was like someone turned off a fucking spigot. It's killing our cash flow, Tony."

DiPrizzio chewed idly on his lip, considering the problem. The CDFS was having more of an impact than he had expected. But he hoped to avoid restructuring the organization based on what he assumed would be a short-term problem.

"Do we have enough cash to get us through the month, Randy?"

"Yeah, but we're gonna have to pull from the offshore accounts. And it's gonna cost us to carry all this inventory. We probably should have refused delivery on that last shipment."

DiPrizzio nodded. "We only pay for it if it's good, though. Go ahead and bring in some cash. I don't want to do anything drastic until we see what's gonna shake out."

Matlin looked worried. "What if it takes a while for the Feds to catch these assholes, Tony? Hell, what if they aren't even looking that hard? Our cash reserves are gonna run out sooner or later."

DiPrizzio smiled. His counselor knew the streets better than anyone, and he was insanely loyal. But he was old school.

Matlin had been his father's counselor and had been a part of DiPrizzio's life since he was a small child. It had been Matlin who recognized young Tony's intelligence and convinced the old don to send him to Wharton for an MBA, and later to put him in charge of the Family's growing concerns.

"Times change, Randy. This could turn out to be a hell of an opportunity for us."

Matlin dug around in his pocket for a cigarette, but didn't find one. "You're a miracle worker, Tony, I'll admit that, but I sure don't know how the hell you're gonna turn this into an opportunity."

DiPrizzio stood and walked to the opposite end of the room, opening a small hutch and pouring himself a cup of coffee. He dropped in a couple of sugars and started back for his desk. "We've got it too good now, Randy. The Colombians take on the risk getting the stuff here, then we buy it, cut it, and sell it for one hell of a profit margin. Demand is unlimited, and our customers depend on us. The cops make trouble every once in a while, but that risk is built into the price. It's the perfect business."

Matlin nodded his agreement. He had a nostalgic look on his face, as though he thought that those days were gone forever.

"Think about IBM," DiPrizzio continued. "They'd been making business machines forever—stuff like typewriters and cash registers. But then computers come along. That could have driven them out of business. But it didn't. Why? Because they changed with the times.

"And what about the music industry? Do you think that the record album manufacturers were happy when they found out that albums were going to become obsolete? They had to throw out millions of dollars in manufacturing equipment and buy millions more in replacements. But now they're selling CDs—that are cheaper to produce than records—at twice the price."

"But we're not IBM, Tony."

"Sure we are. What happens if the FBI doesn't ever get these guys, and the floor drops out of our market?"

The look on his counselor's face told him that he didn't have any idea.

"We adapt, Randy. I haven't given it that much thought—'cause I think the Feds'll come through—but off the top of my head, I think we'd start with a vertical integration."

"A what?"

"Vertical integration. Set up a partnership with the Colombians, get more involved in street-level dealing—regulate it. That way we can watch the drugs from coca leaf to when it goes up our customer's nose. Before, all you had to do was be breathing to sell the stuff. That'd be over. We'd differentiate on quality. Our customers would know that the stuff was safe, and they'd easily pay double the price for a little peace of mind. I see us packaging in those tamper-proof bottles—like Tylenol comes in now. The price increase should more than make up for higher expenses and loss in volume."

Matlin laughed and clapped his hands together. "I always said you were a goddam genius, Tony. Now I'm sure of it. Hell, you almost got me hoping that the Feds blow it."

DiPrizzio sipped at his coffee. "Yeah, we'll be okay in the long run—it's the next few months I'm worried about. It's gonna cost us a lot of money to wait around and see what happens."

"What about trying to get these guys ourselves?"

DiPrizzio shook his head. "Don't see how. We're working with the Colombians to help them figure out where the stuff was hit— but whoever's doing this knows we'd do that. No, I think we pretty much leave it to the Feds." He chuckled. "I never thought I'd be counting on the goddam Bureau's efficiency to save my ass."

22

Near Baltimore, Maryland, February 24

The weatherman's promise of a beautiful late winter day had been broken. The Reverend Simon Blake increased the speed of the wipers as the slightly frozen raindrops splattered against his windshield like bugs.

He slowed the car slightly, bringing it back under fifty-five, and glanced nervously in the rearview mirror. His paranoia and depression had been deepening over the last few weeks, and his wife was near panic. The face that looked back at him in the mirror was almost unrecognizable. The twenty pounds he had lost looked great at his waistline, but his face had become gaunt. Combined with the red-rimmed eyes and shadow of a beard, he looked like a completely different person.

He shook his head violently, clearing his eyes of his image, but not the other image. The one that wouldn't leave him alone. The one that God himself had planted. It was hell, he knew now. In it, people writhed in agony on a cracked asphalt playground. Behind them the face of Satan laughed. Others watching the news report had only seen a dilapidated public apartment building. He knew better. It hadn't been God who had sent him down this path, it had been his age-old nemesis.

The Reverend caught a glimpse of a Days Inn in the distance and veered the car onto an off-ramp. He passed by the hotel, circling to the rear. The Mercedes splashed loudly through a large puddle as he entered the parking lot.

He slipped the car into a space between two trucks, thinking it would make his vehicle less conspicuous. Taking a deep breath, he got out and jogged through the rain toward room 115. He exhaled loudly as he stood in front of the door, realizing that he had been holding his breath. Panting slightly from the run, he rapped sharply on the door. A moment later it seemed to open itself. He stepped in. The door slammed shut behind him.

"Nice to see you, Reverend," John Hobart said. His back was pressed against the wall, so he could remain out of sight with door ajar.

"This has to stop, John."

Hobart slipped gracefully around him, and sat at a table next to the door. He picked up a can of Coke and took a long swig. With his free hand he pointed to the seat across from him. Blake took it.

"Did anyone see you come in here?"

Blake shook his head. "The parking lot was empty. It's raining pretty hard."

"Your car?" He knew that Blake drove a rather conspicuous Cadillac with "AMEN" on the plates.

"Erica's."

Hobart set the can down. "This isn't such a good idea, Reverend. For you I mean. You're risking a lot."

"I know, but I had to talk to you." Blake's eyes silently scanned the room, though there wasn't anything to see. Hobart had seen him do this a hundred times. He was rehearsing a speech.

"I saw a news report a few days ago. It looked like the hand of God had reached down and was twisting people's bodies—trying to rip them apart." His eyes had become unfocused. He didn't seem to realize that Hobart was still in the room. It was as if he was talking to himself.

"Let me explain about that, Reverend . . ."

"Twenty thousand people are dead, John. I heard twenty thousand people are dead." His eyes finally came up. "It has to stop, John. Everything stops now."

Hobart pushed the half-empty Coke can around the table with his index finger.

"Little late for that now, isn't it." It was a statement, not a question. Nothing was going to get between him and the success of this operation.

"This ends now," Blake repeated.

Hobart looked up and suppressed a smile. Blake's voice was thin and he looked sick and weak. His attempt to give an order was a joke. Control of the situation had shifted.

"Have you seen the report that CNN started running today?"

Blake shook his head "Did you hear what I said, John? We've got to . . ."

Hobart cut him off. "They quote anonymous sources in the DEA. Casual use of cocaine is down seventy percent—habitual's down thirty-five. Heroin use is down forty percent. Enrollment in drug rehab programs is up nine hundred percent—hell, they got people sleeping on the floors." He took another swig of his Coke and threw the empty can into a wastebasket across the room. The clattering of the can punctuated the Reverend's words.

"Didn't you hear me, John? Twenty thousand people are dead! We've killed twenty thousand people!" Speaking the words out loud seemed to jar Blake fully back into reality. He put his head in his hands.

"Christ, Reverend. There are probably fifty drug-related deaths every day in the U.S. We'll be net ahead in two years." He looked at Blake with what passed for sympathy. "Look, the big stuff's over. People know we're serious. Now all we're going to do is hit a few shipments here and there. Keep people scared. You don't really want to stop now. If we do, all those people would have died for nothing. Drug use would go right back to where it had been before."

Blake nodded and began studying the room again. His entire demeanor had suddenly changed. Behind the pale face, a flicker of his powerful television persona appeared.

"What's this maintenance phase going to entail?"

Hobart relaxed slightly. "Not that much, really. We'll hit a ship-ment every month or so probably. I want to do some manufactured stuff here soon, too. Amphetamines, X—that kind of stuff. You've heard of Anthony DiPrizzio, haven't you?"

Blake nodded. "Some kind of Mafia don in New York."

"Yeah. I've got a man working in one of his warehouses on the waterfront. Word is that there's a good-sized shipment of coke that's going to be passing through there on the twenty-eighth. I've autho-rized my guy to hit it. Then that'll be it for another month or so."

Blake stood and moved for the door. He paused with his hand on the knob. "Where on earth did you find that poison? The papers say it takes two weeks for it to work."

"It wasn't easy. A few hours west of Warsaw."

"Poland?"

"Yeah."

Blake pulled the door open. The clouds had parted, and the sun blinded him for a moment as he walked quickly to his car. Once inside, he took a deep breath and held it for a moment. It shook as it came out. He rested his head against the steering wheel, fighting the urge to vomit. The image of hell came flooding back. Could he ever redeem himself in the eyes of the Lord?

23

Washington, D.C.,
February 25

Mark Beamon pulled his briefcase from the back seat of the car and made a grab for the door handle. "Here is good, Stan," he said to the young agent driving.

"This traffic'll let up just ahead, Mr. Beamon. I'll have you there in less than five minutes," he pleaded.

"Yeah. I'd just like to get some fresh air, you know?"

"Lots of people on the streets this time of morning—somebody's bound to recognize you."

The controversy regarding the effectiveness and morality of the CDFS's actions had reached a fevered pitch in the media, and Mark Beamon was right in the middle of the debate. His face had been plastered across nearly every newspaper, magazine, and TV screen in the country over the past few weeks. In fact, it was rumored that GQ was running an article on him in their next issue and would be giving him two thumbs up on his fashion sense. It appeared that his nine-year-old, too-tight suits were considered "retro."

"Don't worry about it, Stan. Nobody'll recognize me. I'm told that I look much smaller in person." He jumped out of the car, slammed the door, and leaned in through the open window. Horns began to sound behind him. "Call Laura and tell her I'll be a few minutes late. Thanks." He slapped the windowsill and disappeared into the herd of people shuffling off to begin their workday.

Special Agent Stan Paulous frowned deeply. The party line was that Beamon had been provided a car and driver because of his well-known hatred for and lack of skill in maneuvering an automobile. Paulous had later been informed that the real reason was to impose a more predictable schedule on the investigator. His job was, in essence, to keep tabs on Beamon and make sure he was where he was supposed to be, when he was supposed to be there. He dialed the phone slowly, silently composing a report that would deflect the wrath of Laura Vilechi.

Mark Beamon jammed his free hand inside his raincoat and breathed the late winter air deeply into his lungs. It smelled of car exhaust and aftershave.

He had felt too confined lately. House to car to office to house over and over again—no doubt, exactly what Laura had in mind. What she didn't understand was that that kind of rigidity eventually imposed itself on his mind. His thoughts became confined, commonplace. Beamon's haphazard lifestyle was designed to keep the hemispheres of his brain slightly off center. Just where they should be for artists, and investigators.

Beamon took a right, escaping the thick crowd, and headed directly away from the JEH Building. He would treat himself to a quick trip around the block.

Halfway around, he ducked into a small convenience store.

"Pack of Marlboros in a box, please," he said, reaching into his back pocket and pulling out a tattered wallet.

The old man behind the counter eyed him curiously as he reached under the counter for the cigarettes. He placed them on the counter and punched the price into an ornate old cash register. One eighty popped up in the register's window on what looked like miniature tombstones.

Beamon handed him a five and watched the man's expression as he counted out the change. He could see that the clerk was desperately trying to make a connection. The face in front of him must be irritatingly familiar.

Back out in the cool air, Beamon cupped his hand against the wind and lit a cigarette. He quickened his pace slightly, beginning to feel a little guilty about ducking out on his driver. He seemed like a good kid.

As he approached headquarters, the normal D.C. morning chaos melted into the background, eclipsed by the ongoing activity around the building. Beamon paused, tapping ashes onto the sidewalk. It got worse every day.

There were two camps. Directly across the street from the building were the pro-CDFS demonstrators. Beamon counted heads and came up with roughly fifty. About a third were holding signs that poked up from the crowd like the sharp spines of a poisonous sea animal. Their organization had improved, Beamon noted. When they had first appeared, it had been just a bunch of right-wing loudmouths with a few hand-painted signs. For a day there had actually been a guy in a fucking Klan robe.

Things had changed. The group was now more uniformly dressed in dark suits and skirts. Their signs were clever and professional. The wind changed slightly, making their chant intelligible from where he stood. *You roll the dice, you pay the price.*

About fifty yards farther down the street were the anti-CDFS protesters. They were equally well dressed, with equally clever and professional signs. Beamon couldn't make out their chant.

The two groups looked well matched. The five or six policemen keeping them apart looked as though they were in danger of being swallowed up—or worse, choosing sides. Beamon tossed what was left of his cigarette on the sidewalk and ground it out with his shoe. He immediately lit another.

The country hadn't been as divided since the Vietnam War, and the U.S. government, in its infinite wisdom, had seen fit to charge him with repairing the rift. He laughed quietly to himself.

The President seemed to be doing everything in his power to ignore the issue. Sure, the papers ran quotes about his devotion to finding the people responsible, his horror at the deaths, and so on and so on. What Jameson didn't seem to realize was that something had started here, and its momentum was increasing geometrically.

Beamon pictured it as a large rock rolling down a hill. If he'd been able to apprehend the members of the CDFS a week after they'd started this thing, the rock might have been stopped.

But it wasn't the first week anymore. He would catch these guys eventually, of that he had no doubt. But when he did, and he threw himself in front of that rock—it might just roll right over him. Did the issues relating to Vietnam end when the helicopters pulled the last Americans from Saigon? No, they grew to define a generation.

And this was no different. The growing problems of drugs and crime in America had been receiving lip service for years. But now somebody had offered an effective solution. America seemed to be finding that it liked the taste of blood and the changes it could bring.

Beamon held up his hands, attempting to silence Laura before her mouth was fully open. There was no chance of it working, of course, but it was worth a try.

"Out for a stroll, I hear?"

"Fresh air. Good for the little gray cells," Beamon replied, tapping his head and imitating the Belgian accent of his favorite fictional detective.

She grabbed his elbow and leaned in close to his ear. "You can't keep doing this, Mark. Every time you're late for a staff meeting, Tom and the rest of them end up running around loose, looking over people's shoulders and making them nervous. Takes me an hour to get everyone calmed down and back on track."

"I just do it so I can watch the tops of your ears turn red."

Her right hand went up to her ear and then immediately back to her side. "You just live to get under my skin, don't you."

He grinned and made an exaggerated gesture toward the conference room, where the other members of their morning meeting were already gathered.

"Out for a little stroll?"

Frank Richter and Laura had obviously been talking.

Beamon ignored him and turned to Tom Sherman. "Sorry I'm late." Sherman shrugged.

Besides Richter and Sherman, Dick Trevor and Trace Fontain were the only other people present. Beamon squeezed into his chair. The table they had chosen was a bit too small for the group.

"So what have you got for us, Mark?" Sherman asked.

"Good stuff, actually. Things are starting to look up a little." He snapped open his oversized briefcase and pulled out a complicated-looking portable stereo and a slightly crumpled piece of paper that contained his most recent notes on the investigation.

"The first good news is that poisoning deaths are way down. Coke-related deaths are almost nonexistent—not counting that recent episode in D.C. That seems to have been an isolated incident. Heroin deaths seem to be slowing down.

Laura's graphs had proven to be surprisingly accurate, and had become popular tools in estimating future deaths. The fact that estimating future deaths was a pointless exercise seemed to have been lost in the FBI's sheer love of statistics.

"What have you been able to find out about the episode here?" Richter interrupted.

"Not much. Strychnine was the poison—probably household rat poison—we should have confirmation on that this afternoon. Obviously, we're working to track it back to its source, but as you know, that line of investigation is turning out to be a disaster."

"Why?" Sherman cut in.

"Well, three quarters of the witnesses are dead and the other quarter won't talk. It seems that the narcotics-using community has convinced itself that this is all the government's doing and that we're just pretending to investigate, when what we actually want is to collect intelligence on distribution lines . . ." He left the sentence hanging.

Tom Sherman looked at him strangely. "Is there something else?"

"Well, yeah. Laura has a theory on the strychnine poisoning. And I hate to admit it, but she might be right."

All eyes turned to her.

"Um, yes. Well, it seems like this was a pretty sloppy operation. The fact that now, two days later, we haven't seen any more of this type of poison appear, and the isolated geography—one housing project—seems to indicate that the drugs were hit pretty far downstream. Also, the poison was unsophisticated, probably something that anybody could pick up at any of a hundred stores in the D.C. area. It makes me—us—wonder if the CDFS was behind it at all."

"A copycat," Sherman proposed.

"It's a possibility. I think everybody would agree that this doesn't really jibe with what we've learned about the CDFS to date."

"I hope you're wrong," Sherman said.

The thought of copycats cropping up across the country made everybody's head swim. A red herring in every state from here to California.

"And we may well be," Beamon said. "I mean, if it were me, I'd mix it up a little. Different drugs, different poisoning methods. It keeps us off balance and it keeps the drug users guessing. And scared."

The group nodded in general agreement, and Beamon decided to move on. He pointed at Trevor. "DEA's got some new info."

"Yeah." Trevor's voice was quiet. He sounded almost depressed. Beamon understood and sympathized.

"Luis Colombar, whom I'm sure everyone here is familiar with, has put the word out that he's looking for information regarding an American asking specific questions about his drug-manufacturing facilities. The word is that he suspects that someone poisoned his coke during the manufacturing process."

Frank Richter stood and walked over to the coffeemaker and poured himself a cup. "That makes sense—it's what I'd do. You figure that security isn't all that great at the manufacturing stage. And what security you have is aimed at people stealing stuff."

Beamon nodded gravely and continued the thought. "Right. And what better way to hit a lot of stuff with only one operation."

"Do you know if he's gotten any bites?" Sherman asked.

Trevor shrugged. "As you probably know, we've been unsuccessful at putting anybody into Colombar's operation. At this point we don't know what he's got."

A long silence ensued. Finally Sherman spoke. "Been watching TV lately, Dick? Your statistics seem to be on every channel."

Trevor winced. "We're trying to track down the leak, but I don't see much hope. I gave the order to stop keeping statistics the day we spoke—but I can't keep the street agents from talking to each other."

"Are the numbers accurate?"

"I don't know."

Sherman's voice softened. "Are the numbers accurate?"

It was well known that the quieter Sherman got the madder he was. If you had to strain to hear him, you were on your way out.

"Yeah. They're accurate. Give or take five percent. The numbers on the drug rehab clinics I can't vouch for. At this rate of decline, we could see the complete eradication of coke and heroin within our borders in a couple of months."

Beamon reached for the briefcase that he had brought into the meeting with him. He opened it and pulled out a T-shirt. "You guys seen this? I picked it up yesterday." He shook out the shirt, presenting it to the group. The front depicted a chalk outline of a man traced on a sidewalk next to a smoking crack pipe. The caption read: "I've fallen and I can't get up."

Beamon tossed the shirt to Laura. "Souvenir."

"Let's face it, public opinion was moving away from us anyway," Beamon continued. "DEA's little leak is just gonna speed things up a little."

"Okay, enough of this," Sherman said. "What's going on in Poland?"

"I think everybody's heard that Scott over in Bonn found the guy who collected the mushrooms. Apparently he runs a business supplying exotic produce to restaurants. Our man posed as an academic who was going to use the mushrooms to study cancer or something."

"Description?"

"Yeah," Beamon pulled his glasses from his shirt pocket and began reading from the paper in front of him. "Short—five foot eight or so—and thin. Long, light-brown hair and beard, wire-rimmed glasses and—this is interesting—he goes on to describe him as kind of cold."

Richter looked perplexed. "Why is that interesting—I could have told you this guy was one cold son of a bitch."

"If you remember, the girl who helped him at the bank said the exact same thing."

"So it's the same guy?"

"Laura and I would bet our respective asses on it."

"So where does that get us?"

"Nowhere, really. Scott's convinced that this mushroom guy—Lech something or other—was involved in smuggling them out. You'll recall that customs has no record of anything like that coming through them. Anyway, he's following up. And on that note, Trace has some information that I know is near and dear to your black hearts. Now that we know how many mushrooms were transported, we can take a shot at estimating potential deaths. Trace?"

Fontain cleared his throat. "Uh, yes. Mr. Orloski estimates that he provided our suspect with approximately one and one eighth tons of mushrooms. Assuming that the CDFS's distilling process is reasonably efficient, that translates to around ninety-seven thousand kills."

Sherman groaned.

"Actually, it's not as bad as it sounds."

"My analysis of the tainted drugs shows that the CDFS used about half again as much poison as was necessary—which explains the limited number of nonfatal incidents. So that knocks back our kill potential pretty significantly. Also, you have to make an assumption about how many times someone is going to use the stuff. For instance, a heroin addict might buy a two-week supply and unknowingly take fourteen lethal doses. In essence, he's wasted thirteen kills."

Beamon cut the scientist off. They would be here all day if he let him start in on his assumptions. "Okay, Trace. Boil it down. How many people can they kill with what they've got?"

"Best guess. Thirty-six thousand."

Beamon nodded gravely. "Assuming that they don't branch out into other types of poisons."

Fontain shrugged and nodded.

Beamon could see from the faces around him that the scientist was in danger of an endless Q&A. He decided to put a stop to it before it started. "Thanks, Trace. We won't hold you up any longer. I know you're busy."

Fontain stood and scampered out of the room before anyone could start in on him.

"Well, there you have it, for what it's worth. Now let's get down to some real cop stuff." He reached into the pocket of his jacket and produced an unlabeled cassette tape. It took a few moments for him to figure out how to get the tape into the portable stereo on the table, but the machine finally accepted it upside-down. He pushed the door shut and hit Play.

"I saved the best for last."

Nothing happened.

"Do you have batteries in that thing, Mark?" Laura asked, looking smug.

"Batteries? Uh, no. Don't these things come with batteries?"

She sighed and pulled the rubber band off the tightly wound cord, running it to an outlet behind her. The recorder came to life, spewing out loud tape hiss. A moment later the hiss deadened, and Beamon managed to find the Pause button. "One of the operators on the deathline brought this up to me yesterday."

The hotline set up to collect anonymous tips on the case had become known as the "deathline" because of the reams of death threats that Beamon received on it every day. It seemed that there were more than a few people who were concerned about the FBI's thoughtless interference in the CDFS's solution to the national drug crisis.

"I had the tape washed through the computers. It was pretty hard to understand at first. The guy used the old towel-over-the-mouthpiece trick."

"Traced?" Richter asked.

"A pay phone between here and Baltimore." Beamon pressed the Pause button again, setting the tape back into motion.

The tape noise deadened and the operator's voice came on. It had a strange mechanical edge. "FBI."

The other voice on the line was clearly nervous, even through the towel and computer tampering. "Hello . . . I, uh, thought that you'd want to know that they're planning on poisoning a shipment of cocaine on the twenty-eighth. It's going to be in one of Anthony DiPrizzio's warehouses on the New York waterfront." Pause.

The operator's voice: "Sir, can you give me your name and how you came by this information?"

"No. But so you know I'm telling the truth, I'll tell you this. The poison came from mushrooms growing a few hours outside of Warsaw." Dial tone.

Beamon reached over, ejected the tape, and stuffed it back into his suit pocket.

"You all know that we've kept the source of the poison pretty quiet."

Sherman looked doubtful. "Well, we've done our best, but there are a hell of a lot of people in the health care community who have figured it out. You think this might be something?"

"You never know. I'm meeting with DiPrizzio at four this afternoon. Joe up in New York set it up."

"That ought to be an interesting get-together. Anything else?" Sherman scanned the faces at the table. No one spoke.

"Okay, let's get back to work."

The group stood, pulling jackets from chair backs and tucking notebooks under their arms.

"Not you, Mark. Have you got a few minutes?" It wasn't really a question. The others picked up their pace. Laura was the last one out, struggling to pull the door shut while holding a coffee mug in one hand and the portable stereo in the other. Sherman got up and handed her the dangling cord. He quietly closed the door.

Beamon pushed the chairs next to him away, giving himself enough room to stretch his legs out. He had an overwhelming desire to smoke, but resisted.

"So you think this DiPrizzio thing might come to something, Mark?"

"Probably not—but we've gotta cover all the angles. So what's up, Tommy? You didn't keep me after class to ask me that."

"Same shit, different day. Problems, problems." His smile was forced. Beamon waved him on with an exaggerated motion.

"Calahan and I met with the President yesterday."

"I heard—my condolences."

The weak smile again.

"The President's not happy, Mark. I'd go so far as to say he's panicking." Beamon opened his mouth to speak, but his friend cut him off.

"He's pretty surprised by the public's reaction to this thing. It's put him in an impossible political position. He's got to condemn the CDFS as radical vigilantes, but he can't speak out too forcefully without pissing off all the people who are pro-CDFS."

"I've got a crazy idea, Tommy. Why the hell doesn't he just pick a side and say how he really feels, instead of hiring a bunch of weasels to tell him what the voting majority wants to hear. It's their goddam fault. If the boys on Capitol Hill didn't spend all their time chasing girls and rounding up campaign funds, maybe these guys wouldn't have found this necessary." The frustration he felt was quickly turning to anger.

"That's not the way of the world and you know it, Mark. You like to deal in facts, so here they are. The only way for President Jameson to win is for these guys to get caught. He hopes that the issue will fade in the two years before the next election. He's serious, Mark. He actually intimated that it might be better for the country if there wasn't a drawn-out trial.

Beamon's eyes widened. "He did not! What did you say?"

"I told him we didn't do that kind of thing."

Beamon snorted. "Christ!"

"That doesn't go beyond this room, Mark. I just want to get across to you where you stand."

"Where I stand? What do you mean?" He knew perfectly well.

"This is all going to come down on your shoulders in the end." Sherman couldn't meet his eyes. "I'm sorry I got you into this."

Beamon slapped him on the shoulder.

"Jesus. Cheer up, Tommy. I knew what I was getting into." That wasn't entirely true, of course. No one could have predicted the way this case would consume the nation.

"Who was it that said there's no such thing as bad publicity? You wouldn't believe the calls I've been getting from private industry— I'm not gonna have to fill my pockets with the salmon at my retirement party, you know? I'm thinking about getting a fucking agent."

That *was* true. There was nothing the American public respected more than fame. Private companies were virtually beating down his door, making him various offers of employment. Each one was more spectacular than the last. And that didn't include the $1.2 million guaranteed advance on his autobiography.

Sherman perked up a bit and remained silent when his friend gave into temptation and lit a cigarette in the poorly ventilated room. At least the filter was still attached.

"You know I'm not screwing around here, that I'm doing everything I can, right, Tommy?" Beamon's tone had turned serious.

"I'm not second-guessing you, Mark. You're the best man for the job. I told Jameson that again yesterday."

"Did he buy it?"

"Good to see you, Joe," Beamon said, extending his hand. He had to raise his voice a bit to be heard over the chaotic background noise that was a constant at the FBI's largest office.

"Welcome to New York, Mark. Come on back." Joe Sheets motioned toward the open door of his office across a sea of agents and support personnel.

Beamon hadn't seen Sheets for years. Shaking hands with his old friend had brought back a flood of memories. They had been roommates at the academy and had become fast friends during their twelve weeks there—despite the fact that they were very different people. Beamon had been first in his class academically but had been less than impressive in the physical fitness category. In fact, his performance had been bad enough for Sheets to call him when women were first being accepted as agents, just to point out that Beamon's time in the mile wouldn't have passed him in the women's category, either.

Sheets hadn't shone in any one category—but had been a solid all-around performer. Fairness, reliability, and hard work had landed him an assistant director's slot and the helm of the New York office. Well deserved, as far as Beamon was concerned.

As he pushed the door shut and looked around his friend's spacious office, he pointed at a picture on the credenza. "Jesus, is that Bobby?"

Sheets sat on a slightly threadbare sofa and smiled. "It's Robert now. He's a commercial artist in Chicago. Wouldn't you know that my son would be the only artist in the world who doesn't want to be in New York."

Beamon chuckled. To say that Sheets and his son didn't see eye to eye was an understatement. If he remembered correctly, his old roommate's idea of a good painting involved dogs playing poker, and his son saw all FBI agents as fascist scum. A little distance probably wasn't an entirely bad thing.

Beamon filled a cone-shaped cup from a water cooler in the corner and sat at the other end of the sofa. "You can't keep 'em from spreading their wings, I guess."

"That you can't," Sheets agreed, looking at his watch. "You're late. Our guest should be here any time now."

Beamon nodded and took a sip of water.

"So what's this all about, Mark? With this CDFS thing going on, I wouldn't think you'd have time to worry about New York's organized crime problems."

Beamon looked behind him, confirming that the door was completely shut.

"We got a tip that they're gonna hit one of DiPrizzio's shipments."

"The CDFS? Who gave you the tip?"

"Nobody. Anonymous."

A timid knock at the door interrupted their conversation, and a round-faced woman poked her head in. "Mr. DiPrizzio is here for his three o'clock appointment." Her tone was bored, as though the most powerful man in the New York mob always dropped by around this time.

"Conference room two please, Joan." Her face barely cleared the doorjamb as she closed the door behind her.

Beamon stood and tossed the crumpled paper cup at the trash can, missing by a full three feet. "Game time."

Sheets picked up the cup and sank it.

"Mr. DiPrizzio—I'm Mark Beamon." The two men shook hands.

"I recognize you from your photos, Agent Beamon. I'm pleased to meet you. And it's nice to see you again, Agent Sheets."

"Tony." The use of the mobster's first name was less familiarity than contempt.

"I'm not sure you know my attorney, Glenn Montrose." DiPrizzio motioned to the heavyset man standing next to him. Montrose didn't offer his hand, but immediately went for a seat. His build seemed to make standing uncomfortable.

Beamon watched DiPrizzio walk smoothly across the room to take a seat with his back to the wall. Despite his relative youth—he had turned thirty-seven only a week ago—he moved with extreme self-assurance. If he was the least bit uncomfortable being summoned by the FBI for unknown reasons, he didn't show it.

"I don't want to take up any more of your time than necessary, Mr. DiPrizzio. I'll get right to the point," Beamon said.

"I'd appreciate that," DiPrizzio replied, glancing at an expensive-looking watch for added effect.

"We have information that would lead us to believe that the CDFS is planning on targeting one of your drug shipments."

DiPrizzio's expression didn't even flicker. He looked from Beamon to his attorney and then back at Beamon. Finally he spoke. "This is ridiculous. I am a legitimate businessman. Let me repeat that—a *legitimate* businessman. I am constantly amazed that the FBI continues to harass me and my family simply because we are successful Italian Americans. You have no absolutely no evidence that I have ever done anything more heinous than park at a yellow curb."

DiPrizzio seemed to be warming up to his victimization speech, and Beamon was on a tight schedule. Beamon motioned to the windows lining one side of the conference room. The rain drove against them, making it look like the building was going through a carwash.

"It sure is a nice day. How would you like to show me a few sights—you did drive, didn't you?"

DiPrizzio looked surprised for a moment, but regained his composure quickly. "Of course."

"Great. Joe, why don't you give Glenn here the ten-dollar tour. Tony's gonna show me Times Square."

Montrose started to protest, beginning the long process of extricating himself from the narrow conference room chair. But his client was already up and heading for the door, with Beamon close behind.

"Jesus!" Beamon shouted, his voice echoing off the walls of the parking garage. "What the hell are you trying to do, sterilize me?" DiPrizzio's chauffeur had his testicles in a death grip.

"I'm sorry, sir. It seems a popular place to put wires." He had a sadistic smile on his face. Probably always wanted to have an FBI man by the balls.

"Well, I hope you're satisfied," Beamon said, gently rubbing his scrotum.

"Almost." The chauffeur reached into the passenger side of the limousine and pulled out a metal detector like the ones used in the airports for people who have baffled the walk-through unit. He ran it carefully over every inch of Beamon's body. It beeped on his belt buckle and watch.

DiPrizzio looked surprised. "No sidearm, Agent Beamon?"

"Ruins the hang of my suit." He tugged at a frayed lapel.

DiPrizzio laughed and opened the back door for him. Beamon climbed in.

"Just drive around, Billy." The chauffeur grunted and slammed the back door.

"Nice car. Is that a bar?" He pointed.

"That it is. Can I interest you in a cocktail?"

"Are you having one?"

DiPrizzio answered by pouring two Bushmills. The car moved smoothly out of the parking garage and into the crowded New York streets.

"So you were saying, Agent Beamon?"

"Mark, please."

"Mark."

"I was saying that I think that the CDFS is going to hit one of your shipments."

DiPrizzio nodded thoughtfully and sipped from his glass. "Well, that is a problem. What do you propose we do about it?"

Beamon didn't let show the relief he felt. For a few moments he had been sure that he was going to get nowhere. "We have a date and a general location. I propose that you give us an exact location, and we catch this guy—as they say—red-handed."

DiPrizzio laughed out loud. "Your friend Sheets has been after me for almost five years, Mark—and now you want me to just lead you to my product and say, 'Here it is, officer.'" He was dabbing at the corners of his eyes with a linen handkerchief. "I don't think so."

"Look, I hate to say this, but we're on the same side here. We both want these guys stopped—you want to see demand for your merchandise rebound, and I don't want anybody else hurt. I can guarantee that we'll forget everything we see." Beamon reached across the compartment and grabbed the bottle of Bushmills. He refilled his empty glass and topped off DiPrizzio's.

"Now that you've warned me, I don't really need you. Do I?"

"Come on, Tony. It could be anywhere, anytime. You'd have to quadruple your payroll for the next goddam six months—and it still wouldn't guarantee that you'd catch this guy."

"I have a proposal for you, Mark. I think we can solve both of our problems quickly and painlessly. With a little luck you could be sitting by your pool this time next week."

Apparently DiPrizzio had done some homework too.

"I'm listening."

"I think you'd agree that I have . . . interrogation techniques that aren't at your disposal."

Beamon nodded. He knew where this was going.

"You give me the wheres and whens, and I'll capture this gentleman. The next morning you'll have a FedEx with everything you ever wanted to know about the CDFS. I believe that solves both of our problems. I keep the FBI out of my business, and you clean up this mess faster than you could have on your own."

The car lurched sickeningly, and Beamon turned his eyes to the tinted window next to him. A group of men clad in orange coveralls talked heatedly near an open manhole. The sound didn't reach him.

"It's a tempting offer, Tony. Very tempting. But I'm not sure we're that desperate yet."

DiPrizzio smiled almost imperceptibly. "You've got to be getting damn close."

"Damn close," Beamon repeated, eyeing the cellular phone cradled next to his leg.

"I think I've got some bad news," Robert Swenson said, dropping into a chair. He tossed his damp coat out the door of the office, landing it expertly on the arm of a sofa. Hobart held up his index finger, indicating that he was concentrating, and continued to tap figures into the computer.

The initial costs of the operation had run over a bit, but he was quickly getting back on target. The contingency fund he had set up for any unpleasant surprises hadn't been touched in over a month. Hobart had made it perfectly clear that Bill Karns's relocation was to be at his own expense—and that no more unauthorized operations would be tolerated. Karns made a feeble attempt to defend himself, but in the end had apologized profusely and assured Hobart that he would be a model soldier from here on out.

Satisfied with the bottom line, Hobart saved the spreadsheet and flipped off the computer. "Beer?"

"Sure, why not."

He fished around in the small refrigerator and produced the last two bottles, making a mental note to bring another six-pack down from his apartment. "So? What's the news?"

"Looks like your friends showed up."

Hobart chewed on his lip silently and twisted the top off the bottle. Letting Reed Corey escape had been the biggest screwup of the operation—potentially a hell of a lot more damaging than putting Karns on too long a leash.

When Hobart returned from Colombia he had instructed his partner to drive by his house a few times a week. Look for loiterers.

"I saw them for the first time Tuesday and made a mental note. When I drove by today, they'd moved about half a block, but they were still there. Two Hispanic males, between twenty-five and thirty-five, driving a red Nissan Maxima. Well dressed, but they've got the look, you know. The car and the clothes fit the neighborhood, but they don't fit their faces.

The first rule of surveillance, Hobart reflected. Blend in. No small feat for two young Hispanics in Roland Park—one of Baltimore's most prestigious neighborhoods.

"Fuck," Hobart said simply. He had seen it coming, but there had always been a glimmer of hope that Corey wouldn't make the connection, or better yet, that he had stepped in front of a speeding bus.

"Well, we're gonna have to take care of that."

Swenson looked apprehensive. "Hey, I know that most of these cartel enforcers are idiots, but you never know when they're just gonna be luckier than you. Why don't we just leave 'em alone? We know they're there and you never go within ten miles of the house."

Hobart shook his head. His partner needed to learn chess. It wasn't the next move that got you, it was the one after that. "If I thought they'd just sit there with their thumbs up their asses, I would. But they're not going to."

"So what? You've altered your appearance and rented this place under an alias. Get a rental car and there's no way they'll ever track you down."

"Probably true," Hobart agreed. "But it's not them I'm worried about. When they figure out that I'm not coming back, and that they can't find me, they'll tip off the Bureau. As the de facto leader of the cartels right now, Luis Colombar's gotta be under a lot of pressure to get this thing wrapped up quickly."

Swenson looked as though he still didn't see his point. "So what good's killing them gonna do? They'll just call the FBI that much sooner. And we expose ourselves for nothing."

Hobart took a long pull from his beer, wondering how his partner could have spent so many years in drug enforcement and still not understand the mind of his opponent.

"Trust me on this one, Bob," he said standing and heading toward the door to the office. He walked around the perimeter of the building in his shirtsleeves, ignoring the damp cold. In his apartment he walked directly to the chess board sitting next to the television and advanced two blue pawns to threaten the king. He stood over the board for a long time, mentally reconfiguring the players, conjuring elaborate attacks and defensive strategies. Finally he tore himself away and walked toward the refrigerator and another cold beer.

24

New York City,
February 28

Phil Newberry—at least that's what he'd been calling himself for the last few months—was running out of tricks. He had watered down drinks, poured them on the floor, "forgotten" them in the bathroom, and switched them with his companions' nearly empty ones. Now he was immersed in a deep personal conversation with a man big and dumb enough to be a professional wrestler.

They had met a few times at the warehouse where he had been working for what seemed like forever. Their friendship had grown stronger with every drink The Giant had put away. At last count, fourteen.

Worse yet, his new friend had just purchased him an imposing vodka shot and was leaning close enough to be heard over the noise of the jukebox and patrons of the bar.

Not much hope of getting out of this one.

The Giant—Tim Carey, if he remembered correctly—raised his beer and held it motionless above the table. The gesture was obvious. Newberry raised his shot, tapped the glass against his new friend's bottle, and tossed it back. The red-hot fluid seemed to stick about halfway down. He reached across the table and took the beer from Carey, finishing it one gulp. He shook his head wildly, slammed a fist into his chest, and grinned.

Carey laughed and waved to the bartender for another round.

"Gimme a beer this time, man," Newberry shouted over the din. "A couple more of those and I'm gonna fall right off this fucking bar stool." Carey held up his empty bottle and two fingers.

Newberry surveyed the bar. Dark and foul smelling, just like a waterfront dive should be. He theorized that all bar scents had the same components—sweat, smoke, beer, perfume, mold, grease. What made each particular establishment unique was the combination of those universal aromas. The Rat favored mold and grease.

"I got this one, man," Newberry said, grabbing Carey's rock-hard right arm. He reached into his jeans and pulled out a wadded ball of bills, making a show of carefully peeling off a ten dollar bill and laying it on the bar.

Carey leaned close again and started back into his story. Newberry only half listened. He had too many things on his mind to give the conversation the attention necessary to hear every word over the background noise. Somebody fed a few quarters into the jukebox and it blared a distorted version of an unidentifiable country song, making the conversation even harder to follow.

Undercover operations were hard. Though he didn't know Carey well, he liked him. Despite his imposing figure, Carey was known to be about as violent as a baby seal. His story related to problems that he was having at home with his son. He was afraid that he'd fallen in with a bad crowd. It was a story that Newberry had heard hundreds of times during his years as a cop. He turned his eyes away when the concerned father speculated on the possibility that his son was using drugs—and how dangerous that could be these days.

Carey wasn't the only friend he had made in his three-plus months at the warehouse. He had been to people's homes for dinner, watched their children play in the Little League, lost money at drunken late-night poker games, and helped them move. A professional liar. His old boss used to say he had a real flair.

A woman backed into him as the bouncers continued to herd people through the door with disinterested glances at their driver's licenses. His beer sloshed over and splashed into his lap. Less he would have to drink, he reflected, taking a measured sip of what was left in the bottle.

This assignment was better than most, he remembered, still half listening to the increasingly incoherent discourse from the next bar stool. At least he wasn't setting up to arrest one of the people he had come to know so well. The thing he hated most about under-cover work: the inevitable end—the arrest. Instead of a feeling of triumph, he always saw himself reflected in the eyes of the suspect. A betrayer.

"I gotta go, man," he said apologetically, leaning heavily on Carey's leg. "I'm way too fucked up."

"You all right, Phil?"

Newberry stood. "Yeah. I just need some fresh air and a bed, you know?"

Carey gave him the thumbs-up. He knew.

Newberry grabbed a small black backpack sitting at his feet and made his way across the bar with practiced unsteadiness. He waved clumsily to a knot of men playing pool and continued staggering toward the door. They shouted a few good-natured insults and turned back to their game.

He took a hard right as he left the bar, breathing in the cool New York air. It wasn't exactly the mountains, but it tasted just as sweet after six hours of nursing drinks in The Rat. He slipped the backpack on and tightened it around his waist. The illuminated dial of his watch read 12:13 A.M. as he passed through a narrow, trash-strewn alley.

The warehouse was only about a ten-minute walk from the bar, but his indirect route increased the time to almost a half an hour. As he approached it, he rolled his head on his neck, checking for any effect from the vodka shot. None was apparent—undoubtedly the liquor had been absorbed by the cheesesteak and fries he had wolfed down right after work.

He paused next to a large Dumpster overflowing with the by-products of waterfront commerce and scanned the street for almost five minutes. Satisfied that its daytime inhabitants were nestled into their beds, or propped up in a rickety bar somewhere, he pulled off his bright blue sweatshirt and stuffed it behind the Dumpster.

Padding quietly across the dimly lit street in dark jeans, black turtleneck, and black hightop basketball shoes, he became aware that he wasn't nervous at all. When Hobart had okay'd this operation, his stomach had leaped into his throat, making it difficult to finish the conversation. His head had been spinning when he replaced the receiver.

In the days since then, he had been mesmerized by the news reports. Every night he threw a bag of popcorn in the microwave, popped the top off a beer, and rested his tired body on the sofa. The rest of the night was spent surfing the channels, watching myriad reports on the CDFS's actions from every possible perspective. He had come to three conclusions.

One: If you had cable you could find some kind of related story twenty-four hours a day.

Two: The public was getting more and more behind them.

Three: *It was working.*

Fear and apprehension had given way to pride and a sense of purpose. There had been endless rhetoric from the politicians about taking back America from the drug pushers—and now *he* was doing it.

Newberry pressed his back against the warehouse and looked up. From this angle, it looked like a mile to the third-floor windows—the first ones not guarded with bars. He slipped along the wall, stopping at a squared-off alcove in the exterior wall. The warehouse wasn't just a box—it was from an era when all structures were held to a certain standard of aesthetic beauty. The incut corner, in which he now stood, was adorned with creative brickwork, leaving two-inch ledges every few feet. Newberry tightened his pack one last time, and started his ascent.

By carefully placing his feet on the small ledges and moving them up one leg at a time, he didn't expect to have any problem getting to the third-story windows. He had been practicing this technique in his garage between a couple of two-by-sixes set up specifically for the purpose. Technically, it should be much easier on the actual building. The ledges were sharper and bit into the bottom of his shoes, and the alcove was quite a bit deeper than six inches, making the balance easier. For some reason, though, it seemed much harder.

He was looking straight ahead. The dark alcove made the brickwork in front of him look blank. Finally he dared a look up—he felt like he had been climbing forever. The act of leaning his head back make a surprisingly drastic change in his equilibrium, and he jammed a foot back to keep from reeling over into space. His heart raced and his entire body tingled from the adrenaline forced into his system. He wanted to take a few moments to collect himself, but the burning in his forearms and calves made him press on.

His estimate hadn't been far off. Another five feet brought him to the foot-wide ledge under the unprotected third-floor windows. He steadied himself and carefully shed his pack, pushing it onto the ledge. Finally he pulled himself up and sat, feet dangling, on the narrow ledge. He remained there for some time, catching his breath, oblivious to his exposed position. The night was calm, and he could see the flickering lights of New Jersey in the distance. Ships moved lazily across his field of vision, looking like constellations against the black water.

Realizing that eventually someone was bound to walk by and think he was a jumper, he scooted slowly left, pushing the backpack in front of him. It was less than ten feet to the first window. He twisted precariously on his narrow seat and pushed hard on it. It didn't move. He pushed again, wondering for a moment if he had disabled the lock on the wrong window. It wouldn't be hard to do: The old warehouse's design made it difficult to judge interior versus exterior features.

He pushed one more time and it opened with a dull crack. He slid in belly first and poured out onto a metal catwalk. Pulling the pack through after him, he hurried for the stairs.

It was dark. The only significant light came from the streetlights filtering through the windows and the second-floor office, a square box perched improbably on the second-floor wall. The venetian blinds were closed, but glowed white with the interior light. The sound of muffled voices floated through the dusty air. He slowed his progress on the metal stairs, making no sound at all.

Reaching the bottom floor, he rushed expertly through the maze of towering crates to the far corner of the building. He was forced to slow his pace slightly, as the pathways became narrower and the turns sharper. Finally he was stopped by a chain-link gate. He took off the pack and pulled out a pair of bolt cutters, making short work of the lock. He stuffed it into his pocket and pulled a matching one from the pack, hanging it on the dangling chain. When they came to open the gate in the morning, their key wouldn't turn. They would be confused for a few minutes and protest that the key had worked fine the day before. Finally they would cut it off and forget all about the incident.

Newberry padded silently into the cage and weaved through its contents, stopping at a box that looked like an old army footlocker. It opened easily after a few nails were pulled. The light was too dim to see into the box, so he reached in. His hand caressed a hard rectangular plastic bag, covered with some kind of textured tape. Duct tape, he guessed, as he pulled the first brick out.

He sat down on the floor, making himself as comfortable as possible, and reached into the open backpack, pulling out a bundle of drinking straws. The ends of each straw had been carefully sealed with masking tape. He pulled his turtleneck over his nose and mouth and punched a small hole in one end of the brick lying in front of him. Then he pulled the tape off one end of a straw and forced it into the brick until it hit the plastic at the other end. Upending the brick, he pulled the tape off the exposed side of the straw and pulled it slowly out. It worked just as Hobart had promised, distributing the poison in a deadly cylinder through the middle of the brick. When the brick was divided and the cocaine cut, the orellanin would be evenly distributed.

He was into his third brick when he heard movement behind him—actually, he felt it more than heard it—a stirring in the still air. Turning, he was blinded by a striking match. The hissing of the flame was deafening as it cut through the silence.

The match was held to the end of a cigarette, illuminating a familiar face.

"I'm Mark Beamon," the figure said, shaking out the match, leaving them once again in darkness. Newberry couldn't see a thing. His pupils had contracted violently in the face of the unexpected light. That had undoubtedly been the plan. Beamon's eyes had been closed when he lit the cigarette.

Newberry's mind raced. He once again became aware of the weight of the gun under his arm. Beamon seemed to read his mind.

"Don't do it, son. You know us FBI guys—we never fight fair. I got at least three guns aimed at your head."

Newberry carefully weighed Beamon's words. From what he knew of FBI tactics, he concluded that it wasn't a bluff. He looked one last time toward the gate, and freedom, as his eyes finally began to readjust to the gloom. Then he kneeled down and laced his fingers on top of his head.

25

The White House, Washington, D.C., March 1

Tea?"

"Thank you, Mr. President," Tom Sherman said, holding the cup steady as Jameson poured. He took a couple of sugars from a silver tray and leaned back, stirring. The President finished his tea ceremony, pouring cups for the attorney general and FBI Director, who Sherman knew hated tea. He watched as Calahan politely took a sip and smiled approvingly.

"I thank you all for coming so early. I'm pretty booked up during the days." The antique clock on the wall read 5:05 A.M. "So I hear you're the expert on the CDFS, Tom."

"That's not entirely true, sir. Mark Beamon is more in tune with the details of the investigation."

"Yes, well, Bill apparently didn't want to subject me to your Mr. Beamon, and suggested that I be briefed by you instead. I assume that you're up to the task."

"Yes, sir."

"I hear we've had a major break in the case."

"Yes." Sherman drew the word out longer than necessary. His tone was hesitant.

"You don't sound sure," the President observed, reaching for a cookie. The others took the cue and grabbed a few for themselves.

"It's true that we did capture one of the CDFS's operatives—but he isn't talking."

"He won't talk?" The President enunciated the words carefully, as though Sherman was an idiot. Undoubtedly just the effect he was shooting for.

"I'm not sure you understand the situation, Tom," the President said. "We have to stop these people. You have my authorization to make any kind of deal you have to." He looked smug, as though this was some kind of revelation.

"We've offered him complete immunity to prosecution and a place in our witness protection program," Sherman said. "He's not interested."

A confused look came over the President's face. He leaned forward and set his empty cup on the table. "This guy's gonna go to prison when you've offered to let him walk? I don't understand what you're telling me."

I wouldn't expect you to, you political hack.

"He believes in what they're doing, sir. In his mind, he's a captured soldier. A patriot putting America back on track."

The President looked around at the other two men in the room. "A little cocky for a mass murderer, isn't he?"

"Maybe," Sherman replied, though the question clearly had been rhetorical. The President let it pass, but the look he gave Sherman would have filled most bureaucrats shoes with sweat.

Sherman couldn't bring himself to care. He had twenty years in and more money than he could possibly ever spend. The picture of him fly fishing on a quiet river surrounded by willows was destroyed when Jameson began speaking again.

"So after one day, you've decided that there's no way we can make him talk."

Sherman reached for another cookie. "You haven't asked me anything about this guy, but let me tell you about him anyway. He was a cop for ten years in Atlanta. Apparently he quit to take this on. His former supervisors have nothing but good things to say about him. Honest, smart. His record's spotless. He knows exactly what's going to happen if he ends up in prison. They're not crazy about cops, but I expect they like the CDFS less. He's a tough guy, but I doubt he'll last two days."

"You sound like you respect him," Jameson goaded.

"I don't feel one way or another. He's willing to put himself on the line for what he believes in."

Another thinly veiled insult. This time Jameson pretended he didn't hear.

"Your recommendation?"

"We throw some manpower at it. Track down everybody this guy knows and find the ones who recently dropped out of sight. It's only a matter of time."

The Director cut in, speaking for the first time. "Mr. President—Perry and I were discussing the situation earlier. We think we have a better plan."

Uh oh. Sherman looked at Calahan with apprehension. The President looked with hope.

Perry Trent started. "Bill and I feel that we should put out a press release saying that this guy's gonna make a deal. Force the CDFS's hand."

"Force their hand to do what?" Sherman wondered aloud.

"A hit. Bring the guy in and out of the courthouse on a set schedule every day. Make it look easy."

Sherman mouth gaped, revealing a half-chewed cookie. He slowly scanned the faces of the three men across from him. They all looked deadly serious.

Calahan continued the thought. "We can position enough men around the courthouse to guarantee catching the assassin. Maybe we'll have more luck with him."

The President nodded thoughtfully. "And what's your opinion, Tom?"

Sherman had managed to close his mouth and begin chewing again. A thousand smart-ass comments came to mind. "This is a joke, right?"

"You have a better suggestion?"

"Yes. Track down all this guy's known acquaintances. I know it's not a particularly sexy plan, but, Jesus . . ."

"Hundreds of people are dying each day," the President began. The sympathetic tone didn't play as well in person as it did on TV. "Drastic circumstances call for drastic measures, wouldn't you agree?"

"Drastic, yes. Desperate, no." The eyes of his boss and the AG bored into him. "Look, sir, there's no guarantee that they'll try a hit. And if they do, there's no guarantee that we'll get the shooter alive—at all, for that matter. And even if everything goes right, there's no guarantee that he'll talk."

Jameson buttoned the top button of his shirt and tightened the tie that had been hanging loosely around his neck. "As I see it, we've got nothing to lose here. If they don't try a hit, we've in essence taken your road." He pointed to Sherman. "If they do and you kill the would-be assassin, or he won't talk, it's still a productive operation. I assume that having two suspects will narrow down your search significantly. Won't it?" The President looked pleased with himself for that piece of detective work.

"Yes," Sherman conceded.

"Unless you have a better suggestion—and by better, I mean a faster way to stop these maniacs—I believe we've found our course of action."

Sherman shifted uncomfortably in his chair. His resignation was on the tip of his tongue, but something was stopping him from uttering it. "Yes, sir," was all he could get out.

"They want us to what?"

Beamon actually jumped from his chair as he spoke.

"Sit down, Mark."

He ignored the advice and began pacing violently around the small conference room.

"You told them no way, though, right?"

Sherman's tone was sarcastic. "Yeah, Mark. I told Calahan, the President, and the AG, no. And they said, 'Hey fine, if *you* don't want to do it, we won't.'"

Beamon ran his hand through his hair as he marched across the room, grabbing what was left on his crown. He stopped and stood motionless in that position for a few seconds. "Why are you still here, Tommy? All you talk about is retiring. I'd have thought this would be the perfect opportunity."

"I guess that, when I was faced with it, I just wasn't ready to leave."

That was a lie and Beamon knew it. He wouldn't pull out and leave an old friend twisting in the wind. It just wasn't in him. He went for the chair across from Sherman, deciding to let the subject drop. "Got any aspirin?"

"Took my last five an hour ago," Sherman replied. They both giggled like schoolboys.

"So what do you think, Mark?"

Beamon pulled at his lower lip. "None of these young guys gets hurt." He was referring to the team of agents assigned to protect the suspect. "If you and I don't have the guts to stand up to the President, we've gotta be the ones in the line of fire."

Sherman nodded in agreement. "This is gonna blow up in our faces, you know."

"Oh, man," Beamon slurred through the unlit cigarette clenched between his lips.

26

Baltimore, Maryland,
March 2

There they are."

John Hobart followed his partner's gaze up the street. A red Nissan Maxima sat inconspicuously between two other cars parallel parked on the quiet, tree-lined street.

"They were there yesterday," Swenson continued, pointing to a narrow side street along Hobart's east property line. "And there on Tuesday."

Hobart grunted an acknowledgment, pulled back around the corner, and walked back to his Jeep.

His house was perched on a steep, one-acre lot. The trees scattered across the property were old and plentiful, blocking the structure from view. Hobart had taken his privacy seriously, even before his recent change in profession.

He turned the key in the ignition halfway and punched a button on the CD player. A Bach concerto surged through the interior of the car as he watched Swenson stroll casually down a side street, finally turning and leaving his line of sight. Hobart leaned forward and looked at the sky through the front windshield as raindrops began to slap the glass.

The wind started to pick up, gently rocking the Jeep. Sturdy-looking trees bowed submissively as the first thunderclaps echoed down the streets. Hobart smiled. The large, well-kept houses surrounding him were almost invisible now, obscured by the coming darkness and thickening wall of water. The weather gods were smiling down on him. The street was deserted.

The shrill ring of his cellular phone interrupted his musings. His partner was on the other end.

"There's no sign that anyone's been in here—it'd take a wizard to beat your security system. I walked around the grounds. No sign of anyone there, either."

"Are you ready?"

"Whenever you are."

"I'm coming in." Hobart flipped the phone closed and laid it on the seat next to him. He started the car and moved slowly around the block, passing close to the parked Nissan and turning up his driveway. He couldn't see the expression on the faces of the Nissan's occupants, but he could detect excited movement in the car as he passed. A feeling of relief passed through him. Amateurs.

Hobart hit the garage door opener well before getting to the house and was able to pull in without pausing. He hit the button again and watched his rearview mirror to see if his admirers had followed him up the drive. They hadn't.

Climbing out of the Jeep, he pulled on a Gore-Tex jacket that had been lying in the back seat, and escaped out of the garage through the side door. The rain hadn't let up, and his boots sank in the softened earth. He struggled through his thickly landscaped backyard and alongside the house, finally stopping in a dense group of trees. In theory, his position should have given him an unobstructed view of the front door about twenty yards away. Through the storm, though, all he could see was the dim glow of the carriage lights.

Hobart crouched down and waited. The driveway was the only practical entrance to his property, due to a tall wrought iron fence protecting the perimeter. While the fence had been installed by the previous owners for aesthetic effect, its arrowlike pinnacles effectively discouraged climbing.

He didn't have to wait long. A few minutes after he took up his position, two shadowy figures could be seen hurrying up the steep drive. About halfway to the front door, one of them broke off and positioned himself twenty-five feet to the right of the door. The man stood motionless next to a tree, melted into it by the rain.

Hobart walked carefully along the edge of the lawn, staying out of sight. He stopped ten feet behind the figure. The man's shoulders were broad, and well-defined muscles could be seen through the cheap suit plastered to his back by the downpour. A .45 dangled loosely from his left hand.

Hobart crept up behind him. His feet made an inevitable sucking noise as he moved, so he walked slowly, stopping at odd intervals to mask their rhythm. The combination of the noise from the storm and the man's focus on the door made him an easy target.

He stopped just behind the man—so close that he had to control his breathing for fear his quarry would feel it on the back of his neck. Gazing down at the man's gun, he confirmed that his finger was not on the trigger.

In one swift motion Hobart grabbed the gun, switched hands, and pressed the barrel into the man's cheek. The man stood in the same position as before, except that his eyes strained right—focused on the barrel of the gun.

Hobart grabbed his shoulder and pressed down. The man sank slowly to his knees and then lay face first in the deep mud. Hobart knelt over him, keeping the barrel behind his ear, and watched the activity at his front door with silent anticipation.

The other man, who was still only a vague form to Hobart, had moved to within a few feet of the front door and was standing on tiptoe, peeking in a large bay window. He stood like that for almost thirty seconds, despite the downpour from the overflowing gutters. From that position, he reached over and rang the doorbell, and then pressed his back against the wall next to the door.

Swenson began moving along the front of the house. He would have been in full view of the man at the door, had the man's attention not been focused in the other direction. Swenson moved smoothly, trying to keep out of the waterfall coming off the roof.

It would have been impossible to hear Swenson's approach.

Hobart later theorized that the cartel enforcer had been alerted by the water splashing off his partner's body. Whatever it was, he spun to his right just as Swenson moved within three feet of him.

The struggle was short. Swenson was able to block the gun arcing toward his face and charge the man, lifting him off his feet and landing him hard on the brick porch. As his back impacted, the gun went off. Hobart tensed, inadvertently pressing the pistol harder into his captive's ear. To his surprise, the pathetic whimper floating up from beneath him was more noticeable than the gunshot, which had blended seamlessly with the crash of the storm.

Hobart grabbed his captive by the back of the hair and dragged him to his feet. They marched toward the door. A scared-looking Robert Swenson was standing over the man's companion, gun shaking slightly.

"You all right, Bob?"

Swenson swallowed hard and nodded, stepping back and inviting his prisoner to stand.

As they descended the basement stairs, Hobart came to the realization that he would never live in that house again. Nor would he ever be able to exist under the name John Hobart. The drug cartels had a nasty way of holding a grudge. In essence, the thing he prized most—his privacy—had been stripped away. The price of fame in this case would be a bullet in the head.

"Gentlemen. I always like to know who I'm talking to. What are your names?"

The two men sat under a bare bulb, wrapped in an almost comical amount of rope. Coils of white nylon twisted and turned across their bodies, pinning their arms painfully behind their backs. Swenson had gone back to the warehouse after he had finished tying them.

The basement was typical of Baltimore's older homes. Rotting overhead beams dripped wood on the dirt floor. The cement walls were pockmarked and stained by a dark line running horizontally about three feet from the floor, suggesting that the basement at one time had been under water.

Hobart rarely used it, and with the exception of the large, well-equipped tool bench, most of the junk in it belonged to prior owners. Old bicycles, golf clubs, a bathtub. He had been meaning to clean it out for years, but had never received the proper inspiration.

"Fuck you, man," spat the one who had grappled with Swenson. Hobart looked at his deeply lined face for a moment. The man's stare glowed with hatred and sadism. Hobart moved his eyes to the man's partner, who didn't meet his gaze. There was weakness there. It could be seen in the curve of the mouth. The slightly flared nostrils.

Hobart stood and walked past the men toward the work bench.

"What if we just start yelling, man. Your neighbors won't like that too much," the angry one said in thickly accented English.

Hobart shouted for him. "Help! I'm being murdered!" He lowered his voice to a conversational tone. "You're in the basement of a house sitting on an acre of land in a rainstorm. Who the hell's gonna hear you?"

He selected a scratch awl from the tool bench. The angry one was straining his neck, trying to see what Hobart was doing. The quiet one was dead still, head drooped forward.

The angry one gave up trying to see what was going on, shouting an idle threat instead. "You're dead, man. Dead." The sentence had a practiced finality to it.

"Maybe," Hobart answered, "but you first." He clamped his hand over the man's mouth and nose, and pressed the awl into the base of his skull. The bone resisted at first, but gave way with a sickening crunching sound when Hobart put his full weight behind the tool. Once inserted to the handle, he rotated it in a slow circular motion.

Hobart felt the muscles in the man's jaw go slack, and he released him.

The surviving man, who had appeared dead before, jumped as if someone had run an electric current through him. His head snapped up and every fiber in his body tried to move away from Hobart, who was busy wrapping duct tape around the corpse's neck, sealing the small, oozing wound. Despite the man's valiant effort, the chair only teetered slightly. A tribute to Swenson's overzealous rope work.

Hobart walked around the chair-bound corpse and took his seat. The quiet one stared at him, wild-eyed.

He had the look of a flunky. No doubt he had hung on his companion's every word, convinced that he was the ultimate killer. Lean, mean, fighting machine. What little strength he had, had drained from him with the blood and brains of his companion.

"So what was it you said your name was?" Hobart played with the bloody awl suggestively.

"Jesus, my name is Jesus." He barely spoke English. Hobart switched to Spanish.

"Pleased to meet you, Jesus. Now why don't you tell me who sent you here?"

The young man thought for a moment, weighing his options.

"Look, Jesus. In an hour you'll be dead—no matter what. The question is how comfortable you are during that hour."

It was a psychological trick that Hobart had always been fond of, but had found little opportunity to use. In the face of certain death, earthly loyalties and conventions held little meaning.

A brief look of despair crossed Jesus's face and he drooped as far forward in the chair as the ropes would allow. Hobart waited quietly. Finally Jesus's head rose. The expression of despair had been replaced with one of resignation.

"Luis Colombar," he said in a breathy voice that Hobart had to strain to hear.

"And his orders?"

"To kill you."

"Why?"

"He did not say."

Hobart walked back to the work bench. His captive craned his neck, as his companion had, with similar futility.

As he passed Jesus on his way back to his chair, Hobart swung a heavy hammer into the man's immobilized knee. Jesus howled in surprise and pain, eyes rolling back in his head.

"Why?" Hobart repeated, settling back in his chair and placing the hammer next to the awl on the floor.

Jesus coughed violently, turning his head to the side as though he was going to vomit. Blood soaked through his pants where the shards of what had once been his kneecap had sliced through the skin.

"I swear, he didn't tell me!" There were tears in the corners of his eyes. "Why would he?"

Hobart had believed him the first time, but it never hurt to be thorough. Satisfied that he had the information he needed, he grabbed the awl and walked behind the young man.

Jesus jerked his head side to side and back and forth violently, grunting with every move, trying to delay the inevitable. Hobart grabbed a handful of his hair and forced his head forward, exposing the base of his neck.

Hobart eased Robert Swenson's Cadillac over the steep hill leading to his cabin. The bottom scraped loudly, as though it was intentionally reminding him that it had been made for the highway and not weed-choked dirt roads. The tires spun a bit, but he made it over the rise and began down the steep slope to the cabin.

Pulling up next to the house, he killed the engine and the lights, letting the dark quiet wrestle its way into the car. He sat for a few minutes with the door half-open, letting his eyes adjust and listening for any sign of life in the dense woods that surrounded him. He heard nothing but the wind.

Despite the cold dampness of the night, Hobart was sweating profusely. He had one hand on the collar of Jesus's jacket and the other wrapped around the handle of a rusted shovel. It never ceased to amaze him how heavy corpses felt. Unconsciousness added a few pounds to be sure, but death . . .

He had to stop every ten feet or so to catch his breath and regain his bearings—a flashlight seemed ill advised. The work gloves weren't helping matters, either. The loose leather made gripping the rain and blood-dampened wool of Jesus's jacket nearly impossible.

A half hour's walk brought him to the edge of a small clearing less than a quarter of a mile from the cabin. He stopped a few feet from it, positioning himself where he could make the most of the moonlight while still staying under the cover of the trees. Finding a piece of ground relatively free of rocks and roots, he began to dig.

It was an hour before dawn when Hobart dropped Jesus's name-less companion in the hole on top of him. Despite the moonlight, it was inky-black in the four-foot-deep grave—something he hadn't entirely counted on. He jumped in, landing on the bodies with a muffled thud. He reached down and ran his hand up one of the men's chests until he felt the smooth duct tape wrapped around his neck. He removed his hand and replaced it with the blade of the shovel. He worked it back and forth with his heel, feeling it slowly bite into flesh and finally into bone. One last push severed the man's head. Hobart reached into the darkness and retrieved it. He stuffed it into a thick Hefty bag and tied off the top. As he walked back to the cabin, the head bounced playfully against his knee. It too seemed heavier than it should be.

The theory was simple. When Colombar found that his men had disappeared, he would get impatient. And if he got impatient, he would probably end up calling the Bureau. Hobart couldn't allow that to happen.

His years in the DEA had taught him a few things about the minds of these men. He would FedEx the head to Colombar. Boxed up nicely—possibly with a bow. More important, he would include a note, preferably with something attacking Colombar's manhood in some way. The drug lord's reaction was absurdly easy to predict. He would fly into a rage. He would send more men, ordering them to capture Hobart and bring him back to Colombia. Hobart smiled and tossed the bag over his shoulder. Some things were constant in the universe. Pi, gravity, time, and the fact that drug dealers thought with their balls and not their brains.

27

New York City,
March 5

Bill Karns pulled himself from the cab with some difficulty and hurried down the sidewalk.

The New York streets were relatively quiet. It was three o'clock—the late lunchers had all finished their martinis and returned to work, and the people contemplating sneaking home early were going to give it another hour or so.

When John Hobart had called about the strychnine poisoning in D.C., Karns had thought he was out. He had never heard Johnny like that. Hobart's calm composure under stress was a big part of his personality. Hell, it *was* his personality. The screaming, swearing person on the other end of the phone had taken Karns off guard. And scared him.

He had moved out that day and headed for Oklahoma City. Not exactly a hotbed of high-dollar narcotic traffickers, but it looked like it was where he would stay. Missionless for the rest of the operation.

The call last week had been a shock. Hobart was flying to Oklahoma City and they were to meet. Hobart said that he had a critical mission and needed someone he could trust. One of the CDFS's men had been caught and, according to CNN, was going to talk. He hadn't yet, but unnamed FBI officials were confident that their negotiations were headed in the right direction.

Hobart had arrived the next day and charged Karns with taking care of the problem. The hit was already completely planned, right down to scale models and carefully drawn diagrams. Karns had listened silently, struggling not to let his face reveal his relief at being reinstated as one of Hobart's top men.

And now it had begun.

Karns approached the doors of the building across from the jailhouse where Phil Nelson, as his name had turned out to be, was being held. On the other side of the street, the inevitable crush of reporters and protesters ebbed and flowed across the sidewalk, barely contained by wooden barriers and police. Some had spilled into the road, and the combination of their bodies, and the interest of passing drivers, had caused a near standstill in traffic. The cars sat helpless, horns blaring, and drivers shouting inane obscenities.

He pushed through the glass doors and turned left. The entrance to the stairwell was right where Hobart said it would be. He paused, looking up at the seemingly endless flights of concrete and metal stairs as they rose into the gloom above his head. Finally he took a deep breath and started up.

Under his dirt-streaked coveralls, one hundred and fifty feet of nylon rope was coiled around his torso. A climbing harness clung to his ample waist, and a rifle hung under his right arm. On the outside of his work clothes, an overflowing tool belt hung lifelessly, full of oddly new-looking tools. The weight of these items, combined with years of inactivity, made it necessary for him to stop on each landing for increasingly long periods. The farther he ascended, the harder it was to catch his breath and clear his swimming head.

Almost there.

He could hear the unmistakable sound of power tools and hammering coming from above. Hobart had told him that the last two floors were undergoing a major renovation. No one would notice one more worker making his way up the stairs.

One more flight.

He was bent over as low as the tightly coiled rope would allow. It felt like someone was twisting a knife in his side. He ignored the pain and continued on, finally arriving at the door leading to the roof.

The old hinges had been recently oiled, and the heavy wooden door opened easily. Karns slipped through and pushed it shut behind him. He walked nonchalantly to a pile of debris stacked over eight feet high on the west side of the roof and began picking through it. Typical construction debris—pieces of drywall, insulation, and lumber, mixed with old furniture that couldn't handle the onset of the information age, and the computers that came with it.

After about twenty minutes of seemingly aimless scrounging, Karns straightened out and stretched his back. He looked around, casually scanning the roofs of the surrounding buildings. Then he bent again, squeezing himself into the insulation-lined hole that he had made for himself. He worked his body back and forth, trying to flatten out the sharp edges caused by the haphazardly stacked debris. The rope coiled around his torso was a blessing now, keeping nails and glass from cutting into him.

Satisfied that his comfort had been provided for about as much as it was going to be, he pulled a large piece of drywall in front of him. That, combined with his dull gray coveralls, would make him invisible. Unless of course someone needed something from the pile. That didn't seem likely, though. It was four-thirty, and construction was winding down for the day.

He shifted his position one last time—something was sticking into his neck. The weather was getting noticeably colder too, cooling the sweat that had begun to soak through his coveralls. It was going to be a long night.

The last two hours had seemed as long as all the others combined. Bill Karns twisted his wrist painfully and looked at his watch for the hundredth time. Nine-thirty. Just a few more minutes.

The rubble that surrounded him like a cocoon had provided surprisingly little insulation over the last seventeen hours. The climbing rope that was such a burden on the way up the stairs had been his savior—keeping the cold night air from penetrating his torso, but not doing much for his extremities. His hands were stiff, and his legs felt completely lifeless. He could feel the warmth of the sun in the few places that it filtered through the debris.

Nine thirty-five. Hobart's plan had Karns waiting as long as possible before emerging from his hiding place, lessening the chances of him being spotted from one of the surrounding buildings. He decided to revise the plan slightly. The shot wasn't going to be particularly difficult by his standards, but it would help if he could actually make his finger squeeze the trigger.

He began pushing the large piece of drywall lying on top of him to the side. The noise startled him a bit after spending the entire night on the quiet roof, with only the drifting sound of traffic to keep him company.

His legs were in even worse shape than he had thought. He had to literally drag himself from the hole, scooting on his belly to the northwest and nestling himself in the crook of the four-foot wall that surrounded the roof. He stretched his legs out painfully and began balling and unballing his fists. When his fingers loosened up, he tucked them under his armpits to warm.

Nine forty-five. Time to move.

Karns dropped his tool belt and pulled out a hammer and two six-inch nails. Crawling quickly, he made his way to the only door opening onto the roof and drove the nails through the door and into the doorjamb. Hobart had really done his homework. He had told Karns that the large air-conditioning unit would obscure him from prying eyes as he sealed the door. And there it was, right where it had been on Hobart's elaborate cardboard model.

Karns crawled back to his corner and began unwinding the rope from his body, stacking it next to him. Pulling the covers off the scope on his rifle, he sighted carefully across the roof at a flag just visible on the top of the building next to him. Other than a small amount of condensation on the scope's optics, everything looked good. He chambered a round.

Hobart had definitely been on the roof. Karns had suggested that he bring a mirror or something to set on the wall so that he could watch for his target. But Hobart told him that he would be able to hear the commotion when they brought Nelson out. Karns had been doubtful during their conversation, but had to admit now that Hobart had been right. Some kind of acoustic anomaly seemed to quiet the traffic noise and amplify the sound of protesters and reporters. He could hear their excitement growing as he continued to flex and stretch his legs.

As he had for the last three days, Mark Beamon stopped ten feet from the glass doors leading to the steps of the building. From where he stood, he could see six or seven agents holding back the reporters and interested bystanders, cutting a twenty-five-foot-wide swath in the crowd. He couldn't see the dark blue LTD waiting for him on the street, or the one hundred and fifty other agents stationed on roofs, sitting in cars, and casually strolling through the neighborhood. A nervous sweat trickled down the back of his neck and behind his bullet-proof vest.

He had thought that the first day would be the worst. He had been dead wrong. The tension seemed to grow every day, like the crescendo at the end of a symphony.

"Are you all right, Mr. Beamon?" Philip Nelson asked, as he had every day since Beamon had replaced his original escort. Beamon nodded, but didn't move.

Finally he glanced at his watch. Ten o'clock. Time to go. He began moving forward, right hand gripped tightly around the chain on his prisoner's handcuffs. Nelson looked relieved.

Wait for it, Karns told himself. The reporters and onlookers' excitement level was rising, but Hobart had told him that they could see through the glass doors, and to wait until he could actually hear them shouting questions. Then he would have about eight seconds with a clean shot and another two with a shot partially blocked by a car. Karns took a deep breath and held it, adjusting the rifle slightly in his grip. It felt strange through the surgical gloves, as if it wasn't real.

The shouting started and he wasn't ready. He let the breath out and took another one, wasting two seconds.

His legs were sore from the previous day's exercise, but the blood was back in them. He rose smoothly to his feet and steadied the gun. No one in the crowd noticed the small figure leaning over the roof.

There was no need to adjust for drop due to the angle and distance. Nelson's head was directly in his crosshairs. He lowered the barrel a fraction, repositioning the crosshairs on Nelson's chest. Head shots were sloppy. It was astonishing what the human skull could deflect. He still hadn't been noticed by the crowd when he squeezed the trigger. The rifle cracked loudly, jerking against his shoulder. A fraction of a second later, he had dropped the rifle and was running for the back of the building, rope in hand.

The sound of the shot and the sound of the bullet as it ricocheted off the cement stairs behind him were virtually simultaneous. Beamon expected to feel his prisoner torn from his grasp and to have to watch him cartwheel away with the impact of the shot. In that split second between awareness and action, though, Nelson remained perfectly still.

Beamon dove to the left, pulling his prisoner by the chain between his handcuffs. They landed heavily on the stairs, Beamon on his stomach and Nelson on his back. With a shooter on a roof, it wasn't a much more desirable position than standing, he reflected, watching the crowd scatter. He was counting slowly to himself. It was a habit he had formed years ago. Time seemed to slip away in situations like this, and more often than not, it was helpful to know when things happened. When he reached five—an eternity in a gunfight—he sat up.

The other agents were still crouched behind the LTD parked at the base of the steps, as was Tom Sherman. They were aiming their guns in the general direction of the top of the building across the street. A couple were touching their ears, listening intently to the chatter on the FBI radio.

"Get up, you lucky bastard," Beamon said, poking Nelson's still prone form in the ribs. Nelson didn't move.

Oh, oh.

Beamon ripped open Nelson's shirt, finding a neat hole in his bullet-proof vest. Blood was just beginning to flow through the tear.

"Fucking Teflon bullets!" he shouted, standing up and dusting himself off. He had probably made it to the four count before the poor bastard even knew he was dead.

"Get down, Mark," Sherman yelled.

Beamon thrust his hands into his pockets. "Oh, shit, Tommy, that guy's burnin' a hole in his sneakers by now."

Sherman poked his head up from behind the car, looking indecisive. Finally he walked over and stood looking down at their dead prisoner. His gun hung uselessly in his hand. "Jesus."

Motherfucker didn't even know what hit him, Karns thought to himself as he secured the rope to a thick ventilation pipe on the roof. He hadn't stuck around long enough to watch his target fall, but he had a hunter's sixth sense. Dead center.

Adrenaline coursed through him as he anchored the rope into his harness and climbed to the edge of the roof. He hadn't rappelled since the army—thirty years and fifty pounds ago. And he hadn't been crazy about it then. He felt suddenly dizzy as he teetered on the edge, becoming aware for the first time of the whistle of the wind. The sight of his motorcycle, and freedom, steadied him.

The gear had improved, that was for sure. He slid smoothly down the rope, gripping and releasing rhythmically with his gloved hands. About halfway down he stopped with a vicious jerk. His head snapped back and he nearly turned upside down. Confused, he looked at the metal loop at his waist. Nothing caught. He looked at the rope below him and discovered the problem. Four men in street clothes were standing in the alley, each one with a pistol aimed up at him. A fifth man was pulling hard on the rope, effectively locking him in place. Karns looked up at the roof. Three clean-cut faces peered down at him over the sights of their sidearms. He looked at the window in front of him. Plexiglas.

He ticked off the facts: He had no gun, he was stuck fifty feet above the ground, and there were no fewer than seven guns pointed at him. Options? Surrendering seemed the only logical choice, though the thought of grabbing for an imaginary gun was pretty attractive too. The young FBI agents had set up quite a crossfire for themselves.

He was leaning toward surrendering when his body was slammed face first into the side of the building. As he swung back out, he felt at his nose. *Fucking FBI. Couldn't they just let me sit and think for a minute?*

He looked down, expecting to see the young agent holding the rope swinging it back and forth, trying to hurry his decision. Surprisingly, he wasn't anywhere near the rope anymore. The agents had scrambled behind an overflowing dumpster and were shouting at each other and pointing their guns at a faraway rooftop.

Then he saw it. There was no blood on his shirt, but he could see it running down the neon green rope. First he looked up, thinking that maybe one of the agents above him had accidentally shot himself. No, they were in the same position as their cohorts.

Karns tore open the front of his shirt to find a bubbling hole in his chest. He never felt any pain. The last sensation he had was that of a gradual acceleration toward the ground.

John Hobart dropped his rifle onto the asphalt-shingled roof and walked casually toward the door to the stairs. He walked down two flights and came out on one of the posh upper floors of the hotel. Finding the elevator, he pushed the Down button and waited. A woman came up behind him and pushed the button a few more times for good measure. She was wearing a well-coordinated track suit, and her blond hair was tied back with a thick white ribbon. She pulled one of the ears on her Walkman out as she stretched a shapely leg against the marble wall. "You been outside yet?"

"Sure haven't," Hobart replied in a friendly tone.

"Hope it's not raining," she said to the wall.

Mark Beamon shielded his eyes from the sun and moved away from the Dumpster and the smell of rotting vegetables.

"So he shot from that hotel over there?" he asked the young agent standing next to him.

"Yes, sir."

"You make that three hundred yards, Tommy?"

"At least."

Sherman walked over to look at the body. The impact with the concrete had done even more damage than the bullet.

Beamon turned back to the agent. "So you're telling me that some guy hit a moving target from three hundred yards in this wind?"

"Uh. No. He was stopped about midway down."

"Still," Beamon said with a hint of admiration in his voice. "One hell of a shot."

Beamon slid behind Tom Sherman's desk and grabbed a coffee mug off the credenza behind him. Pulling a bottle of Jack Daniels from the brown bag on the desk, he filled it almost to the rim. He wanted a cigarette too, but he knew his boss would have his ass for smoking in his office.

It had been one hell of a day. The second shooter had walked away scot-free. He'd had a hundred and fifty agents on the street, but they were only covering buildings that you could hit Nelson from. His mistake—and a pretty fucking big one at that.

He took a heavy slug from the mug.

And don't forget the guy you killed today.

He took another slug. He could still see the surprised expression frozen into Nelson's face. In many ways, Nelson was far more deserving of respect than the flip-flopping politicians who had sentenced him to death. Beamon had spent quite a bit of time with him in the interrogation room. Right or wrong, the kid had believed what he was doing, and was willing to put his ass on the line to see it through.

The liquor was starting to go to his head, just where he wanted it. He spun the chair around and looked out the window at the fading light washing the color from the nation's capital.

"Mark?"

Beamon spun back around and motioned toward the chair in front of the desk.

"Got one for me?" Laura asked.

Beamon filled a green mug with *National Park Service* emblazoned across it.

"Quite a day," Laura probed.

Beamon let the remaining half inch of Jack Daniels slide down his throat and poured another one to the rim. "Yup."

"So what happened out there today, Mark."

Beamon shrugged. "I got a couple of men killed."

Laura took a long pull from the mug and leaned back in her chair. "You know, Mark, I sometimes question your methods—no, that's not true, I *usually* question your methods. What I've never questioned, though, is your judgment. What's going on? You knew damn well that Nelson's security was inadequate."

Beamon smiled. She had yelled at him for almost twenty minutes about that very subject last week while he had made stupid excuses. It was nice of her not to say 'I told you so.'"

"Maybe my judgment's not as good as you think it is."

Laura scowled and took another slug. "This is me you're talking to, Mark."

The less Laura knew the better, but Beamon couldn't bear the thought of her believing he'd planned this stunt.

"It seems the powers that be thought using Nelson as bait was just one hell of a fine idea."

Laura let out a long sigh. "You couldn't do anything to stop it?"

"This didn't come just from Calahan, believe me." Beamon shook his head. "I thought that if I stuck it out, I could control the situation." He raised his mug. "Here's to controlling the situation."

"So where are we now?"

Beamon thought for a moment. "It sure as hell would have been a lot cleaner to have two live suspects instead of two dead ones. But—and I hate to say it—we're better off than we were yesterday. It should narrow things down a bit, having two names."

Laura held out her mug and Beamon filled it. "You gonna let me get you drunk?"

"I'm tempted. Do we have a name on the shooter yet?"

"No, but I'm sure you'll get me one tomorrow."

"So do you still think that the organization's centralized? That one general recruited all the soldiers?"

"Hoping, anyway. Figure it this way. The same guy got the mushrooms and the money. It stands to reason that he also hit the sources of the coke and heroin. Well, maybe him and one or two other guys . . ." Beamon shook his head and went for the bottle again. "Aw, hell, who knows? There could be hundreds of these guys running around—each one only knowing one other operative. You know, like the spooks do it. If so, we're screwed."

Laura raised her glass. "Well, then, here's to the General Theory."

28

Near Bend, Oregon,
March 6

Matt Fallon slowed his '72 VW microbus and turned left off Highway 97, passing briefly through Terrebonne, Oregon. The cool, dry wind blowing through the window quieted as he slowed, and he turned down the stereo to compensate. It wasn't long before he could see the volcanic spires of Smith Rock State Park rising in the distance. He smiled and breathed in the sweet, pine-tasting air. It was Friday, and he was anxious to get out of the van that had become a prison over the last three weeks.

The FBI had tried conventional means of finding Lance Richardson, the missing witness from the bank, and had failed miserably. Finally management had been forced to admit that they just couldn't fathom the rock-climbing-bum mentality.

And that's where Fallon came in. He had risen to the top of the U.S. competitive climbing circuit while getting his Ph.D. in physics from the University of Colorado. On the night of his graduation, he had hiked up to the cliffs above Boulder, Colorado. There, accompanied by a case of his favorite beer, he had carefully appraised himself and what he wanted out of life. He had a shot at the climbing thing—power, balance, drive. But where would that get him? Climbers were viewed by most people as a bunch of long-haired lunatics with death wishes. The best in the U.S. would be lucky to feed himself from sponsors.

He had also decided that while he had a real love and aptitude for physics, he wasn't brilliant enough to be a driving force. He would probably end up teaching, or worse, sitting behind a computer at some crazy defense contracting firm.

And then it had come back to him—the days spent riveted to his television as a small child, watching Efrem Zimbalist, Jr. catch the bad guys. He'd finished the case of beer, and the next day, suffering from a near-terminal hangover, he had applied to the FBI.

The funny thing was that they accepted him. The well-rounded agent was what they were looking for, they told him. His Ph.D. and dominance in a sport—even one as esoteric as rock climbing—had apparently qualified him as well rounded.

Fallon shook his head, remembering that it had almost been three years since that night in Boulder. Einstein had been wrong about time. It accelerated as you got older.

He had spent the last weeks scouring America's premier climbing areas—the New River Gorge, Hueco Tanks, Wild Iris, to name only a few—asking questions and running into way too many old friends. He figured that he had packed at least five beer pounds onto his painfully thin frame.

He turned left into a crowded pullout and hopped out. He shouldered a small pack full of climbing gear and headed down the steep trail toward the cliffs.

After only five minutes on the trail, he heard a familiar voice floating through a narrow passage in the rocks. He turned off and danced gracefully up the steep boulder field. At the top, he found a young woman watching a shaking figure fifty feet up a sheer rock face.

"Hi, Sara. Remember me?" he asked, approaching her quietly. She looked up, confused for a moment.

"Matt!" She looked up. "Scott! Matt Fallon's standing right here!"

The man on the rock face struggled a few more feet, finally reaching a bolt that he could clip into. He leaned back on the rope and jabbed his finger downward. Sara obligingly lowered him to the ground.

At the bottom he threw his arms around the agent. After a moment he pulled back, giving Fallon's arms a squeeze as he went. "Still feel pretty strong," he observed. "Three years in the CIA doesn't seem to have hurt you much."

"FBI," Fallon corrected. "There's a difference."

His friend looked like he was about to make a smart-ass comment, but before he could open his mouth Sara pushed him out of the way and ran her fingers through Fallon's closely cropped hair. A sad look came over her face. "What happened to your beautiful hair?"

"Cut it off—the Bureau doesn't take kindly to that shoulder-length look."

"So why didn't you call us and tell us you were coming?"

"I wasn't sure I was. Actually, I'm on business."

She snickered, looking at the climbing harness peeking out from the top of his backpack.

"No, seriously," he protested. "I'm looking for somebody. He's a climber. Name's Lance Richardson. Five foot ten, long blond hair. You know him?"

"Did he kill somebody?" Scott asked,

"Nah. He might have seen a guy we're looking for when he was working for a bank in Saint Louis. That's all."

"Well, you came to the right place," Sara said.

Fallon looked at her with surprise. After all this time on the road, he hadn't been prepared to actually find the guy. "You're kidding. You've seen him?"

"Yeah. He's been around for about a week. I think he's living in his van back in the National Forest somewhere."

"Do you know where, exactly?"

"No. But I think he's probably working Chain Reaction."

Chain Reaction was debatably Smith's most renowned climb. And it was less than a quarter of a mile away.

"You mean right now?" Fallon asked, still in a daze. The realization that his paid climbing trip might be nearly over was sinking in.

"Right now."

Scott was getting impatient with all the business talk. "So are we gonna do some climbs while the sun's still up, man?"

Fallon reached behind him and felt the pack, confirming that his notebook was in it. "Hell, yeah—just let me go ask this guy a few questions. I'll be back in less than an hour." He started back down the boulder field. Stopping about fifty feet away, he turned back to his friends. "Oh, can I stay at your place for a couple of days?"

Sara sat back on the rock behind her. "We've got a wedding to go to tonight. We'll leave the front door open."

Fallon sat down in the dirt and pulled the notebook from his backpack. He lay back and put on his sunglasses. The blond figure was about halfway up the climb, and struggling. Despite his long arms, he missed the hold he was aiming for and fell six feet or so before the rope stopped him. Fallon looked on calmly, silently critiquing his technique.

"Shit, man, I'm never going to get this—too late in the day."

"You want down?" his partner asked.

"Yeah, might as well."

Fallon watched as the climber slowly lowered. When his feet hit the ground, Fallon interrupted what sounded like the beginning of a long conversation about tomorrow's climbing strategy.

"Excuse me. Are you Lance Richardson?"

The young man looked up from the knot he was untying. "Yeah. Do I know you?"

"Nope." Fallon didn't get up, but leaned forward and pulled a pen from his pocket. "My name's Matt Fallon."

Richardson wagged his finger up and down, trying to remember something. Finally it came to him. "Hey, aren't you that guy from Boulder who quit climbing to join the CIA or something?"

Fallon frowned. "FBI. There's a difference."

"So how do you know me?"

"I've been trying to find you for weeks, actually."

Richardson's climbing partner was looking at him strangely.

Fallon figured he was wondering if he'd hooked up with a mass murderer or something.

"We're looking for someone who was a customer of the bank you used to work for." The climbing partner relaxed a bit and began slowly coiling his rope.

Richardson sat down next to Fallon. "Seems like years ago, man—bank jobs, you know?"

The agent nodded, remembering the shit jobs he had taken to finance climbing trips. "You might actually remember this guy. It was right before you left. He brought in a suitcase full of cash to buy some cashier's checks."

"Oh, him. Yeah, I do remember him, sort of."

Fallon shook his head. This guy must not have looked at a TV or newspaper since he had left Saint Louis. It made him long for the good old days. "So what can you tell me about him?"

"Nothing really—don't remember his name or anything," Richardson began, spreading his legs wide and beginning to stretch. "He came up to the teller window where I was working—but we didn't do cashier's checks there, you know. So I sent him to one of the customer service reps. I don't remember which one."

Fallon decided to pass on asking for a description, they had twenty already. "Nothing else?"

He continued stretching. "Actually, I saw him later that day, now that I think about it."

Fallon perked up. "Where was that?" he asked, putting the list of climbs that he wanted do that afternoon out of his head.

"Up the street at a little shopping mall. I didn't talk to him or anything. I was just stopped at a light and he was getting into his car."

Fallon scribbled in the notebook. His heart was beating faster and faster. "Remember what kind of car, by any chance?"

"Sure. It's not every day somebody walks into the bank with a suitcase full of cash—we thought he was a drug dealer or something. Was he?"

"Not exactly."

Richardson looked disappointed. "It was a red Cherokee. Not one of those cool new Limiteds—just one of the old boxy ones. I remember thinking that a guy with that much cash ought to have a nicer ride, you know?"

"Do you remember anything else about the car? Things hanging from the rearview mirror, dents, bumper stickers—anything, really."

"Nothing like that—it was really clean. Looked new. It did have those Save the Chesapeake plates on it, though."

Fallon looked at him with a confused expression.

"You know—from Maryland. I went to school there. The climbing sucks."

29

Baltimore, Maryland,
March 6

What the hell's going on?" Robert Swenson demanded in a loud voice, bursting through the front door of the apartment.

Hobart looked up from a thick computer printout, annoyed at his partner's untimely entrance. He had a headache that no aspirin seemed to be able to cure.

"What's the problem, Bob?" he asked calmly, already knowing the answer.

"I just watched one of our guys get blown away on the steps of some jail in New York and now I'm hearing that the guy that shot him was shot from another building when he was getting away."

Hobart leaned back in his chair, turning the printout to face his desk. "I saw the report," he said cheerfully. "A stroke of good luck— looks like we won't have to close up shop as soon as we thought."

Swenson eyed him suspiciously. "How do you know he didn't already talk?"

"I have a well-positioned . . . friend. He confirmed it."

"Is he reliable?"

Hobart nodded. He had caught his "friend" stuffing his pockets full of cash at a drug bust almost ten years ago. He could have turned him in but decided against it. Better to hold out for a favor if he ever really needed one.

After confirming Nelson's silence, this particular friend had made it clear that all debts were repaid. He had slammed the phone down before Hobart could threaten him again. There had been no answer since.

"They haven't released the name of the shooter, but they're broadcasting a picture. You wouldn't be acquainted, would you?" Swenson asked.

"Karns," Hobart said, feigning disgust. "I was wrong to have let him back on board. Loose cannon. He must have heard the report that Nelson was talking and figured he'd try to make up for the strychnine thing."

"And who do you figure got him?"

"Oh, hell, probably the Bureau. They fucked up and now they're covering up. Doesn't look too good, them blowing away their star witness." Hobart could tell from his partner's expression that he wasn't buying it.

"And where were you yesterday at ten o'clock?" Swenson asked, an edge of nervousness in his voice. Hobart smiled. He could tell that his partner desperately wanted to believe that he hadn't been involved. People with that kind of bias were easily convinced.

"I was in the office working on our budget."

He knew that Swenson had been in D.C. the entire day of the shooting and had no way of knowing whether that was true or not. He would undoubtedly check the time and date of the budget file on the computer the minute he got the opportunity. Hobart had temporarily reset the internal time clock on the system when he had saved it. It would read 10:35 A.M., roughly a half hour after the incident. Not proof positive, of course, but it should ease his partner's mind long enough to finish this thing.

"They're gonna trace Nelson and Karns back to you sooner or later," Swenson said. "We've still gotta get out of here."

"Yeah, but I didn't know them that well. Even with a couple a hundred agents on it, they won't get back to me for at least four weeks. So I figure we've got two weeks to wrap things up and get a little more work done."

Swenson looked doubtful.

"I've got some stuff I've really got to finish up, Bob. You mind?"

Swenson stood. "So what's your plan for today?"

"I'm heading out in about an hour or so. Be back tonight."

"Maybe we can get together and talk about how we're gonna wrap this thing up," Swenson said hopefully. On his way out, he paused and looked down at the chess board sitting next to the television. Two white pawns, representing Nelson and Karns, were lying on their sides. Two blue pawns representing the dead cartel enforcers were in a similar position.

Alone again, Hobart flipped the printout on his desk over and continued running down the endless columns of numbers with the aid of a ruler.

The list had been provided by an old acquaintance who worked for C&P Telephone. Phil Nelson's capture had jolted him like a bolt of lightning. He'd spent hours running though the operation in his mind, trying to find where he might have screwed up.

In the end, he had decided that Nelson had blown it somewhere. That was a risk you ran in this type of operation—it was impossible to do everything yourself.

He had gone to bed that night chalking up Nelson's capture to the fortunes of war—confident that in the next two weeks he could continue to turn public opinion, and then slip silently out of the country.

It had been almost three in the morning when he had bolted upright in his bed. He had mentioned the DiPrizzio operation to Blake at the hotel. Could the Reverend have called the Bureau? Hobart dismissed the idea at first, but had been unable to get back to sleep. In the end, it had nagged at him enough to spend an entire day on a tour of the pay phones of the greater Baltimore metro area. He had pulled off every freeway exit ramp between Blake's office and home, and between the hotel where they had met and Blake's home, copying down the numbers of the first pay phones that he saw.

His acquaintance at the phone company had almost choked on the list of numbers, but Hobart had explained that the Reverend was getting death threats and that this was an integral part of the investigation. A devout follower of Blake, his acquaintance had called in some favors and retrieved a list of the long-distance numbers called from those phones on the dates that Hobart had supplied him.

He rubbed his eyes, painfully aware that the phone company could have had their computer search specifically for the FBI hotline number and saved him hours of tedium and a migraine headache. Everyone in the country knew that number, though. It had been running along the bottom of every TV screen in America for the past two months.

He was on the second-to-the-last page when he found it. Leaning back in his chair, he tossed the thick stack of paper in the garbage. He had underestimated his former employer. Blake was a consummate actor. He had left the hotel with just the right mix of nervousness, sadness, and growing calm. Not overacted, not underacted.

So now he knew. The question was, what could he do with the information?

Mark Beamon paused in the open door to the SIOC. The normally fast pace of the agents inside had been accelerated to a fevered pitch. People talked loudly on phones, typed furiously on laptop computers, televisions blared CNN. The increased activity further tightened the hand that gripped the back of his head every time he walk into the JEH Building.

Laura was leaning over a man's shoulder, reading off his computer screen. Beamon threaded his way toward her, nodding to the hustling agents who bid him a good morning.

"Jesus, Laura—do you live here?" It was seven-thirty A.M. He had hoped to beat her to the office for once, but as usual he felt like he was strolling in at ten.

"Just like to put in a full day at the office," she said, walking around the table.

Beamon grunted and made his way to the coffeemaker. "Want one?" he asked her.

She shook her head. "Had two already this morning. I'm wired."

"Well then, why don't you step into my parlor," Beamon said, heading toward an empty conference room. "Tell me what's going on."

Holding a manila folder under her arm, Laura closed the door behind her and began in as excited a voice as he'd ever heard from her. "We've got guys waiting at the front door of the MVA—Maryland Motor Vehicles Administration. They'll start running down Cherokee registrations this morning."

"What's our time frame on getting a list cross-referenced with the driver's licenses of people who fit our guy's description."

She shrugged. "I have no idea. State motor vehicle departments have different database capabilities. I should be able to give you a pretty good idea later today."

She took a seat at the small table across from Beamon. "Our dead shooter's name is William Karns." She slid the manila folder across the conference table. Beamon picked it up and began reading.

"His prints were on file 'cause he was an ex-cop."

"Seems to be a pattern emerging."

"It gets better. We have three witnesses who place Karns living in an abandoned house only a few blocks from the site of that strychnine poisoning."

"So he's probably not just some crazy—and it looks like you were wrong about the strychnine poisoning being a copycat."

"It looks like we were wrong," Laura corrected in a slightly annoyed tone. "We've got agents digging into his background and known acquaintances right now."

"I didn't catch the morning paper. What's the press got?"

"Wild speculation, mostly. They don't have his name, obviously, and they're running theories from suicide, to the FBI killing him, to one of his own getting him . . ." Her voice trailed off.

"Come on, what else?"

Laura looked down at the table. "You're taking a lot of criticism for letting Nelson get shot."

"Yeah, I seem to be developing kind of a love/hate thing with the press."

"I don't know how you can joke about this, Mark. The thing with Nelson wasn't even your idea and now you're going to be left holding the bag while everyone runs for cover."

Beamon nodded thoughtfully. "It's just politics, Laura. I hope you're taking notes. Always make sure you've scoped out a comfortable chair before the music stops."

"Well, you're setting one hell of an example."

Beamon laughed. "This is one of those 'do as I say and not as I do' situations. You'll find there are a lot of those where I'm concerned."

Laura leaned back in her chair and relaxed a little. "Well, I hope you know that I'm behind you, Mark."

"No, you're not. You'll run for cover too if you have to."

An expression of deep hurt crossed Laura's face. "How can you say . . ."

Beamon held up his hands, silencing her. "I know you're willing to go down with me in this thing, Laura, and that means a lot. But there's no point to it. Besides, I'm counting on you being Director someday and giving me a big promotion."

Laura forced a smile. "And maybe I just will."

Beamon pushed his chair back on two legs and balanced precariously with his feet on the edge of the table. "Enough of this political crap. Chasing criminals is supposed to be fun. Are you ready for our field trip?"

"What do you mean?"

"What do you mean, what do I mean? I mean, let's get out there, have a greasy breakfast at Denny's, and do detective stuff. You and me—the whole day. It'll be just like Starsky and Hutch." He dropped the front of the chair back to the floor and stood.

"Mark, I can't just leave . . ."

He waved his hand dismissively. "The Bureau can survive without you in the office for one day, Laura. Delegate. We're leaving in a half hour."

He slugged down the last of his coffee and headed for the door. Laura scrambled out ahead of him to try to get a day's worth of work done in thirty minutes.

"Don't get me wrong, Laura. Eggs fried at a mom and pop diner have a certain subtlety that just can't be achieved in a chain restaurant." Beamon was gesturing wildly with his right hand, paying little attention to his left, which was steering the car. A toothpick hung loosely from his lips. "But to me, Denny's had the best quality/price/quantity ratio."

Laura was feeling sick from the Grand Slam breakfast lodged in her stomach and Beamon's wild driving. His dissertation on the history of the greasy Southern breakfast wasn't helping any, either. She decided to change the subject.

"You still haven't told me where we're going."

"Baltimore."

"Baltimore. Okay. Why?"

"I told you already—to do detective stuff." He dug a wad of yellow paper from his shirt pocket and handed it to her.

She unfolded the pages. They were from the phone book. The word "Theaters" was in the top right-hand corner of the first page.

"We're going to see a movie?"

He gave her an exaggerated look of disgust. "No, we're not going to see a goddam movie. Flip the page."

She turned it over. The heading "Theatrical Makeup" was highlighted in green.

"We've theorized that the guy in Poland and the guy at the bank were one and the same and that he was wearing sophisticated makeup. A wig, fake beard, that kind of stuff, right? Now, if he is from Baltimore, it stands to reason that he got the disguises around there. So, all we have to do is find a shopkeeper who remembers a short, thin guy buying those particular items about two months ago. Show him the driver's license pictures we're gonna get from the MVA, and budda bing. We're done."

"Why Baltimore?" Laura asked, concentrating on keeping her voice even. *Why hadn't she thought of that?*

"Well, what do we know about this guy? We know he's not from D.C. or Saint Louis, 'cause both those cities were implicated with the cashier's checks—the FedEx place was in D.C., and the bank was in Saint Louis. Now we find out he has Maryland plates. D.C.'s an easy drive from Baltimore, and you can make it to Saint Louis in a day—I looked it up. Also, our anonymous informant called from a pay phone near Baltimore. My gut's never failed me in almost twenty years—and it's screaming Baltimore."

"Are you sure it's not the three eggs, bacon, ham, hash browns, and biscuits and gravy."

Beamon chuckled. "Stop—you're making me hungry."

"What about somewhere else in Maryland—say Rockville? It fits the facts too."

Beamon shrugged. "Yeah, you could be right. If we don't get what we want today, we'll get some guys to expand the search."

Laura leaned forward and flipped on the radio. She had grown accustomed to having the news blaring in her ear twenty-four hours a day. "It's a long shot . . ."

"Hey, at least it got us out of the office."

Laura juggled her legal pad and the large map of Baltimore that they had picked up at a gas station on the way there. Map reading was just not her forte.

"Turn right here," she ordered at the last minute. Beamon turned the wheel hard, squealing the tires.

"Jesus, Laura. A little advance warning would be nice."

"Why don't you let me drive and you navigate," she asked hopefully. The words 'suicide seat' had taken on real meaning in the last couple of hours.

"Nah. Reading maps in the car makes me sick."

They were on their last costume shop in the Baltimore area. No luck so far, though Laura had a list of names to follow up on the next day. People who may have been working on the dates in question, but either weren't in today or had changed jobs.

"There it is." She pointed across Beamon's nose and out the

driver's side window. He wheeled the car around unexpectedly, making a U-turn in the middle of the street, and pulled up in front of the shop. Laura gripped the dash.

"Everybody out," Beamon announced unnecessarily. Laura had the door opened and was hopping from the car before it had entirely stopped.

"Hi, I'm Mark Beamon from the FBI and this is my associate, Laura Vilechi. There was no need to flash his credentials, the man behind the counter recognized him as soon as he said his name.

"Wow, nice to meet you, Mr. Beamon. I've seen you on television." He nodded a greeting to Laura. "What brings you to my store?"

"This is your place?" Beamon asked, carefully examining a luxurious blond wig on a white Styrofoam head.

"Yes, sir."

Beamon nodded and wandered off to look around.

Seeing that Beamon was beginning to lose interest in this investigative avenue, Laura decided to start questioning the shopkeeper without him. "We thought you might have some information that we need."

"Sure, anything I can do to help."

She smiled engagingly and sat down in an antique barber's chair in the center of the room. "What we're looking for is a man approximately five foot eight or less, thin, between thirty-five and forty-five, who might have come in here about two months ago and purchased, at the least, a long gray wig and beard and a long brown wig and beard, as well as makeup to perhaps make his features look different and darken his skin. He probably wouldn't have known much about using the stuff—might have asked for some advice . . ."

The man leaned against the counter behind him, a thoughtful look on his face.

"Is this about the CDFS?"

She nodded.

"Does he have short dark hair—kind of a crew cut?"

"Maybe, we're not sure."

"Yeah, I remember a guy like that. Wanted only the best. Must have spent a small fortune."

Beamon, who until a minute ago had seemed completely oblivious to the conversation, was suddenly at the man's side.

"Excuse me, Mr. . . ."

"Reasor. But call me Chris."

"Chris. You say you might remember this guy?"

"Yeah, sure. He kind of stuck in my mind, you know. Most of my business is kinda regular—so it's pretty unusual for a guy I've never seen to come in and make a big purchase like that. He also didn't really seem like the acting type."

"Did you ask him what he was going to use it for?" Laura asked.

Reasor thought for a moment. "Now that you mention it, I don't think I did. He wasn't really very friendly—hard to warm up to. He was in here a long time, too—didn't know the first thing about makeup."

"Chris, would you mind coming back to D.C. with us for the evening? We'll be happy to put you up in a nice hotel and compensate you for the time your shop's closed. I'd like to have you get together with one of our sketch artists."

"Hell, yes, I'll go. Those CDFS guys are crazy. Let me go grab my coat."

Beamon watched the store owner hurry to the back of the store. When he was out of sight, Beamon turned and gave Laura a hard spin in the barber chair. She gripped the handles tightly and laughed. "Looks like we might just save your butt after all, Mark."

Alejandro Perez hurried through the plush gardens surrounding Luis Colombar's estate, nodding to the guards as he passed them. Spring was fully upon them, and the cool evenings had turned sticky. The sun had just set on the horizon and its light was bouncing off the humid air with a spectacular effect. The sunset, combined with the quiet beauty of the garden this time of year, cast a false peace. Perez knew better.

He left the well-tended brick walkway, turning onto a narrow dirt trail. Through the trees he could see the glimmering lights of a greenhouse in the distance.

He stepped through its door, quickly closing it behind him so as not to release the warm air into the quickly cooling Colombian night. He felt his brow break out in a sweat from a combination of the heat and Colombar's tone when he had summoned him.

"Alejandro. I'm over here."

Perez caught a glimpse of his boss behind a table covered with tall and colorful flowers. He walked quickly across the wet concrete, noticing a strange and foul odor that gained strength as he approached the table. He wondered why Colombar would keep flowers that smelled so noxious, even if they were beautiful to look at. "I came as quickly as I could, Luis," he said, trying to look slightly out of breath.

"I suppose you haven't yet seen the package that I received today." Colombar wasn't looking at him, but was concentrating on the bright pink bulb in front of him.

"What package?"

Colombar gestured toward the back of the greenhouse with his shears. Perez looked at him strangely, then set off in the direction his boss had pointed. On a table in the back, next to a group of half-full sacks of fertilizer and soil, sat a box with a Federal Express sticker on the top. The tape had been torn off, but the flaps were closed. The odor continued to grow.

Perez reached out and pulled back the flaps. He gasped, the smell of the rotting head choking him. He pushed the flap closed and stumbled backward, bumping into Colombar, who had crept up silently behind him.

"Read the card," he invited, pointing back to the box.

Perez swallowed hard, and moving forward, reopened the box. There was a blood-smeared envelope lying across the head's mouth. One yellow eye stared up at him as he snatched it and retreated to the other side of the greenhouse.

NEVER SEND A SPIC TO DO A MAN'S WORK, YOU DICKLESS FOOL

SINCERELY,

JOHN

"I hoped that you might translate the note for me, Alejandro. As you know, my English is less than perfect."

Perez considered softening the language a bit, but thought better of it. Colombar's English was undoubtedly good enough to have read the note. The question was why Colombar wanted to hear it from his mouth?

He translated the note verbatim.

Colombar leaned against an empty table, motionless except for his right hand that twirled his shears ominously. "Do you know who that was?"

Perez answered quietly, trying to hide his nervousness. "I can only assume that it is one of the men that you sent after John Hobart."

"Our little plan didn't work very well, did it?" Colombar observed.

Our little plan?

Perez mopped the sweat from his forehead, thinking before answering. He decided against correcting his boss's faulty memory. "I guess not."

It seemed to be what Colombar wanted to hear. He turned and went back to working on the sick bulb. "I want you to go find this John Hobart. When you do, call me, and I will take care of the arrangements."

Perez winced. "Luis, this is just the reaction our Mr. Hobart was trying to provoke. We must inform the FBI. They are much better equipped to find him than I am. Especially now that he knows we're looking."

"No," Colombar replied calmly. "You'll go and find him. I want to hold this man's eyes in my hand."

Perez shuffled uncomfortably. He had seen Colombar in this

mood only twice in the years he had known him. The cartel leader's levels of rage went from shouting in his practiced European Spanish, to screaming in the Spanish of his youth, to killing people with his bare hands, to dead calm. Dead calm was the worst. That's when he had someone pick you and your family up for a long, slow appointment with death.

"I'll leave immediately, Luis. Should we inform the others of this development?"

"No."

30

Near Baltimore, Maryland,
March 8

The Reverend Simon Blake watched his wife over his pool cue as she walked across the spacious basement. She was carrying a silver tray with a single mug on it.

"I was making hot chocolate for the kids and thought you might like some," she said, setting the mug on a long table behind a leather sofa.

Blake eyed her sadly, wondering how his actions would affect her. Things were out of control, and for the first time in his life, he wasn't sure what he was going to do. God's voice had been silenced.

"Thanks, honey," he said, missing the side pocket with the two ball.

"Are you having fun?"

The pool table had been a gift from her and the kids for his birthday. Erica had read somewhere that pool was an especially therapeutic and relaxing pastime. He could feel her eyes on him, and made an effort to look happier and more energetic than he felt.

"Sure am. I'm starting to get pretty good, too." The statement was accentuated with another miss. He was having trouble concentrating on anything these days.

She nodded, and padded silently out of the room. As he watched her go, he felt tears well up in his eyes.

His plan hadn't worked. In retrospect, it had been a stupid and desperate move. The man he had informed on was dead, as was his killer. And John Hobart was still a shadowy figure perched at the edge of every news report. Why hadn't he just told the FBI Hobart was behind it? He had asked himself that question a hundred times a day since Nelson's death. In the end, he discovered that the answer wasn't complicated. Fear. He had always been afraid of John Hobart—his cold demeanor, the eyes devoid of passion and morality. That twinge of fear had been a small price to pay to have Hobart's ruthless efficiency behind the workings of the church. But now control had shifted. Hobart was clearly in charge. Unhampered by Blake's values and religious sensibilities, he had no limitations.

Blake leaned his cue against the table and reached for the hot chocolate. Steam rose around the whipped cream piled on top. He sipped the hot fluid loudly, knowing he would regret it later. These past few months he had suffered from a constant sense of anxiety. It was an indescribable sensation—as if he was always on the verge of hyperventilating. As if something dreadful waited for him just around the next corner. Sugar and caffeine were definitely contraindicated.

He was nestled into the sofa, finishing his drink, when his cellular phone rang. It was always with him, used to transact business that his parishioners might not fully understand.

"Hello?"

"Hello, Reverend."

Blake's breath caught in his chest. Hobart.

"What can I do for you?"

"I know it was you."

"What are you talking about, John. I fired you months ago. What are you doing calling me at my home?"

He had devised this plan over the past week. There was no real evidence connecting him with the CDFS. He had never really been involved, beyond letting Hobart drain some insignificant dollars from the church's accounts.

There was silence on the other end of the phone. Blake waited anxiously to see if his plan had worked.

"If you want out, Reverend—fine. But you better stay out. If the Bureau gets another tip, I'm coming for your family."

Blake's jaw dropped.

"I'll make you watch while I cut them to pieces. And if I'm caught, I'll have someone else do it for me. Do you understand?"

Blake's mind churned uselessly, words not able to escape his throat. How could he have put his family in the middle of something like this?

"Do you understand?" Hobart's voice repeated. There was no hint of annoyance or threat in his voice. It was cold and matter-of-fact.

"Yes."

"That's good, Reverend. Good-bye."

The phone clicked, but Blake didn't move. When the dial tone started, he put the phone on the table next to him and wept.

Fifty miles away, John Hobart flipped on his computer. Things were going to have to be wound up pretty quickly. He still had the number to the church's computer, and the passwords necessary to access all of its accounts. It looked like he was going to have to get out of Dodge, but there was no reason to take off without a little extra pocket money.

"Reverend Blake? There's a man here to see you. He says it's urgent," Blake's secretary said quietly.

"Does he have an appointment?" Blake asked, peering at the calendar at the top of his desk. It was blank.

She stepped through the door and closed it quietly behind her. "No sir, but he's from the FBI."

Blake's expression didn't change. The adrenaline that had been coursing through him for the past two months had finally dried up. He didn't care what happened anymore. He just wanted release from the pressure.

"Please show him in."

"Reverend Blake, I'm sorry to disturb you without an appointment, but it is an urgent matter."

Blake took the agent's hand. It was cool and dry. "Don't think anything of it." He pointed toward the conference table in the corner of the office.

The FBI must be paying pretty well, Blake thought, watching the sheen of the man's expensive suit as he walked toward the table. The watch on his wrist looked like a Rolex.

"I am special agent Alejandro Martinez," the man said, flashing his credentials. His speech had more than a hint of accent. It reminded Blake of Ricardo Montalban in "Fantasy Island."

"What can I do for you, Agent Martinez?"

"I believe that a man named John Hobart once worked for you. I'd be interested in any information that you could provide me on him. Especially in regards to his whereabouts."

The last of his adrenaline was squeezed out into his bloodstream at the mention of Hobart's name. "I really have no idea where he is, I haven't seen him in some time. Have you tried his home? I can get my secretary to get you the address."

"We've been by his home, yes. It would appear that he hasn't been there in quite a while." Martinez smiled engagingly. "And I already took the liberty of asking your secretary to copy Mr. Hobart's personnel file."

Blake shrugged noncommittally. "May I ask you why you're looking for John?"

"I apologize, but I am not at liberty to say," he answered gravely. "But it is a matter of the utmost importance, I assure you. I would also like to stress how important it is that you do not mention my visit here."

"Of course. Sorry I can't be of more help, but as you probably know, John's employment here was terminated a couple of months ago."

"Yes, we were aware of that." The agent pulled out a small notebook from his jacket pocket. "If you have a couple of minutes, I would like to ask you a few general questions about Mr. Hobart. Things that might make it easier for us to locate him."

Blake adjusted to a slightly more comfortable position in the chair.

"Sure, go ahead."

31

Washington, D.C.,
March 9

Mark Beamon nimbly sidestepped a young man with a box-filled handcart and walked through the door to SIOC.

The place was a mess. The conference table had been pushed against the wall, and a stack of large cardboard boxes had taken its place as the focal point of the room. Around the boxes were endless piles of car registrations, each with a copy of a driver's license attached with a paper clip.

Laura saw him come in and strode over with a wide grin. "We're just getting rid of some of the low priority stuff. It's getting hard to move in here."

Beamon nodded in agreement. "So you've got registrations to every red Cherokee in Maryland?"

"Actually, we have registrations for *every* Cherokee, period. Maryland doesn't put the color on the registration. Laura beamed. She was in her element now. As much as Beamon hated details, she loved them.

"How many?"

"Let's see . . ." She chewed the end of her pen thoughtfully. "I think it ended up being almost seven thousand."

Beamon let out a long breath. Thank God she was here to sort through all this crap.

"So where are we?" he asked through a yawn.

"We started investigating our top thirty this morning."

The suspects were being prioritized by matching the pictures, height, and weight on the license with the descriptions obtained by eyewitnesses, and the rather vague drawing obtained from the costume store shopkeeper.

"Already?" Mark replied "Now how the hell did you manage to go through seven thousand documents that fast?"

"Only about fifteen hundred, actually. We started with the red ones."

"But you said that the color wasn't on the registration."

"It's not, but the VIN numbers have color information in them. We got Chrysler to cross-reference for us."

He bowed deeply at the waist, almost dropping his old trench coat. "As always, my dear, your efficiency leaves me speechless."

She smiled. "The thirty in process are over there if you want to take a look." She pointed to a blackboard that was covered with neat rows of driver's licenses. In the top right-hand corner of the board was the artist's sketch of their suspect.

"Why not? Let's grab a couple of cups of coffee and take a look."

Beamon looked ruefully at the nearly empty coffee pot, and glanced back over his shoulder. "Who drank all the coffee and didn't make more?"

The agents in the room suddenly got busier, redoubling their efforts on whatever they were working on.

"So what have you been doing all morning?" Laura asked. It was almost ten o'clock.

Beamon made a face like he had just bitten into a lemon. "You know that senator who's son died from bad coke a couple of weeks ago?"

"James Mirth?"

Beamon nodded. "I just spent the morning with him. He wanted me to come by personally and tell him why I hadn't caught the people who murdered his son yet."

"Oh," Laura said sympathetically. "And how did that go?"

"Shitty. Now let's see what you've got." He headed for the blackboard, patting his pockets for his reading glasses. Tom Sherman gave him a wave from the corner of the room, where he was talking quietly into a phone.

"Here they are," Laura said, gesturing to thirty color copies of driver's license pictures taped onto the blackboard. Each had a name and brief description of the subject next to it. The description at this point consisted of little more than basic driver's license information. Finding his glasses, Beamon began inspecting each picture, starting at the top left. Somewhere into the fourth row, his face went blank for a moment.

"Son of a bitch!" he shouted loudly enough that Laura sloshed a good portion of her coffee on her blouse. "I know this asshole!"

Beamon ripped the picture off the blackboard and moved past Laura, who was walking in circles pulling her shirt in and out, trying to cool the dark stain spattered across her chest. He slapped the picture down on the conference table. "Christ, Laura, quit playing with yourself and come over here. This is him!"

The agents in the room suddenly finished the tasks that a moment ago were so important, and began crowding around him, looking at the picture that was now stuck in the middle of the conference table. Sherman hung up his phone and took a seat at the end of the table.

"I worked an investigation in Baltimore with this guy—must have been ten years ago," Beamon started. "He was working for DEA at the time. I was impressed with him at first—he was quiet, but really bright and insanely dedicated. So he's got this informant that he wants me to meet. I get there a little late and he's beat the shit out of him. Broke his arm. Lying son of a bitch almost got me thrown out of the Bureau."

He turned away from the table and went through a rather elaborate pantomime of a football player spiking a ball.

"Call up the guys investigating him. Tell 'em he's damned dangerous." He was grinning from ear to ear and seriously considering breaking into song.

"Sorry to ruin the mood, Mark," Sherman cut in, "but aren't you forgetting something?"

Beamon thought for a moment. "Let's see, find out the identity of the criminal, catch the criminal. Nope, I got it covered."

Sherman pointed to a phone anchored to one of the room's glass walls. "Call Calahan."

"Don't suppose you'd like to do it for me."

Sherman shook his head. "You did the work, Mark. Can't hurt for you to take the credit."

Beamon sighed and dialed the direct line to the Director's office. It was picked up on the first ring.

"Calahan."

"Mark Beamon, sir—I think we've identified our man. We believe he's an ex-DEA agent named John . . ."

"When can you pick him up?" came the Director excited reply. He sounded like he was already planning his press conference.

"I don't really know, sir. We believe he's in the Baltimore area. Hell, we may just be able to pick him up at his house—but I doubt it. If he hasn't been seen there in a while, we'll have to assume that he's relocated somewhere else in the city. In that case, I figure we bring in a bunch of guys from New York and Philly to help out. With that kind of manpower, and assuming we're right about him still being in the Baltimore area, we should have him in a couple of weeks at the outside."

There was a long pause on the other end of the phone. "If he isn't at his house, bring the Baltimore Police in on this. They've got far more manpower than we can muster."

In the back of his mind, Beamon had known that the Director would make that suggestion. He had been hoping that the back of his mind would be wrong this time.

"I don't think that that's such a good idea right now. I wouldn't want to do anything that could tip this guy off."

Beamon knew he was treading on thin ice here. The Director had been a street cop early in his career. It had only been for about a year, but he never let his subordinates forget that he had once "walked the beat."

"I've had it with this us-and-them attitude between the FBI and police." The volume of Calahan's voice had risen a notch.

Beamon interrupted before Calahan could get both feet firmly planted on his FBI/local police relations soapbox. "Sir, with all due respect to the Baltimore Police Department, I think we can count on the fact that a man like John Hobart is going to be keeping an eye on what's going on there."

Calahan was yelling now in that high-pitched whine that Beamon remembered so well. "If I want the Baltimore Police Force brought in on this, you'll goddam well bring them in on it."

Beamon tried to imitate the calm, humble tone Tom Sherman used when trying to placate the Director. "Sir, you agreed to let me head this investigation because of my experience and track record. Please, just let me do my job and I'll get this guy."

Calahan laughed bitterly. "Your experience and track record? My, we do have a high opinion of ourselves, don't we? I let Sherman bring you in on this because you're expendable. Don't ever kid yourself that it was anything more than that."

Beamon felt control slipping away from him. Thousands of people were dead, and Calahan was off on another one of his personal power trips. "Sir, I don't think that even you can be this fucking dense. Is there another agenda here that I'm not aware of?"

The room behind him went completely silent. For a moment, Beamon thought that the CNN commentator on the TV above him had even stopped talking. As he leaned back to check, Tom Sherman snatched the phone out of his hand.

"Sir, this is Tom Sherman."

Beamon noticed how effectively the plush carpet muffled his footsteps as he walked back to the conference table and fell into one of the chairs. The unintelligible high-pitched shouting coming over the phone was audible even over the sound of the television sets.

Everyone was still silent, and they were all now looking at him with faint smiles of admiration. Beamon figured that every one of them went to bed at night fantasizing about doing what he just did. He turned his attention back to Sherman as he replaced the receiver.

"Could you give us a few minutes, please?" Sherman said to the agents grouped at the other end of the room. As they filed quietly out, Beamon felt a pang of guilt. Sherman had blocked a number of vicious political blows meant for him over the years. He also knew that Sherman had put his reputation on the line in giving him this job.

"Not you, Laura," Sherman said, taking the seat across from Beamon. Laura sat down as far from them as the conference table would allow.

"What the hell are you doing, Mark? Couldn't you just finish the job and add another chapter in your legend? I could have turned this case into a real leg up for you."

"Bullshit, Tommy. It's not that I don't appreciate your effort, you know I do. But let's face it, my condition's terminal here. I never thought I'd say it, but I'm ready to put this case to bed and get back to my little life in Houston."

Sherman shook his head and let out a long sigh. "It's not your case to put to bed anymore. It's Laura's show now."

Both men turned toward her. She looked like she wanted to crawl under the table.

Beamon stood and stretched his arms wildly. "Well then, it looks like I've got a plane to catch."

"No you don't. You're staying on the team. Calahan seems to think that working for a woman might teach you a little humility."

Beamon resisted the urge to look over at Laura as he sat back down. She wasn't going to take that insult lightly. "I don't know, Tommy, has working for a moron taught you humility?"

Sherman stood and headed for the exit. "I don't care how you delegate the authority here, but I will tell you this. If we don't have this guy by tonight, get on the phone to the commissioner and get the police in on this. That's not a request."

Sherman stopped at the door. "Oh, and Laura. That woman comment came from Calahan, not from me. When Mark asked that you be brought in on this, he told me you were one of the best investigators in the Bureau. I haven't seen anything to suggest he's wrong."

*　　　*　　　*

"Nice job, Mark," Laura said after Sherman had pulled the door fully closed. "What were you thinking, talking to the Director like that?"

Beamon pushed violently on the table, rolling his chair back a couple of feet. "Why the hell shouldn't I? Calahan spends a few years as a judge and plays golf with a couple of political hacks, and that qualifies him to tell me how to run my investigation? It'd be funny if there weren't fucking twenty thousand people dead."

Laura moved to the chair that Sherman had vacated. "Okay, so Calahan's an idiot. That's no reason for you to push your personal self-destruct button. It's starting to get a little worn out, Mark."

"So am I."

Laura bounced her fist playfully against his knee. "Well, we better catch this guy and get you back to Houston before Calahan puts you in charge of the janitorial staff. What's the plan?"

"I'm thinking that we have to count on the general APB going out. Hobart's one smart son of a bitch. I can pretty much guarantee we won't get him by tonight."

"We'll have them announce the APB at roll call. At least we can keep it from going out over the radio."

Beamon nodded. "May I make a couple of suggestions?"

Laura smiled almost imperceptibly. "I don't think I've ever heard you *suggest* anything before. Maybe working for a little ol' girl *is* going to improve your social graces."

"Don't count on it."

"Believe me, I'm not. So what are your suggestions?"

"Well, if we find out that Hobart isn't living at his house—and I think we will—he must be living somewhere else; probably a rental. Get some guys to run down all the houses rented from around the time the neighbors said they stopped seeing him. They should be able to get a handle on that through the local realtors and old newspapers."

"Anything else?"

"Yeah. As soon as he hears that we're onto him, he's gonna have to get rid of his car—if he hasn't already. I want the car rental agencies around Baltimore faxing us copies of the driver's licenses of everyone who rents a car. We should probably try to get that going tomorrow."

Laura nodded as she scribbled on the legal pad in front of her. Finally she looked up. "So did you really say that about me?"

"What."

"You know. About being one of the best investigators."

Beamon smiled. "Nah. Tom's a little senile—gets things confused. I've been covering for him for years."

Officer Larry McFee pulled his cruiser up behind another just like it on the crowded West Baltimore street. He turned on his lights and got out of the car, slipping his nightstick into his belt.

A small crowd had gathered and was milling around lazily in front of a crumbling row home. Domestic disputes were commonplace in this neighborhood, but could still be an interesting diversion. A brief respite from the boredom of the unusually hot March afternoon.

McFee pushed silently through the crowd. It offered token resistance, the people displaying their lack of respect for the law. He hated domestic disputes more than any other kind of bust. They were dangerous and generally pointless—charges were almost never pressed. All in all, one big waste of time.

The row home had been divided into four small apartments. The door to the apartment at the end of the hall on the right was wide open, and the shouting that had been muffled outside was now clear as a bell. He put his hand on his nightstick and walked quickly toward the noise.

He stood for a moment in the open doorway. A heavyset black male, approximately forty-five years of age, was brandishing a rolling pin threateningly. His bare chest was spattered with blood. Less than ten feet from him, a young cop was pointing a .38 at his head. The yelling was coming from the cop, as he urged the man to put down the rolling pin and lie down on the floor. McFee grimaced and scanned the rest of the room. Behind the sofa, a burly woman cop was helping a severely battered woman to her feet. Her face looked to be the source of the blood on the man's chest.

McFee shook his head, feeling a familiar hatred rising in him. A friend of his had been killed in a situation not unlike this one.

"So what the fuck's going on in here?"

The young cop shifted his eyes slightly to the right, spotting McFee. A look of relief crossed his face. He nodded toward the man in the center of the room.

"He won't put down the rolling pin."

McFee grunted and pulled his nightstick from its place in his belt and began walking toward the man.

His eyes were glassy, and McFee noted that his body was swaying slightly.

When he got within striking distance, the man backed up half a step instead of swinging, just as McFee had expected. Fifteen years on the beat had taught him a few things about people.

McFee didn't make the same mistake. He jabbed the nightstick hard into the man's stomach, doubling him over with a loud rush of air from his lungs. He then brought the nightstick down hard across his back, dropping the man to the floor with a loud thud.

Breathing hard, McFee pulled out his cuffs, and closed them around the man's thick wrists. Behind him he heard the battered woman, who had presumably called them, go from whimpering to screaming and clawing at the cop holding her. Her partner rushed over to help.

McFee stood, hauled the dazed man to his feet, and began walking toward the door.

As he started down the steps with his prisoner, the noise from the bystanders increased. The crowd parted even more slowly than when he had arrived. He was almost to his car when he was hit hard from behind, almost knocking him off his feet.

The woman who had been half beaten to death by the man he now had in custody had apparently changed her mind about the arrest. She was now firmly attached to McFee's back, making every attempt to sink her teeth into his neck. He spun wildly, releasing his grip on his prisoner's arm, and managed to grab the woman's hair before she could get her teeth into him. The fear of AIDS was firmly planted in the mind of every cop who worked in the inner city. He slammed her hard into the side of the cruiser, and hearing the wind go out of her, managed to flip her over his head onto the sidewalk.

The crowd's volume had grown another notch, and they looked energized by the spectacle. McFee knew how important it was to regain control immediately, and he pulled his gun. The two young officers, now at the top of the stairs, followed his lead.

"Now, why doesn't everybody just calm down and go home," McFee suggested. No one moved. The two cops pushed their way toward him and handcuffed the woman writhing on the sidewalk.

McFee kept an eye on the crowd as he pushed the squabbling couple into the squad car. He walked back to his own unit and pulled into the street, watching the happy couple beginning once again to scream at each other in the back seat of the car in front of him. Something bounced off the trunk of his car. It sounded like a can.

Fucking niggers, he thought, pulling his car onto Pratt Street and heading east.

He glanced at his watch. Eleven forty-five.

When he reached Canton, he turned right and headed for the warehouse district. There was a dive pub on the water that served a cheesesteak, fries, and a Coke for four dollars. As he crossed Boston Street, a red Jeep Cherokee appeared in front of him.

At morning roll call, their Captain had told them to be on the lookout for a similar vehicle and had given them the license number. He had gone on to say, to the amusement of everyone in the room, that the man's capture was a top priority but that he was extremely dangerous and that they were not to try to apprehend him without the FBI. An anonymous voice had spoken for everyone. "Oooh, that makes me feel a lot safer." Laughter had drowned out the rest of the Captain's speech. While he hadn't seen fit to tell them just who this desperado was, it had taken less than an hour for everyone to figure it out.

McFee shuffled through the papers on his passenger seat, finally finding the yellow Post-it note that he had jotted the license number down on. He glanced down at it and squinted through the glare of his dirty windshield.

The numbers matched.

He felt adrenaline surge through him. Taking a few deep breaths, he pulled within ten feet of the Jeep and flipped on his lights.

John Hobart had noticed the police car behind him the minute it pulled across Boston. He had checked his speed—he was going just under the thirty-five mile an hour limit—and continued to flick his eyes periodically to the rearview mirror. He swore quietly when the lights went on.

His hair had been dyed a sandy brown, and he was wearing a matching false mustache. It was the same disguise he had been wearing around Baltimore for two months now, but it didn't match his driver's license picture. And he didn't feel like explaining his change in appearance to some dumb-ass Baltimore street cop.

He eased the Cherokee to the side of the road, trying to figure out why he was being pulled over, finally deciding that it must be a brake light or something equally trivial. Even the widely heralded Mark Beamon couldn't have identified him that fast. And even if he had, he wouldn't send one lone cop to pick him up.

Hobart examined the police officer as he stepped from his cruiser and began walking toward his car. *Too slow*, he thought watching the man's gait. He also noticed the fact that his right hand wasn't swinging as he walked. It was being held unnaturally close to his gun.

That just wasn't normal. He was a middle-aged white male in an expensive automobile. This guy should be cool as a cucumber.

Shit.

He reached between the driver's seat and console and pulled out a .45. He slid the lever back and switched it to his left hand, where it would be out of sight. The cop was close enough now that he could see his nervous expression reflected in the Jeep's side mirror. His grip tightened around the gun as the cop came abreast of his open window and crouched down, bringing his face level with Hobart's.

"FBI's on to you Mr. Hobart. A lot of us are behind what you're doing."

With that, he stood and walked back to his cruiser. Hobart sat silently, watching the cop's stiff stride. He looked like he wasn't entirely sure if he was going to get a bullet in the back or not.

The cop slid back into his car. His engine roared loudly as he pulled into the street. Hobart sat and watched the car as it grew smaller and smaller, finally turning off onto a side street and disappearing into a landscape of mountainous piles of black coal.

32

Baltimore, Maryland,
March 10

Looks like he does okay," Mark Beamon commented as the elevator door slid open. The decor in the hallway that stretched before them was understated, but reeked of wealth. It didn't seem to reflect the man that they had come to see.

"Nice vase." Beamon stopped to admire it further. "My mom used to love this stuff. Had a house full of it when I was a kid."

"I don't think that one's in your price range," Laura said, continuing down the hall. They were already five minutes late for their appointment.

"Hello, can I help you?" the receptionist asked as they approached.

"Yes, I'm Laura Vilechi, and this is Mark Beamon. We're here to see Reverend Blake."

She nodded, appearing not to recognize Beamon's name. She looked like she was used to powerful people dropping by. "Go right in."

They walked through a beautifully etched glass doorway and into a large waiting area dominated by flowering trees. The air smelled fresh and sweet.

"Hello, I'm Terry, the Reverend's personal secretary. You can go right in. Can I get you some coffee or perhaps some tea?"

They politely declined.

"It's nice to meet you, Reverend," Laura said graciously, extending her hand. "I've seen your show." Beamon knew both statements to be lies.

"It's nice to see that our law enforcement officials know the Lord. I imagine it's difficult not to become cynical and hard—the things you must see." He turned to Beamon. "And you're Mark Beamon. I recognize you from your photos." They shook hands.

Beamon examined the Reverend carefully. Blake's expression was the serene mask required of men in his profession.

"Please sit down. So what can I do for you today?"

"We'd like to get some information on a former employee of yours. A John Hobart," Laura said.

Blake laced his fingers together and laid his hands on the table. He seemed to be deep in thought. "No, I can't think of a single thing that I haven't told you."

The two agents looked at each other, confused. Blake elaborated. "In my meeting with Agent . . . Martinez, is it?"

"Let me get this straight," Beamon started slowly. "You've had an FBI agent in here recently asking about Hobart?"

"That's right. You didn't send him?"

"When did you meet with him?"

"Just yesterday, actually."

Laura broke in. "Could you describe him."

"Sure." He paused. "About thirty-five, I think. Very well dressed. Slight Spanish accent. Not Hispanic—Spanish. I'd peg him as a European. He said his name was, uh, Alejandro I think. Alejandro Martinez."

Beamon shook his head, a thin smile on his lips. *The cartels are smarter than the whole goddam FBI.*

"Do you know where Mr. Hobart is?" Laura asked.

"No. As I told Mr. Martinez, he's probably at his house. I can have Terry pull his personnel file if you like."

"We'd appreciate it. "

Blake leaned back in his chair, looking around Laura. "Terry!"

She peeked in the door.

"Could you copy John Hobart's personnel file for me please." She disappeared without a word.

"Just a few more questions, Reverend," Beamon said. "We'll try not to take up too much of your time."

The questions took less than a half an hour but had still been a complete waste of time. Like Hobart's neighbors, Blake knew very little about his old employee. Personal interests, friends, hobbies. No one seemed to know the first thing about John Hobart.

"We really appreciate your time, Reverend. We know how busy you are." Beamon shook his hand. Laura was already out the door.

"Anytime, Mr. Beamon. I'm sorry I couldn't be of more help."

Beamon strode purposefully across the office. In the doorway he stopped and turned around.

"Oh, I almost forgot, Reverend."

"Yes?"

"Did this Martinez tell you why the FBI was looking for John?"

Blake's jaw clenched slightly. "No. No he didn't."

"Thanks, Reverend. It was nice meeting you." He hurried off to catch Laura, who was standing at the elevator, jabbing at the Down button.

Laura maneuvered the car through the thick traffic, leaning down over the steering wheel so that she could read the street signs hanging from the traffic light wires. She seemed to never be able to remember which street took them back to D.C.

"Oh, he's in on it all right." There was a note of happiness in her voice.

"Why?"

"Too cool. Not curious enough. Did you notice he didn't even ask why we were looking for Hobart? Besides, it would take some serious cash to get an operation like this off the ground."

"What if our mystery agent—Martinez—told him why we were looking?" Beamon tested.

"He still would have asked something about the case. Especially when we didn't know who Martinez was. I mean, come on. He's got the infamous Mark Beamon sitting in his office, and he doesn't even bring up the CDFS. Please."

"Yeah, you're probably right. It'll be hell to prove, though."

Laura flipped on the radio to a news station. It was playing the tail end of a report on the President diverting millions of dollars to drug rehab clinics and away from enforcement programs. Beamon ignored it. It was the same story they'd been running all morning.

"He really did it, though," she observed. There was something in her voice that made Beamon a little uneasy.

"What?

She looked over at him. "What do you mean, what? He's damn near killed the coke and heroin trade in the U.S. And the few people who are still using are trying to get help." She pointed to the radio to punctuate her remark. "How much have we spent over the last ten years—and never gotten close to what he's accomplished?"

"I'm embarrassed to say that I don't even know . . ."

Laura's voice softened a bit. "Yeah, me neither, but I'll bet it's a hell of a lot. Time and money that could have been spent better somewhere else."

It was something that he had been struggling with for months. The pro-CDFS arguments, hawked by the media for their sensational, audience-grabbing effect, rang true more often than he liked to admit.

The constant media coverage, with its thoughtful sound tracks and high-tech graphics, had been very effective in desensitizing the public to the carnage associated with the CDFS's actions. In his opinion, the coverage was more to blame for the public's increasing support of the CDFS than the DEA's leak of drug-use statistics.

And now the number of deaths had dropped dramatically. All that was left was fear. But when he captured Hobart, that fear would disappear. He would go back to Houston and the drug users and dealers would let out a collective sigh of relief. The lines at the rehab clinics would disappear, and twenty thousand people would have died for nothing.

There were only two things keeping his heart in the investigation, Beamon knew. The thought of his nephew rotting in the ground, and the fact that he couldn't bear letting John Hobart get the better of him again.

It was just barely enough.

His thoughts were interrupted by a breaking news story. Laura leaned forward and turned up the radio.

"We have a report that the FBI has put out a statewide APB in Maryland for John Hobart in connection with CDFS activity. He is described as a forty-year-old Caucasian male with short dark hair. He stands five foot eight and weighs approximately one hundred and fifty pounds."

Beamon reached to the dash and turned the radio off.

"Man, that was fast," Laura observed.

He just shook his head and dialed the cellular phone anchored to the floor. He put it on speaker.

"FBI."

"Carol? Hi, it's Mark."

"How are you, Mr. Beamon."

"Oh, you know. Could you patch me through to Tom Sherman?"

The phone went dead for a moment, then began ringing.

"Tom Sherman."

"Hey, Tommy, you watching the news?"

"Yup."

"Who won the pool?"

There was a pause and the sound of shuffling paper.

"Looks like Laura did. Six hundred and thirty-five dollars."

Beamon looked over at her and scowled. She flashed a wide smile and gave him the thumbs-up sign.

"Do we have that press release ready?"

"It went out an hour ago. Hobart's picture will be on every TV in the world in a few hours."

"And we've got our men in place."

"Yeah. A mouse couldn't get out of the country without our knowing it. The SAC's aren't too happy about it, though. We're draining off a lot of their manpower."

"Fuck 'em. Let 'em complain to the President if they don't like it. See you in an hour." He reached over and disconnected the phone.

"So you're sure he's going to skip the country?"

"Probably. Too many people looking for him here. And it's not just us, it's every drug dealer and addict, too. Europe's the way to go. Nobody's too mad at him there."

"Getting him at the airport's going to be tough. He'll spot our guys the minute he walks through the doors," Laura said.

Beamon shrugged. "I'm sure you're right. Hobart didn't get drummed out of the DEA 'cause he was stupid. He's not going to just waltz into an airport when he knows we've got guys crawling all over 'em."

He leaned the seat in the car all the way back. Staring up through the skylight, he pulled out a cigarette. "If I was in his position, what would I do?"

He didn't light the cigarette but just let it perch between his lips. Laura had made it clear that if he ever lit another one in the car, she'd put it out on his scalp. They remained silent for almost a half an hour. A few minutes from the J. Edgar Hoover Building, Beamon sat upright so fast that the seat belt caught, snapping him back. "Jesus, how much more stupid could I be?"

"What?" Laura asked anxiously.

"The question isn't what I would do in John Hobart's position. It's what would I do if I were John Hobart."

She failed to see the difference.

"That's the ball game," Robert Swenson said with a hint of relief in his voice. He and Hobart were sitting in his apartment above the warehouse that they had been using as a base of operations for the past two months. Both were intently watching the news report on the television in front of them. On the screen, a computer-generated image of Hobart's head was slowly rotating. After each full revolution, minor changes were made—hair, eye color, facial hair. They matched his elaborate makeup jobs surprisingly well.

"Looks like it," Hobart agreed. "I'll call our guys in the field and tell them it's time to pack it in."

"Where are you going to go?"

Hobart shrugged. "Don't know. Somewhere where I'm getting a little less press. Can you stick around for a day or two? I can't imagine they have anything on you—and I could use the help wrapping things up."

"They're looking for me, though. I doubt that they missed that I quit the church right after you did."

"Oh, they're looking all right. But what will they charge you with when they find you? Getting tired of your job?"

Swenson let that sink in for a moment. In the end, he decided that staying on would be less dangerous than leaving Hobart in the lurch. He knew better than to cross him. "Okay. I'll stick around and help you wrap things up—then I'm out of here."

"Good. Why don't you call our people and tell them to go home. I'll figure out a way to get rid of the orellanin."

"That ought to be a trick."

They were both driving rentals now, having dumped their cars in a manufacturing plant's expansive parking lot. Swenson was trying to picture how Hobart would get the large metal storage drum into the trunk of a Subaru.

"I'll figure something out," Hobart said, rising. "With a little luck, we'll be out of here tomorrow."

Those were the words that Swenson had been waiting to hear. It seemed they'd been at this for years. He turned back to the television and watched Hobart's disembodied head spin slowly around. It was somehow entrancing.

Less than two miles away, Alejandro Perez was watching the same program while he carefully tucked his clothes back into his suitcase. Luis wasn't going to be happy, but he would just have to take it like a man. With Hobart's identity public, the chances of finding him before the FBI were a million to one.

He pressed hard on the top of the suitcase and latched it. His first-class flight to Bogota left in an hour, and at this time of evening, the traffic was unpredictable. He didn't want to be stuck in Baltimore for another night.

The Reverend Simon Blake took another pull from the vodka bottle and went into an inevitable coughing fit. He had once experimented with alcohol as a college freshman, and it was an episode that he didn't look fondly back on. Since then—almost twenty years—he hadn't touched a drop. Until today.

He laughed bitterly when his throat loosened enough to allow it. Quite a pickle he had managed to get himself into. He thought back to his meeting with John Hobart, how sure he had been that they were on the righteous path. How he was going to single-handedly bring America back on track. He laughed again and took another pull. The alcohol in his empty stomach felt like the fire of hell.

Events had conspired against him in the last few days. His clumsy attempt to put an end to the CDFS through snitching on Nelson had backfired. Now Hobart's face was plastered across every TV in America. Blake could hear the threats Hobart had made against his family as clearly as if the phone were still pressed to his ear. Threats he knew that his ex–security chief was fully capable of carrying out.

And then there was Mark Beamon—who Blake was convinced knew of his involvement. Finally, there were the countless thousands dead because of him.

Blake put the bottle down on the floor next to him and listened to the silence reigning in the house. He had sent his wife and children away for a few days. Erica had been needing to see her mother for some time.

He closed his eyes and reflected on the brief moments in life that so easily turned into milestones. His agreement to finance Hobart's eradication of narcotics. His forgetting to ask Mark Beamon why they were looking for Hobart when he'd been so careful to ask Martinez. His call to the FBI about the DiPrizzio episode. All in all, these three events made up less than twenty seconds of his long life. But those seconds would define him, and overshadow everything he had built.

He reached for the phone and dialed 911.

"Hello," he said into the mouthpiece when the police operator answered. "I heard gunshots at the Reverend Simon Blake's home." He could hear the operator asking for details as he let the receiver fall between his chair and the table next to it. He picked up the revolver sitting on the floor next to the nearly empty fifth of vodka and put the barrel in his mouth. The taste of steel almost gagged him. "I love you, Mary," he slurred over the barrel.

The good thing about having your picture all over the TV is that you know what not to look like.

Hobart tossed his backpack on the bench next to him and watched a tugboat struggling into its slip. Pigeons flapped around his feet, waiting to be fed.

His hair was long and blond, the color that suggests years of surfing in Hawaii, or birth in Southern California. A large earring dangled from his left ear—he'd pierced it himself only an hour ago. Torn canvas pants, a turtleneck, and a brightly colored vest completed the effect. He nodded a silent greeting as a group of skateboarders strolled by. Normally they wouldn't have given him a second look, but they seemed to identify with Hobart's new image, and returned his greeting.

Satisfied that he was drawing no attention whatsoever, Hobart grabbed the army surplus knapsack next to him and headed for a pay phone perched on the side of the ice cream shop across the street. He shoved a quarter in the slot and dialed the warehouse.

"Clipper City Antiques and Oddities." Swenson's voice.

"Could you do me a favor, Bob?"

"Sure, what do you need?"

"Look something up on the computer for me."

The skateboarders began to do tricks on the steps of the large brick square in front of him. He watched with mild interest, listening to his partner walking and finally sitting down.

"How many times have I told you that you don't have to turn the computer off every time you leave, John. It's got a screen saver. You're gonna have to wait till it warms up."

"No problem."

A skateboarder took a hard fall into a steel railing. His friends laughed.

Being almost a mile from the warehouse, Hobart hadn't expected the explosion to be quite so loud. The skateboarders ducked involuntarily, then straightened up and looked around with confused expressions. Everyone else on the street did the same. Cars stopped, drivers leaned out their windows.

Hobart replaced the receiver and strolled casually to his rental car. Once inside, he retrieved a small chess board from the pocket in the passenger side door. The board had been designed for travel, and the pieces had been replaced by small magnetic discs that allowed the player to fold the board up midgame and continue later. The position of the pieces matched the board that until a few minutes ago had rested next to his television. Hobart pulled the white queen—Robert Swenson—off the board and threw it on the floor of the car.

The driver of the car behind him was still looking around, trying to figure out what had happened. Hobart gave a short honk on the horn and began backing out onto the cobblestone street.

Hobart had planned on shutting down the CDFS before his identity was discovered. That had been plan A. Mark Beamon's artful meddling had forced him to switch to plan B.

He had been careful in diverting the funds from Blake's accounts, but he wasn't so conceited as to believe he was smart enough to fool the army of CPAs the Bureau would throw at the church's books. At least he hoped he wasn't. He had used Robert Swenson's terminal number and password.

He slowed slightly as he passed within a few blocks of the warehouse. Smoke curled into the steel gray sky. The wailing of sirens echoed through the narrow streets.

Beamon was clever—he had to admit that. But what did the Bureau actually have on him? Sure, they could prove that he knew both Nelson and Karns, but so what? He could produce at least four other DEA agents who had also been acquainted with the two men. And with his death, Swenson had gone from partner to reasonable doubt. Dead men could be very useful that way.

Hobart eased the Subaru onto I95 North, careful to constantly monitor his speed. The Jeep protested at speeds much over sixty-five, but this one could get him in trouble.

Hobart was almost halfway to his destination when a police car passed him going south. He followed it in his side mirror. It was almost out of sight when it slowed abruptly and bounced across the grass. He switched to the rearview mirror and watched it overtake him. Three cars back it slowed and matched his speed.

Coincidence?

He pulled into the right lane and touched his brakes. The cars behind him began to pass by. The cruiser stayed in the left lane, but again matched his speed, staying about fifty yards behind. Hobart checked his speed. Sixty mph. Cars were beginning to pile up behind the squad car, afraid to pass.

They continued like that for almost five miles, with no cars between them. Hobart spotted another state police car driving too slowly on the overpass ahead of him. This one was unmarked, but its ugly brown color and bristling antennae announced it just as loudly. He shifted his rearview mirror so that he could see the top of the overpass as he came out from under it. The car gained speed and turned sharply onto the on-ramp. It fell in about twenty-five yards behind the black and white.

God damn Mark Beamon, Hobart thought, slamming his hands into the steering wheel. *He must have the cops chasing every fucking rental car in Maryland.*

To his right, Hobart saw the enormous structure of White Marsh Mall and the brightly colored IKEA store that shared its parking lot. He flipped on his blinker, and eased the car onto the off-ramp, keeping one eye on the squad car behind him. The driver slowed slightly, then regained his speed, trying to decide what to do.

As soon as he was around the corner and out of site of the trailing cars, he slammed his foot to the floor. The Subaru jumped satisfyingly as he accelerated into the gently bending road, tires protesting with a low, constant scream. As he curved left through a stand of trees, he caught a glimpse of the two police cars speeding toward him.

He slammed on the brakes and skidded into the vast parking lot of the shopping complex. Pulling into oncoming traffic, he took his first left and sped toward one of the many entrances to the mall. He skidded to a stop in front of the bank of glass doors, and, leaving the car running, walked briskly into the building. Once through the doors, he looked back. The people behind him looked interested, but not enough to follow.

He worked his way into the crowd, turning abruptly onto a down escalator, and bumping hard into a woman with an armful of bags. She didn't drop them, but gave him a dirty look anyway. At the bottom of the escalator, he hurried for the nearest exit.

He burst out the doors, and walked purposefully toward a white Mercedes illegally parked in front of him. Inside, a bored-looking woman examined her fingernails over the steering wheel. He grabbed the handle of the passenger door and jumped in.

"Sorry I'm late, hon, let's go," he said to the woman, pushing the barrel of his .45 into her ribs. A look of terror spread across her face. She froze.

"Smile and press the accelerator or I'm going to kill you." His tone and message woke her from her trance and she pulled out into the parking lot.

"Very good. Now just take it easy, and get us going south on 95."

"What do you want?" she stammered.

"I just want to get back to Baltimore, that's all."

She pulled out onto the freeway, her knuckles white against the steering wheel. Hobart settled back into the soft leather seat and flipped on the radio. The announcer was talking about him. He flipped it off, and began going through the woman's purse.

"I have money—credit cards too—take it all," she begged.

He laughed. "Thanks, but you can keep them. He pulled out a worn leather wallet held together with a rubber band. Pulling the rubber band off, he began going through it.

"Your kids?" he asked, holding up a picture of two blond boys of early grade school age. She nodded. A tear was running down her cheek. He pulled the picture out of the wallet and dropped it and her driver's license onto his lap. He picked up the cellular phone nestled between the seats. "You mind? It's a local call."

He dialed the number of the warehouse, getting a recording that the number was temporarily out of service.

"Charley? It's me. I'm in a car with one Carol Lundan. That's spelled L-U-N-D-A-N. She lives at 506 Pullman Street. Yeah. She's got two kids—look to be six and eight. Blond. If I don't make it back tonight I want you to kill 'em all. Got that? No, 'Lundan' with an 'A.' Yeah. Okay."

Hobart hopped out of the car near Baltimore's Inner Harbor, studying Carol Lundan's face as he slammed the door shut. She wouldn't say a word. Probably not even to her husband. The terror etched across her face was as good a guarantee as a bullet in her head.

33

Baltimore, Maryland,
March 11

John Hobart pulled his new rental car into a nearly empty public parking lot and climbed out. He glanced briefly at his watch as he locked the door, calculating that he had at least two hours before the FBI sent word to start looking for the car. In fact, he probably had much more time than that, but where Mark Beamon was concerned, it didn't pay to take chances.

He jogged across the quiet street and began walking along the storefronts. Many were vacant, their large front windows cracked and duct-taped. Street numbers weren't plentiful, either. He glanced down at the section of Yellow Pages in his hand and stuffed it back into his pocket. He probably should have just gone back to the same store. Despite his elaborate disguise, he was feeling exposed on the empty sidewalk.

There was no sign on the shop, but the mannequins in the window were dressed in outrageous wigs and period costumes. A flyer taped to the door announced that it was Scarlett O'Hara week—whatever that was.

The bells on the door chimed as he opened it, and the man sitting behind the counter tossed his magazine on the floor and jumped up.

"Can I help you?" he asked, sounding elated to have a customer.

"I think you can," Hobart replied, flipping the dead bolt on the door.

"Uh, we're still open . . ."

Hobart pulled his gun from the knapsack slung over his right shoulder. "This'll only take a little while."

The man started to raise his hands but Hobart discouraged it.

"It's been a slow day," the shopkeeper explained as Hobart marched him into the back room. "There's not much cash in the register, but you're welcome to it. I've got a few bucks in my wallet too."

Hobart grimaced. It was the second time in as many hours that he had been mistaken for a common thief.

The back room of the shop was piled high with costumes in no apparent order. One of the walls was completely covered with floor-to-ceiling mirrors. On the far side of the room sat an old makeup table. Two halogen desk lamps looked out of place on its weathered wooden top.

"Turn around," Hobart ordered, pulling off his wig. "I want to leave here a woman."

He almost laughed out loud at the absurdity of his statement. His plan to solve America's most devastating problem had fallen apart. And now, not only was he being forced to flee the country that had been his home for his entire life, he was being forced to do it in drag. God damn Mark Beamon.

The shopkeeper looked at him blankly. Hobart raised the gun again and made a move toward him. The implied threat had the desired effect, and he began milling around the room, grabbing clothes, makeup, wigs, and elaborate-looking pads. Every few moments, he would look back thoughtfully, sizing up his customer.

It may not be the most dignified way to get out of the country, Hobart thought, but it seemed the safest. The FBI had sewn up the airports tight, but were looking for a Caucasian male. His friend in the forgery business could have him a fake passport and driver's license in an hour. With a little luck, he would be on a plane tonight.

"If you could just come out here for a moment where the light's better."

Hobart stepped back out into the front of the store and allowed the shopkeeper to walk slowly around him.

He was surprised when he felt a strong hand wrap tightly around his wrist.

Christ—a fucking hero.

He raised his free arm, preparing to slam his elbow into the man's head, when he felt the unmistakable coldness of the barrel of a gun on the back of his neck.

"FBI, Mr. Hobart. You're under arrest." The nervousness had drained from the shopkeeper's voice. In front of him, another man walked slowly from the bathroom, holding a lighter to a cigarette.

"Yeah, I liked this store best too, John," Mark Beamon said, taking a drag on the cigarette. "Quiet part of town. Lots of empty storefronts."

Hobart relaxed and dropped the gun. He allowed himself to be pushed face down on the floor and his arms to be pulled painfully behind his back. From his position on the floor he could only see to Beamon's knees.

It took a full two seconds for Hobart's mind to process what had happened.

The young agent, who a moment before had been pushing a pair of handcuffs to his wrists, was lying face down on the dirty shop floor next to a blackened mannequin. Both man and model bristled with countless shards of glass, brick, and wood.

Hobart scanned the room, finally spotting Mark Beamon through the quickly dispersing smoke and swirling dust. Beamon was struggling to sit up, apparently oblivious to the bullets flying overhead. He looked a little groggy, but hadn't sustained any obvious injuries. The brunt of the blast had been taken by his partner.

Hobart rolled carefully onto his back, ignoring the sharp debris beneath him. Most of the front of the store was gone. There was no sign of the large picture window that a few moments before had displayed the shop's costumes, except on the floor around him. What was left of the window's wood frame was burning.

The ringing in Hobart's ears was beginning to subside as he rolled back onto his stomach and began slithering toward a sturdy-looking island of cabinets in the center of the room. He kept his chin close to the floor, lifting his eyes occasionally to watch reddish explosions erupt from the back wall as bullets slammed into the old brick. At least one per second he estimated—standing and making a break for it wasn't an option.

Beamon was on his stomach now, moving across the room toward his partner, the human pin cushion. He passed within a few feet of Hobart, still too dazed to realize the young agent was dead.

Hobart stopped for a moment, laying his cheek on the floor and watching Beamon struggle across the room. He remained motionless for a few moments, waiting for a bullet to catch Beamon in his ample side and flip him over.

He sighed quietly when Beamon began splashing through the puddle of blood that was starting to flow across the uneven floor, finally reaching the man and beginning a futile search for a pulse on what was left of his neck. Hobart started back for the cabinets, astounded at Beamon's charmed existence.

It seemed to take forever, but Hobart finally managed to slip behind the island. Remaining on his back for a moment, he examined the cabinets carefully. When he was satisfied that no bullets were penetrating, he sat up and cradled the gun that he had found on the trip across the floor. It was a .45 automatic, not unlike the one he usually carried. He pulled the lever back and examined it for damage and debris. It looked good.

Mark Beamon's faculties were beginning to return to him as he reached his partner, though he wasn't entirely grateful. If there was ever a situation where ignorance was bliss, this was it. The front of the store was missing, and it seemed as if half the population of North Baltimore had picked up machine guns and were now busying themselves trying to knock a similar hole in the back of the building. And to make matters worse, Bobby had definitely seen better days. The young agent's unblinking eyes had gone a pinkish white from blood and the thick dust in the building.

Number thirty-five.

In less than a second, he'd gone from husband and father to the thirty-fifth name on the plaque commemorating agents killed in the line of duty. Bad trade.

Beamon turned and began crawling toward the heavy group of cabinets in the middle of the room. He put the image of his partner's broken body out of his mind and began dealing with the problem at hand. Who the fuck had blown off the front of the building—and more important, who was shooting? And another interesting question—where was Hobart?

As Beamon came around the corner of the island, he felt a pistol barrel press against his cheek. Question number three answered.

He pushed himself into a sitting position and pressed his back against the cabinets. The gun barrel stayed with him.

"I saw a wet spot on the floor back there. I was hoping it was you," Beamon shouted over the gunfire and the ringing in his ears.

Hobart shook his head "Thanks to you, I had the best seat in the house when the front blew."

Beamon sighed and slumped further against the cabinets, reminded of the corpse in the middle of the room. He reached into the breast pocket of his suit, ignoring the increased pressure of the gun barrel on his cheek, and pulled out a small cellular phone.

"Do you mind?" he said pushing the pistol away from his face. "We can settle our differences later."

Hobart looked at him suspiciously for a moment and then lowered the gun.

Beamon flipped open the cell phone and dialed Laura, who was coordinating the SWAT team that was supposedly backing him up. She picked up on the first ring.

"Laura! Guess who? Why are you letting people shoot at me?"

The answer was unintelligible.

"You're gonna have to speak up, hon. I can't hear too well," Beamon yelled, pressing the phone to his right ear until it hurt, and sticking a finger in his left one.

"Mark! Are you okay? Most of the front of the building's gone!"

"Yeah, I'm fine, but that's not gonna last."

"We've got twenty or thirty mostly Hispanic males out here, Mark. They're armed to the teeth. Looks like at least one of them's got a grenade launcher."

Beamon looked over at Hobart, who was trying to get a glimpse of what was happening out front. "My male ego wouldn't be bruised if you were to come in here and rescue me."

"I'm sorry, Mark, but there's no way I can approach your position—it's too wide open. The good news is that our Hispanic friends can't, either. Looks like they're planning to just stay put and wait to get lucky."

Beamon watched a particularly large chunk of the cabinet island that they were hiding behind fly over his head and bounce off the brick wall in front of him. "At the rate my cover is disintegrating, they're gonna get lucky sooner rather than later, Laura. I'm open to suggestions."

"They probably have orders to see John Hobart dead. If you can, toss his body out where they can see it—they'll probably take off."

Beamon scowled. "Easier said than done. Is the alley in back of the building clear?"

"Last time I heard."

"You're a real confidence builder."

Beamon flipped the phone shut and stuffed it back into his jacket. "It seems that there are some South American gentlemen out there who'd like to speak with you."

Hobart pulled back against the cabinets. "Can't really see anything. Doesn't look like anyone's on the street, though." He looked up. "What do you think about a truce until we get out of here?"

Beamon chewed his lip. He had been about to suggest the same thing. John Hobart was a sadistic sociopath—of that there was no doubt. But, while you wouldn't want someone with those failings to marry your daughter, they weren't bad allies in a gunfight. Beamon nodded almost imperceptibly. "Truce."

Hobart seemed satisfied with that, and popped the clip out of his gun for one last inspection. "You got any ideas, Mark?"

"Going out the front ain't gonna happen."

Beamon motioned with his head to the archway that led to the back of the store. It was fifteen long feet away.

"If we can make it through there, there's a back door that opens out onto an alley."

Hobart nodded slowly. "If they've got guys on the roof, we won't last very long in an alley."

Beamon shrugged. "We won't last long here."

Hobart considered this for a moment, a thin smile spreading across his face. "You first."

Reluctantly, Beamon rose to a crouched position and backed far enough away from the edge of the cabinets to give himself room to build up some speed before leaving his cover. Hobart edged to the other side. "On three, Mark. One. Two. *Three.*"

As he sprinted toward the back room, Beamon heard Hobart's gun begin to fire.

He landed rolling, finally coming to a stop when he hit a mannequin dressed like a turn-of-the-century Southern belle. It took him a few seconds of thrashing to untangle himself from the elaborate hoop skirt.

He walked back to the archway and pressed himself against the wall. Hobart was already up and crouched, ready to spring.

Beamon held up his hand and extended his index finger. One. He put up his middle finger. Two. Ring finger. Three.

As Hobart shot across the room, Beamon fired through the gaping hole that used to be the front of the building, deliberately aiming low to prevent injuring any of his own men. Hobart moved like lightning, making it through the archway in half the time it had taken Beamon. He also had managed to stay on his feet and come to a graceful stop at the back door.

"You first this time," Beamon said, taking a position to the right of the door. Hobart gave a short nod, grabbed the knob, and threw the door open.

Beamon tensed and pressed himself harder against the wall, expecting a flurry of bullets to come bursting into the room.

Nothing. He peered out into the alley as Hobart moved silently through the doorway. It was empty except for a cat lying in the middle of a discarded toilet lid. The animal looked at them through bored, city-bred eyes, oblivious to the sound of gunfire echoing eerily off the weathered brick walls of the alley.

Hobart signaled "all clear" and began running lightly through the puddle-strewn alley. Beamon loped after him.

They broke out onto a wider, though equally deserted, road, crossing it quickly and slipping into another narrow back street.

They crossed three more streets that way, putting a reasonable distance between them and what Beamon guessed was a group of Luis Colombar's attack dogs. Despite their slow, careful pace, Beamon felt as though his heart was going to dislodge itself from his chest and skitter off to find a more sedentary home. The image was almost enough to make him laugh.

Hobart, who was about twenty-five yards ahead, slowed to a walk and then turned. Beamon stopped short, keeping the distance between them.

"Sounds like your boys are cleaning things up, Mark," Hobart said in a conversational tone. The acoustics of the alley made it sound like he was only a few feet away.

Beamon cocked his head to the side, listening intently. He hadn't noticed that the gunfire had slowed almost to nonexistence. It sounded like microwave popcorn right before you pulled the bag out of the oven.

"Looks like our truce is about over," Hobart said.

Beamon slowly brought his gun to waist level and stuffed it in the front of his pants. He hoped that the nonaggressive gesture would keep things from getting out of hand until he had time to think the situation through.

"Looks that way."

He pulled a cigarette from a pack in his jacket and lit it, surprised that his hands didn't shake. "Why'd you do it, John?"

"Why do you think?" Hobart said, following Beamon's lead and stuffing his .45 in his belt.

Beamon relaxed a little. "God and country?"

Hobart laughed. "No, I guess I just wanted to see if I could."

Beamon exhaled, watching the slight breeze dissolve the cigarette smoke.

"So how do you want to play it, Mark?"

"I guess I'd like you to throw that pistol on the ground and put your hands on top of your head."

Hobart shook his head. "I don't think so. Tell you what. Why don't you just turn around and walk away. No one would blame you for letting me get away, with all that shit going on."

Beamon took another drag from his cigarette. "I'd blame myself."

Hobart shook his head again, looking at the ground. "Then I'll ask you again. How do you want to play it?"

Beamon looked around him. The alley was only about ten feet across—barely wide enough to drive a car through. There were a few windows in the brick buildings that lined the little street, but they were all at least six feet off the ground and covered with chicken wire. A Dumpster overflowed with boxes of rotting vegetables eight feet in front of him and three feet to the side.

There weren't a hell of a lot of choices. A running gunfight was out of the question—too athletic. Hobart moved with the speed and grace of a college track star and he didn't even look winded from their cross-town run. Beamon's knees felt like they were full of gravel, and his heart was still considering vacating his chest cavity.

The Dumpster was interesting. He could dive behind it, leaving Hobart out in the open. But what would be the point of that? Hobart was only about thirty feet from the mouth of the alley and would be long gone by the time Beamon finished pulling the lettuce out of his ears.

That didn't leave much.

Beamon dropped his cigarette on the ground and crushed it with the toe of his shoe. Hobart was standing with his arms hanging loosely at his sides. Beamon hoped he didn't feel as relaxed as he looked.

"If you won't surrender, I guess we'll just have to end it now."

The bend in Hobart's arm tightened slightly, bringing his right hand an inch closer to his pistol. "Come on, Mark, why do this? Look at you."

Beamon glanced down at his protruding stomach and then to his yellowed fingertips. Finally he looked back up at Hobart. "I remember you being a real trick shot with a rifle, John. But handguns were always more my territory."

"I've been practicing."

Beamon hoped to hell that wasn't true. "One more chance, John."

Hobart stared back at him. His eyes were as lifeless as glass. Windows to his soul.

Hobart was the first to move, bringing his hand up in a lightning-quick motion. Beamon's breath caught as he grabbed for his own gun. He was slower, as he knew he would be, and he saw the flash of Hobart's pistol a split second before he himself fired.

Beamon felt a flare of pain in his chest and then numbness as he watched Hobart jerk backwards and fall onto his back.

Beamon dropped his gun and desperately clawed open his shirt to examine what he had already decided was a fatal wound.

Nothing. Not a scratch. He marveled at the power of the human mind to play tricks as he quickly bent to retrieve his gun.

Hobart was still alive, though most of the flesh between his right pectoral and shoulder was missing.

"Let go of the gun, John," Beamon shouted as he slowly advanced. Hobart was still clinging loosely to the .45, though he didn't look like he had the strength to pull the back of his hand off the pavement. He rocked his head toward Beamon, causing a thin line of blood to flow from his mouth and make swirling patterns in the puddle he was lying in.

He shook his head weakly and began to slowly raise his gun hand.

Beamon stopped short and aimed his .357 directly at Hobart's heart. "Stop it, John. That wound doesn't look fatal. Let me get you to a hospital."

"Won't need one," Hobart croaked.

Beamon estimated that he had two more seconds before it was aimed directly at his chest."

"Drop the fucking gun, John."

There was no more time. Beamon squeezed the trigger and watched his gun and John Hobart buck simultaneously. Hobart's hand dropped back to the cobblestones, still clutching the pistol.

"Mark! Jesus, are you all right?"

Beamon continued unsteadily up the middle of the street, his gun dangling from his hand. Laura ran up to him and threw an arm around his shoulders. "Come over here and sit down."

She led him to the sidewalk and sat him down against the wall of an empty auto parts building.

"What happened, Mark. Where's Hobart?" she asked, crouching down beside him.

"Dead."

"Did the blast get him?"

"Nope. I did."

Beamon tilted his face toward the sky as a light mist started. He still couldn't believe he was going to walk away from this. "So what's the situation?"

Laura sat down next to him. "Looks like we got almost all of them. A couple probably slipped through the cracks—took off when the tide started to turn."

"Any casualties on our side?"

"Bobby didn't make it. You probably know that."

Beamon nodded.

"Other than that, we had a guy catch some shrapnel in his leg—nothing serious. Oh, and another guy ran through a glass door. Broken nose and a few cuts. Overall, we were lucky."

Beamon looked over at her. She was wearing fatigues, a bullet-proof vest and a metal helmet with a face shield. He began to laugh.

"What's so funny?"

Beamon patted her on the knee. "I'm sorry. It's just that you look ridiculous."

Laura grabbed his hand and slapped it back down on his thigh.

"I'm sorry Laura, I can't help it," Beamon said, trying to stifle his laughter.

She stood up and put her hands on her hips, starting him laughing even louder. Her boots almost reached her knees.

"You know, I don't have to take this, Mark. You work for me."

Alejandro Perez squeezed himself through the window and onto the roof of the abandoned North Baltimore row home. The distant sound of gunfire had nearly stopped, reduced to an occasional pop carried by the cold wind.

Perez pulled a pair of compact binoculars out of his breast pocket and peered down the street toward the billowing smoke that he knew was coming from what was left of Samuel's Theatrical Supply. He sighed quietly as he watched a body-armored FBI man drag the corpse of one of Luis Colombar's enforcers to a lengthening line of similar bodies lying motionless in the middle of the street.

Perez had been on his way to the airport when the call had come. Colombar had managed to discover where and when the FBI would attempt to apprehend Hobart and was sending a hit team on the next flight to Baltimore. Perez was to meet them at the airport and wait with them until the appointed hour.

It had been another serious error in judgment. Colombar had indebted himself to two very powerful and very ruthless men in order to get the likely location of Hobart's capture. And for what? To kill a man who could have been taken so much more easily in jail. Perez could not even confirm that Hobart had been killed, though it seemed unlikely that he would have survived a blast that had been powerful enough to rip the front off the store.

Frustrated, Perez slipped the binoculars back in his jacket and turned to the open window he had come through. He would wait to confirm Hobart's death before getting on a plane back to Colombia. If Hobart had survived, it might be wise to wait a few days before leaving. Give Colombar some time to cool off.

34

Houston, Texas,
March 15

Can't tell you how happy I am to be back," Beamon said.

Laura Vilechi grunted from behind a smoking grill. When Mark had invited her to barbecue by the pool she hadn't actually thought she would be doing the cooking herself.

Beamon was flopped over a lawn chair that looked too small for him, sipping a drink with an umbrella in it. It was a scotch, but he had decided when he'd pulled the tarp off the pool that everyone should have an umbrella, no matter what they were drinking. It had taken no small effort on Laura's part to convince him that it was impossible to drink a beer with an umbrella stuck in the neck of the bottle.

"How're those steaks coming—I'd like mine bloody. Really, really rare."

"You'll get it the way I make it."

Beamon jumped out of his chair as the sound of the doorbell floated out to the pool. "I'll get it."

Laura watched him disappear through the sliding glass door and turned the grill up on his steak.

Beamon reappeared in less than a minute with a package under his arm. "UPS guy."

"What'd you get?"

"Dunno." He tore open the box and pulled out a beautiful gray pinstripe suit. Laura came from around the grill, wiping her hands on her apron.

"Nice," she commented, opening the jacket and looking at the label. "Hugo Boss? Geez, this is probably a three-thousand-dollar suit."

Beamon took her word for it and shuffled through the tissue paper, finally finding a small envelope. He pulled out the card. The message was written in a flowery but masculine scrawl.

Please accept this as a small token of my gratitude. Have your tailor bill me for any alterations.

Anthony DiPrizzio

Beamon laughed until tears streamed down his face.

"What is it? Who's it from?" Laura asked.

Beamon handed her the note. "A gift from Anthony DiPrizzio. Thanking me for putting him back in business." Saying it out loud got him chuckling again. "They should put this one in the dictionary as the definition of irony."

Laura frowned, apparently not fully appreciating the humor.

"Don't be mad, Laura. I'm sure your gift's on its way."

Beamon picked up the phone sitting next to him and hit the speed dialer for the JEH Building. "Tommy's gonna love this."

"Tom Sherman, please," he said to an unfamiliar operator. Sherman's secretary picked up. "Hey, darlin'. Is Tommy around?"

"Hi Mark. No, I think he's in his car. Let me patch you through." There was an audible click and pause, then Sherman picked up.

"Hey Tommy! I got a story you're gonna love. DiPrizzio just sent me a three-thousand-dollar suit as a gift for putting him back in business! He'll probably start paying his taxes if we keep helping him out like this."

There was silence on the other end of the phone.

"You still there?" Beamon asked, shaking the phone.

"Yeah. Sorry, Mark. I just got some bad news."

Beamon stood and walked over to the pool, sitting down and dangling his legs in the cool water. "What?"

"We've just gotten reports of narcotics poisonings in San Francisco and Atlanta."

"Bullshit! Hobart's organization's going on without him?"

"I don't think so. The poisons were household items—nothing sophisticated. I don't think it's organized."

"They probably won't be too tough to catch, Tommy. Get 'em and make an example out of 'em. That'll put a stop to it." He wasn't as sure as he was forcing himself to sound.

"I don't suppose that I can convince you to come back and head up the investigation?"

"Not a chance."

"Somehow I knew you'd say that."

The sun had completely dropped behind the horizon, and the automatic lights by the pool switched on. Laura walked over and sat next to him, dropping her feet in the pool. She was holding a long fork with a charred steak on the end. Part of it was still on fire.

"Looks like my steak's done, Tommy. Gotta go. And hey, good luck."